Praise for

THE LOVE CONNECTION

"A delectable romance . . . about two people who are hopelessly in love yet hesitant to take the next step."
                                                            —*AudioFile*

Praise for

THE MISSED CONNECTION

"There's a ton of chemistry between the witty, mismatched duo, and their heated rivalry, sensual sex scenes, and snappy dialogue will surely charm readers. This is a bite-size treat."
                                    —*Publishers Weekly* (starred review)

Praise for

THE SWEETEST CONNECTION

"Punchy dialogue, unforgettable characters, and some light, good-natured intrigue make this story one to devour like a box of duty-free truffles."
                                                    —*Publishers Weekly*

Praise for

THE FASTEST WAY TO FALL

"This entertaining read will have you sweating through your next workout."
                                            —*Good Morning America*

"There's a lot to like in this romance, with its supportive leading man, delightful heroine, and dynamic secondary cast. There's more than just romance going on, and Williams excels at juggling all the parts. . . . An emotionally resonant and thoughtful novel."

—*Kirkus Reviews*

"*The Fastest Way to Fall* is not a story about weight loss but about learning to love who you are and about falling in love with someone who helps you feel strong. Britta's triumphs over her former insecurities concerning her body, her goals, and her job are transcendent moments thanks to Williams's sensitive and masterful storytelling."

—*BookPage*

Praise for

HOW TO FAIL AT FLIRTING

"In this steamy romance, Naya Turner is an overachieving math professor blowing off work stress with a night on the town, which leads to a night with a dapper stranger. And then another, and another. She's smitten by the time she realizes there's a professional complication, and the relationship could put her job at risk. Williams blends rom-com fun with more weighty topics in her winsome debut."

—*The Washington Post*

"Denise Williams's *How to Fail at Flirting* is absolutely SPECTACULAR! Ripe with serious, real-life drama; teeming with playful banter; rich with toe-curling passion; full of heart-melting romance. . . . Her debut grabbed me on page one and held me enthralled until the end, when I promptly started rereading to enjoy the deliciousness again."

—Priscilla Oliveras, *USA Today* bestselling author of *Anchored Hearts*

"*How to Fail at Flirting* is a charming and compelling debut from Denise Williams that's as moving as it is romantic. Williams brings the banter, heat, and swoons, while also giving us a character who learns that standing up for herself is as important—and terrifying—as allowing herself to fall in love. Put 'Read *How to Fail at Flirting*' at the top of your to-do list!"

—Jen DeLuca, *USA Today* bestselling author of *Well Matched*

"Naya and Jake's relationship is both sexy and sweet as these two people, who love their work but are not skilled at socializing or romance, find their way forward. Academia is vividly portrayed, and readers will await the next book from Williams, a talented debut author and a PhD herself."

—*Booklist*

"*How to Fail at Flirting* is a powerhouse romance. Not only is it funny and charming and steamy, but it possesses an emotional depth that touched my heart. Naya is a beautiful and relatable main character who is hardworking, loyal, spirited, and determined to move on from an abusive relationship. It was thrilling to see her find her power in her personal life, her career, and through her romance with Jake. And I cheered when she claimed the happily ever after she so deserved."

—Sarah Echavarre Smith, author of *On Location*

"Williams's debut weaves a charming, romantic love story about a heroine rediscovering her voice and standing up for her passions."

—Andie J. Christopher, *USA Today* bestselling author of *Hot Under His Collar*

"*How to Fail at Flirting* delivers on every level. It's funny, sexy, heart-warming, and emotional. With its engaging, lovable characters, fresh plot, and compelling narrative, I did not want to put it down! It's in my top reads of the year for sure!"

—Samantha Young, *New York Times* bestselling author of
Much Ado About You

"The warmth in Denise Williams's writing is unmistakable, as is her wit. She tackles difficult subjects, difficult emotions, with such empathy and thoughtfulness. Best of all: Jake is just the type of hero I love—sexy, smart, sweet, and smitten."

—Olivia Dade, national bestselling author of *All the Feels*

TITLES BY DENISE WILLIAMS

Love
and Other
Flight
Delays

DENISE WILLIAMS

Berkley Romance
New York

Berkley Romance
Published by Berkley
An imprint of Penguin Random House LLC
penguinrandomhouse.com

Library of Congress Cataloging-in-Publication Data

Names: Williams, Denise, 1982- author.
Title: Love and other flight delays / Denise Williams.
Description: First Edition. | New York : Berkley Romance, 2023.
Identifiers: LCCN 2022025328 (print) | LCCN 2022025329 (ebook) |
ISBN 9780593441077 (trade paperback) | ISBN 9780593441114 (ebook)
Subjects: LCGFT: Romance fiction. | Novels.
Classification: LCC PS3623.I556497 L68 2023 (print) | LCC PS3623.I556497 (ebook) |
DDC 813/.6—dc23
LC record available at https://lccn.loc.gov/2022025328
LC ebook record available at https://lccn.loc.gov/2022025329

First Edition: March 2023

The Love Connection, *The Missed Connection*, and *The Sweetest Connection*
were originally published separately as audio editions, April, May, and June 2022
respectively, and then as ebook editions, May, June, and July 2022 respectively,
by Jove, an imprint of Penguin Random House LLC.

Printed in the United States of America
1st Printing

Book design by Alison Cnockaert

*For you, who always makes me feel like
I've been upgraded to first class.*

Contents

Love
and Other
Flight
Delays

The
Love
Connection

For Jay, who is the best risk-taker I know
(and also a pretty phenomenal brother).

1

Ollie

"FLIGHT 682, DIRECT service from Miami, has arrived at Gate C7."

I normally tuned out the constant stream of announcements from the disembodied voices over the PA system—flights arriving, flights delayed, gates changed, personal items left at security—but this announcement caught my attention. Pre-Flight Paws was right across from Gate C7. If the airport was a small town, which it often felt like, that gate was our neighbor.

Jess walked from the back, calling over her shoulder, "Pepper is an escape artist—be careful when washing him!" After two years of continued popularity and an incredible response from travelers to the idea of having their animals groomed during layovers, we had a staff. Jess let the door swing closed behind her and joined me behind the counter. "You're staring again." My best friend and business partner's voice interrupted me from what wasn't staring but simply observing the passenger exiting the jet bridge.

The tall, broad-shouldered, sharp-jawed mystery passenger.

"I am not staring."

"You didn't even look away when you answered me." She bumped her hip with mine, nudging me toward the counter.

I didn't know his real name, but around 11:15 a.m. every Tuesday, I watched an Adonis in a dark tailored suit leave the jet bridge, check his phone, look around, and then walk out of my neighborhood to some unknown destination. The only thing that could have possibly made him sexier was if he were holding a book. I was always a sucker for a fellow reader.

Jess tsk-tsk-tsked and nudged me out of the way to access the computer. "It's sad, really."

Mr. Tuesday looked serious all the time, and today a crease formed between his brows as he paused, leaning against a wall, and stared at his phone. "What's sad?"

Her fingers clicked across the keyboard. "That your Diet Coke break is going to be the highlight of your day."

I sipped from my straw, keeping an eye on him. "It's iced coffee."

"You remember that commercial from the nineties where the women ogled the shirtless construction worker drinking a Diet Coke at the same time every day?"

I finally dragged my gaze from Mr. Tuesday. "That sounds . . . problematic. What are you talking about?"

Jess rolled her eyes. "So young." She pulled her phone from her back pocket and searched YouTube. She was only ten years older than me, but apparently that meant I'd missed an entire world of advertising-related pop-culture references. "Hold on."

"Speaking of Diet Coke, how did Pepper end up covered in it and in need of a bath?" I'd returned from the restroom to find his owner, breathless and handing over her little terrier, wet and unhappy, though calorie-free.

Jessica held up her phone to me proudly, showing a video of a shirtless man in a hard hat being ogled by women with big hair and bigger glasses. "Apparently, he wriggled away from her and had a run-in with an open bottle someone was drinking. Pepper. Not this actor. I don't know about his wriggling habits."

I glanced back at C7, unwilling to miss more of my Mr. Tuesday moments, even for a Pepper story. "This is not a Diet Coke break," I said, acknowledging in my own head that it was; I just had smaller hair than those women. "It's . . . curiosity."

Jess laughed, the lively sound filling the small check-in area. When some policy changes made it possible to move our mobile grooming business into the terminal, we'd sunk all our savings, all our connections, all our favors, and all our time into getting it off the ground. Time I still had, though the rest of it was short, but I loved this space, especially with my best friend's voice bouncing off the walls. "Curiosity about what he looks like without the suit on?"

I grinned and watched Tuesday stash his phone, look around, and then head toward the other end of the terminal. "No, just . . . who he is. Where he's going."

Jess walked toward the back with a knowing smirk. "Diet Coke break," she called over her shoulder, letting the door swing behind her.

With Mr. Tuesday off to his flight, I returned to the computer, where I'd been reviewing our finances. Jessica was the groomer. I was the adorer of pets, and while I could help with the basics, the business side of things was my contribution. After a moment of looking at the screen and skimming through the numbers one more time, I glanced back up at the spot on the wall where Mr. Tuesday had been leaning. Him suitless would probably not be so bad. A suitless guy in an airport was fun. A suitless guy in an airport didn't date you for three years, convince you a long-distance relationship was better than you moving to DC for your dream job, and then lead a double life for a year.

I shook off the memory because that betrayal had changed me into someone who was scared to get into anything romantic—but also into the river-rafting, skydiving, business-starting, fearless woman I was. Some risks were worth it to prove to myself I wasn't a timid person anymore. People risks . . . well, I had book boyfriends for that. I glanced at the novel tucked into my purse under the counter, eager to get back to it later.

Back to the hustle. I scrolled through the accounting software, double-checking my work, the proposal to expand in another window.

The muted sound of Pepper's sharp, high-pitched bark came through the usually effective soundproofing door. "Hey, Ollie, Jess is in the middle of it with that chihuahua. Can you help me with—" Jeremiah pushed through the swinging door, his hands covered in suds.

It never occurred to me that we'd have so many regular customers in an airport, and I turned immediately, knowing how squirrelly Pepper could be when motivated. "Sure, just close the—"

A young couple holding an animal carrier walked into the shop, but before they could say anything, Pepper, covered in soapy water, made a run for it, leaving a trail of suds across our floor and out into the terminal, trailing his lead behind him like a snake.

Damn it! "I'll get him." I pushed from behind the counter, giving our new clients the best possible impression, and sprinted after Pepper. "Jeremiah, please help them!" I cursed the devious little animal I used to find adorable and ran after him through the crowded walkway, calling after him. "Pepper!" I dodged a family staring blankly at the arrivals and departures board, ignoring my instinct to help them. "Pepper! Come!"

Ahead of me, the dog bobbed and weaved and I swear the little jerk slowed down until I got close, probably laughing maniacally in his head. I'd planned to land in DC as a power player in a corner office for high-level campaigns. As I slid on one of Pepper's wet paw prints and hurtled to the ground, banging my forearms on the tile, I questioned the life choices that had brought me to this point.

Scrambling to my feet, I searched the area and followed his wet trail. "Pepper!"

The crowd had thickened, but I heard a deep voice say, "Gotcha," and I breathed a sigh of relief, hoping the voice didn't belong to one of my fellow business owners who were lobbying to get us kicked out. *Please don't let him stop by Julianna's Candy Shoppe. She already hates us.* I wasn't sure whether she didn't like animals, didn't like us because we took over her friend's storefront when that shop went out of business, or didn't like us because she didn't like anyone. Regardless, I did my best to avoid her cutting glares.

I walked through the crowd, searching for Pepper and following the trail of soap along the tile to trace his whereabouts. The one time Pepper was quiet was, of course, when I needed to find him in a crowd.

We are banning Pepper.

"This is yours, I presume?"

I narrowly avoided a collision with a family running for a flight when I snapped my gaze up to find a bedraggled and gleeful Pepper wiggling in the arms of my Diet Coke break.

2

Bennett

I DESPISE AIRPORTS.

"Hold on," I said, looking around the gate area for an open out-let. My phone hadn't charged the night before and now my battery rested at eleven percent. When it dipped below thirty, my anxiety started to roil, much like when the fuel gauge reached twenty-five percent. I never saw any point in taking chances.

"Where are you?" My best friend shouldn't have had to ask, be-cause my job always left me in the same place, and I grumbled my response, going in search of an available spot to charge my phone.

"Where else?" I attempted to navigate around the group ahead of me, who had decided four people at a leisurely stroll was the ideal spread and speed for the middle of the crowded walkway. I didn't have somewhere I had to be, not for another hour and thirty-three minutes, but that didn't lessen the rising frustration at having to slow my pace.

"Why haven't you quit that job yet?" I heard conversation and birds chirping in the background and assumed Gia was walking outside on the college campus where she taught chemistry.

"For starters, I quite enjoy the paycheck." I finally eased past the left-most person, earning a cutting glance as if I'd used my roller bag as a battering ram. "Things like that tend to come in handy for food and shelter." Ahead, a kid stood and reached for the cord attached to his device, and I quickened my pace.

"Sure, but you have another source of income."

My best friend hadn't been shocked when I told her I wrote a romance novel, much like she hadn't been shocked when I told her I'd gotten a job in risk assessment. She'd simply demanded I send her the draft, and five published novels later, she was still the first person to read my work, only I hadn't sent her anything in a while because I hadn't written anything in a while, not since turning in my last manuscript. It was as if all my creativity was in a piece of lost luggage, with my next deadline looming ever closer.

"Attention in the terminal: If you lost your phone, wallet, and cigarettes, please return to the security checkpoint."

That person is having a bad day. I stepped around two young people cuddled together on the floor, basking in the warm light of an iPhone. Immediately past them was an elderly couple, both in wheelchairs being pushed by two young men. Young love. Old love. Love was all around me, and even though it was my job—my second job—to write love stories, I had no new ideas. The well was dry.

Gia pulled my attention back. "You still with me?"

"Sorry. And I can't quit my job, but I especially can't quit my job if I can't finish this manuscript."

"Maybe you'd be able to finish if you took time off to let your creativity replenish. Or if you went on a few dates to get *inspired*."

"It's not like inspiration is going to jump out at me just when I need it."

"It might," she said. "You might meet the girl of your dreams in line to buy a cinnamon roll if you put down the carrot sticks and let yourself enjoy something."

I remembered the first time I'd flown, when my parents brought

me to the States. The smell of cinnamon when we passed a Cinnabon smelled like opportunities. I glanced at the storefront to my left.
Now I barely registered the scent. I spotted someone else eyeing the
kid's outlet and ticked up my speed. "Why did you call? Other than
to question all my decisions?"

"That was the main purpose." She laughed into the phone and I
felt the pang in my chest of missing her. My best friend since my first
day at uni—or *at college*, as she would challenge me—Gia and I
lived half a country apart and I'd never found anyone else I could
connect to like that. I missed her laugh. The colleagues I spent all
my time with chuckled, but I hadn't been around real laughter in a
long time.

"All right, then. Good to chat," I said, already reaching into my
messenger bag for the charger.

"Wait, wait, wait," she said. "You're not bailing on me for the
week at the beach, right?"

Stuck behind another glacially moving group of people, I reluctantly slowed, looking for a way through the crowd, until I felt a tap
on my shoulder. A woman who looked to be roughly two hundred
years old stood next to me, her slight frame coming to my shoulder.
"Excuse me. Can you point me to baggage claim?"

No one could have stopped me from getting to that outlet and
the power of a charged phone except this woman. "Hold on, Gi," I
said into the phone, and came to a stop to help the woman find the
right direction, asking her, against my better judgment, if she needed
any assistance. She reminded me of my gran, who wasn't really my
grandmother but our neighbor. She'd been the closest I'd had to a
reliable adult growing up.

Gia waited until she heard me say goodbye and then asked,
"Were you saving old ladies again?"

"I was assisting someone elderly. Why do you say it with such
derision?"

"It's not derision. You just can never not help someone. It's cute."

"Well, as you know, cute is what I'm going for." My competitor for the outlet beat me to it and I began my search again. "And yes. Next month will be great."

"A week at the beach. I can't wait to get sun, surf, and a hot beach hookup."

"You plan to limit yourself to just one?" She'd strong-armed me into taking a vacation and we'd rented a house on Tybee Island in Georgia. I fully expected her to find a long line of adoring fans while we were there, but she ignored my question.

"You could make your own hookup plans," she chided. "It's been a while. Maybe a little no-strings fun would clear your writer's block."

I rolled my eyes. This conversation was also not new, and I had just as much interest in it as in the one regarding quitting my job. Unfortunately, being unable to write was the number one reason I couldn't quit—sometimes the stories didn't come. My mind wasn't always reliable when it came to getting my words on paper. She was right and I had been blocked, but a no-strings thing wasn't the answer. I liked strings. I liked tethers to something and someone.

Gia laughed again. "Are you ignoring me?"

"I am." I shoved my charger back into the bag and looked longingly at the outlet that I had failed to snag. "I would settle for a hookup with an available outlet right now, though."

"Kinky."

"I'm hanging up on you."

I smiled to myself at her laugh as I ended the call. I was looking forward to the vacation and seeing Gia, and hoping the change of setting had the desired effect on my writer's block.

"Pepper!" a voice in the crowd called out, and I glanced around in time to spot what looked like an oversized wet rat with perked ears darting at full speed through the crowd.

I could have ignored it. I should have ignored it, but damn it all if Gia wasn't right about my need to help people when I could. I bent and snatched the creature from the floor, holding the squirming, slippery rodent-looking animal with both hands. On closer inspection, I saw the rat was actually a dog. "Gotcha."

I couldn't see the person looking for it, but I heard their voice again. "Pepper!" I scratched the dog behind the ears and it stopped squirming, and then I heard, "I could have been in a corner office." A moment later, a woman squeezed between two travelers, head down. She wore a lime green T-shirt that read PRE-FLIGHT PAWS, and I recognized the name from the little shop near the gate I flew into often. I hadn't noticed her before, but her curly hair was pulled back from her pretty face, and jeans hugged her hips.

It took me a moment to find my voice. "This is yours, I presume?"

At my words, she looked up and almost ran face-first into a man and child dashing by.

When they passed, I saw her whole face—a complexion like warm amber, clear skin, and full lips. Her brown eyes were wide and landed on me, quickly skating to Pepper.

"Yes. I'm so sorry." She held out her arms to take the dog, who had made a little home in the crook of my arm. "He's an escape artist."

"I hear Houdini started out in airports," I said, giving him to her, my hands momentarily brushing the smooth skin on her forearms.

She smiled at my joke, a slow grin as she held Pepper to her chest, her fingers scratching behind his ears as mine had. "Impressive, since there weren't many airports to speak of in the 1920s."

"Well," I said, stealing a glance at the logo on her shirt as she readjusted Pepper. "That's a trailblazer for you."

I wanted to know her name. It was a bizarre thought needling into my brain. I hadn't needed to know the elderly woman's name or the name of the person who'd glared at me for passing. Hell, I didn't know the names of most of my neighbors, but I wanted to know hers. Her gaze fell to my chest and I felt myself flexing. *Maybe Gia was onto something.*

"Your suit," she said with a grimace. "I'm so sorry. Can we pay for your dry cleaning?"

The suit. I laughed at my instinct to flirt with the strange woman. "No," I said, waving her off and removing the wet jacket. "It's fine."

She examined me again as I lifted my bag onto my shoulder. "Are you sure?" She held the slippery dog firmly in her arms while he tried to lick her and possibly find a way to escape again.

Logically, I knew she was studying my wet jacket, the smears of suds slowly soaking into the fabric, but I had the strangest sensation that she might have been checking me out. I rather liked it. "I'm sure. No bother."

"Sorry again, and thanks. I won't keep you."

"You're welcome," I said, not quite ready to look away from her. A woman hadn't captured my attention like this in a long time. "I'm Bennett," I said, holding out my hand. "In case that one tries another escape, you can shout for me."

She grinned and I wanted to make her smile again. "Ollie," she said, trying to hold out a hand but pulling it back when Pepper shifted, ready to jump. "Olivia. I run the grooming shop back there," she nodded over her shoulder. "Thank you, Bennett, for saving me a much longer run through the airport."

I gave a little wave when she took a step back. "My pleasure."

"If you're ever here and in need of pet grooming, stop by." She nodded toward the aisle again. "I promise Pepper is the only animal who has ever escaped." The dog wriggled in her arms, whining. "But good to know I can shout for help."

I nodded, taking one last glance at the splash of freckles I'd noticed across her cheeks. "I don't have any pets, but if I happen upon one, I definitely will."

Then, for the first time in my life, I considered adopting a puppy.

3

Ollie

I MERGED ONTO the interstate and waited for the call to connect. The sun hung low in the sky, the summer day sinking into a warm night. I left my window down to breathe in fresh air and listen to sounds other than the soundtrack of the airport. I held my palm out the window to make waves like I had as a kid.

"Shouldn't you be out on a date or something?" Harriet was my mom's aunt, and when I was five, she said if she could call me Ollie, I could call her Harry. It stuck.

I slowed behind a sea of undulating brake lights. "Shouldn't you?"

"Getting ready for one right now." She would have sounded impatient to anyone else, but I knew better. "And before you ask, it's probably just a one-night thing. He's very cute but I don't know if we have much in common."

My sixty-eight-year-old aunt was well entrenched in hookup culture, and I had to applaud her. She looked great, but she exuded this bad-bitch energy I had a hard time picturing anyone ignoring. It didn't seem like many men did.

"Another twenty-five-year-old?"

"There's no need for hyperbole. He was twenty-nine. Almost thirty, and that was one time." I could hear the eye roll in her voice. "Anyway, he was lousy in bed. Nice to look at. Stamina for days, but no technique. No finesse. Is that what you have to put up with from men your age?"

I laughed, enjoying the breeze, but before I could answer, she added, "Look who I'm asking. If he ain't in a book, you don't want him."

"I mean . . . I'm okay with men in movies, too, but yes . . . sometimes there's a dearth of finesse."

"Damn shame. This one is fifty-four. I'm holding out hope." Her tone softened. "Now, why did you call?"

I debated putting the car in park—this congestion stretched as far as I could see. "Just checking in."

"How's the shop?"

She knew well enough as our first investor, but she always asked like that, voice gruff and like she didn't really care, when I knew she did. She'd been the one to give me the money to start the business, the money she'd set aside to help pay for my wedding. "It's good. Pepper escaped today. I had to chase him through the terminal."

"That dog is a menace."

"He's free-spirited, for sure."

"Free-spirited my ass; that dog is a troublemaker. No shame in calling someone what they are, especially when what they are is a dog."

My face flushed and I knew she was referring to my ex. "A helpful stranger snagged him and saved me from a much longer run." Mr. Tuesday. Bennett. His British accent was unexpected but fit him so well. Sitting in my car, I remembered how I felt his voice in my spine when he spoke—my spine and other places.

"I guess there are some helpful people out there." Harry's voice grew faint, and I imagined she had walked into her closet, setting down her phone on some surface as she thumbed through her jeans and skirts. If my butt looked as good as hers at that age, I would count my lucky stars. "Something else on your mind?"

"I'm curious if you think I should start dating again."

Harry was quiet for a few seconds, and I heard the rustling of fabric. "Well, how would I know? Do you want to date again?"

"No," I said automatically. That wasn't fully true. I liked dating. I enjoyed flirting and having someone to share jokes with, to have meals with. I didn't miss the being-tied-down part, the being-tethered part. I sure as hell didn't miss the careful part where I shaped myself to fit someone else's life and came to expect disappointment in return. "I mean, not really."

"It's okay to be skittish. A little fear is probably normal after the way that lying sack of refuse treated you."

Harry had said much worse and much more colorful things about my ex-fiancé, not that she was wrong.

"I'm not scared," I said, tasting the lie. Scared wasn't part of my new brand, the new me. When Harry had handed me a check, the money she was going to give me to spend on my wedding, she'd clutched my hands and told me I didn't have to fear life, that I could take it in both hands. I did. So I wasn't scared of something as basic as dating. *Right?*

Harry laughed. "Keep telling yourself that. I know you dive off cliffs and take chances left and right. You're not scared of dying, but you might be a little scared of meeting a nice man and living a little."

"I'm not," I said again. Nice men were in short supply anyway. I went to work and I went home. Unless I wanted to start something up with Martin, the custodian at the airport whom I adored and who was a widower with seventeen grandchildren, I was fresh out of luck. But I thought about Bennett. "I mean, I don't think I am. I don't want to be."

"It's not rocket science, girl. Go on a date and see if you enjoy it. Otherwise, enjoy those men in your books."

My phone pinged with an incoming message.

"Just sent you a photo. How does this look?"

Harry had slid into a form-hugging red dress that popped in every possible way.

"How do you always look this stunning?"

"Good genes, good luck, and good use of my alimony." Harry laughed and I assured her the outfit was perfect. She air-kissed the phone before we hung up, and I stared ahead at the traffic. Her comments about me being afraid of living a little rankled me, and I didn't like the idea that he whose name shall not be uttered was still influencing my life. I wished there was a way to get all the good things out of dating without the risks. I'd fiddled with the apps but hadn't committed. The entire vetting process seemed like so much work.

My mind drifted to Bennett again and his deep voice and big hands. In an ideal world, I could date someone like him—handsome, funny, and only in my life for increments of thirty minutes to two hours.

Traffic finally started to inch forward, and I looked ahead to see movement.

If only.

4

Bennett

"BEN, WE'RE GOING to need you in LA week after next," my boss said without preamble, his voice loud through the phone. He looked like how I imagined Humpty Dumpty might in real life, only with a mild addiction to orange Tic Tacs and hemorrhoids he was inclined to mention in conversation.

"I'm out the week after next," I said, standing in the aisle of the plane, waiting for the doors to open. "Can Carter do it?"

"Oh, that's right, the book thing," he said. "Sure. Sure. I'd rather have you, but Carter can handle it. Are you ever gonna give me a sneak peek of the next book? I didn't expect the cliffhanger with the viscount in that last one."

The decision to leave the job might have been easier with a boss who was a tosser or judgmental, but as it was, he was always interested in my writing and supportive of my side hustle. He preordered my books and read them with his wife—it was nice. He was nice, and even though I didn't have time, I added, "I can work with Carter ahead of time to help him prep if you want, and I'll make sure you get an early copy."

"That'd be great. Thanks, Ben."

The doors opened and I pressed forward with the rest of the travelers, the routine so ingrained, I could do it in my sleep, but this time when I stepped out of the Jetway doors, I ignored my waiting emails. I threaded between a family of four making plans for their layover and spotted the storefront across the hall. Pre-Flight Paws was brightly painted, with a small lobby area, where the woman I'd met the week before stood, helping a customer. She was in the same lime green shirt and smiling at someone while stroking a dog's head. It didn't look like the same dog as last time. This one was dry, for starters, and not trying out to be an Olympic sprinter.

The customer and the dog pushed out of the glass door and I had a full view of her face. Olivia. Ollie. She was focused on her computer, and I cut my glance away when a short elderly man shoulder-checked me as he passed. I'd become one of those people I hated, blocking the flow of traffic.

"Apologies," I said. My words were met with a grunt from the man, but when I glanced back up, Ollie was looking at me, smiling. I'd hoped to see her—the shop was right across from my gate, after all—but I hadn't planned on talking to her. I waved, which felt like the dumbest thing to do, but she waved back. Then we stood there, both our hands raised like someone had hit pause, but she looked away first, saying something over her shoulder.

Before I got knocked over by another senior citizen, I stepped aside and opened my emails, my mood instantly sinking. There were seven urgent messages from my boss, none of which he'd mentioned when we were on the phone. Risk assessment had seemed like a job I'd enjoy—it wasn't sexy or glamorous, but it fit me. I grew up in a house where betting it all on the next big thing was a love language. Risk was all around, and as an adult, I enjoyed identifying and hopefully minimizing risks with my clients, which I never could with my family. The emails sat on my phone like talismans of doom. I was drafting a quick reply to the first one, which wasn't as urgent as my boss had made it seem with the subject line. I had fantasies of deleting the mail app I used for work, hitting uninstall, and watching the messages disappear in a flash.

"Are you on the lookout for wet dogs?"

I shot my head up in surprise—dropping my phone and two file folders I'd pulled from my messenger bag to get my boss the information he needed—at the sound of her voice and the sight of her approaching. "Should I be?"

"Pepper just left, so you're relieved of duty," she said, bending with me to pick up the papers, our knees bumping for a split second. I couldn't remember ever touching knees with someone in a memorable way before, and I made a note to include it in a book, as there was something exciting about that brief contact.

"Shame—I liked the little guy." I shoved the folders into my bag and we both stood in the mostly empty gate. That flight always cleared fast.

"Maybe we should hire you." Her gaze cut to my tie and swept over my suit. "Not sure we could afford it, though."

I hoisted my bag onto my shoulder. "As luck would have it, dog catching is a hobby. I'd prefer to maintain my amateur status."

Ollie crossed her arms over her chest and tilted her head. "Sounds nefarious. Are you a bad guy?"

"I don't think so . . . I always give the dogs back. I'm not Cruella de Vil or anything."

Her laugh filled the gate area, and I wanted to make her laugh again. She grinned before speaking, continuing the joke. "You sure? You didn't just leave your dalmatian coat in an overhead bin?" She tipped her head back in a way I wanted to record so I could write it accurately later, the lines around her smile and the arc of her neck. I had an overwhelming urge to drop everything and write down the description that came to mind, but now she was looking at me, unaware I had been turning her into my main character.

"Best to check the coat. It's insured, after all."

"Prudent." She leaned against the column, her crossed arms still folded under the swells of her breasts.

My phone buzzed in my hand and my boss's face flashed on the screen.

"Go ahead. Thanks for checking to see if we needed any animals corralled." She took a step back, still facing me. "And thanks for not kidnapping any baby animals in the middle of the concourse. I consider it a personal favor."

"Who knows what I would have gotten up to if you hadn't arrived."

She smiled again, and, God, she had a great smile. I felt something shift in me, a rock rolling out of the way. "Good luck with the coat." She waved again and turned to walk back toward her shop.

I took a moment to appreciate the way she moved and the curves of her body as she walked away. It was like I could feel her smile in the bounce of her step. I turned back to the urgent messages and rolled my eyes at my cheesy internal monologue but still made note of the line in an email I sent to myself. Ideas suddenly started flowing, but a text notification from Carter flashed over my screen as two more urgent emails arrived. I gave Ollie's retreating form one more glance, amazed at how that short exchange with her had lit a fire under my creativity.

5

Ollie

JESS ADJUSTED THE camera for Harry to see us both.

"So, what did you decide?" Aunt Harry asked. She never spent much time on small talk, and I always liked that about our relationship. We video chatted with her every couple of weeks to talk about the store.

Jess and I exchanged a look. "We want to do it," I said in a confident tone. The opportunity to expand, to join with a parent company to get Pre-Flight Paws locations all around the country, was a huge risk. It would mean changing the way we functioned as a company; it would mean traveling to new locations, and it would mean facing the unknown.

"Hot damn!" Harry's smile was wide and she clapped her hands together. "That's my girls! Taking chances and taking names!"

"It's a big risk," Jess hedged.

"Big risk. Big reward. To that end, I have some news for you girls. I'm getting hitched again."

Jess and I exchanged shared jaw drops.

"Oh, don't be so surprised. I'm old and impetuous."

Jess shot me a did-you-know look. "Who is he?"

"Well, remember that date? The red dress? Well . . . I like him. He likes me. We're gonna try marriage on for size."

"What if it doesn't work out? You haven't known each other long," I said, worry taking hold at the base of my spine.

"Then we'll get divorced. It's fast, but we're old and he makes me happy. Don't make other plans for August ninth," she said. "Gives you plenty of time to find a date if you decide you want one, Ollie."

"Wow," Jess said. We exchanged another look and said "Congratulations" at the same time.

"Go big or go home," Harry said, her face lit up. "Right, girls?"

I glanced over the top of the laptop. We'd closed the shop before jumping on the call, and the area outside was mostly free of passengers. The airport was always brightly lit, but the giant windows from Gate C7 showed an inky sky, and it made me miss looking up at the stars. I loved so much about Atlanta, but the city lights made it hard to stare up at the stars.

"Right," I said. In addition to the lights of the flight line and the inky night, I saw someone familiar walking down the concourse. "Go big or go home," I said, half listening to the two of them talk and watching Bennett. I usually only saw him on Tuesdays, always at the same gate and in a suit. Tonight, he'd lost the jacket and his sleeves were rolled up to showcase forearms that made me want to run my fingers over them. He paused as he neared the store, seeing the closed doors and the dimmed front lights, but he approached and smiled when he spotted us inside.

"Ollie, are we boring you?" Harry's tone drew me back to the screen. "I'm over here making dirty jokes about going big and I don't think you heard a one of them."

"Sorry," I said, shooting a quick glance over the screen again, hoping she wouldn't repeat the dirty jokes. Bennett was crossing the shiny tiled walkway with a wave.

"The cute guy she's been stalking just walked by," Jess added. "Well, I guess it's not stalking anymore. Maybe it's just flirting now."

"I'm not stalking him or flirting," I said, returning his wave with a quick one of my own and earning a smile. I held up a finger off-screen and he shrugged, waving a hand. The international talking-through-a-door sign for "take your time." *Is it common body language or did I just understand him?*

Either way, he settled in the mostly empty area around Gate C7 and pulled out a laptop.

"Cute, huh? How old is he?"

I laughed along with Jess. "Didn't you just tell us you're engaged? You already have a younger man at your beck and call."

Harry waved a hand in front of the camera. "I grew up in a time where you had to pretend your hoo-haw didn't have needs and that men were always right. There will never be enough young, attractive men at my beck and call for me to not appreciate a nice, firm butt."

Jess and I both laughed again, and I peeked at Bennett working across the hall, a crease between his eyebrows and his mouth in a firm line. "He's just a nice guy who I met in the airport," I said.

Harry kept going. "But does he have a nice butt?"

I was about to cut the conversation when Jess jumped in. "I don't know, but he is handsome and seems to like our Ollie."

"I'm going to stop talking to you two. What does it matter if he's cute? I only ever see him when he has a layover."

"Are you trying to marry him? I know you think you get enough romance from books, but there are a few things books can't do I wager that man could."

"No. Too complicated." Dating meant being boxed in by someone else's needs and wants, someone whose plans might not always be in my best interest, and I wasn't interested in a hookup.

"Is he still out there?"

Jess nudged me. "Yep. Go talk to him." She looked back at the screen. "We've got things to catch up on anyway, and we'll make sure he doesn't snatch you up and drag you off somewhere."

"Unless you snatch him up and find a nearby Ramada," Harry added.

"I'm done with both of you," I said, sliding off my stool and walking toward the door. "I'll be right back."

The music was playing through the overhead speakers. It was usually too loud to hear anything, but the area was mostly still with just the normal background noises and announcements piping through the space. I stepped into the hall and walked toward Bennett, aware I was wearing the same thing I'd been wearing the first two times we'd met. We didn't always wear the shirts, but it was familiar, easy, I had a ton of them, and I never cared if they got animal hair all over them. Still, I wished I looked a little more impressive.

"I think you might have a while to wait for this flight," I said, pointing to the blank screen.

Bennett's head tipped up in surprise and he smiled. He smiled like I was wearing something impressive. "Hey." He tucked his laptop away and stood. "I wasn't certain you would be open this late."

"We're not," I said, pointing over my shoulder at the obviously closed shop. "Just working late."

"I know it's strange, but I was out in Anaheim on business and I saw this," he said, pulling a Cruella de Vil figurine from his bag, a small plastic toy with moving arms and legs. "I couldn't really explain to my colleague why I laughed when I saw it or why I bought it, but I thought it was . . ." He handed it to me, our fingers brushing.

"Hilarious," I finished, studying the small toy, my belly fluttering in a way I had not given it permission to do. "So perfect. Now when you're not around, I'll still have a reminder to protect the puppies from would-be villains."

A splash of pink covered his cheeks and I had a sudden impulsive urge to kiss him. I took risks and did impetuous things a lot—well, a lot more than I used to—but not the kind that involved kissing a stranger at work. Still, I grinned.

"Reminders are important. I'm glad you like it and don't think it's too silly."

I turned the toy in my hand and imagined him purchasing it. "I'm a fan of silly." I wanted to ask him why he was flying at a different day and time than usual, but even in my head that sounded less silly and more like the stalking Jess had accused me of. Though, if I thought about it, we weren't normally in the salon that late—we'd only stayed to discuss the expansion and to call Harry. Maybe Bennett had been in my airport on Friday nights, waiting to be adorable, this whole time.

He glanced down at his hands. "I don't want to keep you; I just wanted to give that to you. Looks like you're busy."

I nodded and glanced over my shoulder, where my friend was staring at us and had turned the laptop for Harry to see. *How embarrassing.* "Thank you," I said. "I am. We're having a meeting with my aunt—well, an investor; she's both, so I guess I should get back in. Clearly, they're just watching us."

"Good to have people looking out for you." He gave a little wave to our audience.

"I guess so." I held out my hand, which seemed odd and too professional, but also, I was kind of giddy to touch him again, because the first time the sparks had been like a shot of adrenaline. "It was nice to see you again."

My hand was small in his, and he shook it slowly, giving me time to soak up the sparks. "You, too."

"Maybe next time you come through," I said, not pulling back my hand. *When you come through next Tuesday at 11:15 a.m.* "Maybe we could get coffee or something."

He hadn't let go of my hand, either. "I'd enjoy that. Maybe tea instead of coffee for me. I'll be through again in a couple of weeks."

"I guess I'll see you then." This was good! This was human interaction with a man and I wasn't scared. My ex's cheating, lying butt hadn't held me back.

The speakers came to life. "Flight 7816 to Miami is now boarding at Gate C24."

"Oh, that's me," Bennett said, glancing down the hall. It was a bit of a walk to get to C24, with a myriad of shops and busy intersections along the way. "I guess I should get going."

I finally pulled my hand back from his, knowing Jess and Harry were going to give me a world of shit about this. "Yes, sorry! Don't miss your flight on my account."

I think he realized how long our hands had been clasped, too, and shoved his hand into his pocket. "I guess not, though talking to you is more fun than the work I'll do on the plane."

"I won't tell you not to work, but I hope you get a break soon."

He hoisted his bag onto his shoulder from its place on the seat behind him. "Soon. Taking a little vacation to the beach next week."

"You'll have to tell me about it when we have that drink."

He grinned again, a dimple popping on his cheek. "Definitely." He paused, his eyes on my face, and I used my hand to do the shooing motion.

"I'll see you in a couple of weeks."

"Count on it," he said before beginning a jog toward his gate.

6

Bennett

"BENNETT!"

I heard Gia, but it was the kind of passive hearing I could do when in the zone, and I waved at her without looking away from my screen. Something had pushed the boulder that had been blocking my creativity out of the way, and I'd flown through the first half of my draft in the last two weeks.

"Ben?" Gia was standing behind me now.

"In a minute," I said, raising my hand. "I'm almost done with this."

I furiously tapped out the end of the chapter. I glanced over the words on the screen. *Not bad*, I thought to myself.

"Ooh! Spicy," Gia said from over my shoulder, and I hit save and closed the laptop.

"I did not grant you permission to read that yet."

She sank into the deck chair across from me. "Well, I have excellent eyesight and I haven't met any sexy strangers on this trip, so your drafted sex scenes are all I have to hang on to."

I made a hushing noise, nodding to the trio of older women walking nearby.

I was used to Gia's eye rolls, but when the women looked over and she waved and called out to them, I wanted to roll up in a ball and strike out toward the ocean.

"My best friend writes the best romance novels, and the love scenes are perfect!"

I wasn't embarrassed that I wrote romance novels, but the combination of Gia loudly extolling the virtues of my more explicit writing skills along with promoting me by literally yelling at people on the beach was more than I felt like experiencing.

"Oh, what's your name? Iris loves a good steamy read," one of them said, giggling and pointing to her friend as they walked over to us. I normally enjoyed meeting fans, and after the moment of surprise when they learned that D.A. Bennett wasn't a woman, they usually seemed to enjoy meeting me, too. But normally, I wasn't half-dressed, unshowered, and coming off an almost nonstop writing binge.

Gia handled the conversation for me when I didn't chime in. "D.A. Bennett, and he wrote *The Duchess Affair*, *To Loathe an Earl*, and The Scoundrels of Maleficent Falls series." Gia popped up. "I can grab a piece of paper to write them down if you want."

Two of the women had pulled out their phones. "No need. I'll buy it right now. You should hire her to do all your marketing," the woman in front directed at me, taking in my hobo-like appearance.

"You know, I should."

"So, I've always wondered," her friend said. "I always assume romance writers have these epic, sweeping love stories in their own lives. Is that you two?"

Gia laughed. The laugh was so sudden, so loud, and so uproarious, I should have been offended. "No, absolutely not," she said while gulping in breaths.

"We're friends," I interjected, cutting my eyes away from my friend, who now had tears streaming down her face. "Despite how hilarious the idea of dating me is to her. I am single."

The woman patted my hand. "I bet your love story is out there waiting for you." She waved her phone at me. "And thanks for the recommendations," she said to Gia. "A good hot scene is all I need to turn me on to an author!" The women waved and continued up the beach as Gia's giggles subsided.

"Was it really that funny?"

"It was," she said, pushing a wayward curl behind her ear. "Not only us together, but your expression."

"I didn't have an expression."

"You did. With your hair all messed up and your writing-zone face, it was a cross between horror and confusion, like you'd forgotten I was a woman, that you are attracted to women, and that love stories exist in the real world." Gia settled back in the chair, bringing her glass of iced tea to her lips once she'd finished mocking me.

"I don't even know what you're talking about. How could you get all that from a split-second expression?"

"I know you. Tell me I'm wrong." She didn't wait for me to tell her she was wrong and pointed at the laptop. "Is the beach helping? You've barely looked up from your computer since we got here. Writer's block defeated?"

"I think so." I reached for my own tea and found three different mugs and an abandoned sandwich. Blessedly, my friend didn't say a word, though she gave me an arched I-told-you-so eyebrow raise. "Ideas just started flowing during my last couple work trips."

"Did you meet a sexy fellow risk assessor who turned your mind to thoughts of love and steamy carriage activities?"

"Definitely not. Fred in California just doesn't do it for me. Plus, his motion sickness would make carriage activities decidedly less fun." I'd been struck with a flood of ideas after running into that cute dog groomer in the airport again, and she'd been on my mind the entire time I was in California. Ollie. Our brief exchange along with the smell of the dog's soap on my jacket had been stuck in my brain, and the block had begun to crumble. By the time I gave her that silly toy, the wall was a memory. She was pretty, the kind of pretty I wrote into my characters, with wide, expressive eyes and full lips, and she was funny. *Have I ever babbled on like this in my own head?* "The only thing of note was catching a runaway dog and meeting the owner of a grooming salon in the airport."

"You caught a runaway dog and met a pet groomer inside the airport?"

"I know." I chuckled. "Cute dog."

"Cute groomer, too?"

Stunning groomer. I set my tea aside—it was cold and I didn't remember the last time I'd gotten up from my computer to refill it. "Her name is Olivia."

"So, you met the sexy groomer. Are you going to call her?"

"I didn't say sexy."

"It was implied from your dopey expression."

I waved her off and laughed. "And of course I'm not going to call her. We live in different states and we met three times for like five minutes."

"Three times? Long enough to get you writing again."

If I was honest, and I didn't plan to be, I'd thought about her more than once. The way her lips tipped up in a smile was so memorable. Instead of admitting that, I stood. "You're too much of a romantic."

Gia laughed again and motioned to herself. "I am not the romantic in this friendship. I'm the flirt."

"Fair. Are you planning to bring some strapping man or devilish woman back to our place tonight? Will I need earplugs?"

Gia held up crossed fingers. "I hope noise-canceling headphones.

I bet—" She stopped mid-sentence when a kitten stepped onto the deck, a little gray, dirty, mewing kitten. It wasn't tentative but walked toward Gia's leg like it owned the house. "Hello," she purred, lowering her hand for the animal to smell. "Are you lost?"

The animal didn't look like it lived with people, or people who took care of it. It was thin, even for a cat, and with something black and sticky streaked along its back. "Looks like a stray," I said.

Gia was checking for a collar, and I had a feeling that cat had found its owner. Gia said she wasn't romantic, but she loved easily. I was envious. She was a sucker for taking in stray animals and stray people. It was how we'd ended up friends—she a popular, bubbly student, and I the quiet, reserved kid in the corner unsure how to make friends.

"You can't adopt any more pets," I commented. She had two cats and a turtle at home, plus her elderly dog, who for the last five years had looked like he had only ten minutes left. "You're going to get kicked out of your apartment."

She waved me off. "My landlord loves me. Can you find him something to eat?"

I hustled into the house, wondering why so many pets were coming into my life lately and what she would name this one. With the appearance of the cat, Gia had forgotten about goading me, but I still thought about Olivia. I couldn't just use her as a muse. That would make me kind of a dick. Still, I couldn't shake the fact that her smile and meeting her were the catalysts to words actually flowing again. Maybe if I was up front with her, she wouldn't think it was weird. I rolled the potential request around in my head. *Hello, would you like to spend time with me so I can continue to write romance novels? I promise it won't be weird.* I rolled my eyes as I rooted around the kitchen. I'd never be able to ask that. The idea of a muse wasn't real, but even just thinking about the conversation with her made my fingers itch to write.

When I emerged from the kitchen with some water and sliced lunch meat, Gia and the cat already seemed to be fast friends, the furball tentative but winding in and out of Gia's legs. "You've picked out a name already?"

"I'll try to find his owner."

I nodded, knowing she would and that the cat would still be getting on a plane with us. I examined the black substance stuck to his fur. "Should get that looked at."

7

Ollie

"OH, MY SWEET baby," the woman said, holding out her arms for Pepper. "Was he just a perfect little guest today?"

In the back, Jess snorted. I accepted the woman's credit card. "Just like always."

The woman cooed over Pepper. We saw him without fail, every two weeks, and I kept meaning to ask her where she traveled every two weeks that required that her dog be bathed. I had an idea it was some kind of love affair and was curious about the person who would want Pepper around on a date. I leaned an elbow on the counter, enjoying the slow moment. Gate C7 was still, with nothing posted about upcoming arrivals or departures.

"You're staring at that gate like it's Tuesday," Jess commented, wiping her hands down the front of her smock.

I was hoping Bennett would show up. Bennett, who had pulled some knight-in-shining-armor stuff, interrupting Pepper's unplanned marathon through the C terminal and then bringing me a gift. "I am not," I said, shooting a quick glance at the groups of people walking by in hopes of spotting him. I hadn't at all thought back on our loose plan to have coffee. "Even if I was, he's just nice to look at."

"And has a great voice," she said, parroting my words back.

"And a nice suit," I said with a sigh. "He might not come back through." It was on brand to meet a cute, funny guy while he was on his way to somewhere else.

"Shame," she said. "Too bad you can't find a guy like that to take to Harry's wedding. Show that jackass ex what he missed."

Harry and my ex's grandma were close friends. We'd practically grown up together. The likelihood that he'd be there with his grandma was high, even though Harry would grumble. The idea of showing up alone made my stomach churn, but that might have just been the idea of seeing him.

The door chimed as a woman walked in, mid-conversation with the person behind her. She was tall and curvy and carrying a cat case. "The love of my life," she said with a smile over her shoulder.

I smiled at her open expression, the affection clear on her face for whomever she was speaking to behind her. I didn't want that but I kind of wanted it. *I really do need to try dating again.*

"Welcome to Pre-Flight Paws," Jess said with a smile, but it took me a minute to catch up because Bennett, Mr. Tuesday with the ruined suit and the quick hands, walked in behind her, returning her adoring smile.

He was dressed casually this time, in jeans and a long-sleeve T-shirt, the sleeves rolled over those very impressive forearms. "Hello again," he said, meeting my eyes.

"We found this little guy at the beach and couldn't find an owner. The vet said he's healthy, but there's something stuck to his fur. Would you be able to give him a wash or maybe cut it out? We have a long layover and Bennett said he knew this place." She motioned over her shoulder at Bennett. Tall, handsome, funny Bennett, who had openly flirted with me yet was apparently the love of this woman's life.

Jess reached for the cat carrier. "Oll, can you get them checked in and I'll take a quick look?"

I snapped my attention back to the woman and her cat and away from her presumed boyfriend or husband, whom I'd agreed to have coffee with. That, right there, was the prime reason to stick with my books. "Of course." I handed her a tablet to fill out the needed information.

"I'm sure this cat will not give you the same chase as Pepper," he said from over her shoulder. "He's not near as clever."

I nodded with a tight smile. He hadn't propositioned me or anything, but his tone still felt too familiar, especially with this woman standing right here. "That is helpful information."

He glanced around before landing back on me with a boyish smile that just felt slimy now. "It's nice to see you again."

"It is." I accepted the tablet back from the woman, my face heating with guilt. "Thank you. I'll check with Jess, but I think probably forty minutes. Will that work?" I was trying my best to be professional, but disappointment clawed at me. *He has a girlfriend.*

The woman nodded. "Perfect. I can pick up some chocolates from that shop I love. Ben, can you wait here for the cat?" She gave him a side hug once he nodded, and dashed out the door.

"She loves that chocolate shop. I get truffles for her sometimes."

He was sweet. He bought chocolates to take home for her. The sweetness made my teeth hurt because I realized with striking clarity that either he was a cheater or he hadn't been flirting with me at all; he'd just been nice and my radar was off. I would reinstall the apps later. Normal no-strings dating was the best way to avoid this faulty-radar thing happening again.

"You can have a seat if you'd like," I said, motioning to the small waiting area. "Or we can text you when the cat is done."

He looked around, taking in the place. "I was, uh, glad to see you again. While Gia's at the shop, I was wondering . . ." He adjusted his glasses, ears tinted pink like he was nervous. "Would you maybe want to get that drink with me? I know you're probably busy, but I was hoping we could like we talked about . . ."

Nope. Nope. Nope. I held up my iced cold brew, as evidence for why I wouldn't get coffee while his girlfriend was off buying chocolate truffles for them to take home. "I'm all set."

"Oh. I apologize." He didn't even look ashamed that I refused to be part of his cheating ways.

Internally, I pumped my fist, but I was also sad for the gorgeous woman who'd made the mistake of loving a cheater. He didn't say anything else and walked toward the seating area, leaving us five feet apart and not speaking until Jess pushed out from the back, thankfully breaking the tension.

"Hi there," she said, approaching him, the scent of the pet shampoo surrounding her, which was comforting since it blocked out the whiff I'd gotten of his aftershave or deodorant or whatever made him smell as good as he looked. "I don't know what's on the cat, but I don't think it's going to wash off. Is it okay to trim the fur?"

He glanced at his hands. "Oh, let me ask my—"

The woman in question pushed through the door, holding a paper sack from Julianna's Candy Shoppe, spelled with two *p*'s. The woman was from Missouri, where I was pretty sure only one *p* was the conventional spelling. I chided myself. I didn't really know her well enough to say that, but it irked me that she disliked Jess and me so much.

Jess repeated the question as Bennett rose to stand next to his girlfriend. I expected him to touch the small of her back, but he just stood by. I still couldn't believe my crush, the guy I'd been admiring for so long, was the kind of guy who would ask me out while traveling with his partner. I lifted the coffee to my lips when his arm brushed the counter.

Jess confirmed with the woman. "You and your boyfriend can wait here or we'll text."

The woman chuckled. "Oh, I am a single pet parent. He's not my boyfriend."

"My mistake. I really shouldn't assume," Jess said cheerily, disappearing into the back.

The woman by Bennett turned to me with a smile. "You must be the woman he ran into with the wet dog, though."

"Gi, drop it," he said flatly. "She's busy."

"I will, but we're not together. I promise," she said, meeting my eyes. "Oh no! Did you think he was some kind of a jerk? I would, too!" I was initially skeptical, but she talked like we'd been friends for years and had this energy that made me wish we had. "He's a great guy, just not my type."

My eyes flicked to his face, where his mouth was set in a line, face a little pinker than the last time. "Good to know he's not asking me out while dating someone."

Gia swung around to look at Bennett. "You actually asked her out?" As she moved, she knocked over a cup of pens, and when he and I reached to catch it, my iced coffee went tumbling, the lid popping off and cold brew flowing everywhere . . . including onto his white shirt.

I slapped my hand over my mouth and he jumped when the cold liquid hit him. "I'm sorry. I'm so sorry." I searched for paper towels behind the desk.

"It's okay," he said, holding out the fabric from his body.

"The benefit of being a traveler is having spare clothes." His friend smiled and wordlessly reached into one of their bags, pulling out a T-shirt and handing it to him. "Did he ask you to go have a hot beverage? That's his go-to first-date move."

I nodded, glancing between them but stopping on him as he pulled his wet shirt over his head and pulled the clean T-shirt on. I hadn't known how much muscle was under those suits, and a smattering of hair covered his chest. I shouldn't have been looking, but I certainly wasn't looking away.

"I do not have go-to moves," he said to his friend. "And she already has coffee so it doesn't matter anyway."

"Looks like you don't have coffee anymore, though," she said, motioning to the now empty cup next to the spilled drink I was sopping up.

"I suppose I don't."

A drink with a good-looking guy was still a date, and I could start my practice without the task of getting back on the apps. The idea of showing up to Harry's wedding alone and running into my ex without being able to show him how well I'd moved on clawed at me. "Can I buy you a hot beverage as an apology?"

8

Bennett

WE SETTLED AT a café table near a coffee kiosk, snagging a spot as two people left. "About what happened in the shop." I needed to make sure she believed that Gia and I were just friends.

"Sorry, again," she said, brushing condensation off her cup. "I assumed you two were together." She held another iced coffee in her hands, black with one sugar. "And then I accused you of being a cheater . . . and then dumped coffee on you."

"You're going to be a hard person to forget," I joked, using a napkin to clear a few crumbs off the table. I racked my brain, trying to remember the last time I'd gone on a date with a woman. It had been when I first started writing the last book, and there hadn't been a second date. Now I wished I was in something nicer than the T-shirt Gia had bought for me that read SASSY AND SALTY AT TYBEE ISLAND. I'd told her I had no intention of wearing it, so the irony was not lost on me that I was now wearing it on a date with a woman I kept wanting to describe as "enchanting." "I'm not sure my wardrobe will survive many more encounters with you."

"I'll make sure to have a Pre-Flight Paws T-shirt ready for you next time your friend drags you in," she said with a smile.

When Gia decided to adopt that cat, I'd thought of Ollie immediately. "She didn't pressure me," I said, staring into my cup of tea. *Get it together, man.* "I was interested to hear more airport trivia."

She looked confused for a moment.

"From the first time we met?"

She laughed, the sound filling the little bubble we were in. "That was a solid throwback. You're kind of smooth, huh?"

"I am unequivocally not smooth."

She sipped her coffee. "How long have you lived in Florida?"

"How did you know I live in Florida?"

Her eyes widened. "Oh, I've . . . Shit," she said with an embarrassed laugh. "I've noticed you getting off the flight from Miami a few times."

Ollie was adorable when she was embarrassed, and I sipped from my cup to temper the smile. "I fly from there most weeks for work lately. You really noticed me?"

"I thought dumping coffee on you while accusing you of being a cheater was going to be the embarrassing low point of my day."

"A man can always hope to be someone's low point."

She tapped her cup to mine. "I don't usually say the right thing. I haven't had coffee or anything else with someone new in a long time."

"Same for me. I guess we can practice with each other, huh?"

She looked interested, her eyes flicking up. "Practice is good."

"If I'm honest, I've had writer's block for a while, and I guess talking to you helped."

She tilted her head in the way people do when they hear something unexpected. "What do you write?"

"Romance novels," I said, glancing down at my cup. "Not that I think this is a romance between us," I clarified. "I mean, not that it's not, just that it's—"

Her wide smile made me pause in my rambling.

"When you get nervous, you keep talking, huh?"

"Don't tell anyone. It's not very dignified."

She laughed again and ran a finger over her lips. "It's our secret, but somewhere in there you told me you write romance novels? I love romance novels. I read two or three a week."

"That's amazing." My face heated. "I've been getting stuck lately. That's why I wanted to see you. I've been writing again since I ran into you."

"I think you technically ran into Pepper. Maybe he's your muse," she said. "What are your books about?"

"They've all been historical. The next one is due soon." I didn't often talk about my writing away from writing-centered spaces, and I wondered what she might say, if she'd ask why or ask about sex scenes. That was usually what people asked.

"What made you want to write love stories?"

I'd been asked that a lot, especially as a man writing stories featuring men and women. I had my canned answer. *There's so much going on in the world that I wanted to write happily ever afters for those who have found love or those who hope to.* I didn't want to tell her that, though. "Honestly, I started reading romance to figure out how to do it."

"To do . . . it?"

"To do romance . . . not 'it.' I mean, I figured that out mostly on my own; I mean . . . not just on my own, well, kind of on my own, but . . ." I sucked in a breath. "I'm doing the rambling thing again, aren't I?"

She held her delicate index finger and thumb together. "Little bit."

"I wanted to learn how to have a great love story in my own life. I didn't grow up with that in the traditional sense and I thought maybe I could pick it up in books. It didn't work, so I thought maybe if I started writing them . . ."

Ollie smiled and rested her chin in her hand. "And it worked?"

"Well, no." I gave a nervous laugh. "Turns out reading and writing about chemistry doesn't make you any better at actually sustaining it."

"Chemistry is hard to get right," she said, sipping coffee through her straw. "Sometimes you think you have it, and then . . ." She made an explosion motion with her hand. "So, that's why you wanted to see me?"

I didn't have a good answer other than I couldn't stop thinking about her, but that would sound weird after we'd just met. "I thought maybe if we spent some time together, I could keep writing and we could both . . . practice, like you said. I've never been this blocked or been around someone who so . . . well, inspired me, I guess."

"Oh. Wow." I couldn't read her expression, but she shifted to a tentative smile.

"It sounds a little strange when I say it out loud, I guess." In my head a giant neon sign was flashing BACK UP! and ABORT! "You're not . . . I mean, I'm not writing about you, if you're worried about that, but being around you, well, I couldn't not ask."

She glanced at her watch. "So, you want to hang out with me to finish your book?"

"Yes. I mean, I like you, too, of course." I glanced at my own watch. I didn't have much more time, and I didn't get the sense this was going well. "I have to catch my flight soon. Maybe we could meet again?"

She looked uncertain, so I rushed to add more. "I mean, maybe we could talk next time I fly through. Obviously, we would stay in. In the airport, that is . . ." I would never recount this conversation to Gia after this woman flatly refused me.

"Can I think about it? I like you—you're kind of funny and strange—but I've never been someone's muse before."

Bollocks. That backfired.

She stood. "I should get going. Sorry again about the coffee."

"Sure," I said, half standing and bumping the table. "I mean, no problem."

She walked backward, literally backing away from me, but paused. "What name do you write under?"

"D.A. Bennett," I said, handing her a card from my wallet. "All the information is on my website. Of course, you probably want to make sure I am who I say I am."

She took the card and tucked it into her pocket. "I'll think about it." She started back toward the grooming salon, and I watched her walk away, worried my writing mojo was taking the same path.

I buried my head in my hands and then felt my phone buzz.

> GIA: I have the cat. How's the date?
>
> BENNETT: Over.
>
> GIA: Thumbs up or thumbs down?
>
> BENNETT: 🧛
>
> GIA: Did you make it weird?
>
> BENNETT: On a scale of normal to 100? 98.

Gia didn't immediately respond, which meant she was effectively flirting with someone she met while walking to our gate or slamming her head against a wall at my ineptitude.

> GIA: They're about to board—how about we debrief on the plane.

9

Ollie

THE NEXT TUESDAY I volunteered to do inventory, making sure I was buried in the back at the time Bennett's flight normally landed. Jeremiah eyed me curiously when I sent him out to the front and got to work unloading boxes and making sure everything was stocked. There weren't any animals in back, and the cozy space was kind of comforting. I'd told Jess about the disastrous date, or maybe it wasn't even a date. Bennett had been so cute and I'd been intrigued when he told me he wrote romance novels. Even though he'd left things between us in a weird place, I'd wandered down to the bookstore on a break, but the romance section was crowded with shoppers and I couldn't get close enough to spot his books.

"Are you having fun hiding?" Jess strolled in holding an iced coffee.

I added another bottle of the special shampoo we used to the shelf and wiped my brow. "I'm not hiding."

"I think Mr. Diet Coke Break got to you," she said, leaning against the doorframe.

"He said I inspired him."

"That sounds like fun. Who better to inspire a romance novel? You read them all the time."

"Sure," I said, hoisting two more big bottles onto the shelf. "I mean, that would be cool." Also, I'd wanted him to be a little interested in seeing me because he liked me. It had seemed like he did, with his nervous rambling.

My phone buzzed and Jess handed it to me from the place I'd set it on the counter. "Oll, you have like ten messages on this dating app."

I rolled my eyes. "They're mostly dick pics," I said, dismissing the notifications. "It's exhausting."

"I don't believe they're all dick pics," she said, grabbing for my phone. "Surely—" She stopped mid-sentence as she entered my passcode and scrolled. "Wow. Those are several poorly photographed penises. Do they have no sense of lighting or good angles?" She studied the photos with an incredulous smile. "There are a few normal messages, though." She handed back my phone.

"I know," I grumbled. The normal messages were tempting to respond to, but every time I opened them, I fast-forwarded to getting hurt, to feeling betrayed, and I froze. Then another poorly lit phallus would land in my inbox.

"Are you sure the awkward frequent flier isn't a better option?"

I tucked my phone into my pocket, ignoring her probably good advice. "He wasn't interested in *me*, anyway; he just needed my presence to help him write. So . . . what's the point?"

"Are his books any good?"

Even though I hadn't been able to get to them in person, I'd checked out his website and reviews of his books, and people seemed to like his writing. "I was too scared to read them. What if they're all really good and this one he's writing because of me bombs? That's a lot of pressure."

"I . . . guess? It's not like you have to *write* the book." Jess handed me the coffee and a slip of paper. "Here."

"You got this for me?"

"Nope," she said with a smug grin and walked out. "But maybe you could think about this whole muse thing."

I took a sip from the coffee, bitter with just a touch of sweet, how I liked it. I flipped over the note.

Olivia,

I wanted to apologize for last time and if I made you feel uncomfortable. I don't know if you'd want to talk to me again, or spend time with me, but I wanted to reiterate that there is no pressure to go along with my request, even if we spend time together.

Bennett

He'd left his phone number, and I read and reread the note.

It would have been nuts to contact him. For starters, even for a friend, he'd be in the airport for an hour or two tops.

"Gonna text him?"

I jumped at Jess's words. She stood in the doorway holding Pepper with a vise grip on his harness. "You scared me! Also, why are you accepting beverages for me from strange men?"

Jess laughed and fastened Pepper in to be washed, tossing a treat on the surface in front of him to keep him occupied. "He dropped it off while running for a flight, and I made him pour a little into a cup and taste it himself."

"You did?"

"No," she said, turning on the water and holding Pepper steady. "But that would have been kind of badass, huh?"

I eyed it and brought it to my lips. "Would it be weird to accept his offer to hang out? I kind of love being the idea behind a novel getting written, but . . . it's weird, right?"

Jess shrugged. "Weird because you've been eye-banging him for a couple months from afar? Yes, that will be weird, but otherwise . . . I don't know. It's kind of low stakes getting to know someone in an airport. You could ease back into socializing with real people who aren't me. You said you needed practice, and none of those dick pics were very inspiring as a reason to get out there."

She turned and focused on Pepper, and I bit the corner of my lip and pulled my phone from my pocket.

OLLIE: Thank you for the coffee.

OLLIE: I'm in. I couldn't forgive myself if a romance novel didn't get written because I refused to help.

BENNETT: I promise it won't be weird, Olivia.

OLLIE: My friends call me Ollie.

BENNETT: My friends, unfortunately, call me Bennett.

OLLIE: Maybe I'll call you Benny. What do you think?

BENNETT: I think our arrangement was short-lived.

OLLIE: Well, nice knowing you, Benny.

BENNETT: It's been real, Olivia. 😂

BENNETT: But maybe we can have lunch next time I fly through? Probably next week.

OLLIE: Sure. Maybe another hot beverage.

BENNETT: I'll bring a change of clothes.

BENNETT: In case of spills or a wet dog.

BENNETT: Not because I think I'd have to take off clothes.

OLLIE: Benny.

BENNETT: Rambling again. Got it. I have to go into airplane mode but I'll talk to you soon.

I tucked my phone into my pocket with a grin. He oscillated so quickly between charming and awkward. It was all adorable, and maybe this wouldn't be so bad.

Jess washed Pepper, the hose in one hand and the extra-tight grip on the harness attached to him in the other. "So, you're going to be friends with him?"

"You read the note?"

She spoke over her shoulder through the noise of the sprayer. "Of course I read the note. You think I was going to just deliver something to my best friend without checking first?"

I chuckled before I slipped out front. "We're going to be friends."

"Friends who fool around in hidden airport corners?"

"Friends who don't end up on a TSA watch list," I corrected at the same time I imagined kissing Bennett and how his strong arms might come around me, how his lips might feel against my neck.

As the door swung shut, she said in her I'm-talking-to-an-animal voice, "Who wants those kinds of friends?"

10

Bennett

OLLIE'D TEXTED WHEN I was still in the air.

> OLLIE: Lunch still work?

I'd never been more eager in my life to get off a plane, so of course there was an issue with the sky bridge, and the man sitting in front of me apparently thought he had left suitcases in every single overhead bin, judging by the number of times he stopped, set down his things, checked, and picked them back up. I smoothed a hand down the front of my shirt and glanced at her text again. My departure had been delayed because of mechanical issues, and the man with a million suitcases or just a bad memory was moving like molasses.

> BENNETT: Flight delay + slow fellow passenger.
> Can I still see you?

The crowd finally started to move forward again, and luckily the bag man found all his belongings and stopped searching. I'd been antsy all day, waking two hours ahead of my alarm because I was paranoid about missing a flight. I hated being late. Even though my tardiness wasn't my fault, it reminded me of my parents and the constant uncertainty about whether they'd show up or not. I didn't want Ollie to question whether I'd show up, even if we'd established this was just a mutually beneficial friendship.

> OLLIE: Sure. I'll be the woman behind the counter at Pre-Flight Paws.
>
> BENNETT: Or the woman chasing a wet dog.
>
> OLLIE: It's always a possibility.
>
> BENNETT: Even better. It's really Pepper I hoped to see.
>
> OLLIE: See you soon.

My chuckle earned a kind glance from the flight attendant, and I thanked her, navigating around bag man and smoothly circumventing a chatty young couple ambling up the jet bridge. The airport was one of the few places where you could walk fast around people and most didn't mind. They'd assume I had to catch a flight and not the attention of a beautiful woman who'd agreed to practice dating for some reason.

Emerging from the jet bridge into the terminal was like walking out into sunshine, even though the lights were fluorescent. For a moment, there was so much space, I felt like I could spin. I never spun, of course, because that would get me followed and taken in by security. Sometimes I wanted to, though. I'd stepped off a plane three years earlier to find out that my first book had sold to a publisher. This time Ollie was waiting and leaning against a column at the edge of the seating area. She wasn't wearing the same T-shirt I'd seen her in before but rather a blue cotton dress with a belt at her waist that showed her curves.

"I figured I'd meet you," she said, standing straighter. "Not sure how this whole muse thing works."

"I . . . Well, I don't know, either, but I'm glad you're here," I said, returning her wave. I wanted to hug her, but we hadn't set any boundaries yet and I was dragging my roller bag behind me. "I'm sorry I'm late."

She waved a hand. "That's okay. How long do you have?"

I didn't need to look because I'd done the math in the sky bridge, eager to maximize my time with her, but I glanced at my watch anyway. "An hour and seven minutes."

She giggled. God, she had a great laugh. "That's very specific. Are you a specific kind of man, Bennett?"

"Well, I work with risk assessment for an insurance company, so I'd say so."

She nodded toward the terminal and I followed her, standing close to hear her and to be a little nearer. "Insurance and romance novels. That's quite a combination."

"I'm afraid those are the two most interesting things about me," I confessed as we neared an open area filled with different food options. "I want to hear about you, though. How you decided on pet grooming in an airport."

She laughed again and paused, glancing around. "I can share that, but first . . . which culinary delight tickles your fancy? I'm flexible."

I looked for the shortest line. It was hard to hear her in this crowded space, and leaning into her would mean I'd be inhaling the delicious scent of her, which would probably cross a line for friends. "Do you like pretzels?"

"Why? Did you sneak some off the plane?" We walked toward the soft-pretzel vendor and stood behind three other people.

"I always choose the cookies, even first thing in the morning." I had a small addiction, but they were excellent cookies. "My friend Gia found them for me in a store once, but they just taste better on the plane."

"Sweet tooth, huh?" The customer in front of us stepped back unexpectedly and bumped Ollie with his backpack. She braced herself against my arm, and her palm stretched across my biceps.

My face heated for no reason. Liking sweet things wasn't even embarrassing, but her touch sent a warm flush through my body. I'd felt the same thing after I gave her the Cruella de Vil toy and we'd shaken hands. "They're excellent cookies. I, uh, have a stash."

She moved her hand away and I missed the feel but pulled my messenger bag toward her and opened the front compartment, where I had ten or fifteen little packets of Biscoff biscuits. "You have a problem," she said, peering into the bag and then meeting my eyes. "But the bigger question is: Do you share your cookies?"

"Only with my friends."

She grinned. "Good thing we're friends."

BY THE TIME we got our pretzels, we had only forty minutes, which was how we found ourselves on the moving walkway, standing off to the right together, eating our pretzels and watching the concourse move slowly by us. "So, tell me about work. That's what people talk about on dates, right? How did you decide to do this?"

She finished chewing and leaned back against the moving rubber hand belt. "My best friend, Jess, has wanted to open her own grooming place for years, but it's expensive."

I nodded, remembering the woman in the shop who had

trimmed Duke the cat—Gia had named him the Duke of Malefi-cent Falls, from my third book.

"I went to school for management and political science," she added, looking out over the flight line as we passed a series of floor-to-ceiling windows. "I was going to move to DC and maybe try to change the world."

"So, you've never been a corporate drone like me. Perhaps a high-powered lobbyist?"

She smiled without her teeth and shook her head. "No."

"What happened?"

She swung her gaze to mine and fixed a smile on her face. "That's a story for another pretzel. I didn't end up going but came into some money later. Yada yada yada, we did our research and decided the trend of pets flying wasn't going anywhere, and with some policy changes, we were able to give it a try. I'd been trying to take more risks, and . . . well, this was a big one."

"I have limited knowledge of pet grooming," I said. That was a bit of a lie—I'd looked up everything I could find on the business after meeting her the first time. If I'd put that much research into my new book, the writing might go faster. "Seems like the risk paid off."

"It did. We might be expanding into some other airports. It will mean a ton of travel, but that's kind of exciting," she said as we stepped off the end of the walkway and strode toward the next one. I saw my gate in the distance and contemplated missing my flight so I could talk to her longer.

"That's fantastic. Congratulations." I crumpled the wrapper from my pretzel to do something with my hands. "From one fre-quent flier to a soon-to-be one, it can be hard to keep up with people. In my experience, all relationships start to feel like long-distance relationships if you're gone a lot."

She shook her head. "I believe it. I will never have another long-distance relationship."

My heart sank. This was just pretzels on the people mover, and this was just friendship and book inspiration. "Sounds like that's a story for another pretzel, too?"

"Definitely," she said, crumpling her own wrapper. "Is this helping? For the book, I mean?"

I'd forgotten about it, lost in talking to her. "Yeah, I think it is. In the book, the character is heartbroken; not that you're heartbroken, of course. But it's about long-distance relationships and how he might be lonely. How that might shape his actions." I'd pulled that out of the air, but it was a perfect angle for the part I was writing. I glanced away and then back to Ollie, tracing the constellation of her freckles.

"Lonely is definitely a thing," she said, her own gaze wandering. "That's why I love books. Should I read your books? I don't know if that's allowed."

We stepped off the moving walkway again and stood near a wall across from my gate, both regaining our equilibrium. "You don't have to."

She shrugged. "It would be nice to see what this might lead to."

The gate agent's voice startled us. "We will begin preboarding for Flight 2225, service to Chicago, shortly."

"I guess we're about out of time," she said, with maybe a hint of disappointment at the corners of her lips.

"Here," I said, reaching into my bag and pulling out a few packages. "For dessert."

"Three? Wow, what did I do to earn this much of your stash?" Our fingers brushed when she took the cookies from my hand. That same electricity sparked over my skin.

"Just to ensure I get to hear those other pretzel stories."

She ran a hand over her stomach. "Heavy trade-off, but I guess that's fair. I can enjoy the cookies when I start reading your book."

I liked the idea of her holding my words in her hands. "I like to read with something sweet, too."

She pressed her lips together and shifted her gaze, and I wondered if what I'd said sounded as flirtatious to her as it did in my head. She met my eyes again, though. "I'm sure it will only sweeten the reading experience. I'll make sure to leave good reviews."

"Only if you enjoy them," I said automatically, trying to tamp down the smile.

"Oh, of course. If I don't, I'll eviscerate you on every platform I can access."

My laugh came out bigger than I'd intended. "That's all I ask."

"Now, this isn't *101 Dalmatians* fan fic, is it? If so, I just need to mentally prepare."

I laughed again, noticing the looks from a few nearby passengers waiting for our flight. "Just love stories; no puppies were harmed."

She wiped her brow in mock relief. "Whew!" Ollie glanced over my shoulder at my gate. "I think you probably have to go."

"I suppose you're right." There was a crumb under her lip I noticed just then and I had a fleeting fantasy of kissing her there, taking care of the crumb and then backing her against a wall. "You have a little something here," I said, motioning to my own mouth.

She brushed it away immediately. "How long have you let me talk to you with food on my face, Benny?"

"Not long, and I didn't want to interrupt your story." I didn't mention that I'd been so focused on her, I hadn't noticed the fleck of bread.

"Well, I guess that's polite," she said, walking with me closer to the boarding area, where they'd begun boarding the main cabin.

"And I didn't want to brush something from your face without your permission."

She grinned. "It's a good thing we weren't eating chicken wings," she said, brushing her own lips, seeming to check again.

"You're perfect," I said without thinking. "I mean, you got it. The crumb. Not that your face is perfect. I mean, it's a lovely face, a beautiful face, a perfect face, really, but I meant—"

"Bennett?"

I pressed my lips together.

And she laughed again. "You can brush away crumbs or chicken bones or any other food that might end up there. It's something I'd ask of any of my friends."

I had the urge to practice the motion, but the gate agent indicated the doors would close soon. "I will. Thanks for having a pretzel with me," I said, taking a step toward the gate.

"See you soon," she said, waving me toward my flight.

"Definitely."

11

Ollie

OUR BUSINESS SAW mostly dogs, with a few cats in the mix, but every now and then, a customer would throw us a curveball. I accepted the animal carrier from the gentleman across the desk once he was finished talking sweetly to and then kissing on the mouth a sable-colored ferret. I wanted gold stars for maintaining a straight expression. After checking him in, I walked the case to the back for Jess, who was showing Jeremiah a few tricks of the trade.

"Miss Cornelia is here," I said handing over the case. "How do you bathe a ferret, anyway?"

"Carefully," Jess joked. "I read up on it since I knew she was coming in. You want to stay and watch?"

"No, thanks." I liked dogs, but Jess was the animal lover between the two of us. Also, I was stuck on the image of the owner's mouth on the animal's mouth and I was feeling a need to wash my hands. Instead, I pulled my phone from my pocket.

OLLIE: I just watched a man kiss a ferret.

BENNETT: Have you no shame? Some moments between a man and his ferret are private.

BENNETT: Tongue wasn't involved, was it?

I clapped my hand over my mouth to stifle giggles, though the lobby was empty.

OLLIE: Do you really want to know?

BENNETT: On second thought, I don't. Do you have anything unrelated to ferrets to discuss?

OLLIE: Do you have a minute for a question?

BENNETT: Sorry, all my minutes are reserved for answers. You can try again later.

BENNETT: Shoot.

I checked the lobby again and took a selfie with the five books I'd brought from home.

OLLIE: Which one of your novels should I start with?

I waited for a reply and glanced over the book covers, the first two with sweeping covers featuring two people in an embrace, the man's hands always venturing slightly toward indecent and the woman's expression looking perfectly wanting. I wondered how much influence Bennett had in picking the models; maybe that was the type of woman he was interested in. The three in the series were a mix of illustrated backgrounds and half photos and half sketched images, the effect feeling like the artist had been caught mid-render.

OLLIE: Did I lose you?

BENNETT: Sorry, no. I just didn't expect you to buy them all.

OLLIE: I'd already bought your first and then the bookstore in the terminal had them in stock. The owner loves you, by the way. She talked my ear off and two other customers joined in.

OLLIE: You're a little famous, Benny.

BENNETT: I am not famous.

BENNETT: I'd start with *The Duchess Affair* or *To Loathe an Earl*. They're stand-alone books, so if you don't want to keep reading, you're not left with a cliffhanger.

OLLIE: I'm not worried about not liking them.

BENNETT: FYI. They all contain love scenes. They're rather graphic.

I glanced at the books I'd stashed back under the counter. The bookstore owner did tell me the books were "very steamy" and the two customers who joined the conversation said to "have extra batteries on hand while reading." My face warmed. Other parts of my body warmed at the idea of Bennett, my new *friend*, writing sex scenes that were so hot they elicited warnings from well-meaning strangers to make sure my vibrator was charged. I thought about the feel of his hand against mine when we shook hands, the way his grip had been firm but gentle. I wondered how much of his writing translated to real life.

OLLIE: Dedicated romance reader, remember?
Looking forward to those! 🍆🍑🏆

    I sent another text with just a smiley face to balance out the sexting emojis and watched the dots blink back and forth until a customer entered and I set aside my phone. Ten minutes later, once I had them checked in, I looked back at the thread, where I found a GIF of a ferret sticking out its tongue.

LATE THE NEXT night, I set the book aside and let out a deep breath. I wasn't sure what I'd been expecting, but the novel had ticked every box. The characters were interesting and well-rounded, the story kept me turning pages, the romance felt both normal and grand, and, as promised by the women in the bookstore, the sex scenes made me blush. I had a fleeting curiosity about whether his rambling carried over into the bedroom. *Does Bennett just keep going?*

OLLIE: I finished your book.

BENNETT: I'll await your eviscerating review.

    I glanced at the clock. I hadn't realized it was so late, after 1 a.m. my time. I did the math for California, where he was working that week, and I wondered if he was in bed, too.

OLLIE: I loved it. I loved every second of it. How are you this good? Is it too weird that I'm texting you from my bed at 1am?

BENNETT: It's three hours less weird in California, if that makes you feel better. I'm happy you liked it.

I picked up the book again and ran a finger over the raised font of his name. I'd heard his voice in the words and touches of the humor I was getting to know, and a few moments that made me gasp.

> OLLIE: You didn't tell me there was a runaway dog.

> BENNETT: That was a bit of a coincidence.

> BENNETT: Not that it's the same. No nudity for you, and Pepper isn't a pug.

> BENNETT: I mean you weren't naked when chasing the dog. Not that you're not naked now.

> BENNETT: Not that you are naked or not that you'd tell me if you were. Of course, I wouldn't ask you what you were wearing. It's none of my business.

> OLLIE: Benny, you're rambling. Is it rambling if it's in a text message?

> BENNETT: Yes. It is my natural state. Apologies.

I grinned and imagined his expression when he realized he'd been going on and on about me being naked, the words falling out of him like they had nowhere else to go. He'd look a little flustered and a little embarrassed and then he'd flash this smile that was a little bit kissable.

> OLLIE: For the record, I am not naked. I have paired an ages-old T-shirt with my rattiest sweatpants for this conversation. Does that inspire anything for you?

His end of the conversation was silent for a few minutes.

> BENNETT: Definitely. Well, now that you've told me what you're wearing, will you tell me something else?

> OLLIE: Granny panties.

> BENNETT: I just choked on my tea. I wasn't going to ask that. I was only joking about the what-are-you-wearing thing. I know that would be completely inappropriate.

> OLLIE: I know. I just wanted to see you ramble.

> BENNETT: Mission accomplished. What I really wanted to ask was if you'd share one of the 🥨 stories? Why didn't you move to Washington DC?

I swallowed and set the book down, glancing out the open window with the city lights twinkling. I didn't want to type it all out and see the words in front of me, so I hit the call button.

"Hello." His voice was low and soothing, and I liked the unexpected rush I got from the familiar way he answered.

"It's an easier story to say than to type," I jumped in.

"The best pretzel stories are." I heard rustling in the background and wondered again if he was lying in bed like me, a few thousand miles away.

"It's not that great a story. I mean, you wouldn't put it in a book, but maybe it will help."

Bennett spoke a little slower and a little lower. I didn't know if that was because of the late hour or if it showed he was relaxed, but I liked it. "I wouldn't put it in. It doesn't always have to be about the book; we could just talk like friends."

I rolled the term around in my head. Friends. "I had a job offer to work with a campaign strategist in DC. She was supporting a candidate I really believed in who had some sweeping ideas. It was everything I'd worked for, what every internship and late-night study session had led to." I glanced at the space across the room where I had a framed photo of me in DC in college, standing in front of the Capitol with friends during a trip.

"That sounds like an amazing opportunity." He had this way of responding without a question or without prompting me to continue that made me want to tell him everything.

"It was." I settled against my pillows. "My boyfriend at the time had a good job here and asked me to marry him, said he would miss me too much, that he wanted us to have the best chance to make it." I looked at my bare ring finger. "I loved him and I agreed to put off the job and to look for something local."

Bennett didn't say anything, so I kept talking.

"I found a few things here and there with some local politicians, but nothing on the level of the DC job, and then he got a new job in New York."

"And you moved with him?"

"I was going to go. I had to wrap up a campaign here, so he went on without me for the first six months. We planned to get married and live there. Well, turns out he chose New York for more than the job. His girlfriend was there. When I found out, he tried to convince me it was my fault, that if I were with him and not working so much, it wouldn't have happened. That it was just the distance."

"I'm sorry he was such an ass, Olivia. You broke up with him?"

Aunt Harry had advised me to blow up his life and go full scorched earth, but she didn't mean it. That would hurt his grandma, one of her best friends. Jess still offered to bring the matches, though. "I returned his ring to his sweet grandmother—it had been hers—and began to figure out what to do with my life."

"You're much kinder than I would have been. Did you at least tell granny that her grandson was a cheating asshole?"

I smiled. "I should have. I was so angry and sad, I didn't know where to direct it all, but then I channeled it into other things and eventually the business with Jess. Anyway, that is my pretzel-for-another-time story."

"And that's why no long-distance relationships?"

"Yes." I checked out the clock; it was after two in the morning now. "I should get some sleep, though. If I stay up any later rereading passages from your book, I'll be dead at work tomorrow."

"You're right. It's getting late." There was a hedge in his voice, like there was something more he wanted to say but decided against it. "Thank you for telling me your pretzel story, Ollie."

"Thank you for listening to it." Now we were both just breathing into the phone, soft puffs of breath the only sounds between us, and neither of us seemed to be making a move to hang up. I liked the sound of his breaths. I liked the way it was comfortable. And I didn't like how much I wanted to stay on the phone with him. "I'll see you soon?"

"Absolutely. I'm looking forward to it."

"Good night, Benny."

"Good night, beautiful Olivia."

12

Bennett

ASIDE FROM A text here or there, I hadn't really spoken with Ollie since our late-night phone call, which started out with me imagining her naked in bed and ended with me imagining her in her tattered sweatpants reading my book next to me. The second image had been harder to shake away.

As the plane taxied and I powered my phone on, I drummed my fingers on the seat, eager to see her. She'd texted that morning asking if my flight was on time and if I was allergic to anything, leaving me curious.

> BENNETT: Just landed.

> OLLIE: Hungry?

> BENNETT: Famished.

The stars had aligned for this flight—we'd arrived early, I was near the front with efficient travelers ahead of me, and I'd spent the first leg of my trip working on my book, the one scene I couldn't get out of my head since meeting Ollie. The hero and heroine shared their first kiss, a moment of passion alone in a rose garden. The entire time I was writing it, I was imagining Ollie at Gate C7 and the rows of chairs instead of a maze of rosebushes. The fantasy left me eager for a kiss that wouldn't happen, but when I stepped off the plane, Ollie smiled at me like she'd been eager to see me, too.

"What's all this?" I motioned to the two brown paper bags she carried.

"I didn't want to chance long lines, so I picked up lunch for us." She held up the bags and nodded to the other end of the concourse. "There's a gate at the end of the concourse that's usually not busy this time of day."

"You made us a picnic lunch?"

She looked up at me through thick lashes with a sheepish grin. "I bought us a picnic lunch in the food court."

"Still counts." When I reached for one of the bags, our fingers grazed. I still wasn't used to the feeling that shot through me at her proximity. "I have a long layover this time."

"Good, because I acquired a lot of food and have help covering the front of the salon for a while."

I liked that she wanted to spend more time with me. I'd asked my assistant to make sure I had a longer layover in the airport when traveling to or from LA. She'd given me a curious expression—my requests in the past had always been to spend as little time traveling as possible, as I preferred to spend the time doing the work. Despite this job, I didn't actually like travel all that much. Except for Ollie. She made it worth it.

She pulled a blanket from one bag and spread it on the carpet near some empty seats and the airport's floor-to-ceiling windows. "Is sitting on the floor okay?" She looked at my suit skeptically.

I set my bags near the seats and laughed, in awe of this whole setup. "I just can't believe you set up a picnic lunch. I'm so impressed."

She shrugged and joined me on the blanket, her legs tucked to one side. "It's no big deal. I figured sitting down was better than the moving walkway and it would be quieter here."

I accepted the bottle of water she handed me as she begun unpacking things from the bag. I admired the slope of her shoulder—she wore a tank top today, her soft brown skin a contrast to the bright white of the shirt. I wondered if she'd chosen it thinking of me in the same way I'd studied my shirts wondering which might look nicest when I saw her. She smiled when she handed me a wrapped sandwich and placed a container of chips and guacamole between us. "Did I do something special to deserve this level of care?"

"I finished all your books," she said, digging a container filled with chopped vegetables from the bag. Impressively, the broccoli and carrots looked fresh and crisp and not sad and deflated, as could be the case with prepackaged, to-go vegetables.

"All of them? It's only been a few days." I imagined her reading some of the scenes in my second book—the ones Gia said were the hottest thing I'd ever written—and my neck heated.

"You're a really good writer," she said with a wink. *This woman is going to kill me.* "Dig in," she said, motioning to the food. "I have dessert, too."

As soon as I'd seen her, I'd forgotten I was starving, but the sandwich was thick sliced turkey on soft bread, and one bite was all it took to remind my brain that my body needed sustenance. "This is really lovely. You're an excellent picnic curator," I commented.

"I order takeout with the best of them."

"It's an important life skill," I said, reaching for a baby carrot.

We chewed together in companionable silence, enjoying the food. It was so strange that these silences never felt awkward. Other than with Gia, silences often felt so stressful, so anxiety producing, like I needed to come up with the next thing to say. Ollie just made me feel like I could relax, and the conversation would reinstate itself at some point.

"Can I ask you a question?"

"You don't actually have to ask permission before asking." I shifted so I could lean against the seats behind us as I finished the sandwich I'd mostly inhaled. "What would you like to know, beautiful Olivia?"

"No one calls me Olivia. I'm not really used to it, I guess. But no one calls me beautiful, either. Why do you do that?"

"That was your question?" I stalled because I hadn't meant to call her that—her given name or adding on to it. It's how I thought of her in my head, and I knew it was completely wrong to say to someone who'd said they wanted to be friends, and she was doing me this favor. "I apologize. I don't want to make you feel uncomfortable."

"I don't . . . mind; it's just so . . . I don't know."

"I'll stop. I do think you're beautiful—stunning, really." I snapped my gaze up to her eyes from her lips, where it had naturally fallen. "But I know it's odd to say that, to make you believe I only appreciate how you look. And that couldn't be further from the truth, though, of course, how you look is . . . well, you're beautiful, and . . . I'm rambling again."

She glanced down at her hands, as if she were hiding the smile on her lips. "The rambling is kind of adorable," she said quietly before taking a gulp from her water bottle.

We fell into one of our silences again, this one filled with my awkward admission that I thought she was the most beautiful woman I'd ever met and I couldn't get her out of my mind. Maybe I didn't say that out loud, but it felt like I'd told her everything. "So, what was your actual question?"

"In one of the books, the characters' parents were gamblers. You wrote that in such a . . . I don't know, moving way. Was that from personal experience?"

I'd answered the question before. That wasn't fully true—I'd been asked the question before and provided a response, but not the real answer. I nodded. "Yes. Mum and Dad met at a card game. They always joked they bet it all on love."

"That's sweet," she said, studying me.

"It was, I suppose. It is. They're still betting it all on each other, but also on everything else, too."

"And on you?"

"Not so much." I gave her what I was sure was a wry grin. "They're not bad people. They love me; they just love the next big thing a little more, or so it's always seemed."

She chewed her thumbnail, considering my words. "So, you built a career assessing risk."

"Doesn't take a psychiatrist to figure out that one, huh?"

She smiled, one of her familiar soft smiles, and we both watched a small family walk by, one father holding a little boy's hand and talking to him in that way parents always seemed to talk to kids in airports—one part keeping them close, one part teaching them how to behave in the space, and one part awed at the child having this little adventure. The other father pushed a stroller and spoke to the baby inside, making exaggerated funny faces.

"You like it, though? The work?"

I returned my attention to her. "I enjoy it. I'd rather be writing, but the day job is more stable."

"Have you ever thought about writing full-time?" She began to clean up the empty containers and I helped, passing wrappers and lids across the blanket. "Or is that too big a risk financially?"

Gia asked me that all the time; so did my literary agent. I'd never given either of them the real reason I was hesitant to do it. "It's a financial risk, but it's not really that."

She narrowed her eyes and handed me a single serving of cheesecake from inside her brown paper bag. "It's hard to take a chance on ourselves."

I nodded. "If everything goes tits up, it's on me, and in publishing, nothing is guaranteed. You must know that feeling, owning your own business and all. I just don't know if I'm cut out for that."

"You've been able to keep writing, though? No more writer's block?"

"Not since I met you."

She handed me a fork and rested her hand on mine. It was the first time we'd touched in any sustained way since that handshake, and the risk I wanted to take was to link my fingers with hers, or to tip her chin up so our lips could meet. That's what I wrote into my books. It was what my characters would do, but my characters were braver than me.

Her eyes met mine, her cool hand still over mine. "For what it's worth, I couldn't put your books down. It felt like you were next to me when I was reading." She leaned forward and my hands finally took over where my brain had stilled.

I lifted my hand and brushed the pad of my thumb over her cheek, gently, barely touching her, but her eyes fell closed.

"Did I have a crumb?"

My voice sounded foreign to me, rough. "It was a chicken wing, actually."

She chuckled but didn't move her hand. She didn't pull back, and I needed to kiss this woman more than I needed to breathe, but the sound of wheels clattering on the tile broke our connection, as two men chatting animatedly about baseball rounded the corner and sat nearby.

Ollie pulled back and smoothed out her tank top, though it

wasn't unsettled. She nodded toward the cheesecake in my hand. "It's not as good as the cookies, but eat up."

I had a sinking feeling the opportunity was gone and I cursed my parents in that moment for raising me to not take chances. I knew they didn't always come around again, that sometimes being careful meant missing out.

I couldn't believe we'd been talking so long, and when I checked my watch, I knew I'd have to head to my gate soon. As we finished cleaning up and threw away our trash, I didn't want to leave her. "Thank you for the picnic. This was the best layover I've ever had."

She did a deep bow, her tank top dipping low in the front, and *No, I will not ogle her breasts even though they look perfect.* "It was fun. Maybe you can add a picnic to the book." She smoothed a palm down the front of her shirt. "And, for what it's worth, I hope you decide to take the chance if it will make you happy." She ran her palm down my forearm and goose bumps covered my arm at her touch. "It's important to be happy."

The guys behind us were still talking about baseball, loudly and without mind to our conversation, so Olivia had leaned close when she spoke, her hand still on my arm. The flurry of sensation from her touch was the only way to justify what came out of my mouth. "May I hug you?"

"Hug me?"

"I mean, to say goodbye. Well, not goodbye. I'll be back, but goodbye for now. Goodbye until next time. I don't know why I tell you all these things, but I seem to be able to talk to you, and I just thought, maybe we were good enough friends to hug, if you want to, but of course if you don't—"

She cut me off, wrapping her arms around my neck. She smelled like cinnamon and flowers, and the two scents should not have gone together so well, but they did. "Thank you for telling me your pretzel story, Benny," she said as I wrapped my arms around her back.

"And for showing up again without your fur coat. Too bad my aunt Harry isn't getting married in the airport. You'd be a really fun date."

"Would she consider changing the venue?" I laughed from my belly and used the joke to pull us closer, all the while thinking about risks and her enticing cinnamon scent and how much I didn't want to get on that plane.

13

Ollie

"NO PICNIC LUNCH today?" Jess bumped me with her hip at the front desk, practically in sync with yelps from Pepper and his fellow guest waiting to be picked up alongside him in the back.

"I regret telling you about that."

"Why?"

"Because you keep making the whole thing into something more than it is." In truth, she wasn't, because I was making it bigger than it was. When he'd asked to hug me, when he'd pulled me to him and our bodies were close, I'd wanted more, and not just more physically, which . . . Well, of course I wanted more physically, but I wanted more time spent getting to know him. And in the back of my mind, I knew this was for his book, that for whatever reason, I inspired him. But the book would be done at some point.

Jess raised an eyebrow and sipped on the straw of her massive water bottle. Her hydration intake was truly impressive.

"I mean, we're just friends. I barely know him." Except that I felt like I did know him on some level. I'd told him about my ex and he'd shared about his parents—not a lot, but it felt like more than what you'd tell a stranger. "And he lives somewhere else."

"True," she said, skimming through the paperwork on the desk. "Is that the only thing holding you back?"

"Holding me back from what?"

"From going on a real date or at least admitting you want to."

I didn't respond, filing away the stack of invoices I'd just paid. I'd thought he was going to kiss me during that picnic. I'd leaned in and he'd touched my face, and even though we were in the middle of the airport with the PA system and all the background noise and the fluorescent lighting, I thought he would kiss me, and I'd wanted him to.

"You know, you're my best friend, you're my business partner, but I don't get you sometimes. After that jackass cheated on you, you've been all about taking chances, taking risks, and never playing it safe just to play it safe. I love that about you. But you meet a guy who is the exact opposite of a safe choice, and suddenly you don't even consider risking it?" Jess nudged me again and I met her stare.

Her words reminded me of Bennett talking about striking out on his own, on taking a chance on himself. Jess was right; Bennett was not a safe choice—he lived somewhere else and we'd spent a grand total of maybe five hours in each other's company. I'd liked him immediately, though, and nothing about that initial attraction had dampened. He was a risk, a big one, but it wasn't financial or professional. "I like him a lot, Jess," I said quietly. "I think if I opened the door, I'd fall through, and I'm a little skittish about doors at this point."

She wrapped an arm around my shoulders and tipped her head to mine, bumping it in time to another explosion of conversation between Pepper and the poor shih tzu who was his unwilling bunkmate. "I know."

The barking intensified and we saw Pepper's owner approaching the doors. Jess slid away and walked into the back room. "I'm not letting you off the hook about this yet," she called over her shoulder.

My phone buzzed by the computer.

BENNETT: Are you free tomorrow evening? I'm
flying through around seven.

BENNETT: And hello

I made small talk with Pepper's owner, who was, in fact, not visiting a love interest but staying with her grandson every couple of weeks. It made me look at Pepper a little more kindly, knowing she wanted him dapper and clean before he interacted with a toddler with whom he was "a peach." After they left, three more customers arrived, and I didn't get a break to respond to Bennett until almost an hour later, when Jeremiah and Jess had the animals in the back and in the throes of pampering.

OLLIE: I can be here at seven.

OLLIE: Also, can you recommend some more
books since I ran through all yours?

BENNETT: Of course! What do you like to read?
More historical? Lower heat?

OLLIE: I'm feeling historical right now.

I drummed my fingers against the counter.

OLLIE: High heat.

I bit my lower lip, waiting for his response, not because I was basically telling him I liked reading about sex but because he knew I liked reading the sex he wrote. The sex he wrote so well that it transported me into this feeling like I was completely in the moment and experiencing every detail. Bennett was very good at details.

> BENNETT: I enjoy those, too.

I expected him to add a qualifier, to ramble in that way I was kind of coming to love, but he didn't.

> OLLIE: Then send those recommendations that will require me to buy a fan, Cruella!

> BENNETT: Here are some of my favorites.

He sent three texts in a row filled with book recommendations, and I imagined him typing furiously before having to stow his phone for a flight. The last message contained a GIF of a half-naked man sitting in front of a fan, and I covered my grin. I didn't need to—Jess was in the back—but if I covered it, I could convince myself the guy didn't delight me so much.

> OLLIE: Thanks. I'll let you know how it goes.

> OLLIE: I mean, how the reading goes, not how the fanning goes.

> OLLIE: Not that I'll actually be using a fan.

> OLLIE: That would be dangerous and cold, which, I'm not into that . . .

> BENNETT: I think you picked up my rambling habit.

> OLLIE: It's contagious, isn't it?

> BENNETT: I should have given you a warning, but it's cute when you do it.

I'm in trouble. I wasn't sure what to reply. I could have told him I felt the same, but our conversations were getting flirtier and flirtier and I didn't want to lead him on. I didn't want to lead myself on, because Jess was getting to me, and the reasons I couldn't admit this crush out loud kept seeming more and more insignificant.

His next message was a photo from the window of the plane—the sun had cast the tops of the clouds in swaths of orange and lavender like they were a giant blanket.

> OLLIE: Wow, that's gorgeous.

> BENNETT: I'd never paid much attention to the color of the clouds, but it made me think of you for some reason. Couldn't stop looking out my window during my flight.

Deep trouble.

> OLLIE: You should put that in a book. The line about the sky making you think of someone, not the air travel.

The door chimed and a customer clutching a pug to her rushed in needing quick service before a flight. We were slammed for the next two hours solid, customers in and out constantly. When I picked up my phone after things finally slowed down, I had a message waiting from Bennett.

> BENNETT: Good idea. It's probably something you wouldn't say to another person in real life, anyway, huh? Too sappy?

> OLLIE: Maybe just the right amount of sappy.

14

Bennett

I LUCKED OUT and ended up needing to spend a few days in Chicago for work, so I was able to visit Gia. When I arrived at her office to pick her up, a student in a Thurmond University sweatshirt, the hood pulled over his hair, was talking to her. Gia wore jeans and a sweater, and I felt out of place in my suit.

"Thanks, Dr. B," the student said, backing out of her office. He gave me a nod as he moved past me, pushing sunglasses down from his forehead.

"No problem, Quinn." She gave a wave to the student and then turned to me. "Hey," Gia said with a smile.

"Look at you, shaping young minds," I said while taking in her space, every surface crowded with books and papers. She wrapped her arms around my neck.

"Today I'm just giving young minds another chance to pass chemistry." She motioned to the chair across from her. "I just have to finish up a few things and then we can go."

"No problem, Professor. I'll sit here quietly."

She rolled her eyes and spoke while closing things out on her computer. "So, I finished reading the new book."

I always sent Gia my stuff before anyone else read it. I'd been feverishly writing it, the book I was inspired to work on every time I talked to Ollie.

"What came over you with this one?"

"What do you mean?"

Gia studied my face, her eyes narrowed.

"Does that mean you didn't like it?"

She shook her head. "I loved it. It's romantic and moving. The hot scenes were, well . . . damn, Ben. I always love your work, but this one hit different. What changed when you wrote this one?"

I shrugged. "Nothing." That was a lie. I normally plotted my books before writing. I knew each beat of the story, each step of a character's arc. There was no risk in writing it because I knew what would happen when I started typing. After getting so stuck, I'd ditched my plotting for this book—I'd been surprised at my own twists and turns, and it needed editing, but I'd been inspired, I supposed. I'd had Ollie in my head.

"How're things going with the airport woman?"

I pulled my phone from my pocket to have something to do with my hands. "Fine. Why do you ask?"

She arched a brow. I'd told her about my screw-up and our decision to be friends. She'd eventually pried out of me how we texted and that we'd gone on dates in the airport. "Just curious when you're going to tell me you're completely falling for her, which is why this book feels different. Like, now? Or will I have to wait until we get our entrées?"

I didn't respond to the text waiting from Ollie. It was a picture of her holding one of the books I recommended and a series of emojis. Her smile was wide and I saw her bedroom in the background, the space I imagined her texting me from late at night. I flicked my eyes up to meet my friend's. "I might need my dinner in front of me first."

• • •

SEEING GIA WAS good for my soul. We laughed and caught up and she told me I needed to get my head out of my ass about quitting and about Olivia in the way only my best friend could. When my flight to Atlanta landed, I'd gone back to sketching the future. I had a plan.

When I powered my phone on, I had a voice mail from Ollie. "Hey, when you get here, follow the signs to walk toward Terminal B."

I rushed toward the underground walkway between terminals and spotted Ollie standing near the escalator in jeans and a loose-fitting shirt that somehow still hugged the swell of her breasts. I walked down the escalator, sliding around people who were more patient to get to the bottom.

"Welcome back," she said when I neared the bottom and stepped from the metal steps onto the tiles. She paused for a second and then pulled me into a hug. She was soft, her body pliant against mine, and even the feel of her back under my palm was inviting. We talked most days now, so even though I hadn't been near her in a few weeks, seeing her again felt like coming back to someplace familiar.

"It's good to be back," I murmured near her ear, holding her a few beats longer than was probably normal for that section of the airport. I grudgingly let her go, holding on to her sweet scent. The shuttle groaned to a halt and a hundred feet shuffled on or off, eager to get to baggage claim or their connecting flight. The automated voice announced, "Attention, passengers, the train doors are closing."

"I wanted to show you something," she said, nodding to the left.

"Lead the way." I placed my hand at the small of her back and wished I hadn't, because I didn't want to pull it away. "How did the meeting go?"

She'd told me she and her partner had a meeting with the company that wanted to work with them to expand the business. She took risks the way I admired, after researching and strategizing, but there was still a lot up in the air.

"I can't believe there are going to be Pre-Flight Paws locations in other places."

We navigated around the crowds waiting for the train and into the long tunnel connecting gates for those who wanted to walk, and the entire time I longed to touch her lower back again. "Do you ever miss politics? The kind of work you thought you'd do?"

She shrugged. "I do, but running the business has been more fulfilling than I thought it would be. The new challenge is exciting." She motioned around as we stepped into the tunnel and began walking next to the moving walkway. There was a display that stretched the length of the long hall with depictions of historical figures and people through time connected to social movements. It felt like walking through a museum. Ollie bumped my shoulder with hers. "Kind of a hidden gem, huh? Well, as hidden as a gem can be in an airport that sees tens of thousands of people a day."

"Perfect airport date location," I said, looking around, catching my words after they left my lips.

I risked a glance to catch her reaction, but it didn't seem she'd made anything of my comment. "Are you ever going to tell me what this book is about? Every time we hang out, I'm dying of curiosity about what I say that shapes the book."

I should have told her it was done, but I didn't want this arrangement to end. "No book today," I said, searching the display without really looking. "I just wanted to see you."

"Pressure is off, then, I guess. I've never been this creative with dates before," she said, pausing to read a display about a prominent Black transgender woman who'd pushed for changes in the 1990s. The crowds had thinned, most people taking the moving walkway or the train to their next destination. "I never actually enjoyed dating."

"Me, either. Always felt like a job interview, and when it worked out, it felt like being at a job I didn't deeply care about."

"So, you quit?" She was still reading the sign and not looking at me, which made it easier to answer.

"I was usually fired before I could quit." I chuckled.

She gave a wistful smile and I wanted to kick myself. "Not that that's what happened with you. I know being engaged is a whole other thing."

"No, it's pretty much what happened to me." She turned to face me, but she didn't look sad. She smiled. "That's okay, though. There were better dates ahead." The back of her hand brushed mine and that now familiar sweep of sensation rushed through me.

"With friends?" I shifted my fingers so they touched hers lightly, feeling like I was holding a breath, waiting for this to go wrong.

She held my gaze, though, and linked her finger with mine, her middle finger sliding against mine before I curled my fingers to bring them together.

We stood together for only a few moments, but it felt like longer. "Could I take you on a real date?"

"Are you saying the Cinnabon outside the men's room I have planned after this isn't a real date?"

Her wry grin made me laugh, and the tension was gone. We were just two people holding hands and learning about the history of the city, not that I was paying attention to the display now that we'd made this jump to something new. "I love Cinnabon."

"I knew you weren't a total cartoon villain," she said as we walked. "Sure, you make questionable fashion choices and might be on PETA's most-wanted list, but you can't be all that bad if you love gooey giant cinnamon rolls."

"Not 'all that bad' is what I was going for." We reached the end of the display and passed the next stop for the train into a smaller hallway with large prints of wild animals adorning the walls. There were even fewer people here, and I considered walking Ollie back toward the wall and pressing against her between the macaw and manatee photos where we'd paused. She hadn't answered my question, though.

"What do you think, beautiful Olivia?"

She faced me. She was thinking, her brow furrowed, and I bit my tongue to stop myself from rambling, attempting to play it cool for once in my life. "It's probably good for your writing, right? What would we do on a real date?"

"I don't know," I admitted. I hadn't thought about my writing until she brought it up, and I remembered this was an arrangement. Just because my heart felt like it was beating out of my chest didn't mean she'd changed what she needed. "I'd just like to spend time with you knowing you don't have to be at work and I don't have to catch a flight."

"I could smell like something other than wet dog," she mused.

"It's a good scent on you."

"You and your fetish." She leaned against the wall, pulling me closer.

"It's a fetish now?" I'd stepped nearer to her, inhaling her scent, which was definitely not wet dog.

She raised her eyebrows and grinned when I stepped closer, sliding the pad of my thumb over her soft cheek. Her grin fell and her eyelids were hooded. "Chicken wing?"

"Mutton chop," I said sweeping my touch over her satin skin, feeling a little reckless. "If we went on a real date, I might want to kiss you at the end."

"Ahem." A phlegmy voice behind us coughed and I stepped

back, dropping my hand. "I'd like to see the artwork." A man I would describe as crotchety in one of my books stood with arms crossed behind us.

"Sorry," Ollie said, taking me by the hand and leading me toward the escalator. "Do you think there will be grumpy old men on our real date?" She took the step ahead of me on the escalator and I was happy with my decision to check my carry-on.

"Do you want there to be?"

"I'm not sure. On the one hand, it could ruin the mood." She dragged her palm down my biceps. "But on the other hand, it would be familiar."

"So, is that a yes?" I linked our fingers again.

"To the date or the kissing or the old men?" We neared the top of the steep escalator. "Would kissing me inspire your writing?"

I briefly considered telling her the truth, that the book was finished and that I wasn't looking for inspiration, that I was only looking for her, but I didn't want to risk this thing we had, not yet. "Kissing you would inspire me in a lot of ways."

"Then . . . maybe don't wait until the end of the date."

I was too lost in looking at her and almost tripped when the escalator ended. I stumbled into her and she laughed. "Or I'll just kiss you first. Think about it," she said, leading us toward Cinnabon.

15

Ollie

I SMOOTHED A hand down my dress and examined myself in the mirror from different angles. I'd taken a page from Harry's dating handbook and wore a white dress that fit snuggly over my curves and dipped low in the front. I'd paused when I pulled the dress from my closet because I'd bought it for the engagement party we never ended up having and the tags were still on it, but I pushed my hesitation aside. I looked good in this dress. I checked my phone for the fortieth time.

> OLLIE: I can meet you there.

> BENNETT: I could pick you up.

The annoying butterflies in my stomach fluttered. I was beginning to fall for him, to crave time with him, and that was scary as hell because it wasn't the plan. It was actually the thing I'd been set on avoiding. Me admitting how I felt would just make it awkward between us. I took a slow breath and held my hand to my stomach, calming myself. I checked myself out in the mirror again as I stepped

into my heels. The dress was a good choice. It reminded me to stick
to the plan, to have fun, and not to fall for Bennett, not because I was
afraid of heartbreak but because I was smart about it.

My phone buzzed and I prepared myself to be careful.

BENNETT: Unless you live in the parking lot of
this Zaxby's, I think I am lost.

I GOT HIM turned around in the right direction and peeked out the
front curtains, looking for his rental car to pull into the driveway,
eager to see him again. The red sedan pulled in and I watched him
check his hair in the mirror. I'd always seen him put together—he
usually traveled in suits or business casual—but when he stepped
out, he looked . . . good. Different. The gray suit fit him well and the
shirt was unbuttoned at the top. I snatched my purse and stepped
out my front door before he made his way closer, taking another
slow breath to remind myself this was for fun and not for keeps.

"The Zaxby's is my winter home. I summer here," I said, pulling
the door closed behind me. I thought he would laugh, but he stilled.
"Is something wrong?" I looked down, searching for a stain on my
dress. "Did I spill something?"

"No. Sorry." He shook his head and smiled. "You just . . . you
look wonderful. I mean, you always look wonderful. This dress,
though, it's something else. I mean, it's not the dress, it's you, of
course, and—"

I pressed my finger to his lips, which I meant to be funny but
which felt incredibly intimate, especially when his hand fell to my
waist. "You're rambling," I murmured.

He said, "Sorry," but my finger against his lips muffled the
sound, and we both laughed. It was nice laughing with Bennett, his

hand on my waist, my hand falling over his shoulder and down his arm.

His hand flexed and his mouth drew closer to my lips. I thought he might kiss me there in my driveway. I wanted him to, but at the last moment, he pulled away and opened the car door for me.

He'd picked a nice restaurant on the BeltLine and conversation was easy, comfortable, and just missing the announcements about keeping luggage with you at all times and lost car keys. After our meal, we decided to walk for a while, taking in the families and couples walking the trail and enjoying the night. Bennett's hand found mine and a slight breeze blew around us. "Is this okay, walking in your heels?"

"I was planning to hop on your back for a piggyback ride in the next few minutes."

He nudged my shoulder with his. "Well, that's awkward because I was planning to ask you for a piggyback ride."

"A real one, or is that creative romance-writer slang for you prefer to take me from behind?"

Bennett's head shot up, eyes wide and expression horror-struck. "No, I meant a real piggyback ride. I didn't mean to imply . . . people actually say that?"

"I'm kidding, Benny," I said, putting my hand on his back, feeling the muscles under his shirt. "Breathe." I wasn't exactly kidding. I'd wanted Bennett in my bed for a long time, since before I even knew his name, but we had an arrangement to stick to and I wasn't sure I could sleep with him and pretend it was all casual.

We kept walking and after a couple of minutes he slipped his hand around mine again.

"How is the book?" He hadn't ever told me much about it, and I got the sense he wanted to keep his work to himself until it was perfect, but I was dying to know.

"It's . . . well, it's done."

"Oh." I dragged my gaze forward to the trail. "That's great," I said, making sure my voice was bright. "Are you happy with it?"

"I think so. I sent it to my editor a few days ago."

"That's great. Congratulations." I nodded, an emotion I didn't expect clawing at my throat. "I guess you won't need me anymore, huh?" I nudged his shoulder with mine to temper how sad my voice sounded.

"What?"

"If your book is done, you won't need me to keep your writer's block at bay, right?" I squeezed his hand. "And I got practice, so this is a nice way to finish our arrangement, right? And for what it's worth, I'm really proud to have helped to bring another of your books to the world."

He stopped abruptly in the middle of the path. "You . . . want to be finished?"

"I mean . . . I don't want to be. Just if it's run its course, I don't want you to feel like you have to keep doing this for my benefit." I tugged his hand, nodding toward the path. "C'mon. We can still have a fun last hurrah."

He didn't step forward with me, and I looked over my shoulder and then down at our hands, our fingers still linked. "So, that's what you want?" Bennett gently pulled me back to him, our linked hands against his chest. "Because I don't want that." His free thumb ghosted across my cheek.

"You don't need me anymore," I insisted, not daring to move and risk losing the featherlight touches against my cheek.

"I think I do need you." His thumb grazed my skin again. "Or at the very least, I want you in my life. It feels . . ."

"Too fast," I added.

He nodded, searching my face. "Far too fast."

"Too much." My voice was breathy, odd because I was positive I'd been holding my breath.

"Probably too much."

"You wanted to kiss me tonight."

"I wanted you to know the book was done first, that I was here just for you. That kissing you wasn't some literary exercise."

"And you still want to kiss me?"

"Yes." He brushed my jawline before sliding a finger down my neck, his thumb grazing my throat.

"Mutton chop?" My voice was breathier than I wanted.

"Would you believe it? An entire chicken potpie," he murmured, his gaze on my lips, his body close and his grip firm and possessive. The evening crowds moved around us, unaware of the seismic shift happening to our quid pro quo.

Inside my head my swallow was audible, like in a cartoon. "Do you want to go back to your hotel?"

He dipped his face to my shoulder and laughed against my skin. "How fast can we get to the car?"

16

Bennett

THE HOTEL ROOM was cool, a sharp contrast to the warm weather outside and the overhanging humidity. I looked around the spartan room, aware of her near me, of the pace of her breathing and her scent and how much I wanted to touch her, but I kept my hands at my sides, determined not to mess this up. "Are you hungry? Thirsty?"

She smiled, her fingers continuing the path up my neck and to the back of my head. "In a way."

"Is 'thirsty' some slang I don't know?" I finally snapped into action, fitting my hand to her waist and guiding her to me. Her body fit against mine just like I'd imagined.

Her lips parted, her tongue wetting her lower lip, and I tipped my chin closer.

"What does it mean?" I spoke into her ear, my lips grazing over the shell, the tip of my nose stroking against her skin in a slow path toward her mouth. It was hard to reconcile the feel of her skin with the knowledge that I was able to touch her.

Ollie tilted her head to the side. "It means I want you." Her voice was breathy, open, and inviting, like I might refuse her. "So, if you want me, too . . ."

Our mouths were close, almost touching. I stroked a finger across her collarbone and kissed her there, inhaling her. "That's not a question, Olivia." I tipped up her chin and took a moment to admire the way she slid her tongue along her lower lip, and then her lips were on mine, eager, opening to me as our tongues danced. "I wanted to do this on the moving walkway and the escalator." I kissed her again, my hand sliding up her spine until I could hold the back of her neck, and then back down the glorious expanse of her body.

"That would have been dangerous," she said on a groan as I moved to kiss her neck, to find the hollow of her throat. I trailed lower and kissed her collarbone, a place I'd never been excited to touch on another woman. "We would have tripped when the walkway ended."

Ollie's nails dragging down my back spurred me forward, and I walked her backward toward the bed in the middle of the room as my own hands roamed lower, palming the swell of her backside, where the dress clung to her perfect curves. "Probably."

"We might have fallen," she said, before she pulled my lips to hers again, her mouth against mine, tongue moving over my lower lip and her body in my arms, her softness against my hard length.

"I guess it's good we're not in the airport, then." I found the zipper of her dress and toyed with it. "Can I unzip your dress?"

She nodded and moved her hands to mine, but I nudged them away.

"Let me," I whispered, guiding her to turn toward the bed. "Let me look at you." I pulled the zipper down with as much restraint as I could, watching the white fabric open and gape, revealing her bare skin, a shock of black-and-white-spotted bra strap across her back. "Your bra . . ."

Her back moved in time with her laughter.

Ollie glanced over her shoulder, so I could appreciate the smile on her lips. "I wanted to remind you of our joke."

"I remember everything we've joked about." I slid the dress off her shoulders, tugging it down and enjoying how my palms grazed her hips as I slid it over them. I trailed a finger down her spine, feeling her body react to my touch. "You've been in my head since the day I met you." I kissed her shoulder, sliding her bra strap out of the way.

"Before we met, I used to watch you when you'd get off the plane." She spoke as I continued a trail of kisses across her shoulder and the back of her neck, my finger sliding up and down her spine.

"What did you think about?"

"This." She rolled her body and I let out a low groan. "What this would be like."

I unhooked her bra slowly, letting the garment fall to the floor and sliding my palms up her ribs. "Do you want me to touch you?"

She slid her hands over mine and placed them over her breasts, showing me how to touch her, guiding my fingers.

I knew she trusted me to have listened, to have paid attention to what made her feel good, and her hands fell away. "You're beautiful," I said into her ear, enjoying the way she groaned and moved under my touch. "I am desperate to taste you." I slid my hand down her stomach to the lacy edge of her underwear. "Can I touch you here? Can I spread your thighs and learn how my tongue can make you come apart?"

She was quiet for a moment, and I paused.

"That's a line from your book." She turned in my arms, her fingers working the buttons of my shirt. "That's cheating."

"I still wrote it." I watched her make quick work of my shirt, pushing it off my shoulders. "And how do you remember that line?"

Ollie flashed a devilish grin and pushed her panties down before sitting on the bed and beckoning me forward to the space between her spread legs. "I reread that scene a lot of times."

I kissed my way up from her knee. "If you don't let me do or say things from my books," I said between kisses, nudging her knees farther apart, "there's a lot of things I won't be able to do."

Her nails grazed my scalp. "Like that thing from the carriage?"

I nuzzled her with my nose, letting out a shaky breath at the feel of her hot, wet flesh. "Definitely the thing from the carriage." I wasn't a stranger to sex, more of an infrequent out-of-town guest, and the nerves that usually plagued me were quiet. "Which would be a shame because I rather like the thing from the carriage."

When I ghosted a finger up the crease of her thigh, across her mound, and then down the other crease, she groaned and arched her back. "Maybe a few things from the books is good."

Ollie was just as responsive and vocal as I'd fantasized she would be, sinking her fingers through my hair when I hit the right rhythm and squirming under me when she was close, her breath stuttering. Feeling the rush and pulse of Ollie as she came undone under my tongue was addictive—I wanted to feel and taste it over and over again.

"The carriage," she panted, falling back onto the bed, her hand resting over her heart. "The damn carriage."

I kissed the side of her knee, watching her body buzz. "Do you need a drink of water before I do that again?"

"You're going to do it again?" She smiled as she raised onto her elbows.

"If you'd like me to."

She hadn't stopped smiling, and her eyes fell down my chest, leaving a trail of heat. "I'd like you to take off your pants."

I hurried out of my trousers, conscious of her gaze on the unmistakable erection in my boxer briefs. I liked her looking at me, examining me.

She reached for my hand and tugged me to the bed with her. "Where did I find you?"

I slid my palm over her belly. "Technically, Pepper found me."

"You're saying I have Pepper to thank for that?"

"Well." I slid my hand lower and guided her thigh to my hip. "I had a little something to do with it."

"Sixty–forty." Ollie giggled, a light, airy sound that delighted me.

"Fair, I suppose." I followed the line of her thigh, inching higher, holding myself back as I took in her face. "I meant what I said. I want you in my life. Not for my book and not just in my bed."

Her own hands were tracing my biceps, delicate fingertips playing over the muscles. "We might break each other's hearts."

"We might." I pulled her closer, feeling her heat against me, the swell of her backside under my hands. "You're worth the risk, though."

"Yeah?" She slid her fingers up my neck, and I had to close my eyes at the wave of sensation. When she stroked them through the hair at my nape, I took in her expression, her parted full lips. "You are, too."

I grinned. I couldn't help it, so taken in by her words.

"Now, can you do the *other* carriage thing?"

I rolled her to her back, lowering my lips to her throat. "I thought I might do the first one again and then work my way through the series."

She let out a whimper as my fingers skirted lower, brushing between her slick folds, and my cock jumped at the sound of her voice, the sounds of her reacting to me. "I really like how you think."

I BURIED MY face in the crook of her neck. "Please stay tonight," I panted.

"Well," she returned, her own chest heaving. "You're still inside me, so I'm not going anywhere right now."

I kissed her, already addicted to kissing her, addicted to the way her tongue swept over mine. "Maybe I was a little overeager." I slowly pulled from her, both of us reacting to the loss of contact. "Stay, though? We get so little time together, and I know we haven't talked through how this will work, and of course there is a lot to talk through, but mostly I just don't want to let you go and I'd—"

Ollie pressed her finger gently to my lips. "I'll stay," she said, looking up at me with a dreamy expression that made me want to rally and go again. She brushed a finger along my hairline. "I'll stay, Benny. I'm not going anywhere."

I grinned, kissing the tip of her finger, loving the sound of those words, the definitive Olivia-shaped tether to the ground they felt like.

17

Ollie

I WALKED THROUGH the security checkpoint the next Monday humming "Feeling Good" by Nina Simone, waving to Martin on my way into the shop and suppressing the grin I felt in my whole body. My body was sore in the most delicious way, and the sense of having landed somewhere, of establishing something new with Bennett, was disorienting.

> BENNETT: I hope I didn't keep you up too late last night.
>
> OLLIE: You were the one who had to leave for the airport at 4am.
>
> BENNETT: You're right—you should be apologizing that I was half asleep on the plane imagining being back in bed with you.
>
> OLLIE: Isn't it too early in the relationship to say sappy things like that?

BENNETT: I'll rephrase to be less sappy. I couldn't lower the seatback tray because thinking about being back in bed with you had *that* kind of effect on me. 😏

OLLIE: Definitely less sappy. More awkward for your seatmate, too.

Sex with Bennett had not been what I expected. I'd fantasized plenty, first when he was the guy I watched from afar, then after I got to know him as the rambling, adorable nerd, and especially after reading his writing, but he was somehow all those three fantasies and more. He was creative and methodical but playful, even sometimes a little dominant. I sighed as I unlocked the grate for the shop, remembering how he looked after the first time, breathless, with a wide grin, like we'd just been on the best roller coaster.

BENNETT: Heading into a meeting and then a call with my agent. Talk to you later, Beautiful?

OLLIE: 😃 Definitely.

I sang to myself inside the empty shop, powering on the computer. I'd wanted to add something else. Not "I love you." It was way too soon for that. Even with my ex, I hadn't been someone who texted throughout the day. We said what we needed to say and then didn't talk until we saw each other. I'd liked it. Texting with Bennett made me want to cuddle up on the bed with my phone like a preteen, though.

OLLIE: Please tell your agent I'd like more carriage scenes if possible.

BENNETT: You've inspired a few, but please leave
that for later so I'm not turned on when my boss
walks into my office in a few minutes.

OLLIE: I promise.

"Hey," Jess said when she walked in a few minutes later. This was a busy time in the airport, but we didn't usually see a rush of clients until a little later in the morning. She sidled next to me, glancing over my shoulder at the schedule for the day. "How was the date?"

"Did you have to practice that casual tone?"

She laughed, her smile cracking wide. "I totally did on the way in. Tell me everything."

I glanced around, making sure no one was coming in, and shared about dinner and the conversation on the BeltLine. "We spent the rest of the weekend together," I said, pressing my lips together.

"And it was good?"

I nodded. "We're together now, I guess. It sounds weird to call him my boyfriend."

"I bet." Jess took a swig from her massive coffee cup. "Does it feel different than with your jackass ex?"

"You know, it's hard to remember the beginning, but something I thought about when I was driving in this morning was that I was never sure I could rely on him. Even before everything that happened, I'd need to remind him about things, have a backup plan in case he didn't show, and he never called me back. It's such a small thing, but Bennett calls back; he shows up. He's conscientious."

"That's sexy," Jess said. "Competence porn, for real. My ex-husband was never sexier than when he remembered to do shit and didn't leave me hanging."

"Right?" We exchanged a look and both laughed. I clicked

through our emails and the scheduling software, confirming a few appointments. "I don't know. I didn't realize that was such a big deal until I had it. Until I had someone I knew would be there."

Jess gave me a side hug, squeezing me to her. "I'm proud of you. So proud that I will not ask for more details about the sex until later."

"That's very selfless."

"Not really . . . I'm expecting a lot of details and we have two dogs coming in fifteen minutes." She hugged me again and walked into the back room to prepare the bathing and grooming stations, leaving me alone to grin to myself and smile at my text messages.

18

Bennett

I SCRUBBED MY palms down my face, the stubble on my cheeks longer than normal since I hadn't taken time to shave early that morning, preferring the extra moments with Olivia in my arms. That bed seemed years away now.

I flipped my phone over, the screen black. I hadn't touched it in hours, since the meeting with my boss where he'd dropped a huge project in my lap in addition to offering a promotion. That was before I learned the book I'd turned in months earlier needed major revisions fast if I had any hope of salvaging it. The phone buzzed in my hand and it was only a lack of sleep and muscle memory that made my thumb swipe up to answer the call from Gia.

She launched into conversation without preamble—she always did, which was a blessing when I was short on time. "I met someone."

My stomach growled and I looked around my office as if a taco truck might be hiding between the bookcases. "It's not another cat, is it?"

"It's a human woman, thank you. My new next-door neighbor, Elena. We're going out for drinks tonight."

I didn't get too excited about the new love interests of my best friend—she was someone who flirted easily, fell hard, and fell out of love even faster. "What happened to Dustin, the yoga instructor?" I asked, opening the DoorDash site in my browser. I wasn't leaving the office anytime soon, and it was after eight.

"Dustin is a great guy. We're going to just be friends."

I clicked through and gave up, hungry but not sure for what. I could always pick something fast—it was my superpower. Even if I didn't crave it, I'd pick the first thing that looked decent and call it good. "Careful, you said that about me back in the day, too."

"I was right. We are great friends. We would have been a disaster couple. You're too nice for me." The phone rustled and then I heard the unmistakable mewing and chirping of her menagerie. "Speaking of couples, how did your weekend with the indelible Olivia go?"

I'd let my gaze drift back to the Corterian Incorporated file on my desk—a huge project that would mean more travel, a staff, and the promotion. It was more money, which would mean more financial security. I wasn't sure I could turn it down. It would mean less time for writing and anything else, though.

"She's fantastic," I said, knowing I wasn't fully answering her question. Holy hell was she beyond fantastic. Olivia made me feel like I'd hit the jackpot, and for the first time in my life, I understood my parents a little, the high of winning they seemed to be chasing their whole lives and their laser focus on only each other. Olivia made me want to block out everything else. That was why I hadn't called her after I spoke with my agent or my boss. I never let myself get swept up—that was something other people did, and I had to wrap my head around all this before I could share it.

"Yes, you've mentioned she's fantastic, once or a thousand times. Did you tell her how you feel? Did you tell her you're planning to quit the job now that you've finished the new book?"

"Turns out, the new book might not matter."

"What do you mean?"

My agent never minced words with me, which was why I liked working with her. My editor didn't like the book I'd turned in before I began the book I'd written with Ollie in mind. I'd need to make major revisions and make them fast before turning it in again. Those kinds of revisions would take all my time and still might not be enough. "I have a lot of work to do on the last manuscript before they'll accept it."

"Maybe it's a good time to quit the day job, so you can take the time you need."

It was the worst time to quit my job. When I was with Olivia, I'd thought about it more. She inspired me, the way she bet on herself, and it felt like the right time. But getting the news the book didn't measure up put in sharp perspective what it meant to take a risk on myself, that it could all crash down with one book.

"You're in your head," Gia said. "A stumble is not a fall."

"A stumble is also not proof you should be a professional sprinter." I stared at the extensive notes from my editor outlining the issues. They made sense, and I wasn't sure why I hadn't seen them myself. "I don't think it's the time to put all my eggs in one basket."

Gia was quiet for a minute. "Maybe you should talk to your new girlfriend about this. See what she thinks?"

An email came in from my boss marked urgent and I was skimming it as I responded. "I don't want to bother her with it."

"You're bothering me with it," she said, and I heard the raised eyebrow in her voice.

"I think that's the other way around," I muttered, knowing she would read my tone for what it was—frustration with myself. "I need to go, Gi. There's no way I'm getting out of here for another few hours, and then I need to start on these revisions."

She promised to bother me again later, and when we hung up I let out a slow breath. I wanted to read through the revisions and figure out a plan for attacking them, but the voice in my head—the voice of caution and intentionality and not taking chances—yelled to focus on the safer bet, so I started working, leaving my phone on the other side of the desk.

THE NEXT MORNING, I woke groggy and stiff at the desk in my apartment. The sky outside was gray, rain falling in sheets, and the clock read quarter after five. A clap of thunder shook my fourth-floor apartment and I stretched, blinking away the bleariness and waking up my sleeping computer. The manuscript came to life, red and marked with my tracked changes. The screen looked like it had gotten as much sleep as I had, and I shuffled into the kitchen for tea. It was Tuesday and normally I got to see Ollie on Tuesdays when I flew to LA, but I'd canceled the trip, needing to attend meetings in town for the new client.

As the kettle heated, I searched my desk for my phone, finding it hidden under a stack of binders filled with reference materials and research from previous books. I had four texts and a missed call from Ollie.

> OLLIE: How did it go with your agent? More carriage scenes coming soon?

> OLLIE: Guessing it's a busy day—text me tonight to let me know if you'll have time to do lunch tomorrow when you fly through. Is it sappy to say I'm looking forward to kissing you?

> OLLIE: In an uncharacteristic moment, I'm fine with sappy. I really can't wait to kiss you.

The last was timestamped around eleven. I vaguely remembered hearing my phone buzz, but I'd been trying to untangle a mess I'd made in a subplot and ignored it, assuming it was Gia. I hadn't considered it might be this incredible woman who'd just agreed to be part of my life.

> OLLIE: I'm getting a little worried. Are you okay?

> BENNETT: I'm okay. Sorry I didn't respond.

I thought about telling her the whole story, but the idea of admitting I'd messed up so badly made me want to shrink into the wall. I didn't want her to believe I wasn't someone who had it together. Someone she could count on.

> BENNETT: Something came up, so I won't be
> flying through this week.

I didn't expect a response—it was still early in the morning and I was sure she was asleep, but I still stared at the message for a few moments, listening to the rain against the glass and the water beginning to boil in the kettle.

> BENNETT: I'm sorry. We'll talk soon!

I set the phone on the counter and grabbed the kettle—I could work for a little bit before I showered and headed into the office. I wanted to feel better about my plan before I told her what was going on.

19

Ollie

BENNETT: I'm sorry. We'll talk soon!

I hadn't heard from Bennett since early the morning before when I'd woken up to two texts and no real explanation. My brain immediately flashed back to the months before I found out what my ex was up to, and the years before that when I'd receive texts and no real explanations.

An explosion of barks erupted from the back, where Jess and Jeremiah were washing and clipping two shih tzus and Pepper. "You need my help?" I called through the door versus opening it, not wanting a repeat of Pepper's last adventure. My stomach sank. Bennett wasn't going to be there to snag him for me.

"We're good," Jess called through the closed door. "They're just making friends." A series of yelps erupted, along with a bark so deep I had a hard time imagining any of those little dogs making it.

I returned to the desk and glanced at my phone again, angry with myself for checking. On the one hand, I understood being busy and knew that Bennett was not the type to do what my ex had done. On the other hand, we'd slept together and then I barely heard from him, and it was hard to know for sure he wasn't like my ex. I was in the middle of weighing this out when the chime sounded as a customer walked in the door.

No. Not a customer. He was tall and toned, a swimmer's build and an easy, too-wide smile, as if he knew he'd popped into my head and then taken shape.

"Well, look at you," he said, walking toward me. "I couldn't fly through and not come see you. My grandma said you'd opened a little store. This place looks great," my ex said, looking around.

I hadn't seen him in a couple of years and was too surprised to respond.

"You look great. How are you? If I'm honest, I always saw you doing something like this versus working in Washington." He said it like he still knew me, and my blood pulsed in my ears. "Washington was too serious for you. Too demanding."

"How is . . . what was her name? Amy?" I knew her name and I'd long moved past the idea that she was to blame, but her name still felt like acid in my mouth.

He laughed, but kind of a humorless bark. "Oh man. I haven't thought about her in ages. That didn't last long."

I wanted to say a lot of things. Among them, that she lasted long enough for us to end our engagement, but that seemed somehow unfair to her, this woman I didn't know, whom he'd probably ignored or cheated on like he had me.

Before I could say any of that, he glanced at his watch. "Gotta catch my flight, but I had to pop in. I'll see you at the wedding—I'm my grandma's date." He raised his palm and I think he was planning on me giving him a high five, but when I didn't, he just waved and walked out.

"Was that . . ." Jess stepped out from the back.

"Yep."

"And you let him walk out with his legs and other extremities still intact?"

I nodded. "I barely said anything. How weird to see him."

"Are you okay?"

I'd thought about what I'd do if I ran into him again, wondered if I'd cry or yell, if I'd feel sad or angry, but I didn't feel much of anything. I did glance down at my phone to see no new messages, which somehow felt worse than running into my cheating ex. "Better off without him," I said with a shrug.

"Exactly." She pushed back into the mayhem of Pepper and the Pips, calling over her shoulder. "You've got hot Bennett now!" I looked at the spot where my ex had stood, and a chill gripped me. I didn't miss him, but I remembered how it felt when he'd go quiet on me, not responding. It felt like he was gaslighting me, and in the end, he was. I'd tie myself into knots worrying he was no longer interested in me or that he was with someone else and then tighten the knots when I convinced myself that those thoughts were silly.

Bennett canceling his trip and not responding to me wasn't the same.

I could have sworn the disembodied voice of the announcer was calling me out. *Attention, passengers in the terminal. Olivia Wright, please report to a security checkpoint. You seem to have lost your mind.*

I started sorting through invoices and receipts, double-checking our books. *It feels the same, but it's not the same.* I drummed my fingernails on the countertop. *Sure, he slept with me and then kind of ghosted me, but there* has *to be an explanation.*

I heard the disembodied voice in my head: *Attention in the terminal. Keep telling yourself that.* I didn't like how familiar this feeling was, and I reminded myself that I didn't have to feel this way, that I could cut ties and move on. In this instance, I could play it safe. I thought about Harry's wedding—the only thing worse than being

there alone and near my ex would be getting stood up at the last
minute and still having to walk in alone.

> OLLIE: Not sure what's going on, but I think we
> should maybe cool it. Long distance might not
> have been a good idea.

I expected a quick response, maybe for him to explain or re-
assure me that I was overreacting. I looked at the screen, but my only
response was another round of somewhat soulful barks from Pepper's backup vocalists. After a couple of minutes, I set my phone
aside and got to work.

Four hours later, I looked again, taking a deep breath to prepare
for what the response might be. I straightened my back in preparation to defend my decision, the decision that had started to feel less
correct.

Nothing.

The same when I left the airport.

By the time I checked before going to bed, I wasn't sad or even
mad. Well, I was a little mad. I was mad at myself, mostly, because
I knew better than to trust someone again. I'd wanted practice and
I got it, and I didn't need to stick around again to see if it got better.

20

Bennett

I ROLLED MY shoulders and stretched my neck from side to side, allowing the words in front of me to go blurry. It was after two in the morning and I'd been up since five again, writing before work, working through lunch, and then diving into writing as soon as I arrived home. My eyes felt dry, my five-o'clock shadow something closer to a seven forty-five, and I wasn't sure I'd eaten anything besides popcorn since lunch, but I was finally moving the book into what my editor wanted it to be. When I stood, my body protested the move from the seated hunch I'd adopted over the previous days, but after hitting save three times and backing the book up to the cloud, I walked away from the desk.

Gia kept texting me about taking care of myself and trusting myself, and I finally muted my phone because every time she brought it up, I started spiraling. *Keep the job, quit the job, trust yourself, you're fixing a big mistake—don't put your trust in you.* I was glad I hadn't told Ollie about everything. I didn't care that Gia saw me out of sorts and uncertain, but I didn't want to be that guy with Ollie.

I fell onto my bed and unmuted my phone, seeing a missed text from Ollie from around lunchtime. I grinned and settled against the pillows. She'd be asleep but I couldn't wait to talk to her. The last thing I'd told her was we'd talk soon, and a few days had gone by where I hadn't let my focus leave the book and the job. Of course my mind had wandered, wandered to how her lips felt when she kissed me first thing in the morning, sleepy and relaxed. It wandered to the feel of her under my tongue and how she shivered when I kissed her neck. To the way she sounded when she laughed.

> OLLIE: Not sure what's going on, but I think we should maybe cool it. Long distance might not have been a good idea.

I reread "cool it," my own body going cold and my exhaustion temporarily shocked out of me.

> BENNETT: Cool it? What does that mean?
>
> BENNETT: I'm sorry I went quiet. Please don't be angry.

The dots bounced next to her name.

> OLLIE: I'm not mad, but I don't think this will work. It was a mistake to make it more than it was.
>
> BENNETT: Olivia, I know it's late, but can we talk? Please?
>
> OLLIE: No. I don't think so.

The chill I'd felt at her words was replaced by heat over the back of my neck. I didn't want to tell her a lie, but coming clean meant showing her all my messy, disorganized cards.

BENNETT: I've been working a lot, writing and
day job.

OLLIE: Ok.

I took a chance and hit the call icon next to her photo, one I'd
snapped while we ate Cinnabon huddled close together outside my
gate. She was laughing after telling me I had icing on my cheek, and
I wanted nothing more than to hear her laughter.

When she picked up, the silence crackled through the phone.

"I'm sorry," I repeated. "Please don't give up on me."

"I'm not giving up on you," she said. She sounded tired, her voice
resigned. "But I spent years with someone who disappeared with no
explanation. I won't do that again, and I know a few days doesn't
matter, but I'm not willing to risk a few days turning into weeks and
months. I'm just not. I don't like the way it makes me feel."

"It will never happen again. I can manage my time better." I
looked through my bedroom door to my desk across the apartment.
The screen had gone dark and shadows played on the small succu-
lent Gia had bought me because she said my apartment was depress-
ing. "I . . ."

"What?"

"They sent back the last book I turned in. I have to make major
changes to it."

Her voice softened immediately. "I'm so sorry, Bennett."

"I can do it; it's just a lot of time, and then work is piling on . . ."
I scrubbed my face again. "That's not an excuse, but that's what I
was doing."

"You're busy."

"I didn't want you to know I'd failed with the book."

"I don't care about the book. I mean, I care that you care about
it, but I wish you'd told me."

"I also wasn't sure how to tell you I was offered a promotion at work and assigned a big local client. I wouldn't be flying near as much, and usually flying through another hub when I had to." I wasn't sure about the response I was expecting, but stone silence wasn't it.

After a few more beats of silence, she finally spoke. "Congratulations on the promotion. I thought you wanted to leave the job, though."

"Publishing is so tenuous . . . I thought this book was perfect when I turned it in, a home run ready to be broadcast, and I was wrong. I don't think I can risk quitting my job yet."

"Well," she said, her voice quieter than I'd ever heard. "Then I think I was right the first time. We should cool it. You have to pursue your dream and you have to keep your job."

I wanted to tell her she was my dream, but it was too soon; that sentence was too big a declaration. "I can—"

"Bennett," she interrupted. "Let's not do this. It could have been good at another time, but you're there and I'm here. I won't settle for a distracted partner, and you can't risk taking anything off your plate."

"I can . . ." I didn't know how to complete the sentence.

"It's late," she said, and I floundered for something, anything, to stop her, but I didn't have a good response. "Good night, Bennett."

I looked around my dim bedroom with blank white walls as if it might have answers, but nothing stared back at me except open, empty space. "Good night, Olivia."

21

Ollie

"MIGHT AS WELL close up shop," Jess said. The terminal was packed with travelers, the thunderstorms outside leaving all flights temporarily grounded. "I think I'd like to get home before it gets even worse."

I nodded from my perch behind the counter, glancing through the crowds to the darkened sky beyond the glass, where rain belted the tarmac and high winds whipped around the building. I'd stared at Gate C7 so often, I could sketch it in detail from memory, but I kept looking for Bennett. It had been two weeks since we'd spoken, two weeks since we'd ended whatever had just begun, and two weeks since I'd felt like myself. "Yeah," I said. "Let's go."

Jess and I closed the shop, locked the grate, and made our way to the exit. "You okay to drive in this?"

I nodded, reaching for my keys as if that were proof. "I'll take it slow." We usually liked to walk the length of the space between terminals, but both of us stood in front of the closed doors, waiting for the train to transport us. "I'm proud of you, you know." Jess nudged my elbow once the train pulled away, heading toward the exit.

"For what? I grew up driving in weather like this."

"Not that." We jostled as the train sped toward the end of the line. "For everything with your Diet Coke Break."

I laughed. Well, I didn't laugh, but I let out a puff of breath that some might have considered a laugh. "I don't think that was anything to be proud of. It lasted like three days."

We flowed with the crowd exiting and stepped onto the escalator. "Well, three days or not, I know you opened up your heart a little, just enough to start again. For that I'm proud."

"That's me ... opening up my heart to be reminded why it was closed off in the first place."

"I don't buy this little I-don't-care routine, you know that, right?"

I tipped my head to her shoulder and she rubbed my arm. "I know."

When the escalator reached the main level, we were greeted by the squeals of a young woman running toward a young man dragging a suitcase. In seconds, she was in his arms, her long legs wrapped around him and her hair flying in all directions.

"I'd like to be greeted like that," she commented.

"That wasn't how you and Jack reconnected when you got home every night?"

"No time," she said with a wink. "It was straight to bed. Who had time for big gestures when *big* gestures were on the table?" She held her palms apart and wiggled her eyebrows. She and Jack split up when he wanted kids and she didn't, but they were the poster couple for mature and friendly marriage dissolution.

I laughed, giving the reunited couple one last glance. They were now staring into each other's eyes. I'd always kind of loved those grand gestures, the public displays of affection, and my heart ached for what wasn't. If Bennett were next to me, he would have said something grumpy, like how they were blocking traffic. I imagined his fingers twining with mine, and my heart hurt anew.

When I was alone in the car, I stashed my phone in my bag and prepared for the long drive home in a thunderstorm. Since traffic was slow, the rain was kind of calming in tandem with the sea of brake lights. Jess was right on some level. I was proud of myself for taking a risk, even though it didn't work out. I was proud that I gave Bennett and me a chance, that I was open to it, but I was also proud that I stood up for what I wanted. I knew he was scared to quit his job, and for good reason, and I knew he loved writing. His face lit up when he talked about his books, and his characters seemed like real people when he talked about them. Maybe the practice had been enough to kick me into gear. I debated the different dating apps as I drove slowly toward home.

As I pulled into my neighborhood, my shoulders ached from sitting tensely behind the wheel and I stretched my neck. A hot bath and a good book, one of the ones Bennett had recommended, waited for me at home, and I was ready, but when I pulled into my driveway, I hit the brakes on instinct.

Bennett sat on my porch, his back against my front door, knees pulled to his chest. He gave a small wave when he saw me, and it wasn't until then that I noticed the rental car parked on the street.

"What are you doing here?" I called through the rain, holding my jacket over my head as I made a run for my porch.

"I wanted to tell you something in person." He had to yell over the whipping wind and sheets of rain.

"What?" I was yelling, too, after ducking under the cover of the porch. It was a little quieter in that bubble, and I already didn't like being near him and not touching him. "It's a severe thunderstorm. Why are you here?"

He scratched the back of his neck. "I should have checked the weather, but I just booked a ticket. When I decided I wanted to see you, I didn't want to wait any longer. I hoped you'd be home at the normal time, and then with the weather it slowed everything down, and then I worried you were out with someone new, and—"

"Bennett . . ."

"I ramble when I'm nervous." His clothes weren't dotted with raindrops, and I wondered how long he'd been on my porch. He glanced down and then back up at me. "And I'm nervous."

A clap of thunder shook the ground and I jumped, inching closer to the front door and to him. "Why are you nervous?"

"Because you might say no."

I searched his face, where dark circles shadowed his eyes; he looked exhausted. "Say no to what?"

Bennett's hands stretched toward mine, glancing at me for approval before linking our fingers, sending that familiar sensation over my skin. "To taking a risk with me."

"Bennett . . ."

"I quit my job. I put in my notice."

My jaw fell open, but he kept talking before I could figure out what to say.

"And the book my editor sent back still needs a lot of work, but I can't wait for you to read it." His smile was earnest and I gave a small one back. "I added a dog."

That made me smile more genuinely. "You added Pepper to your book?"

He nodded. "In case you said no. I wanted a reminder of you, of us, in print, even if it didn't last."

"But in case I said no to what?"

He sucked in a deep breath. "I want to move here—well, not here," he said motioning to the house. "I don't mean I plan to move into your guest room, but to the city or nearby. I could get an apartment or rent a small house and we could try again."

I stared at him.

"I know that sounds absurd," he added.

"Yes, it does." I unlinked our fingers, stepping back. "That's too much pressure. You can't uproot your life for me."

"That's the thing . . . I'm not uprooting my life and it's not just for you. I always wanted to be tethered to something, grounded, but I'm alone in a city I'm ambivalent about and doing a job I don't enjoy, looking forward to landing in this airport because that means I get to see you." He slid the pad of his thumb over my cheek. "I want to uproot that life. I want to replant somewhere else. To belabor the metaphor, you make me feel like I'm blooming, and . . . I want to establish my own roots in soil near you."

"Are you done making plant references?"

"That depends . . . What do you think?"

I tugged on my cardigan. "It's a lot to consider. It's a big risk."

"I know." He linked his fingers with mine again. "And you should probably tell me to get in the car and drive away. You should probably tell me I blew my chance with the most amazing woman in the world because I couldn't get over my own pride and baggage." Lightning cracked in the distance, giving the sky a disco-ball effect for a moment. "But I'm striking out, whether it's here or somewhere else—but I'd really like it to be here because you're here and I'd like to take you to that wedding and then on picnics with or without grumpy old men. I'm flexible on that point."

His hands were big around mine, the way our fingers linked already familiar. "You don't take big risks. What changed?"

"I found something worth taking a chance on."

"Me?"

He shook his head. "Not just you. Us. Me, too, I guess. That probably doesn't make sense, but if you'll give me more time, I'll explain it."

I chewed on the corner of my lip. "You don't have to leaf yet."

"Was that a plant joke?"

I stepped forward into the comfort of his arms, breathing in the now familiar scent of him. "It was."

"So that means . . . yes?"

"It means I'll hear more of what you're planning." I slid my palm up his chest, coming to rest over his heart. "And that you should kiss me now."

He grinned before lowering his lips to mine, his kisses soft and slow, until a clap of thunder made us both jump. "Maybe we could take this inside?"

I dug for my keys. "Maybe a good idea."

His body was warm behind me as I unlocked the door, his hand resting on my hip and anticipation coiling in me. "You know, I thought about meeting you at the airport with a big sign that read, 'I'm sorry.'"

I stepped inside, toeing off my wet shoes after Bennett shuffled in behind me. "Why didn't you?"

He backed me against my door slowly, his hands moving down my shoulders, then my ribs, at a glacial pace. "If it went badly, I figured it would be less embarrassing without an audience." His fingers inched under my shirt, stroking my belly and sides.

"And if it went well?"

"I prefer this kind of thing in private." His lips met mine again as his palms grazed over my skin. "And I want our story to exist beyond the airport."

I kissed him back and ducked under his arm, tugging him toward my bedroom. "I like the idea of that."

Epilogue

Bennett

BENNETT: How many truffles would you like me to pick you up from the candy shop?

GIA: A lot. I'm still nursing a broken heart.

I walked toward Julianna's Candy Shoppe near Pre-Flight Paws ahead of boarding my flight to Chicago. I'd made this trek a hundred times in suits. Doing it in jeans and a T-shirt was better. I'd owed Gia a visit for a long time, and after the book I'd spent so many sleepless weeks ripping apart and reconstructing hit the bestseller list, it felt like things had been nonstop. Aside from a stop at two favorite Chicago bookstores—one specializing in romance novels, where I planned to spend an exorbitant amount of money—this trip was pure vacation.

GIA: Can you bring me someone hot from the plane, too?

BENNETT: I believe that would be kidnapping at worst and solicitation at best?

Gia had surprised me. She and her neighbor had dated for almost two years, and Elena had become part of our circle, a part I
assumed would be permanent, but they broke up when Elena got a
job that would take her to Tokyo for the foreseeable future. It had
been a few months, and I was mostly certain Gia was playing up the
raw pain of her heartbreak to get me to bring her more chocolate,
but I'd bring it anyway because she'd found someone to love and
then lost her.

GIA: And Ollie isn't coming with you?

I'd missed her call when I was going through security, and the
voice-mail notification popped up as I was replying to Gia and making my way through the terminal. I'd planned to listen to it once I
got to my gate, but why wait? I wanted to hear her voice.

"Hey. Just calling to say have a good flight and I hope you can
make some headway on that steamy scene you've been working on.
I'm in meetings all day, but let's talk tonight. I didn't want it to pop
up on your screen, so I emailed it, but I just sent you a photo to help
get you in the mood for writing carriage scenes. Love you, Benny!"

I grinned to myself, thumb hovering over my email icon, but
Gia's last message waited for me.

BENNETT: My lady love is traveling for work this
week. The new salons in LaGuardia and Sea-Tac
open next month.

She loved the traveling and I joked I'd need to get a part-time
job at Pre-Flight Paws or the candy shop so I could watch her cutting through the airport like she used to watch me. She lovingly told
me I wasn't qualified to deal with Pepper and she wouldn't tolerate
me being friends with Julianna. We were making it work.

BENNETT: You'll have to wait until the wedding to
see her.

GIA: I can't believe you're getting married in the
middle of winter. How am I supposed to attract
someone new in my banging Best Woman
ensemble if I have to cover it with a coat.

BENNETT: I'm sure you'll have no trouble
attracting someone.

GIA: You're right. 😏

I ducked into the candy shop, greeting the clerk and determin-
ing whether I would need an additional carry-on bag for all Gia's
heartbreak chocolate. The woman behind the counter was helping
a customer and said she'd be with me shortly, so I took a free moment to open my email, shielding the screen.

The subject line read, Who Knows You, Baby? I clicked on the
attached image, my mind swirling with the idea of her sending me
a provocative photo. What she actually sent was even better. She was
holding two tiny packages, the Biscoff label visible over her fingers,
and in the background was a dalmatian puppy on a leash. I chuckled
to myself and replied, I don't know if I'm impressed that you know
me so well or terrified that you know me so well. I love you, Beautiful
Olivia. I tucked my phone in my pocket and stepped up to the counter.

"Hi. Welcome to Julianna's Candy Shoppe. Is this your first time
here?" She straightened her pink apron when I walked up to the
counter; her gold name tag read TEAGAN.

"No," I said, eyeing the display. "I've spent a lot of time in this
airport. I know exactly what I want."

The
Missed
Connection

For my mom, who taught me to love with my whole heart,
and my dad, who taught me to speak up with my whole chest

DECEMBER 31

1

Gia

I **DIDN'T EXPECT** the ice storm. It seemed, neither did the other few thousand people stranded in the airport.

"Attention in the terminal. Due to inclement weather, your flight may be delayed. Please check monitors for updates."

I glanced up from my e-reader. The man with the bushy mustache and the beginnings of a mullet was still there and staring, but not at me in my cute day-after-the-wedding brunch outfit. He was eyeing the outlet next to me like he was on his way to jail and that outlet was his last shot at a conjugal visit. I pressed my lips together at my own joke and the image of this very large man trying to sate his needs with the outlet. "I'm almost done," I said, hiding my giggle with a cough.

> GIA: I just made myself laugh at the idea of a
> *Duck Dynasty* extra screwing a power outlet.

I stared at the text I had started typing and my laugh fell away. I didn't have anyone to send it to. My best friend's new wife, as cool as she was, would maybe not appreciate me interrupting their honeymoon. And Elena, the person I thought would be my forever New Year's Eve date, was thirteen hours ahead on the other side of the world without me. I was still mentally calculating the time difference every time I saw a clock. Deleting the text, I unplugged my phone. "All yours," I said, rising to my feet.

For a moment, I hoped for some sparkling conversation, maybe a new friend to be made despite the questionable hairstyle choice, but he simply grunted out a guttural "thanks" and took my spot on the floor.

So much for a new friend.

I walked along the crowded hallway taking in the groupings of fellow stranded travelers. I'd spent a while catching up on work, reading a scathing critique of my most recent research findings from an A.F. Ennings, the fellow chemistry professor who lived across the country and loved to pick apart my research. I'd given up on finishing it, deciding people watching was more productive than reading his long-winded opinions about the futility of my experimentalist approach to studying catalytic hydrolysis reactions. It was my life's work, but even I had a limit on chemistry talk on New Year's Eve.

"Five. Four. Three." A very excited mother had her arms around two very disinterested preteens. I respected the energy—I loved New Year's Eve and always counted down even if I was just with an otherwise calm group of people. This woman, though, was doing a countdown for every time zone, and her kids were over it, as were most of our fellow travelers. I was supposed to be at a party back in Chicago, where I would be a little drunk, a little sweaty from dancing, and a little ready to kiss someone shiny and new at midnight in hopes of getting over my ex.

"Two. One! Happy New Year, South Sandwich Islands!" The woman's sugary, bordering on Pez-sweet voice filled the gate area, and I took a hard right toward the nearest bar. That level of sustained enthusiasm for time zones really only worked when everyone was drunk.

The bar nearest to my gate had been packed all evening, so even my plan to be a little drunk in time to ring in Rio de Janeiro's New Year with the mom had been thwarted. I was about to do another about-face and search for somewhere else to go when I saw the familiar shuffle of belongings as someone began to vacate their seat. Elena was a runner. Not me. I preferred to move at a leisurely pace and only get sweaty when it ended in a payoff of the bedroom or dance-floor variety, but I pumped my legs as fast as they would go. That spot at the bar was mine.

Unfortunately, someone else had the same idea, and a middle-aged woman and I arrived at the seat at the same time. I had to act fast. "Do you mind? I'd really like to sit next to my husband." I motioned to the man in the seat next to the vacant one, who looked up at me in confusion from behind glasses, his amber-hazel eyes narrowed slightly. His low fade and edges still fresh from a barber made him look polished, and the wide shoulders hinted at an athletic build. I widened my eyes in a "play along" gesture.

"Hi . . . honey?" he said slowly, and I was certain we were fooling no one.

Still, I flashed the woman my most charming smile and slipped into the seat, looking lovingly at my "husband" until she walked away.

"Do I know you?" He had a nice voice, deep and kind of rumbly, and his defined forearms rested on the bar.

"No," I answered, tucking my roller bag beside me. "But I've been in this airport a long time on New Year's Eve alone and I would like a drink."

He continued to look at me skeptically. He was cute, and the casual long-sleeve T-shirt he wore was doing his body all kinds of favors.

"Thank you for playing along." I motioned for the bartender, ordering nachos and a glass of champagne. "And another of whatever he was drinking," I said.

He still eyed me like I had two heads.

"It's the least I can do for forcing a marriage on you."

"I suppose you're right."

"And there wasn't time for a prenup, so I think if you want them, you're entitled to half my nachos." I sensed I was talking too much, especially since he hadn't really said much of anything, but the worst that would happen would be him getting up to leave and me talking to whoever took his seat.

He glanced down at his phone and after a beat said, "It *was* an asset acquired during the marriage." He wasn't exactly talking to me, and the timing for the joke was off, but it still landed. He seemed funny in a way people are when they're not used to being funny.

He looked up with a small grin when I laughed. The bartender set down my drink and another beer for my husband, telling us the nachos would be out soon. "I'm Gia," I said, holding out my hand. "Desperate to board a flight to get me back to Chicago."

"Felix," he said, taking my hand. It was a normal handshake and not a creepy guy-trying-to-get-in-my-pants handshake, which was as endearing as his little joke. "I'm trying to get to California."

"Home?"

"For now," he said, but didn't explain further, and the murmur of other people's conversations settled in the silence between us.

"Attention in the terminal, Flight 627 with service to Albuquerque has been moved to Gate D24." The disembodied voice was so pleasant, I wouldn't have minded it narrating my life.

Attention in the grocery store, Gia will be purchasing a new detergent today.

Attention in the faculty meeting, Gia stopped listening to this conversation ten minutes ago when it ceased being productive.

Attention at Thanksgiving dinner, Gia is going to take more than her fair share of mashed potatoes and does not require your commentary.

Instead, I accepted the plate of nachos, nudging it between Felix and me. "How many times do you think they've changed the gate for that flight?"

"In the last three hours?"

I loaded a chip with as much topping as I could. "Sure."

"Fourteen."

"You counted?"

He looked down into his beer and I thought he might ignore me again, but then he slid his phone across the bar, the screen waking to show a spreadsheet displaying flights with ticks next to them. When I looked up to catch his expression, it was blank but with a hint of hope, as if he wanted me to have a positive reaction but was prepared for something else.

I leaned in close, waiting for him to do the same. "I say this with all sincerity and swear on the sanctity of our marriage." I braced my hand on his shoulder and let it slide over his biceps. "That spreadsheet is singularly the sexiest thing in this airport right now."

His arm muscles tensed when I finished the sentence, and I earned a small, almost nonexistent, but totally there smile. "I wasn't going for sexy," he said, shoving his phone into his pocket.

"Too bad. My assessment stands."

I bit into a chip piled high with cheese and chicken, and a couple of pieces of tomato fell into my hand.

"There wasn't much else to do," he said, reaching for his own, much more reasonably piled chip. "But thank you."

"This"—I motioned between us—"might be the beginning of a beautiful friendship."

"Just a friendship?"

I cocked my eye at what I was pretty sure was accidental flirting. "Are you hitting on me, Felix?"

His eyes widened and I laughed, waiting for him to laugh as well. "I just meant because of the whole marriage charade."

I angled my legs to him and patted his biceps again with my non-tomato hand. "I'm just kidding." I squeezed his arm, enjoying the feel of the firm muscle under the fabric of his shirt. "I'm more fun to flirt with once I'm fed anyway."

"Oh, I wasn't trying to flirt with you."

I flashed him a smile, feeling more like myself than I had in months, since before Elena broke up with me and the pressure to conform at work to fit in with the mostly white-man culture began to feel bigger. A colleague I worked closely with had recently been awarded a major Department of Energy grant, which was exciting, but pressure to perform and produce was mounting along with the expectation to conform to a more "professional" style, which I took to mean being quieter, more traditional, and less me. I'd felt boxed in at work lately, and there in the airport, I realized no one knew me. Felix wouldn't care that my approach to catalytic hydrolysis reactions challenged my more traditional colleagues. He probably wouldn't understand what I was even referring to if I brought it up. I bumped his arm with mine. "Well, start trying to flirt once we finish the nachos, okay?"

2

Felix

GIA'S HAND FELT small in mine—it was soft and delicate—and I worried I might crush it, but she kept pulling me through the airport. It was the shock of my life that I was letting her lead me to an undisclosed location.

I didn't usually like new people. After a dismal introduction to her best friend's daughter when I visited over the holidays, my stepmom told me I came off as severe. I told her I thought "acerbic" was a better fit, and she promptly threw a pillow at me. I didn't put much heart into her challenge that for the New Year I should try being open to meeting new people. As a social experiment it didn't interest me, but she'd predicted I wouldn't be able to do it. I didn't like to fail at things. Maybe that was why I let this beautiful, outgoing woman pretend I was her husband to get a seat at a bar. "Where are we going?"

She smiled over her shoulder, squeezing my fingers in a way I enjoyed far too much. "It's almost midnight." She said this like it was explanation enough as we traipsed past gate after gate of stranded, sleepy, and annoyed passengers trying to get out of Atlanta. "We have to find a good place to ring in the New Year."

We'd finished the nachos and had a couple more drinks, but we discovered a mutual appreciation for *Doctor Who* and ended up talking more than drinking. She kept touching my arm while we were sitting beside each other. Little touches, brushing her hand over my sleeve, and I liked it more and more. I wasn't touched a lot—it had been a long time since I'd been in a relationship, and I wasn't the type of guy people casually touched. But I eagerly awaited her doing it. "What is a good place to ring in the New Year inside an airport?"

She sped up until we were on the escalator. "The train," she said breathlessly, fingers linked with mine. Gia pulled me toward the empty tram car, and all I could think about was the chemistry of a redox reaction, because all night I'd felt like I was waiting for fireworks that were now about to begin.

"The train? To look in another terminal?"

She tugged on my hand and we walked down the last few steps before reaching the platform. "No, to be on it. Doesn't being in motion when the new year starts sound poetic?"

"Are you a poet?"

She laughed, her head tipping back. "Just about the furthest thing from it."

We'd talked about a lot of things, but I realized I didn't have any idea what she did for a living. "A . . . mime?"

She'd let go of my hand while we waited, seeming to realize she was still holding it, and I missed the contact. "How is that the opposite of a poet?"

The disembodied voice announced the arrival of the train. "Attention, passengers, please stand clear of the train doors, allowing people to exit."

I shrugged. "I guess the only truly logical opposite to a poet is not-a-poet." I didn't exactly hold my breath, but I braced for her to realize we hadn't asked about what each other did. I had a feeling explaining my work might derail this wonderful connection between us.

"What if I was a professional mime?" she mused, and my breathing returned to its normal rate as we stepped onto the nearly empty train and she walked toward the back, where the wide bench was available.

Her arm brushed mine and I followed her lead and sat on the ledge, settling my roller bag at my feet as she did the same. "That might make this night more normal."

"You hang out with a lot of mimes on the regular? You're fascinating, Felix."

I laughed, inhaling the faint hint of whatever scent she'd put on earlier in the day. I hadn't taken notice of how a woman smelled in a long time, and I pushed my finger along my nose to adjust my glasses. "Not really. Now, what are we doing on this train?"

"Attention. The train doors are closing. Next stop, Terminal D."

She waggled her eyebrows and scooted closer to me.

"What does that expression mean?"

"Want to do a little kissing at midnight?"

I glanced around the train to see if anyone overheard her and to avoid how much my answer was a resounding and uproarious yes. Gia was smart and funny and hot, and I was tipsy. Add to that, she didn't know my last girlfriend had referred to me as cantankerous and a little closed off, and that was while we were still dating. "You want to kiss *me*?"

"Who else would I be talking to? It's okay if you don't want to. It's just that it's New Year's Eve, and you're cute and I'm cute and this used to be the kind of opportunity I'd take to make out with a cute stranger."

She tipped her chin up, eyes meeting mine. She was so close to me, and the sum total of the sensations from every time she'd touched me that night pooled at the base of my spine.

A curl fell over her ear, and I brushed it back tentatively. "This is usually the point when I realize I walked away from a pretty woman and left a bad impression."

"You haven't made a bad impression on me." Her breath was warm against my chin.

"No?" That would normally bug me, someone being so close, but she smelled like nachos and that perfume and I wondered if she tasted like champagne.

She shook her head. "Not yet. Are you a bad kisser?"

"I . . . don't think so?"

She grinned, eyes meeting mine in some combination of challenge and invitation I felt in my toes. "Then we should be good."

If Gia was as surprised as I was when my lips crashed down on hers, she didn't show it. The train rumbled under us, with my hand holding her neck and her hand running through my hair. When I lowered a hand to her hip, pulling her closer, Gia let out a little moan against my mouth and I had visions of fast-forwarding to a lot more than kissing.

"Attention, passengers. The train is stopping."

The voice made us both pull apart, and I sucked in a breath. Gia's lips were parted, her tongue darting out over her plump lower lip. "It's not midnight yet," she said, as the force of the train's brakes pushed her thigh against mine and her finger along my hairline, grazing the tiny scar there.

"Sorry," I said, as the doors opened and two people shuffled off, leaving us alone.

Gia glanced at her watch. "A little less than a minute to go."

"Do you want me to wait a minute?" I didn't even recognize my voice, let alone the words I was saying.

She cut her eyes around the empty train and stood, stepping between my legs. "No." This time, she kissed me, her soft lips and eager tongue blocking out the rest of the world. Gia's body molded to mine when she sat on my lap, her hands moving over my chest and stomach. I was sure she would feel the effect she was having on me, but I didn't have the wherewithal to be concerned.

"Attention, passengers. The train is stopping."

We pulled apart again, more reluctantly this time. "Happy New Year, Felix," she said, her palm sliding down my chest. "The train is stopping."

I couldn't quite catch my breath, and the sudden, blissed-out, untethered feeling I was experiencing was entirely unfamiliar to me. I shouldn't have liked it, except that I couldn't remind myself to care with Gia perched on top of me. "Do you want to get off?"

She arched an eyebrow.

"I mean, get off the train, not . . ."

She laughed, which made her body vibrate against mine. "I did not know I needed this, but I did," she said, finally stroking my hairline again, where her fingers traced the line of the scar I'd picked up as a kid when I fell into a pool and hit my head. She slid from my lap and picked up her roller bag. "I'm going to head back to my gate," she said, walking backward. Her teeth sank into that delicious bottom lip I wanted to kiss again.

I wasn't sure what to say as she stepped off the train. Stay? Wait? *For what?* The best-case scenario would be us making a mistake inside an airport, and I didn't do mistakes, so I waved her goodbye instead. "Happy New Year," I said, before the doors closed and I rode to Terminal B, where my plane would eventually depart for LAX.

APRIL

3

Gia

"HEY!" MY BEST friend, Bennett, sounded excited when the call connected. "I thought you'd disappeared on me." His familiar voice and warm British accent made me smile.

"I've been busy with work." I took the exit heading toward the airport. "Do you remember the grant I told you about?"

"Vaguely. Remind me and explain it like I failed introductory chemistry."

"You got a D," I said, slowing behind a long line of cars approaching short-term parking. "The head of my department got a huge grant from the Department of Energy to study solar hydrolysis catalysts."

"Gi, I believe I asked you to explain it as if I'd *failed* chemistry."

I laughed at his response. "Basically using sunlight to split water molecules so hydrogen can be utilized as a cleaner alternative energy source."

"Well, now I feel as if I earned a C-minus."

The grant meant Christopher was bringing on additional people, and it felt like half my new job was wooing research partners. I was part of the conversations about the science, too, but the only time he seemed to trust me to woo solo was during airport transportation. I pulled into a spot on the main level. "Surprise, surprise. He asked the only woman on the team to take airport duty."

"From what you've told me about the man in charge, I must say I am not at all surprised," Bennett said.

"But it's not the hill I'm going to die on today." Between my teaching and research commitments, let alone my volunteer responsibilities, every day felt like it got away from me by ten in the morning. I'd been working more since the breakup and Elena moving, needing the distraction, but also to prove to her in some way she was wrong about me. She'd said it wasn't worth trying to do long distance because she didn't think I was serious or grounded enough to make it work long-term. That had hurt more than any intentionally cruel thing she could have said.

"How did things go with your enemy? Was he as villainous as you feared?"

I rolled my eyes as I grabbed the ticket for short-term parking and drove into the garage. "I'm on my way to pick him up from the airport." Maybe "enemy" was too strong a word, but ever since I first presented my work, A.F. Ennings had been there, waiting to tear it down and challenge me. We'd never met in person, but I could pick his writing out in a heartbeat. Of course, I gave it right back, and now six years later, I found myself picking up A.F. Ennings from the airport to interview for a position in my department.

"And you'll be nice to him?" Bennett asked. He had had front-row seats to my reactions to some of Ennings's critiques of my publications and my spirited responses to his own work over the years.

"I'm always nice."

Bennett laughed, the sound reverberating through my car. "Sure you are."

"It's not like I'm gonna kick him. Helping looks good to my

department chair, and he already hates me." I glanced around the baggage-claim area, where I was supposed to meet Ennings. No one knew what he looked like, which was so weird. No social media, he never attended conferences in person, and the campus-directory listing at his institution was just a blank avatar. "Anyway, I assume he's some trollish narcissist."

"You say that based on . . . ?"

I fumbled in my bag for the piece of paper on which I'd scribbled *Alexander Ennings. Take that, A.F. I know your real first name.* "Based on everything he's ever written. It's—"

"Reminder in the terminal. Please keep your bags with you. Unattended luggage should be reported to airport security."

I stopped mid-sentence when I spotted a familiar figure in the crowd. I didn't think I'd ever have the chance to see Felix again after that strange New Year's Eve night and that searing kiss we had shared—those searing kiss*es* on the train—but there he was standing in front of me, wearing a fitted button-up with a coat tossed over his arm. "I gotta go, Ben," I said hurriedly into the phone before shoving it into my pocket. Ennings could wait.

He stood with shoulders squared glancing around the baggage area. His hair was trimmed short, cropped close to his skin, which, even under fluorescent lighting, looked rich and warm. "Felix?"

His head whipped up from whatever he was staring at on his phone and I caught his dark hazel eyes. He was wearing the same glasses, frames that accentuated the rest of his face, even the light scar that ran along his hairline. "Hi."

I grinned, walking toward him and showing not even an iota of coolness. "I didn't think I'd ever see you again."

"Likewise." He looked stiffer than I remembered, but he had probably just gotten off a long flight, and I should cut him some slack. He still looked as good as he had that strange night in the airport when it felt like we talked about a million different things. "You live here?" He adjusted his glasses. "In Chicago?"

"Well, I figured you meant the city and not baggage claim." I motioned around the space. I suppose I should have been trying to spot Ennings, but this was more important. "I'm picking up some old blowhard for work. Well, he's probably not much older than me, but he's still the one person in the world I wish I could muzzle." I waved a hand dismissively. "It doesn't matter. I can't believe we're running into each other!"

"It's quite the coincidence," he said, glancing around the crowded area. "How . . . are you?"

"Well, I haven't kissed any strangers since getting here, so it's a slow day for me."

His rich baritone made the best sound when he laughed. "That's reserved for holidays?"

"Holidays and guys with outstanding *Doctor Who* recall."

"So," he said, glancing around again and then lowering his voice. "You want to hear my Dalek impression?"

It was my turn to laugh, and at the sound he flashed one of his grins, which felt hard-won. "How long are you in town? Maybe we could grab a drink?"

He pushed a messenger bag up on his shoulder, and I remembered holding on to that firm perfect-for-my-grip shoulder when we were kissing the life out of each other on the train. "Two days, but I'm interviewing for a job here, so maybe if I accept their inevitable offer, we could see each other again."

"I love that you assume you'll be offered the job, but good luck anyway." I crossed my fingers on each hand and held them up. I didn't get the impression Felix was used to asking people out, and it was fun to see him trip over the words. "Why don't I get your number." I pulled my phone from my pocket. The notification that

THE MISSED CONNECTION   151

Ennings had landed sat on my home screen, and I dismissed it before adding Felix to my contacts and sending him a GIF of nachos followed by the kissing emoji. Did I mention there wasn't even an iota of cool? He was a seriously good kisser.

"I have yours now, too." His grin was sweet, if timid, when he tucked his phone back into his pocket. "I should probably find my ride soon."

"Oh! Me, too. I almost forgot." I dug into my purse for the sign without taking my eyes off Felix. "But, wow, I can't believe we ran into each other again. I've thought about that night."

His lips twitched. "Me, too."

I should have stepped back the way I had when I'd gotten off the train. I was into grand gestures and theatrical moments, but even I knew this was not that moment. Still, I didn't want to break that chemical reaction between us, even without touching. "Can I give you a hug?"

His eyes widened but he nodded after a beat. "Sure."

Felix smelled like mint and oranges. It was such a strange combination, but as soon as the scent hit my nostrils, I wanted to nibble him to see if he tasted the same. His hands were flat at my back, and he stiffened under me until our chests touched. Then he relaxed, his hands moving lower down my back—just by a centimeter, but I felt it and I wanted more. When I pulled away, the sign slipped from my hand, but he saved it before it fell to the floor and held it out for me.

"I really hope you get the job," I said, finally taking that step back, our hands still linked like it was a handshaking competition.

His grin was that tiny one that delighted me to earn. Surely he felt what I did in that hug. "Me, too."

His gaze fell to my lips and then to my hand, where I clutched the sheet of paper with *Alexander Ennings* scrawled on it, and Felix's tiny grin disappeared.

"What?" I asked. "Do I have something on my face?"

This time, he took a big step back and stood straighter, glancing over my shoulder.

The abrupt shift made me feel panicky. "What's wrong? Do you see your ride?"

He nodded once. "That old blowhard you're here to pick up? The one you want to muzzle?"

"Yeah . . ." I glanced down at the paper. "Ennings. Why?"

He met my eyes again, his gaze cool, assessing, and devoid of all the warmth and humor I'd just seen, and my stomach dropped. "I'm him." He held out his hand. "Nice to meet you."

SEPTEMBER

4

Felix

I TAPPED MY pen on the table. If I had known being a professor would mean so many hours in meetings with people who couldn't stop talking, I might have considered a different career path. It was three minutes past the planned start time and everyone was still chatting, laughing, and, in my opinion, wasting time. I hadn't been part of the department long. The opportunity to work on the Department of Energy grant at Thurmond had emerged quickly. But five months after interviewing and a few months into my new role, I had learned that the culture of my new chemistry department was much more social and casual than I'd expected, and I missed the distinctly antisocial one at my last institution more and more by the day. "We'll get started in a few minutes," the department chair said to no one in particular before returning to his conversation with a senior professor about golf. I tapped my pen faster to avoid rolling my eyes.

The door to the conference room opened and in walked Dr. Georgia Price. Gia. The woman I'd kissed during a wildly out-of-character night in an airport and whose body had filled my thoughts for months. The odds of her being a chemist, let alone one in my same area of focus, were astronomical. Almost as unlikely as experiencing the best kiss of my life with a complete stranger. But while we studied similar things, I approached the work through computer modeling to make predictions while she took an experimental approach toward testing. The two could work in tandem, but when our findings differed and she challenged the veracity of my approach, I responded in kind. That had been years ago, and we hadn't let up. I'd been a little captivated with Dr. Georgia Price before I knew who she was.

Now she took the seat next to me, her subtly floral perfume tickling my nose as she hurried into the chair, dumping her notepad and tablet on the desk. The purple pen rolled toward me, and I nudged it back before it fell on the floor. I didn't want her things in my space, because I wanted to avoid the temptation to look at her and the fleeting thought that our hands might touch. It was left over from the encounter in the airport, a juvenile fantasy I was quick to squash.

"Right on time," she said to herself, checking something on her tablet.

"The meeting was supposed to begin four minutes ago." I don't know why I said it. I didn't need to, and I was just needling her. It was like every time I was near Gia, I needed to prove to myself that I didn't still harbor those juvenile fantasies, that I didn't want to ask the name of her perfume.

She motioned to Christopher, the department chair. "He never starts on time."

"He would if everyone arrived on time," I commented, scribbling a note on my tablet with my stylus.

She pushed some stray curls back from her face and I caught the flash of purple nail polish. "Did one of your models tell you that?" It wasn't a dig. I developed computer models to answer complex questions, saving time and resources needed to physically experiment. I was good at it. Excellent, really. But her comment still made me want to respond.

"You're the experimentalist. Why not try arriving on time to see the results?"

She smiled sweetly—too sweetly—and pinned me with a stare. "Are these the hard-hitting scientific problems you're spending your time on these days, Ennings?" Gia Price said my name like it had mud on it, and I guess I had that coming. As soon as I realized who she was at the airport, I pushed everything from before out of my head, or I pretended I had. During the painfully stilted drive from the airport, I tried to think of a way to explain why I'd given her my middle name on New Year's Eve. I'd just left my family, who called me Felix. But the real reason was that she'd seemed fun and exciting from the moment she approached me at that bar, and it seemed fitting to be a little different from my normal self. As we cruised down the interstate, I didn't know how to phrase that, though, so the silence hung.

My interview had been awkward, particularly around the aspects of my work that challenged hers, and when I was hired, they gave me a coveted corner office. The one right next to hers, where the low bass of the music from her speakers hummed through my wall. Everything I found captivating about her in the airport felt chaotic at work. She adjusted her necklace and I cut a quick glance to her fingertip moving along the soft skin of her neck.

I could have ignored her. I would have with any other colleague, but she made me want to poke at the wound. "You know we're working on the same hard-hitting scientific problems. I'm just having more luck answering them."

Her eyes narrowed and her nose scrunched, but she didn't have time to respond before Christopher started the meeting.

●　●　●

"ALEXANDER. A MOMENT?" Christopher motioned for me to follow him to his office as the other faculty members cleared the room. I wanted absolutely nothing more than to get out of there. The past two hours had dragged, and all I could think about was how much I wanted to be back in my office, away from people and away from Gia.

"Certainly." I followed him down the tiled hall and into his large office, surrounded by picture windows overlooking the campus quad. Thurmond was a beautiful campus, not that I'd spent much time outside enjoying it.

Christopher slid behind a desk that was a little too big for the office. "How's the transition going?"

"Well. Thank you."

"Everyone is treating you well?" He coughed into his sleeve and looked at his inbox instead of me. "We're glad to have you here with us."

I tipped my chin down. I knew they were—I'd had my choice of institutions and Thurmond had the best offer. I still wasn't sure of the point of the inquisition, though. I'd signed a contract, and whether people were nice to me or not, I wasn't going to break it. "I am doing well," I repeated.

"I know it can't be easy having an office next to Gia." He still hadn't looked away from his monitor, which was fine by me. I wasn't that interested in the heart-to-heart.

"She's unique," I said, not mentioning that her lips were soft and her small hands were strong and I had a hard time divorcing that from my otherwise very clear distaste for her.

He laughed, finally looking away from his monitor. "She's a pain in the ass. In my experience, you don't find women who are attractive, smart, and tolerable. Impossible for them to have all three, even if they've got looks and brains like our esteemed Dr. Price."

My fingers curled into fists at my sides. "That's inappropriate."

He sat straighter, blustering before regaining his composure. "Just a joke, Alex."

The nickname grated on me, but I remained still. I learned young that most people are uncomfortable with a cold stare, and I'd perfected mine. My unchanging expression seemed to throw him when I didn't respond. *Acerbic.* It served me well. Gia wasn't tolerable, not exactly, but I didn't like him framing a fellow professional in that way, and I really didn't like him thinking I was the man he could share it with.

"Anyway," he said, clearing his throat and glancing back to his monitor. "The president wants our department to tour some peer institutions as part of a STEM-teaching knowledge alliance. Basically, we'll be visiting five schools who are doing big things with STEM teaching, and they'll share information. They all visited us two years ago for the same purpose. I'd like you to go."

"There are other faculty members who are better suited to it," I said, not excited about the idea of having to socialize with strangers. Plus, teaching was my least favorite part of this job.

"I agree. You're not the friendliest guy we have, but the president requested you." He pinned me with a flat expression. "I was going to suggest someone else, but now, talking to you, I think you'd be the best one after all." He handed me a printout including dates and locations. The itinerary would include five trips, with two days on each campus. It would be two entire weeks of travel.

"Do I have a choice?"

He flashed a more sardonic smile. "Of course." I took his words for what they were—"not really." "And you won't be alone. You'll travel with another faculty member."

"Who?"

He grinned. "Your very professional colleague, Dr. Price." Christopher gave a little laugh in reaction to the expression I didn't realize I had made. He stood and I followed suit, surprised when he smacked me on the back with a laugh. "Don't look so grim. She'll do all the work and it will be a cakewalk for you. She loves this stuff. Just make Thurmond look good."

I walked back to my office at a normal speed, but my mind ran a seven-minute mile, which upped to a five-minute mile when I caught a glimpse of Gia through her open door. She laughed with a student over her desk, and the sound followed me into my bare, ordered office. *How am I going to spend two weeks with that woman?*

Her voice was a muffled hum through the wall, and I scrubbed a hand down my face and sank down into my chair.

OCTOBER

OCTOBER

5

Gia

I SETTLED INTO a seat at the departure gate and pulled out my phone.

GIA: This trip is going to be awful.

BENNETT: The work trip with your ex-lover? 🍆

GIA: The work trip with the colleague I can't stand.

GIA: Who, fine, I kissed once. But there was no 🍆 involved.

BENNETT: Do you plan to kiss him again?

GIA: Why are we friends? You've become more insufferable since falling in love.

BENNETT: Turnabout is fair play. You teased me for years. Who is watching your menagerie of cats while you're gone?

> GIA: My friend from work, Jill, is going to check in
> on them.

I glanced up from my phone and saw Felix striding toward me, looking far too stiff and polished for seven in the morning on a Sunday. "Good morning," he said gruffly.

"Morning." I waved, trying to make my perusal of him less obvious. "Bet you're surprised I beat you here." I was surprised myself.

"On time isn't what I've come to expect of you. So, yes, somewhat surprised."

> BENNETT: He'll be kind. You'll be lovely.
> Everything will be fine.

I didn't look up from my phone. "Our flight boards in ten minutes. I'm not early so much as you're cutting it close."

> GIA: It's been forty-five seconds since he sat
> down. Kind is already out the window.

I checked my book and dug in my purse for a breath mint, thinking I should offer one to Felix but then deciding not to. He'd probably take it as a come-on or something, so we sat across from each other not speaking. It was my own personal hell. The flight wasn't crowded, and only a few other people sat near us. There weren't any ticking clocks in the airport, but it felt like there was an ominous metronome between us.

"Listen," I said, leaning forward on my knees.

"Yes?" It was hard to reconcile the pretentious asshat I now knew him to be with the fun guy I met on New Year's Eve. He glanced up from his phone but didn't really turn his head toward me, and I knew I didn't have his full attention. He looked poised to return to something more important.

"The elephant in the room."

He didn't say anything, just kept eyeing me with a cool stare.

"We made out on New Year's Eve."

"I was there. I remember."

The airport was the wrong place to put hands on someone, but I was pretty sure no one from security would blame me if they overheard this conversation. "We should talk about it."

He shook his head and glanced toward the boarding gate. "We do not need to talk about it. It's in the past."

"Things are awkward between us," I said, motioning to the space between him and me. "And we're going to spend the next two weeks together. Let's get things out in the open."

He stood when the gate agent opened the boarding door. "I don't think we need to do that. It was a mistake and it's behind us. It's not worth discussing."

For some reason that felt like a very polite punch to the gut. I still thought about the kiss, more than I cared to admit, especially since I hadn't kissed anyone else since then. "So, it's just awkward between us because you're an uptight misanthrope?"

He didn't even look back at me. "And you're kind of cocker spaniel–like in your need to be liked."

I didn't have a response, other than biting the inside of my lip to keep from showing him the emotional reaction I felt working its way into my features, the feelings of hurt, annoyance, and wanting to punch him in the throat. "Fine," I said. "We work together. That's it."

"Perfect."

DURING THE FIRST leg of the trip, we sat next to each other in silence. He was on the aisle and I was in the dreaded middle seat.

He put on headphones immediately, but lucky for me, our seatmate by the window was talkative and friendly, a young guy on his way home to see his family. He reminded me of a young Bennett, all sharp-jawed and classically handsome, and he made me laugh. The few times I peeked over at Felix, he was staring at his laptop with a dead-eyed and somehow intense stare. *Probably drafting an email to complain about the overrepresentation of cute puppy and baby videos on YouTube.*

The guy in the window seat, Jason, glanced out the window at the passing clouds, and I looked over his shoulder to see the sky had turned a soft lavender. "Wow," I commented, leaning closer to see it. I should have considered that meant leaning toward young Jason, but I didn't.

He noticed, though. "So, do you think I could get your number? Maybe I could call you when we're back in Chicago?"

He looked all of twenty-two, and though I firmly believed age to be just a number, he reminded me of my students. Hard no. Before I could answer, the flight attendant interrupted us.

"Can I get you something to drink?" The blond braid fell over her shoulder as she leaned closer to Felix.

He barely looked up, shaking his head and holding up a hand. *Rude.*

"Can I have a Coke?" Jason asked, lowering his tray table.

To my right, Felix rolled his eyes at the drink choice, and the small motion just irked me.

"I'd like one, too," I echoed. I would regret the carbonation and that much sugar first thing in the morning, but I had a feeling it would be worth it, just to bug Felix, whose jaw flexed at my words.

After she delivered our drinks, the sweetness of the soda invaded my taste buds with one drink, but I took another sip anyway. "Ennings, you're sure you don't want anything to drink?"

"Certain." He eyed my and Jason's cups, and then the young

man's face quickly before returning to his laptop, turning the volume up on what had to be the soundtrack to babies crying and forks scraping against flatware.

"So, can I call you sometime?" The kid's expression was so hopefully doe-eyed. I made a note to put in my own headphones soon, but I knew I had to let him down gently first.

"I just got out of a long relationship and I'm mending a broken heart, so I'm not looking for anything now."

"Oh! Me, too! We dated for like five weeks and I really loved her. It's the worst getting dumped."

I smiled to myself because he was right. "It is. Tell me about her. What happened?"

I never put in my headphones, but Jason forgot about getting my number. We talked the rest of the flight.

The second leg of our trip was shorter, and though it was nice to be out of a middle seat, this time there was no one to talk to besides Felix. The gray sky outside my window provided no interesting views. I hated reading on planes—it was an environment where I always craved conversation, but Felix's headphones were already in place, with his fingers moving over his keyboard.

Reluctantly, I pulled the two folders from my bag and handed one to him.

He didn't take it, eyeing the folder with skepticism. "What is this?"

"The itinerary along with some background materials and relevant research I compiled on the work Carr University is doing."

"Oh," he said, taking the folder and flipping through it. "This is thorough."

I shrugged. It was thorough. It was also summarized in an annotated bibliography and included questions to ask of the institution's leaders. "I'm a thorough person."

Felix read through the front-page summary of Carr I'd asked

our department secretary to compile for us. "Very," he mumbled. His tone didn't sound the least bit condescending or derisive for once. Maybe the twitch of his lip was even him being mildly impressed. He looked back at the document and flicked his eyes to me. I thought that might spark conversation about Carr, about the trip, about anything, but all he said was "thank you" before he replaced his earbuds and returned to his work.

I glanced at my watch. *Oh good. Only two more weeks of this.*

6

Felix

GIA SMILED.

Gia smiled at everyone.

Gia smiled at everyone all the damn time.

We'd been with the first institution's faculty and staff since eight that morning, learning about their initiatives, talking to their administrators, and now we were finishing a coffee break with graduate students. I shot a glance at Gia, who was nodding as a PhD candidate droned on about his experience adapting the teaching initiative to his own style.

Of course she was smiling. She'd told the kid on the plane she was heartbroken when I'd been pretending not to listen to them, but it was hard to believe. She just smiled all the time. I'd never seen anything like it.

A blonde whose name I'd already forgotten approached me, sipping from a tall paper cup. She was one of the faculty members who was researching the teaching initiative, maybe from biochemistry. "How's it been today?"

"Informative," I said, finishing my own cup of black coffee. The work they were doing wasn't groundbreaking and I'd been bored for much of the day, but I kept it to myself. I glanced at Gia, whose lips curled from a smile to a laugh at whatever the student had said. Her face brightened the way it had with the guy on the plane, and my stomach clenched at the memory of him hitting on her and her still giving him her attention.

Not that I wanted her attention.

"We're looking forward to hearing your thoughts. You all at Thurmond have been doing such good work." She touched my shoulder as another man approached. His name was Phillip Sauer, which I only remembered because it was on his name tag. "Phil, have you met Alexander Ennings yet?"

Gia's laugh trailed over to our conversation and I made a mental note to tell Christopher this was absolutely the last time I was agreeing to do anything like this, no matter what the president wanted.

"THAT WAS FUN," Gia said when we returned to the hotel after a dinner with Carr's administrators. The lobby buzzed with people, and when the elevator doors closed, we were finally blessed with silence. Silence from the crowds. Gia's presence was always loud even when she wasn't saying anything.

"I wouldn't say fun." I pulled my phone from my pocket to give my hands something to do.

"But would you ever use the word 'fun'?"

"Fundamentals."

She laughed, the sound of it reverberating off the walls of the small space, and I held my breath to keep from smiling as it hit my ears. "That sounds about right. At least you're consistent," she said as the doors opened on our floor.

Our rooms were two doors apart and she paused in front of hers, but her key card wouldn't work. When the light flashed red repeatedly, Gia's eyebrows scrunched each time.

"Try moving it slower," I offered as she swiped it in front of the sensor again. "No, slow." I made a grab for the card. "Like this."

The light flashed red again and I repeated my action but caught her glower from the corner of my eye.

"Were you under the impression that your gender would be a magic screwdriver?" If her tone wasn't so sharp, I would have commented on the *Doctor Who* reference, which made me think back to the airport and that first night.

"Sorry," I said, face heating at the memory of her kisses and how her thighs had settled against mine and how she smelled so sweet. I shook off the memory. "Do you want to call the desk from my room?"

She followed me down the hall and I willed my key card to work on the first try.

"Wow," she said, walking into my room. "You don't unpack much." Gia glanced around, her gaze landing on my zipped suitcase.

"We're only here for two nights."

"Sure, but . . ." She motioned around the room. "I guess I just have to spread out when I have a space."

I imagined her room, clothes strewn across the bed, toiletries across the sink. It fit all my other images of her. "That's not surprising."

She gave me a wry smile and sat on the edge of the bed, picking up the phone to dial the desk. She wore dark slacks, and when she crossed her legs the fabric stretched slightly over her thighs against the stark white duvet.

I pulled my phone out again, sitting as far across the room as I could before opening the familiar app and scrolling through videos, pushing her voice out of my head.

"They said that lock has been acting up. Do you mind if I hang in here for twenty minutes or so?" Her hand slid across the bed absently, like she needed to feel the cool cotton under her palm, like she needed to touch something. *Someone.*

"Sure." I'd thought the same thing when she touched the arm of the kid on the plane, the guy who'd asked for her number and then told her his whole life story. *Ridiculous.*

"Sure, you mind, or sure, I can stay?"

I didn't look up from my phone. "Which do you think?"

I didn't pay attention to how she settled back against my bed. "Don't act like someone wouldn't need to clarify with you." I flicked my eyes up from the video and took in her profile as she glanced out the window. Gia's eyes skipped back from the window and she caught my eye. "What are you always watching? I can't believe you're on TikTok." She arched a brow. "Are you secretly kind of fun after all, Felix?"

I angled the phone to my body. "No."

"What are you watching? Consider it an icebreaker."

I exited the app, worried she'd give up on asking and snatch my phone. "I think our ice is sufficiently cracked."

"C'mon." She sat forward on the bed, tucking her ankle under her. "I'll show you my favorite videos." Before I could respond and tell her I wasn't interested in whatever positive-living, rainbow, and sunshine accounts she followed, she said, "This is it." She pulled her phone from her pocket and scrolled for a minute, holding the screen toward me, where someone mixed paint colors.

I narrowed my eyes, realizing my glasses were in my bag. "Huh," I commented.

"What did you expect? Puppies and thirst traps?"

I grinned to myself. "Yes."

"Well." She laughed and tucked her phone away. "I watch those, too, but this is so fascinating." Gia's black pants and blue sleeveless top along with her warm brown skin formed a contrast against the white of the bed—it made her look like a painting, a study in contrasts. "Your turn."

"I prefer cats to dogs," I said, standing, needing to move.

"I have three cats," she said, following me around the room. "I know. Cat lady, right?"

"I have a cat," I said, touching the cool metal between the windowpanes, but I still saw her reflection against the glass, Gia over top the town's lights.

"Really? Well, look at us having things in common. What's its name?"

"Fred."

She laughed again. That laugh. Damn, I didn't like how it unsettled me, how much I wanted to let go and laugh with her. "I love that. Mine are—"

Gia's phone vibrated, and I caught myself studying the way her teeth sunk into her plump lower lip as she stared at the screen. I turned and cleared my throat, seeking out a blank wall to study instead of Gia's mouth. "Your lock is fixed?"

"No," she said, glancing up. "Phil and Amelia invited us to go out for drinks."

"Phil and Amelia?"

She looked at me like I'd asked for clarification on what state we were in. "The two people who were with us all day?"

"Oh." I sat on the edge of the desk. "Why would we go for drinks?"

"Basic socialization?" She was already standing, and a pang of loss ticked at me because as much as it unnerved me to have her in my room talking about TikTok viewing and our cats, I also knew I didn't want her to leave. "We don't have to drink. I'm sure they'd be fine if we went to a coffee shop or something."

"I'm good," I said, watching her smooth down her outfit.

"You sure?"

I nodded and motioned to the door. "Go wild without me, though."

She didn't move toward the door again. "It's a Monday night in a college town. Do you think drinks with colleagues is code for something? Why not come with us?"

My face heated. "I'm not interested."

She shrugged and I thought she rolled her eyes. "Whatever you want, Felix. I'll see you in the morning."

She held the door handle. "Want to tell me what you were watching before I go? It's all I'm going to think about all night."

"I'm sure you'll have better things to think about than me."

She smiled, and I kind of liked the idea that I'd be on her mind.

7

Gia

"YOU SHOULD HAVE come out with us last night," I said as we cruised down the highway toward the small airport. "The Carr hosts were a lot of fun."

My head gave a dull thud and I made a mental note to grab Tylenol at the airport. We'd been out a little too late and had a few too many drinks after a day and a half of talking about little else besides teaching and learning. I loved my research, but the hands-on teaching and finding ways of making teaching more effective, that was my favorite part of the job. Taking a break from the grant work was refreshing to me, and socializing with colleagues outside the scope of my research filled my cup.

Felix looked down at his phone. The expression on his face hinted that the level to which his own cup was filled remained unchanged. Sometimes I wondered if there was anything in his cup besides vinegar anyway. "I don't make a habit of socializing with my colleagues."

"Do you make a habit of socializing with anyone?" I said it under my breath as I looked out my window. The day before had been inspiring—the work Carr University was doing with teaching

STEM and supporting traditionally underserved students was amazing. Add to that, our hosts in the chemistry department were kind and fun. Not that you would have known any of that from Felix, who sat like a statue, nodding politely when needed but otherwise was like having a cardboard cutout next to me.

"Not often," he said from the other side of the car.

The way he said it almost made me feel bad, but only almost.

It was busy at the airport, with a long security line for such a small airport. "I wish I had TSA PreCheck," I said to myself. I'd meant to sign up for it for years, never more so than when I stood at the back of a very long line like this one, behind a family of seventeen unsupervised children parented by four large roller bags. I looked longingly at the short line for PreCheck and once again lamented putting it off.

"It's convenient," Felix said from behind me, and I whipped around to face him.

"You have it?"

He nodded like I'd asked the most obvious question possible, and I suppose I had.

"You don't have to wait with me." It wasn't like we were going to carry on a conversation.

"It's fine." He said it in the same terse way he said everything, but he didn't move, and we slowly—achingly slowly—inched forward in line as the group of unsupervised children seemed to swell from seventeen plus four bags to twenty-nine and twelve bags.

We finally reached the security checkpoint and began unloading things onto the conveyor belt. There was something about the body scanner that made me want to assume the position and then break into a dance when the beat dropped, like I was choreographing my own music video. Unfortunately, Felix was right behind me, and I had a sneaking suspicion he wouldn't play along.

"Is this your bag, ma'am?" The TSA agent leaned over the barrier, and I nodded. "We need to search it."

Panic crawled up my spine. I wasn't worried they'd find anything, but I hated the idea of other people touching my things. I also didn't look at Felix at all, certain he'd be rolling his eyes again, assuming I left a water bottle in there. *Did I leave a water bottle in there?*

It was much, much worse. Felix took his roller bag and messenger bag off the conveyor belt and waited for me as the TSA agent unzipped and checked my bag. "Did I leave something out of my Ziploc bag?" I asked the question, but the follow-up froze in my throat as the man pulled my ergonomic, gold-accented, sonic-wave toy, purring away from inside my bag. I am a person who would strike up a conversation about sex toys with a stranger because I think everyone should enjoy them if they want, but the man's gloved hands and confused expression while my fully charged device whirred away half out of its cute little travel bag gave me pause.

He raised his bushy eyebrows.

"Yeah, that's my . . ." I glanced at his expression, debating how specific TSA needed one to be. *My clitoral-stimulation device? Pleasure toy?* I could have said "vibrator," but it wasn't exactly accurate. I paused again, debating if I wanted to extol the virtues of sonic-wave technology over traditional vibrators. I must have seemed embarrassed or flummoxed, because someone came to my rescue.

"I believe that is a, um, personal massager," a voice from behind me said, all low and rumbly.

I closed my eyes at the sensation of Felix's arm brushing against mine and the puff of his breath near my ear. The agent's eyes widened further and the device fell from his hand into my bag, where it buzzed against the rest of my things. "Understood." He reached into the bag to retrieve it. "I'd never seen a . . . massager that looked like that before." He pulled a wand from somewhere behind the counter and scanned my toy quickly before setting it back in the bag gently, like it might break. He pushed my bag back onto the belt and it rolled down to my hand. "Have a nice day."

"Thanks." I reached into the bag, pressing the off button. Felix still stood stick-straight next to me, as if a drill sergeant had called him to attention, and I tried to ignore the coiling in my belly at his presence, even though I'd been annoyed when he stepped in. "You know," I said, pushing the bag onto my shoulder. "If there's someone in your life who enjoys that kind of massage, you might look into that brand. They're the gold standard."

The old guy laughed, and Felix shifted next to me. "You've got to be kidding me." I'd never heard an eye roll in someone's voice before, but the footsteps as he walked away weren't hard to interpret. *Good.* A little space would help me forget how his voice had made me feel. I chatted with the agent for another minute before walking toward our gate to catch up with Felix, who had already walked beyond where I could spot him. Something about that made me grin.

"Did you run away from me so you could watch your secret videos?" I fell into the chair next to Felix at our gate. "Makeup tutorials? I'm pathetic with eyeliner. I won't judge, Feels. Can I call you Feels?"

"No." He tucked his phone away and pulled out his laptop. "You could call me Alexander like everyone else."

"You introduced yourself to me as Felix." I'd never asked him why he'd used his middle name in the airport all those months ago. I wanted to know, though. Rather than choose that moment, I focused on my phone, where I saw a few messages from my teaching assistant and began tapping out a reply. "Anyway, I'm not like everyone else."

He didn't respond, but I knew he heard me because of the quirk in his eyebrow. There was something so fun about poking Felix until he finally spoke. "Maybe you're the same as everyone else. You assume I didn't make out with Christopher in LaGuardia?" His delivery was so dry, I almost missed it.

"Was he a better kisser than me?"

"He talked less."

I elbowed him in the side, relieved he wasn't being awkward after that mostly embarrassing moment at security. "Felix, did you actually make a joke?"

"So it would seem."

I grinned and returned to my phone, finishing my reply to the TA's questions and checking a few emails. The gate began to fill with people, and boarding was set to begin in a few minutes, so I stashed my things in my bag. "Dance videos?"

Felix shook his head, not looking up from his computer.

"Time-lapse videos of fruit rotting?"

He finally looked up, mild horror covering his normally flat expression. "God no. Is that a thing?" His indignant reaction was kind of endearing.

I shrugged. "Probably?"

"No."

I leaned close to him, speaking low. "It's not something . . . kinky, is it?" I didn't realize how close I really was until I felt my own breath after it hit his neck and I breathed in the scent of his aftershave.

He stiffened and I pulled back, regretting the familiarity. I was always too familiar too fast. Bennett told me that. Elena told me that. It was true. Felix hadn't replied yet but dragged his eyes to mine. "It's nothing sexual." His voice was pitched low, gravelly, and my stomach fluttered. The actual words were literally not sexual, but the way he said them hit me in a way I wasn't comfortable with from someone I didn't really like.

"Uh, good. I was kidding."

We sat in silence for a few moments.

"We will begin preboarding Flight 1678, service to Indianapolis, momentarily."

I sat forward, fiddling with the strap of my bag while Felix stood and stretched. "Those kinds of videos are probably better on other apps, anyway, if you're looking for viewing material," he said over his shoulder, with a pointed glance toward my bag, walking off toward the restroom.

Felix Ennings was full of surprises.

8

Felix

AFTER A QUICK trip to St. Anne's University, I let Gia take the window seat on our flight to the next institution when she was assigned another middle seat. I didn't think Christopher had that kind of power or influence over the staff who made travel arrangements for the university, but if he did, a steady stream of middle seats was the way to show Gia how he felt.

She made notes in her trip binder as we settled in. I'd watched her take pages of notes over the past two days.

"What else could you be writing?"

She spoke without looking up from the page; a curl that had fallen loose from her headband framed her eye and cheek. "They had so much good information. I wanted to get down a few more thoughts."

My arm brushed her elbow on the shared armrest, and her skin was impossibly soft and warm, even under the chilled air in the plane. I leaned forward, knowing our limbs would brush again. "Their work is impressive."

Gia set down her pen and met my eyes with a playful smile, her teeth just slightly sinking into her full lower lip. "I can't believe you're admitting it."

"I acknowledge excellent work. I'm not actually some kind of misanthrope."

She raised an eyebrow and knocked her elbow into me, another brush of skin and warmth.

"What?"

"You act like it costs you something to give a compliment." Gia smiled and tucked her things away under the seat. "You were just the other side of rude when we were at Carr."

"I wasn't interested in what they had to say. I was professional, though." I'd been told things like that my whole life. I never felt compelled to be friendly for no reason—it always seemed like a waste of time. The way Gia invited people into conversation was so foreign to me, it felt like she was speaking another language.

"I was nice at St. Anne's," I said, defending myself.

Gia smiled again and glanced out the window at the blue sky emerging over the clouds. "I just mean, what does it cost you to show you're interested in what someone else has to say? It doesn't have to entail schmoozing or even that you give a compliment you don't believe. But you can't actually be this unimpressed with everything."

"I was impressed with the work St. Anne's is doing," I said, settling back in the seat, angling slightly toward Gia and not the wide-shouldered man on my right.

"Name something else that has impressed you on this trip. Anything." She cocked her eyebrow again like she had me, like I wouldn't be able to give another answer. She was wrong, though, because she'd impressed me time and time again—from her binders and the way people just wanted to talk to her to the pointed and insightful questions she'd raised in our meetings. And how she was happy even before coffee and calm even when TSA held up her sex toy.

Jeez, the sex toy. I'd had a lot of impressive thoughts knowing she had that, too.

I was trying to figure how to roll that into a response when she smiled again. "I knew it." Gia leaned against the window, resting her curls against the plastic-coated wall. Her eyelids fell closed and I stole a few glances at the curve of her shoulder, the set of her jaw. "It's okay. Wake me up if you think of something to compliment."

I THANKED THE flight attendant, doing my best impression of the man Gia accused me of not being, and smiled. I set the three cups on my tray, trying not to jostle Gia, whose head had fallen to my shoulder during her nap. I told myself I wanted her to stay asleep so I wouldn't have to talk the entire flight, but really the weight of her head and the little murmurs that escaped her lips while she slept, along with how good she smelled, made me hold as still as possible, so I read on my phone instead of pulling out my laptop.

"Oh." Her voice was rough and quiet and she stirred against my shoulder. "I'm sorry," she said, sitting up, her arm sliding against mine.

"It's okay." I motioned to my tray and glanced away from her. "I got Coke and water for you when they came by. I wasn't sure which you'd want."

"Thank you," she said, taking the Coke from my tray. "Sorry I used you as a pillow."

The lights above us flickered as the FASTEN SEAT BELT icons lit up. "Attention, passengers, I have turned on the Fasten Seat Belt sign. We may experience some turbulence as we move through a weather system on our way to Indianapolis."

The plane jostled before the announcement was over and I steadied the cup of water from falling onto Gia's legs. I always liked

turbulence and the way my stomach dipped. I'd never told anyone
that; it felt a little weird or maybe whimsical, but the man next to
me was clearly not enjoying it in the same way. He gripped the arm-
rests, knuckles turning white with exertion.

Gia's arm and leg bumped mine, each touch accompanied by the
swooshing feeling in my stomach, and something else. After soda
sloshed over the edge of her cup twice, she tossed back the entire
drink like it was a shot. Her expression pinched at the sudden hit of
cold and sugar.

"You okay?"

She cringed as the plane jumped again, and her shoulder nudged
mine. "Fine," she said, and I returned to my phone, annoyed I'd felt
the need to check on her and noticing the way her arm felt against
mine and that she hadn't moved it away yet. "What are you reading,
or is this more of your secret videos?"

"An email from Christopher," I said, holding up my phone.

"Warning you not to talk to me too much, no doubt. We don't
get along."

I flashed back to my conversation with him in his office when
he'd made that attempt at a joke at her expense.

"What's that face?" Her damned arm was still against mine.

"I didn't make a face."

"You made a face."

"She's right. You made a face, dude." The formerly terror-
stricken man next to me weighed in, which was so appreciated.

"You don't like him?" She arched her eyebrow.

"I never said that." I didn't, especially after he made that crack
about Gia, but I didn't want to share that with her, and since her
most common reply to anything was, "Let's talk about it," a crowded
plane didn't feel like the place to take a chance, so I changed the
subject. "I also read your latest article in *Journal of Catalysts*."

"And it was impressive?" Her lips curled into the smile I was getting used to seeing when she made fun of me. I enjoyed that smile more than I wanted to.

"No."

"Ouch, bro." Our seatmate was now fully part of our conversation. "That was harsh."

"It's fine," Gia said, leaning forward to speak around me. "That's one of the nicer things he's ever said about my work." She patted my knee without taking her eyes off the guy next to me, not that I was focused on anything other than the feel of her fingers on my leg. "He gets cranky because I'm doing science and he's only doing computer programming."

The man's expression twisted in confusion in my periphery. "I don't know what that means, but was it a better burn than what you said to her?"

It was, and there were a hundred things I could have said in response, but her lips were already tipped in a grin, her body still close to mine. "It was definitely a superior burn."

"Sweet," he said. "You kind of deserved it, man."

9

Gia

IT WAS USUALLY me following Felix through the airport terminal to get to our gate because he was hell-bent on being there immediately. This particular airport was my turf, though, and I glanced over my shoulder to make sure he was keeping up.

"We only have fifty minutes. Get the lead out, Ennings!"

The non-smile he gave me was just as good as a grin. The corners of his lips tipped up when I called him by his last name, and it always gave me a fluttery summertime feeling when it happened. "Your friend owns a dog-grooming place . . . inside an airport?"

I hadn't seen my best friend's wife, Ollie, since this past summer and was excited our layover gave us almost an hour to stop in and see them. Ollie knew about the airport guy because Bennett had a big mouth, so she would know he was now my colleague. "My best friend's wife owns a chain of them. Well, I guess she's my friend now, too. Anyway, pet grooming in an airport. Strangest thing you've ever heard?"

We had started walking side by side and I felt the lingering sensation of his hand on mine, wanting to find an excuse to brush mine against his again.

I didn't expect him to engage with me about this, but he did. "There's a place in the Phoenix airport where you can buy vinyl records," he said as his hand brushed mine.

"You're kidding me. Have you ever bought one?"

"No." He smiled faintly. "Thought about it, though. My dad's a music guy, so I always look for something he'd like."

"I'm trying to picture you with a rock-god father."

He laughed for real this time and we slowed behind a cluster of kids in matching T-shirts dragging backpacks and roller bags. "My dad is probably exactly how you'd imagine an aging colonel looks."

"Ah, but he lets loose behind closed doors."

He nodded, looking over the heads of the group of kids, presumably searching for an escape.

"You let loose with him?"

He didn't answer but met my eyes in a way that made me think he did, that maybe Ennings danced when no one was watching.

"I bet Felix does let loose," I mused. "Even though Alexander Ennings, PhD, is a stick-in-the-mud."

His smile tipped up on one side. "Maybe. But only in the presence of my family, good whiskey, or a beautiful woman."

Before I could pull more of the story from him, he clasped my hand and tugged me to the left, pulling me through a short-lived opening in the group. It was like swimming through a koi pond, the kids moving and gesticulating without regard for anyone around them, but Felix and I moved together, our own tiny adventure, with our hands linked.

Once we made it past the group, we picked up speed again and I guided him toward the end of the C terminal where the grooming salon was located. He was still holding my hand. I suppose I was still holding his. I missed that feeling of someone's hand in mine. Elena and I would hold hands all the time, but it had been a while. "So,"

I said, enjoying the warmth of his hand. "If I want to see you loosen up, I need to find some whiskey?"

He slowed and looked down at our joined hands as if he'd forgotten. He mumbled, "No whiskey needed."

The warmth in his tone was there for only a moment, a subtle shift from friendly to something else, something that took me back to the train on New Year's, but then he quickly let go of my hand, unlacing his fingers from mine as we cleared the crowd.

"Oops," I added in a phenomenally articulate moment. "I guess we're safe now, but if we need to make it through a hoard of third graders again, I'm your woman."

He didn't respond, which was probably for the best. Ahead I saw Pre-Flight Paws and I squealed; the bright colors of the storefront reminded me of Ollie, which reminded me of Bennett, which felt a little like coming home.

"I can head to the gate while you visit with your friends." Felix glanced down at me, his hazel eyes showing something like uncertainty.

"No," I said. "Come with me. You can meet them."

He raised an eyebrow and his expression looked sarcastic, but it seemed there might be a little honesty in there, too. "Aren't you concerned I'll be antisocial?"

"I know you'll be antisocial. I still want you to come with me."

Felix studied my face, and I worried the inside of my lip with my teeth before taking his hand and nodding toward the shop. "C'mon."

Ollie greeted me with a big hug, and her business partner, Jess, joined us in the small lobby, which smelled like soap. I'd let go of Felix's hand well before we reached the shop, not wanting to give the wrong impression to Ollie or her staff or to Felix, or to myself for that matter. But I wondered if I'd somehow hit Felix's secret social switch, because he'd been smiling and laughing and charming since we walked in. He and Jess were talking about cats while Ollie and

I caught up, and when I glanced over the next time, he was leaning on the counter, the widest smile on his face, and Jess was laughing at something he said.

My Felix? He's making someone laugh. I pulled my attention back to Ollie, who was telling me about their expansion plans, but I kept seeing Jess and Felix laughing out of the corner of my eye, an uncomfortable needle in my side.

My phone buzzed in my pocket and I gave Ollie another hug. "We have to get going, but I'll see you guys next month?" When I turned, I expected Felix to be tapping his foot or checking his watch, anxious not to miss the flight, but he was the one laughing now, focused on a story Jess was telling, his eyes kind of sparkling in a way I'd only ever caught glimpses of. "Ennings," I said, stepping closer and flashing a smile to Jess. "We should get going."

"Oh," he said, looking over at me, a little startled. I felt like he'd forgotten I was there, which was like a scratch of that same needle, but I ignored it, smiling anyway. "Of course." He turned back to Jess and jotted something down on a pad of paper. "You'll send me that website?"

Wow, he looks relaxed. He looks fun.

"Absolutely," Jess said with a wink.

Felix smiled at her again and then looked to me. "Shall we?"

I nodded, again pushing down the weird feeling their interaction had given me. I smiled myself. "Yep."

We waited to board our flight, and Felix seemed lighter. *Was he really flirting that effectively with Jess? And do I really care?*

"Are you okay?" His voice pulled me out of my own head as we inched toward the gate agent with our phones out to scan our boarding passes.

"Me? Of course."

No, I don't care who he was flirting with. It was absolutely not something I would let bother me.

10

Felix

OUR LATEST HOSTS drove us back to the hotel after dinner with their committee. Andrews State in North Florida hadn't impressed me like our last stop, but Gia's words had stuck in my head and I'd tried to be more open to conversation with our colleagues. It wasn't all horrible—which I was certain she'd make me grudgingly admit later. Gia's laugh floated to me from the front seat, where she and Dan, the committee chair and our host, were deep in discussion. It was hard to tell if I took an immediate dislike to Dan because he struck me as a disingenuous douche canoe or just because Gia seemed to like him.

"We have a full day planned tomorrow," he said as we neared our hotel. "But we could grab a drink or something if you want to." He directed the question to Gia without glancing in the mirror or over his shoulder at me. *As I said, douche canoe.* I answered anyway. "No, thank you."

In the ambient light from the street, I noticed his jaw twitch at my response, which gave me a petty but satisfying sense of accomplishment.

"A no from Ennings. What about you, Gia? The cocktails at

Dynasty Club are pretty good." He grazed his fingers over her forearm, an act that might have been to get her attention but I suspected was an excuse to touch her.

"You know, I think I'll pass, too. It's been a long day of traveling." I thought she slid slightly closer to the door, but it might have been a trick of the light or my imagination. "Maybe a rain check for tomorrow, though?"

The small bubble of elation I felt inflating when she turned him down popped as we pulled up to the hotel.

"Definitely. Let me get your number," he said, pulling to a stop and digging his phone from his pocket. I sat in the back seat for another few moments, but neither of them seemed to be paying attention to me as they swapped numbers, and so I stepped out of the car, lingering on the sidewalk for Gia to step out. It wasn't as if he tried to kiss or hug her, but I was watching eagle-eyed through the window anyway until she stepped out and waved a farewell.

Once the door closed behind me, my perfectly nice hotel room felt cramped. My suitcase was set along the wall and I took off my shoes, lining them up underneath. I had work to do, a book to read. There was probably even something on TV that might interest me, but I felt like I was caged in. No, I felt lonely. I lived alone, save for my cat, and I grew up an only child, so being by myself didn't usually bother me, but I felt Gia's absence and I didn't like it. I sat on the bed and checked my email, not seeing anything I wanted to respond to.

> GIA: I'm bored. Do you want to do something tonight?

> FELIX: With Dan?

> GIA: With me.

> FELIX: Didn't you tell Dan you were tired?

GIA: It's 8pm. I just didn't want to go out to a bar.

FELIX: We could do something.

There were three raps on my door, and I smiled but then rolled my eyes for good measure. When I opened it, Gia stood on the other side, having changed into jeans and a red T-shirt that hugged her body in a way I tried not to find delicious. "What if I had said no?"

"I would have knocked on the next door down." She grinned and walked past me into the room, sitting on the edge of the king bed. "What do you want to do?" She leaned back on her arms and arched her back, throwing me back to remembering how her kisses tasted, how she felt on my lap all those months before.

"This was your idea. What do *you* want to do?"

"See, I could suggest something, but you'd probably have ten reasons to not do it because you are generally a fun hater. So, if you come up with an idea, we've gotten halfway there already."

Instead of arguing, I tossed her the remote. "Movie?"

"Ooh yes. Horror?"

I shook my head at her eager change in tone. "You like horror movies?"

"Love them. You?" Gia slid up my bed, settling against the pillows, her legs crossed in front of her.

"Definitely not."

"They give you nightmares?"

"Yes," I said, sitting on the edge of the bed. "I'm a normal human."

"That's debatable." She turned on the TV and patted the bed next to her. "I promise not to bite you, Ennings. You look like you're ready to bolt."

Gia flipped through the available movie channel options and stations, and I slid farther onto the bed. There were still a couple of feet between us, but I felt the bed move as she shifted. "Looks like our non-horror choices are an animated film about a robot, a rom-com, and a documentary about ska music in the nineties."

I cringed.

"Don't make that face. You can still choose horror."

I shook my head. "Rom-com, I guess." I hadn't paid close attention when she flipped through the stations to know which one it was because, as usual, I was distracted by her.

"You always surprise me," Gia said, hitting play and settling back on the bed. "I wouldn't have picked you for a romantic."

I mirrored her as much as I could, leaning back with my hand behind my head. "I'm not. But if it's between flirtatious banter I roll my eyes at and ghost stuff that keeps me up all night, I choose the eye roll."

Gia tucked her legs under her, the scent of oranges reaching me anytime she moved. "It's like your default setting is downer," she said, but her grin belied what might have otherwise been a dig. The movie started and filled the dimly lit room with a blue cast as the opening scene began. "Anyway," she said, out of nowhere, her tone casual, "you were pretty good at the flirty banter with Jess."

"Jess? Your friend at the grooming place?"

She kept her eyes trained on the TV. "Sure. You were flirting with her pretty comfortably."

I was ignoring the movie already. "I wasn't flirting with her."

Gia finally met my eye and stretched her arm out to lean against the headboard. "You don't have to be so defensive. Flirting isn't a bad thing."

"Fine, but I wasn't flirting with her. You told me to be social with your friends."

"You never listen to me."

"Well," I said, paying attention to the space between us, smaller now that she'd moved closer and angled herself toward me. "I tried this time."

"Oh." She sank her teeth into her lower lip but didn't say anything else, returning to the movie, dropping the thread of conversation.

I should have been relieved, but I didn't exactly want to drop it. "And you're one to talk. You and Dan were very chummy. He asked you out tonight."

Gia's hand was warm when she gently rubbed my shoulder, not even a push, just the feel of her palm against me and this small pressure that sent goose bumps up my arm. "He asked us both to get drinks."

"No," I said, doing my best to hold still so she wouldn't move her hand. "He asked you; I just happened to be in the car."

Her hand slipped away and I pressed my finger to my palm to keep from reaching for her. "Maybe." Her gaze slid back to the TV and I let mine, too. I'd never wanted a movie to speed up or slow down more. Gia was right next to me, her scent and smile close, and it wasn't unprofessional but I wanted it to be.

We watched the movie in silence for a few minutes. It was funnier than I'd assumed it would be. The characters' comedic timing was pretty good, and I even caught myself chuckling.

"Did you care that Dan asked me out?"

"I'm your colleague. What I think doesn't really matter." And yes. I noticed. I cared. It bothered me because after two minutes with Dan I knew he wasn't interesting enough for her.

"Maybe we're friends a little, too." She tucked both hands behind her head and stretched out on the bed, bumping her foot against my leg.

"I didn't care. I just . . . noticed."

She nodded, eyes back on the movie. "I thought maybe . . ." She let the silence hang there like a weight. "Never mind."

"Did you care when you thought I was flirting with your friend?"

"I noticed," she said, parroting my words back to me. "I hadn't seen you be . . . like that since that night in the airport." She smiled and met my eyes, a playful look on her face. "Here I thought I was special."

"I'm . . . not like that often." Every moment of that night in the airport flew back to me. The memories didn't have far to travel—they were on my mind a lot, especially lately. "You were special." I regretted saying it right away, especially when she didn't respond. I immediately scanned my mental Rolodex for a strategy to walk back that statement, to apologize, but she spoke first, not looking at me.

"Maybe I was a little jealous," she said. "If I'm honest."

Nothing had changed. There was still a good foot and a half between us. We were fully clothed and not even touching, but it felt like my world shifted in that moment, everything moving one step to the left. "I was, too. About Dan. A little."

She gave a little *hm* sound and then there was just the sound of the film. This entire conversation had me on my head and out of sorts, not a place I liked to be, except that it felt better with Gia. She never let silence fall like this, and we were swimming in it until we reached these unexpected islands of conversation. "We were good together that night, before I knew you were the uptight hard-ass bent on hating on my work."

"And before I knew you were a chaos demon whose challenges to my research are ineffective but continual."

"Felix," she purred, feigning a touched tone. "That's the nicest thing you've ever said about me."

"Well," I said, angling toward her and taking her hand, mirroring her fake adoration. "I meant every word."

Her laugh wrapped around me like no one else's ever had.

"We *were* good that night," I added, realizing I was still holding her hand again, but I didn't drop it, not yet.

"Before I was a chaos demon," she murmured, her thumb stroking the side of mine.

"And before I was a hard-ass trying to destroy you."

"Hating on my work," she corrected, sliding to her knees next to me, our joined hands resting over my heart as she steadied herself. Gia's face was close to mine, her soft, full lips I remembered in detail right there. "Get it right, Ennings."

"My apologies," I said, letting my hand fall to her waist, my palm barely grazing her body. Our breaths mingled and we were too close and not close enough. "Gia?"

"We could be good again," she said, her palm sliding up my chest. "Tonight. What if I kissed you again, right now?"

Gia's eyes were locked on mine, her warm, soft curves against me. "You want to kiss me?"

She grinned and guided her knee over my lap so she straddled me, her body against mine sending me into something close to cardiac arrest. "You seem so surprised."

"I didn't think you liked me."

Gia's lips brushed against mine in the softest kiss, almost innocent and sweet. "Sometimes I don't."

When her lips brushed against mine again, I deepened the kiss, my hand moving to the back of her neck. "You do now, though?"

"Do you really want to interrogate me at this moment?"

I shook my head and she kissed me again, lips and tongues gliding against each other in a way that took me back to New Year's Eve and the mystery woman on the train. Her body was pliant against mine, her kisses playful and intense and then soft and needy. I couldn't get enough, and it was like the temperature in the room had reached a blistering high.

When we finally pulled apart, breathing fast, I took in her expression, her soft features and hooded eyelids. "I always like you," I said, dipping my lips to her neck, her jaw, and then back to her lips in order to take more and more kisses, feeling her weight against my lap in the best way, despite her jeans and my slacks between us.

"Felix, I—" She stopped suddenly, and it took me a moment to realize she was vibrating against me. Well, her phone in her pocket was vibrating, and she reached for it, pausing halfway to her hip. "Sorry. Habit."

"It's okay," I said, not recognizing my own voice. "I . . . I don't mind if you check."

She dropped a quick kiss on my lips and pulled out her phone, her expression grim.

"What's wrong?"

"It's Dan," she said.

If it's possible for a person's soul to leave their body and sink into the institutional carpet of a mid-range hotel, that's what happened to me.

"Oh." The last person I wanted between us in this moment was him, and I heard the edge in my own voice. "Can you send him to voice mail?"

"It's a text. I left my messenger bag in his car and he's heading into the lobby to drop it off."

I leaned back against the headboard, taking in a breath.

"It has all my things for tomorrow in it," she explained, sliding back. "Let me go get it and I'll be right back."

I let out another slow breath, trying to get my body under control. "Sure," I said, scrubbing a hand down my face.

"I, uh . . ." She slid her feet into her shoes and glanced toward the TV before dragging her gaze back to me. "I want to see how the movie ends."

She slipped out into the hall and I fell back onto the bed wondering what the hell I was getting myself into. I had a sinking feeling I was going to have a hard time getting back out of it.

11

Gia

FELIX MET ME in the lobby the next morning looking as tired as I felt, his face drawn, despite his otherwise perfectly pulled-together appearance. He scrolled through something on his phone, shoulder and arm muscles tense under the oxford shirt with the pale salmon pinstripes. "How is Dan?" He didn't look up.

I pressed a palm to my mouth, poorly covering the yawn. "A bad ankle sprain and a broken wrist—I left him at his place with some good painkillers." The night before had been wild in the best way with Felix. That kiss on his bed felt like the start of something, the start of something good. Maybe not even the start . . . maybe the next part of something after the long intermission. He'd kind of softened with me, and I got the sense I'd gotten a peek behind the mask of indifference. Well, he'd softened and he hadn't. I'd planned to grab the bag from Dan and head back up as fast as possible to see where things led. I smiled like a goof the entire elevator ride at the idea of climbing back onto Felix's bed and seeing that expression of his, but a puddle from someone's spilled drink had other plans, and before he even got to me, Dan was on the ground. "I guess it's lucky I was there to drive him to the emergency room."

Felix nodded. "Very lucky."

I hadn't texted him until we were at the ER and Dan was being seen. At that point, it had been more than an hour and I'd cringed at what Felix must have thought, must have been worrying about. I had a few missed texts from him by then, and a call.

> GIA: I had to drive Dan to the ER. Sorry, it
> happened fast and I panicked.

It was close to ten when I sent the text, but he'd responded immediately.

> FELIX: Are you okay?

I'd felt even worse, realizing he'd been worried about me. I'd scrolled back to the missed texts and cursed myself.

> GIA: Dan fell in the lobby and couldn't drive
> himself. I'm fine.

> GIA: It will be late when I get back.

> FELIX: 👍 See you in the morning. Call if you
> need anything.

NOW, WITH THE morning light streaming through the windows, we stood together in the lobby, waiting for a Lyft to take us to the campus, the chilled fall morning air breezing through the automatic doors as other guests came and went. Felix stood with his back straight, and the mask was back on. I probably deserved that. "I'm sorry it took me so long to text you last night."

"It was an emergency," he said, putting a hand in his pocket, so casual and cool. "It's fine."

"It's not. You were worried."

"Most people would be when someone they . . ." He trailed off, something he didn't usually do. The Lyft arrived and he stepped toward the exit without finishing, leaving me to follow.

"What were you saying?" We settled into the back seat for the short drive to the campus.

"Most people would be worried when a colleague disappeared. It's fine."

I held my messenger bag to my chest, the one I'd retrieved from Dan after he fell, busting his ankle and wrist on the polished tile floor. "Well, I'm still sorry."

"No apology necessary."

We drove onto the campus, winding through the roads amid the students dashing across the streets, the behavior of college students the same on every campus. I liked that energy, the somewhat blissful ignorance of all the things that could hurt them. Not even ignorance, just the sense that those things, like cars and buses and maybe heartbreak, too, couldn't touch them. *Perhaps I'm projecting.*

We'd spend the bulk of the day in a four-story building with unexpected angles and jutting windows. This was their innovation building we'd read about in the materials about their teaching work. A cool breeze made me pull my cardigan around me as we stepped out, though Felix's one-eighty from the night before might have left me just as chilled.

"YOU'RE THE HERO of the day," an administrator said, approaching me later that afternoon. "We heard you took care of Dan last night!"

"The ER doctors did the heavy lifting there," I joked, noticing

THE MISSED CONNECTION 201

the way Felix stiffened. It had been a good day with them, sharing interesting approaches to instructor education and learning assessment in the classroom. I'd taken pages of notes and even noticed Felix nodding along. After a day of discussion, they'd planned a coffee reception for us in a conference room with sweeping views of campus.

The administrator laughed and shook my hand. "Well, we still appreciate you getting him to the emergency room. He and his wife divorced recently, so he lives alone. Anyway, that's neither here nor there. We appreciate your willingness to help."

My chest puffed up at that, the warmth of having helped someone. I'd been so focused on abandoning Felix and the weird . . . wonderful . . . no, weird moment between us right before that, I'd forgotten I'd helped someone who needed it. I smiled at the administrator and talked with him for a few more minutes as the reception wrapped up.

Felix stood near the exit, finishing a conversation with one of the professors who'd hosted us for the day. He still looked stiff, but not as constipated as he did during our first college visit. "Thank you for having us," he said, shaking her hand. "We can get a car. No need to drive us." His eyes cut to me and then back, and I thanked her as well.

"Ready to go?"

He nodded and we grabbed our coats from the rack. We had a few hours before our flight to the fourth stop, and I was looking forward to a few more days of warm weather before we returned to the onset of winter in Chicago.

"We kissed last night," I said when the elevator doors closed, encasing the two of us alone, the sentence bursting out of me.

His cool gaze cut to me in a very Felix way. "I don't think we need to talk about it here."

"Need? No. But we kissed last night and I left." I tucked my thumbs into my palms. Apologizing and putting things out in the open wasn't always my thing. For all my extroversion and comfort with emotion, I didn't like awkward and I didn't like giving someone else the opportunity to shut me down. Elena and I fought about it when we were together. "I think I hurt your feelings, and I'm sorry."

I was prepared for a few responses from Felix, ranging from ignoring me to telling me the extent to which I'd hurt his feelings.

"We're in an elevator."

"Um, yes." I looked around as if the setting might have changed.

"I can't talk about kissing you with only two floors to go."

Was my mouth open? I didn't think it was, but the mirrored walls of the elevator car showed me differently. "How many floors do you need?"

The doors opened before he answered, something that had happened more than once today and that made me want to corner him, but we walked out to meet the waiting car, the driver a chatty young woman who spoke nonstop from the campus to the airport. Felix ignored me, pulling out his phone almost immediately and leaving me to engage with the driver. Granted, she was interesting, and I was sad when we arrived at the airport before I got to hear the rest of the story about how she met her boyfriend while looking for a lost turtle.

We waited in line for security, a blessedly short line, and I chuckled at the man in front of us carrying a cardboard box with a packing tape handle jerry-rigged to the side. It made our roller bags look so uninteresting by comparison. I was about to point it out to Felix to break the weird post-makeout tension between us, but he spoke first.

"If I talk about kissing you, I'll want to do it again." Felix's voice was low and deep behind me, and his words wrapped around me so intimately for such a public space. My hand smacked into the stanchion guiding the line when I turned to face him, and I grabbed my wrist.

"What?"

"Are you okay?" He motioned to my wrist like he hadn't just dropped a Felix-shaped bomb in my lap.

"Fine," I said, waving him off, my wrist throbbing at the movement. "If you want to kiss me again, why have you been acting like this all day?"

"I don't want to kiss you again," he said, his voice just above a whisper. He held out his hand and motioned to my wrist, inspecting the red, tender spot when I finally acquiesced. Felix was a chemist, same as me, but he was inspecting my arm like it was his duty as a physician, his fingertips grazing, almost ghosting, over my skin. "I don't want to kiss you again," he repeated, gaze focused on my arm. "Because I really want to kiss you again."

"You're not making any sense." We shuffled forward in the line, my wrist still cradled in Felix's hand.

"I know," he grumbled. "I don't make sense to myself when I'm around you. I think you need ice for this."

The spot where I'd slammed into the hard plastic was tender and swelling a little, but the entire moment felt too strange in other ways to focus too much on that. Around us the line buzzed with people, both excited and annoyed.

"Next." The TSA agent's voice was a constant, moving people ahead in the line.

"You don't like it, huh? Feeling out of control?" I saw it in the furrow between his brows, the stiff way he held his shoulders while cradling my arm.

His hazel eyes flicked up to meet my gaze, and if I had any doubt, it was gone in that moment.

"It's okay. That's kind of what I do . . . make people feel a little out of control." I gently pulled my arm back. I wasn't sure why the realization made my stomach dip. It was true—people had told me that my entire life, and I'd always liked it about myself. I helped people bust out of ruts and bubbles they didn't realize were boxing them in. Of course, some people liked the bubbles and maybe saw the rut as more of a path. Felix was a path-and-bubble guy. In the end, my ex had been a path-and-bubble woman. The comparison made my stomach sink.

"We can forget it happened. Not the first kiss," I said, rolling my bag forward, the sounds of the security check becoming louder. "But last night never happened. It was just a weird thing." I waved my hand and regretted it, wincing at the pain.

Felix searched my face like there was a secret code. For a second, I thought he might shake his head and tell me he didn't want to forget it, but instead he motioned to my arm. "Let's get some ice when we get through security."

"Next."

I nodded and walked toward the agent with my driver's license in hand and the sour aftertaste of the declaration that we could pretend the kiss hadn't happened. That wasn't what I wanted at all.

12

Felix

I BALANCED THE three cups with the plastic bag hooked over my finger. The concourse wasn't crowded, and I was able to walk at my normal speed between the coffee shop and our gate, where I'd left Gia with our bags. I'd only been gone ten minutes, but the thought of sitting next to her again had me speeding up and knowing I should slow down. The night before had messed with my head in the best and then the worst way. I hadn't slept and then had felt annoyed all day during our meetings. Then she'd said to forget it.

"Attention in the boarding area, our flight to San Diego is full . . ."

All I wanted was to forget the entire thing had happened, but ahead of me I saw her near the shard of fading sunlight shining in the large window, scrolling through her phone, a few curls escaping the bun on her head and framing her face. She wasn't wearing a lot of makeup, but her lips were a dark red color. The color never seemed to fade, so I assumed it was natural.

"Why are you looking at me like that?" She eyed me skeptically.

Busted.

"Is your lipstick tattooed on?"

She laughed and reached to take the items in my hand. "You ask the weirdest questions. No. It's long-lasting lipstick."

I glanced away and put ice in a bundle of napkins for her wrist, dipping my fingers in the cup of ice, considering the chill a good diversion. When I handed it to her, she held out a red tube to me. "You want to try it?"

I saw the way her features twitched when she put the ice on her wrist. "I don't think it's my color." I took the tube anyway, examining it. POWER POUT. I chuckled at the name before I handed it back. "I've been told I pout weakly."

Gia nudged my elbow. "Give yourself more credit. I'm sure you can pout with the best of them. Give me a duck-lip pose." She modeled, arranging her lips dramatically, as if for a selfie. The expression did nothing to diminish how gorgeous she looked, but I laughed despite myself, setting the soda next to her.

"I'll pass. Thanks." I handed her the plastic bag. "Tylenol and some cookies."

"Thank you. A girl could get used to this, Feels," she said, abandoning the duck face. I let her get away with the nickname. "It's really not that bad."

"Doesn't hurt to take care of it." I settled in the seat next to her, opening the bottle of water I'd bought for myself.

"Thank you." She sank her teeth into that Power Pout–tinted lower lip. "You could do one more thing for me."

Anything. I'd pulled my phone from my pocket already, prepared to check emails and get myself back to a normal place, on steady footing. "You want me to tell you the ways in which your latest paper could be improved?"

"I don't think I'd need to ask to get that from you."

"You're right." Our approaches were different, and we disagreed on many things, but I liked reading Gia's work. She was a good storyteller, a talent that not everyone possessed in science and technical writing. Maybe that's why I so enjoyed getting a rise out of her.

Gia rolled her eyes and motioned to my phone. "You could tell me what you're always watching on your phone."

"No."

"Please?"

"No." I scrolled through my inbox and didn't pay attention to the burst of scent when she moved next to me.

"I'm injured." She whined, holding up her wrist pathetically, the napkin full of melting ice cubes pressed to her soft skin.

"That's low," I said, turning my phone screen facedown on my thigh. "You're manipulating me."

"Obviously." She picked up my phone, her delicate fingers sliding along the side in a way that shouldn't have felt suggestive, but I squirmed in my seat anyway. "Is it working?"

"You're going to be disappointed," I said, taking my phone back.

"I seriously doubt it." She leaned toward me, our skin brushing along the lengths of our arms.

"You can't make fun of me," I said, hedging before I clicked the icon to open the app.

"I do not promise that," she said, moving even closer to me, one of her escaped curls tickling my cheek. "But I will be kind in my mockery."

"You're annoying," I grumbled, but opened the app anyway. "And I'm only showing you because I assume you'll keep bugging me about this."

"Noted." She held the ice against her wrist awkwardly and I stretched my arm across the seat behind her to make room and paused after I realized the placement.

"Uh, is this okay?"

Her body was already against mine, her shoulder resting against my chest, the fingers on my left hand itching to lower and rest on her shoulder. "Perfect," she said, seeming to be unfazed by this cuddle-adjacent position. "Show me. I'm dying of suspense."

"Fine," I said with a sigh. I'd never told anyone else about this weird habit. "It's kind of . . . Well, if you want me to turn it off right away, let me know."

When Gia looked up, she smiled and nodded, and I tried not to let my gaze fall to her lips. "I'm pretty tough, Ennings."

I opened the app and scrolled to the account I wanted, hitting play on the first video.

Gia stilled and then cut her eyes up to mine, wide in surprise but maybe a little gleeful, too. "You're kidding me."

"It's . . . satisfying, I guess." My face felt hot. "I can turn it off. I told you it wasn't that interesting."

"No way!" She pressed into me. "This is a very interesting thing about you." She looked at the screen again.

"It's not like . . ." I wasn't ever at a loss for words, but Gia had me feeling like I needed to clarify. She shushed me, though.

"I totally get it." She focused on the screen, and I divided my attention between the screen and her shoulder just shy of touching my fingers. She lowered her voice. "Wait, this isn't like . . . a sexual thing, is it?"

"No!" I jerked upright, jostling her. "Why would you ask that?"

Gia laughed, settling against me again. "It was a joke, Ennings. I wouldn't assume pool-cleaning videos get you going."

My face was still heated, but the heat moved through my body with her settled against me, both of us watching my phone. "It's just soothing. Something mindless to watch where a very specific problem is solved and all is right again."

She nodded and we watched the rest of the short video quietly, the different solutions and powders shifting the murky green water to a sparkling blue. She sighed when the video ended. "Felix, this might be my new happy place. Who knew you were so brilliant?"

The next two videos played and I didn't move a muscle, not wanting to lose any contact with her skin. I'd hidden those videos from everyone who'd ever known me, worried they'd judge me, certain they'd think it was weird. It was weird. Other than being relatively certain I could avoid drowning, I didn't swim or have an interest in pools, but Gia rolled with it. Gia always rolled with it. "I fell in a pool when I was a kid," I said, looking over her shoulder at the screen. "Hit my head on the edge and got this scar." I touched my fingertip to my head when she looked up. I wasn't sure why I told her that. The story wasn't particularly interesting and she hadn't asked, but I liked the idea of Gia knowing things about me that other people didn't.

"I noticed that scar the first night I met you. Now the videos make sense. You have a dark and twisty past with swimming pools."

"It's my villain origin story." I chuckled and stroked my thumb along her arm. "You know . . ."

When she tipped her head up again, her shoulders shifted and my fingers skirted over her skin. It was one of those moments over-dramatized in movies. The boarding area buzzed around us and a guy a row over coughed into his arm and a group of kids ran in and out of roller bags playing tag. Time didn't slow and nothing around us faded, but it was like the feel of her skin and the feel of her gaze were the loudest things I absorbed.

"What?" She eased her arm away, dropping the melting ice into the cup. "Was I dripping on you?" She studied me, maybe looking for the drops of water, but her gaze disintegrated what was left of my self-control.

"I don't want to pretend it didn't happen." My words hung between us for an interminable amount of time.

Finally, she nodded and returned her gaze to the screen. She didn't say anything else for a while, but then rested her head against my shoulder. "Okay."

"Okay." I let my hand drop to her shoulder, fingers stroking her upper arm experimentally.

"Did that one-word response send you into an overthinking spiral?" Her smile was twisted to the side when she looked up at me.

It had, but I didn't know what else to say.

"We've got two more stops on the trip. Let's just . . . enjoy each other."

"Enjoy each other . . . how?"

"Well, we start with more pool-cleaning videos because I didn't know I needed that in my life, and we'll go from there," she said, with a chuckle that shook her body against mine.

I shook the phone. "I'm going to regret admitting this to you."

"Probably," she said.

My head was filled with a hundred ways I wanted to enjoy time with Gia Price. I glanced around the gate area for something to distract me because only half of them were sexual. Well, maybe more than half, but the space she occupied in my brain kept getting larger. "How does your wrist feel?"

"Should be game ready soon," she said without looking away from the screen.

"I didn't mean like that," I interjected. "I mean, I wasn't trying to imply . . ."

"You're really too easy, Ennings."

13

Gia

EVER SINCE I was a kid, I'd play a game with myself, asking, *Are they boring or am I bored?* In the case of Douglas University in Austin, it was this presenter who unironically read a PowerPoint to us about increasing engagement with students and moving away from technology crutches. He didn't just read it from notes—he turned to face the screen and narrated every single slide.

Felix inched a notebook between us without looking away from the speaker. He'd filled in some of the letters after my guess of *o* for our hangman game. *l _ _ n i e _ _ _ o _ r e _.* I studied his blocky script and the letters, jotting down my guess. *I am Niels Bohred?* I grinned and nudged the paper back toward him, taking my turn to focus on the PowerPoint slide. He would make a science pun. I didn't look over at him, but I wanted to.

The previous twenty-four hours had been strange, but it felt better to have an understanding with Felix. Our flight had been delayed and there had been hiccups getting from the airport to the hotel, so when we finally got to our rooms, we had only six hours until the visit at Douglas started, and both of us seemed to know "enjoy each other" wasn't going to be explored effectively that night. Not that I wouldn't have sacrificed sleep.

At the memory, I snuck a quick glance and caught the edge of his grin as he scribbled on the page. Our hug the night before at my hotel room door lasted a long time, and I knew I was going to kiss him when we pulled apart, but he beat me to it, tipping his head toward mine and asking if he could, his lips tentative at first, the kisses soft and close-lipped. Whenever I thought I had Felix figured out he'd surprise me, like when his fingers sank into my hair and he deepened the kiss, meeting my open lips with his tongue. When we finally pulled apart, I felt how much he didn't want to stop, and it was the same way I felt, but we kissed one more time and went into our rooms.

How did you guess the answer already?

I'm good at hangman and it was easy.

I give up. How long until we can get out of here?

An hour.

You want to check out the library? Or their new labs?

I want to check you out. I wrote it without looking and grinned at the puff of breath leaving his lips with his chuckle.

I thought you were cooler than that.

The presenter turned away from the screen and smiled. "Sorry for droning on. I get so excited about this." He then immediately turned back to read the screen.

Is saying I want to check you out allowed within our parameters?

We didn't set parameters, but I think so. Is saying you look nice today within our parameters?

Well within. Too within. Something you couldn't also say to your grandma?

You look sexy in that sweater set and I want to take it off you?

I squirmed in my seat, suddenly aware that Felix could make me feel things if he ever decided to commit to some actual dirty talk. *I hope you don't say that to your grandma.*

He laughed quietly again, the sound of his sharp exhale only noticeable to me, but it was enough.

I twisted in my seat to speak into his ear. "I don't want to go to the library or see the labs when we're done here."

"And that's why eye contact matters so much when answering student questions," the presenter said to the wall he was facing.

Felix spoke into my ear. "This feels like we're teenagers sneaking around."

I jotted my response in the notebook. *We don't have to sneak around. Want to make out right now? Don't think the presenter would notice.*

He didn't write a response but whispered in my ear again, the feel of his breath on my skin sending a tingle into my belly and lower. "Don't tempt me."

I let my finger drag along the side of his hand before I nudged the notebook back toward him, enjoying the way his breath stuttered. *It would be fun to see you out of control.*

Keep doing that and you will.

I squirmed at the coil of energy his words had me feeling.

"And that's it," the presenter said with a flourish, turning to us and the other people in the room. "That's the foundation of the work we've been doing. Questions?"

Felix straightened next to me and I closed the notebook surreptitiously. "Thank you," I said, struggling to come up with a question so it didn't look like Felix and I had been messing around the entire presentation, but Felix beat me to it.

"How has the focus on increasing engagement affected student involvement in high-impact practices?"

I had just enough cool to not whip around and give him a look that would clearly translate to *I didn't think you were paying attention either.*

The presenter smiled, all his teeth on full display. "Lots of ways, but the main thing is that staying engaged with students reminds them you're paying attention to them. For example, do either of you have a colleague who is particularly critical of your work?"

I laughed at the same time Felix said "Yes" like a robot.

"Dr. Ennings is probably the person most critical of my work," I chimed in to explain the laugh.

The presenter was much more personable with his slide deck complete, and I wondered how I could tell him that without hurting his feelings. As it was, he smiled and continued engaging with us. "So, he's critical of your work. What effect does that have on you?"

All eyes in the room, including Felix's, swung to me.

"I guess it makes me feel like my research is . . . important." I didn't look at Felix but stayed connected with the presenter, whose tongue had never been in my mouth and whose quirks didn't make me feel swoony. "He's brilliant, a rising star in the field, so even when he's challenging my approach, which is often, it makes me feel I'm doing something important, something that rises to the level of him debating it."

The presenter smiled widely. "Exactly. In science fields, we don't spend enough time remembering the meaning for students or colleagues of being paid attention to or acknowledged. It's another way we can promote learning and success through paying attention, which can make students feel supported to engage in high-impact practices." He smiled again and moved across the room to take a comment from another professor.

Felix leaned toward me again, his breath against my ear. "I didn't know you felt that way."

"I've never thought about it before, but . . . yeah, I do."

Felix was quiet for a moment and his jaw was working when I looked back to him. The presenter's Q&A continued and the presentation was finally somewhat interesting, so I didn't notice Felix writing another note until the notebook bumped my hand.

I think you're brilliant, too.

You know, you could stop eviscerating my work all the time.

The tip of Felix's finger brushed against my arm. It was the smallest, quickest possible touch, but my body reacted like he'd slid his palm up my shirt.

I didn't say you were right, just brilliant.

14

Felix

I'D NEVER TAKEN the time to worry about how far my hotel room was from an elevator until Gia Price stood next to me. I hoped no one needed me to share the details of our visit to Douglas University, because beyond how smooth and silky Gia's skin felt and how she looked in profile when she smiled, I would struggle to remember anything pertinent. Christopher would love that report. We were on the same floor but at opposite ends, so when we stepped off the elevator, we paused, both looking down the hall and back to each other.

"So," she said, sinking her teeth into her lower lip. "Your place or mine?"

My entire life, I thought before speaking. I weighed out the correct answer, the socially desirable answer, the most professional answer. In another time and place, I would have clarified her statement, rethought the arrangement completely, or asked her to choose. "Mine is a few doors closer."

Gia grinned. "Ennings. I like how you think."

We started down the hall and I brushed my hand against hers, wanting to link our fingers. "You didn't leave your bag in Dr. Antonio's office, did you?"

"I keep forgetting you have jokes sometimes," she said. "Nothing left in the car. No flight delays. No stroke of midnight. No built-in escape button," she added. "You've just got me."

I stopped in front of my door, pulling the key card from my wallet but waiting to swipe it. "I've got you?"

"For tonight." Gia trailed her nails up my back, something that made my nerve endings vibrate. "And a few more nights." Between the kiss the night before and the wayward touches and glances all day, I wanted Gia. I wanted all of her. She widened her eyes and blinked slowly. "Unlock the door, Ennings. I want to see how we do with no interruptions."

I was sure I took the steps to unlock the door, walk inside, and close the door behind us, but I didn't remember doing any of them before Gia's lips were pressed to mine again, her soft body against me as I backed her up against the wall. We must have looked like lovers if someone had seen us through the window, a couple so lost in each other the outside world stopped existing. That's how I felt with her, though not just in that moment with our bodies pressed together. She had a way of making me feel like we were together in a bubble apart from other people. Maybe that's why it felt so natural to challenge each other professionally.

"You really think I'm brilliant?" Her words escaped in puffs of breath when I lowered my lips to her neck, kissing and nipping at her warm skin.

"Incredible," I said against her jaw. "You think I'd lie?"

"No." She let out a low groan near my ear when I pulled her closer to me. "I just like hearing you say it."

I pulled back and our eyes met, our faces so close our breaths mingled, a phrase I'd never given much credence to in the past. "You want me to compliment your work while we do this?" I nudged my knee between her legs to get us closer, her thighs on either side of mine.

She dragged her lips along my jawline. "Maybe." She tugged on my shirt, pulling it from my pants and sliding her fingertips over my lower back and obliques. "Yes. I think I'd like that." She wiggled her fingers, tickling me, and I yelped. It wasn't a cool yelp, if such a thing existed. I jumped, breaking our connection, and Gia laughed. Not giggled but laughed.

"What was that?"

"I'm ticklish," I said, stepping back toward her, face heating. "Very ticklish there."

"So," she said, stepping forward. "You'd prefer if I didn't—" She reached for my sides, her fingers out. "Do this?"

I held her wrists before she could get to me, attacking me in the most adorable way. "I like being touched, just not tickled," I said, holding her arms.

"I promise I won't tickle you." She met my eyes with the same adorable smile. "But is there another way to get you to make that noise? It was like an inhuman sound."

I still held her wrists, so we stood in the middle of the hotel room in an awkward slow dance, me holding her at arm's length until I tugged her closer to me, her hands held behind her back in a gentle hold she didn't try to wiggle from.

"Felix?"

"Yeah?" My free hand settled at her waist and I brushed my lips against her temple.

"Tell me how you like to be touched."

I released her wrists, placing my hand on the small of her back, the swell of her round backside just under my reach. "Will you tell me, too?"

"We're researchers." Gia nudged me back toward the bed until the back of my knees hit and I sat down, tipping my chin up to her. "No computer models, though . . . hands-on."

I held her hips and pulled her forward so I could kiss her. Every kiss with Gia felt somehow familiar and uncharted. This wasn't a wild kiss, but it kept going, deeper and deeper, until she pulled away and began unbuttoning my shirt. "Firmer touches?"

I nodded, watching her fingers work over the buttons, the color on her nails flashing as she made quick work of my shirt, and I shrugged out of it.

"Kisses?"

I swallowed in a way that felt cartoonish, like the sound was echoing off the walls, because Gia had lowered to her knees in front of me and I'd stopped breathing. "Kisses?"

"Can I kiss you here?" She moved her hands over my side where I was so ticklish. No one had ever asked me that before, especially no one as beautiful and captivating as Gia, and all my years of rational thought slipped away from me.

I nodded, looking up at the ceiling, and exhaled heavily as her lips touched my bare skin, sliding over my abs. "Wait," I said, my head tipping up.

"What's wrong?" A few curls fell over her forehead, and I lifted her arm from my thigh.

"Is your wrist okay?"

Gia laughed but didn't pull her arm away. "That a hint, Ennings? I plan to get there, but give a girl a little time to warm you up!"

I glanced at her wrist, which looked a little bruised but otherwise okay, and it didn't seem my face could feel any hotter, but there it went. Before I could reply, Gia smiled and kissed my fingers wrapped loosely around her arm. "It's fine. Relax, Felix." She nudged me backward and continued a trail of kisses over my stomach, dipping lower and eventually playing with my zipper. I felt like a teenager, so on edge, and I dropped my palm to cover hers.

"Hold on," I said, sitting up and pulling her into my lap. "I need a few minutes to calm down." I slid my hand to her neck, pulling her lips to mine again. I loved kissing her, loved how she felt when I kissed her, loved how I felt when I kissed her. "You're brilliant," I said, dipping her back to the bed.

"I was wondering when you were going to get back to the compliments."

I let my hand wander up her stomach and over her ribs, finally brushing the swells of her breasts through the material of her dress, feeling her nipples react through the fabric. "How should I touch you here?"

"Soft, then hard," she murmured, guiding my hands before she let hers fall away.

"Brilliant," I said, reaching behind her in search of the zipper for her dress, working it off her shoulders, leaving us in a tangle of clothes.

"I guess we should have taken this off before lying down," she said, popping off the bed and sliding out of her dress. "It looks easier on TV."

"Wow," I said, letting my eyes travel over her shoulders to the bright pink lace bra, where her hard nipples poked through. I wanted to drop kisses across her enticing soft belly, and her matching underwear hid every gift I was hoping to unwrap.

"You mean, brilliant?" she said, tossing her bra aside and climbing back onto the bed and into my arms.

"Yes." I ran my palm over her breast, soft, in slow circles, exploring every inch before moving to the other. "Soft?"

"Then hard," she groaned, and I increased pressure and rolled her tight nipples between my fingers, earning a little Gia moan.

I sucked her nipple between my lips, trying to reconcile this moment and all the times I sat in my office hearing Gia through the wall. Gia's music, Gia's humming, Gia's laughter when she spoke with her graduate students. She wriggled under me and I gave up on trying to make it make sense; even my brain thrummed with the reality of going back to hearing her through the wall. But not yet. I kissed her again, letting my fingers trail lower, to the apex of her thighs, and I focused all my attention on her soft places and exuberant reactions until she came apart in my arms. I had Gia in my bed for tonight. Maybe for a few days—and I hoped that would be enough.

15

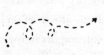

Gia

I GLANCED OVER my shoulder from my spot at the desk when I heard Felix stir on the bed. He looked uncharacteristically rumpled and scrubbed a palm down his face. "Morning," I said, letting my gaze slide down his bare chest.

"Good morning." He looked around with an adorable level of groggy confusion. "What time is it?"

"A little after seven." I wanted to climb onto the bed and snuggle up to him. We'd fallen asleep together. I wasn't sure if it was intentional or not, but we'd collapsed after . . . well, after multiple rounds of brilliance, and it had been nice to feel his arms draped over me. Now, though, it was morning. I wasn't sure where we stood.

Felix searched the floor for his boxers, and I grinned at the pile of clothing on the patterned carpet, my body flushing at the memories of his mouth moving over my body and his hands gripping my hips. Felix did brilliance like he did everything—with incredible attention to detail. Maybe that was why him hunting for his underwear delighted me, and I just admired his body until he looked up, confused, and said, "I didn't picture you as a morning person."

"A long time ago I trained my body to get up early. I can focus when it's quiet. I didn't want to leave without you knowing why, though . . ." I glanced around. "I hope it's okay I snuck off to my room and then came back."

"I don't mind you coming back." His eyes finally roamed my body. I'd pulled on his shirt from the night before, the fabric tight across my chest. "I'm glad you did." Felix rubbed the back of his neck. "I had fun last night."

I narrowed my eyes and studied his posture, the tone of his voice. Felix straightened under my examination "What?"

There was a crease across Felix's cheek from the pillow, and I pushed back from the desk. It took two steps to reach him so I could trace a fingertip down the crease. "Let's skip the awkward morning-after part."

Felix remained stiff and I dropped my hand. "I can go. No big deal."

"No!" He wrapped his fingers gently around my wrist, bringing my fingers back to his cheek. "I mean, don't go. I just don't know how this is supposed to work."

I'd appreciated Felix's body plenty the night before, but that didn't make me any less interested in running my hands up his sides in the light of day, making sure to press against his muscles and not to tickle. "How do you want it to work?"

"Casual is fine, but I don't want just one night and done."

"That's not surprising. I didn't think you were the hit-it-and-quit-it type of guy." I slid my hands around his neck and his palms settled at my waist. Felix had nice hands. "How it works is we have a few hours until we need to be at the airport and should probably shower at some point."

"Mm," he said, unmoving. "I want to brush my teeth before I kiss you good morning."

I grinned, any thought of the work waiting on my laptop forgotten. "I think that's permissible."

"I appreciate your blessing."

"I'm a giver."

He kissed my forehead, the brush of his lips sweet and as intimate as everything we'd done the night before. "I *know* you're a giver." He tickled my side, something I told him I actually enjoyed, and then he teased me in the best possible way. He winked. Felix Ennings winked at me before disappearing into the bathroom, and my silly heart couldn't handle it.

"Though," he said, peeking his head out the door, "we could shower together."

"Save hot water."

"And time."

"Eh. We could take our time."

He walked back out, his toothbrush in his hand, a little more of the normal straight-back strut in the way he held himself. "Maybe you could tell me the merits of your . . . massager."

"Tell you or show you?"

"You are the experimentalist." Felix began brushing his teeth and waggled his eyebrows, leaving me to wonder how he'd hidden this playful side of himself from me for so long.

I PRESSED THE back of my hand against my mouth to hide a yawn so big, I felt it in my toes.

"You should take a nap if you're—" Felix's uninvited suggestion died on his tongue as his own yawn stretched his face.

"You were saying?"

"Yeah, yeah," he said, settling back in the seat. "Fine. We both need naps." He glanced at his watch and I took in his languid form, his body almost unfamiliar without the ramrod-straight spine and stiff movements. "We board in forty minutes."

"I like you like this," I said, mirroring his pose and letting my head loll toward his.

"Like what? Tired?"

"Tired. Sex drunk."

His eyes were closed but he grinned. "I'm not drunk." He grinned again, a little dimple showing on his cheek, and I reached out to tug his ear, for no other reason than to prove to myself I could touch him without feeling the butterflies. It didn't work. "Okay. A little drunk. It's been a long time."

"How long?"

"Last spring."

I couldn't get over how relaxed Felix looked reclined in his seat, his eyes closed and chin tipped toward the ceiling.

"Did you break up because of the new job?"

He shook his head and I searched his face for a pinched brow or a twitch at the corner of his lips, the things I thought might give away a broken heart. The things I knew were my own tells. His expression remained placid, though. "Nah. She broke up with me before I applied, back at the beginning of March."

No matter his relaxed demeanor, I stiffened as something cold tickled the back of my neck. He broke up with someone in March. Had he been dating her when we'd first met? I'd built that moment up in my head, especially since my attraction to Felix had grown. It felt somehow fated and special at the time, but now, sitting at our gate, the sound of suitcase wheels along the tile concourse as background noise, nothing but doubt crept into my mind.

"I was single on New Year's," he said, still not opening his eyes.

"How did you know I was wondering that?" I bumped his leg with my closed fist. "And you're so blissed-out right now. It's off-putting."

Felix flinched but grinned, and his eyes were still closed, which

I was pretty sure was just to bug me at this point. "You already accused me of being sex drunk." He lowered his voice for the last two words, so hopefully only I could hear them. "Isn't blissed-out part of that prognosis?"

I crossed my arms over my chest. "You're annoying."

"So are you."

"Attention in the boarding area, Flight 684 with service to Albuquerque will begin boarding shortly at Gate D5."

Felix opened his eyes as the announcement concluded. "You're the good kind of annoying, though." He trailed his fingertips over my knee, the sensation somehow overtly sexual and completely friendly at the same time, but it did send a trail of goose bumps up my arms. "Sometimes. I knew you were wondering if I was single because I pay attention to you. You're carefree and fun and sometimes just a whirlwind of what feels like disorder, and you care about treating people well and not causing harm, even if it's a kiss with a stranger or"—he motioned between us—"whatever it is we're doing for the end of this trip."

I stared at his relaxed posture and at how his fingertips continued to dance over my knee.

"Don't look so shocked."

"I am shocked," I said. "Who are you with these intuitive takes on human emotion?"

Felix chuckled, the warm sound feeling like it was a secret he was sharing only with me. "You bring it out in me." His laugh subsided and his eyes fell closed again. "She didn't. I think that's why she broke up with me. She said I wasn't fun. That I was too flat."

"Your last girlfriend?"

He nodded. "Summer."

"Well, Summer sounds like a loser," I said nudging his side and letting myself relax again, letting myself fall into Felix's orbit.

"She wasn't. I think she was right. I didn't grow up with fun. Most things other people thought were fun, I thought were kind of a waste of time. We moved so much with the army, it was hard to make real friendships before we had to go again, so I learned to keep myself entertained." Felix's tone was soft, like the words were flowing out without the normal filter, and I grabbed them all up. "Anyway, that night with you felt . . . fun, so I thought maybe it was time to try dating someone again, someone fun and breezy."

"Did you overcorrect?"

A grin cracked across his face. "Maybe."

"What was Summer's job?"

"Guess."

I studied his face and his little silly grin that made the dimples on his cheeks just barely pop. I glanced around the gate for inspiration. A short older man stood on his tiptoes to talk too loudly at the gate agent, and a harried-looking couple chased three kids through the concourse. I couldn't tell if they were running for a flight or the children had escaped containment. "Summer was a life coach? A motivational speaker?"

His eyes popped open and he sat up straight. "How did you guess that?"

"I tried to imagine someone's work life being the exact opposite of yours, and speakers have to be outgoing and always on, right? I don't know."

"Well," he said, shaking his head. "You're close. She called herself a wellness influencer. Has a big social media following. She said I was too stiff and she couldn't relax around me. It's probably good you only want a couple days. I'll sober up soon and be back to stiff."

"I was kind of hoping you'd return to stiff." I copied his eyebrow waggle from earlier and grinned when he rolled his eyes. "What? I can't point out your unintentional joke?"

His phone buzzed between us, and he reached for it without looking. "It's a good thing you're—" He froze mid-sentence after glancing at his phone, and his entire demeanor changed.

"What's wrong?"

"Just got a text. There was a fire at Golson College," he said, skimming through the message. "Everyone is okay. They think it was an electrical issue, but they've evacuated half the campus."

My heart beat wildly, imagining that happening at Thurmond. Things happened with electricity and gas lines and worse. "But no one was hurt?"

"That's what it says," Felix said, draping an arm over my shoulders and pulling me toward him so I could see his phone, too. On the screen was a tweet from the college's communications team. Felix's shoulder was firm and steady against me, and my pulse began to slow, but he didn't let go. "We should reschedule the trip."

"Definitely."

We sat quietly for a few moments, our bodies together, Felix's hand moving up and down my arm and my head resting against his firm chest. I glanced up and he kept staring at his phone. I wasn't sure he was aware of the way he was stroking my arm or if he knew that's how I liked to be touched when I was worried. He kept doing it, though, the strokes even and consistent, until I pulled away to take out my own phone and we decided who needed to do what to begin rescheduling our visit to Colorado.

Felix was sitting straight again, the sex-drunk haze missing from his aura, but he still looked different to me. The same Felix but with something else sprinkled over him. I shut the thoughts down and told him I was taking a walk through the terminal. I was prone to falling for people too fast and too hard. The way I was seeing Felix now was the way I'd seen Elena when we first met, and at that thought, my stomach dipped. I didn't have the time or resilience to deal with that again. I glanced over my shoulder one last time before

I turned a corner and dipped into the Hudson News. Felix was on the phone, his mouth in a firm line, and nodding away.

This short-term thing would be good for both of us. I had the sinking suspicion that Summer and I might have been friends, and he didn't need someone like me in his life long-term, not as anything more than a colleague, anyway.

16

Felix

I **WOKE TO** a dark hotel room, the lights from the city flickering outside against the inky sky. I couldn't fully see the clock over the pillow, but the time started with five and it looked like traffic outside was on the edges of beginning to pick up for the morning. Gia's warm, soft, naked body was pressed to me, and the single queen bed could have been a twin for as close as we were. I didn't care.

I gently rolled onto my back, trying not to disturb her, and stared at the ceiling.

We'd changed our flight to return to Chicago instead of going to Denver, but that had meant spending another night in Austin and sharing the only room left at the hotel, a single. I tried to imagine getting the news of only one room at the beginning of the trip. I might have demanded to speak to a manager in the lobby and gone full Karen.

Gia let out a small, soft string of nonsensical words. She talked in her sleep and it was adorable. I'd thought about telling her but hadn't had the heart. Her hand was splayed on the sheet; the contrast between her skin and the stark white sheet was a play of shadows in the near-dark room. I'd found myself memorizing how she looked from all these different angles, the shape and color of her hands and her bright pink fingernails. I'd read somewhere that comparing skin tone on people of color to food was problematic, which made sense, but looking at Gia's hand and following the line of her arm up to her bare shoulder, which reflected the twinkling city lights outside, all I could think of was the sweet taste of brown sugar on my tongue.

I'm screwed. We had an early flight back to Chicago and we'd need to be up soon to get ready, but this warm cocoon was a place I unexpectedly wanted to stay. I hadn't planned to tell her about Summer, about the embarrassingly short relationship that still felt like a significant commitment to me. I hadn't loved Summer. If I was honest with myself, I didn't really think about her when we weren't together, and she was right that I wasn't fun. I glanced at Gia's still frame again and studied her nose, scrunched for a moment unexpectedly in sleep and then relaxed. She knew I wasn't fun. I was pretty sure she knew what was closer to the real me than I'd previously let most people see.

"No," she murmured. "Gummy bears."

I grinned and made a mental note to buy her gummy bears when we got to the airport, or maybe I'd wait until we were on the plane or until we got home. I imagined her confused and delighted expression. She let out a little groan and rolled to her side, her hand making its way over my stomach before she settled and her warm breath hit against my chest.

We hadn't stayed up late, but we'd depleted every ounce of energy from each other before falling asleep. Gia approached sex like she seemed to approach everything—with curiosity and energy—and I had a hard time not touching her. I gently nudged her closer, wanting more contact.

She'd told me the day before that I looked sex drunk. I was pretty sure that wasn't it. I was Gia drunk, and here I was again, staring at the ceiling with her against me and thinking about the kind of candy I would buy her.

I brushed my lips against her forehead and she stirred.

"What time is it?"

I stretched to see the clock over her shoulder. "It's five twenty. You have a little more time to sleep."

"Why are you up?" Her voice sounded half-asleep and dreamy and she curled into me until I wrapped an arm around her neck, pulling her close. With Gia, I cuddled.

"No reason," I murmured, stroking her back and wishing my first instinct wasn't to roll her onto her back and help her fully wake up.

"It's too early for morning sex," she grumbled, tightening her hold around my waist.

"I didn't know there was a rule book."

"There is," she said with a yawn, stretching in my arms, her full height lined up next to me. "I'll point it out to you when the sun's up. I'm surprised you don't know it already. You love rules."

"You seem to have your own rule book."

She was quiet for a moment, and I wondered if she'd fallen back asleep. "You told me about your ex yesterday."

I hadn't expected those words. For a minute, I couldn't respond, and I noticed the chill of the air conditioner, which we'd set low when entering the warm room the day before and had never gotten around to adjusting. "It's not a secret."

She let out a little *hm* sound and then was quiet again. "My ex moved to Japan and didn't ask me if I'd be willing to go with her."

I stroked her back, unsure what was happening with this early morning confession. "Would you have?"

"I don't know." Her palm slid up and down my side, and I noticed how she pressed down slightly so I wasn't ticklish. "I might have."

I let out my own *hm*, sensing this was an important moment but uncertain what I was supposed to say.

"She didn't think I was serious enough for long-term. She thought she wanted me, but in the end . . . So we're kind of a pair, huh?"

I brushed my lips against her head again. "I'm no fun and you're too fun?"

Gia lifted her head and slid over me so that her head rested on the forearm over my chest. "I guess that's the long and short of it."

I ran my hand down her arm, very aware of the places where her bare skin touched mine. "Well, balance is important."

She glanced out the window, where the tiniest hint of sunrise was beginning to light the edge of the sky. "Back to reality today," she said. "I'm sad losing that last leg of the trip also meant losing another night of our fun."

"Or morning," I said with a grin.

"Or two mornings." She cut her eyes to the clock and then back to me. "Maybe it's not too early . . . for morning activities." Her eyes kind of twinkled and there was an adorable crease across her cheek from the pillow.

When her lips brushed over my chest, my body flushed and the last few nights of touches and kisses and Gia's perfect bright smiles crashed over me. "What if we augmented the existing reality?"

"Felix, I'm propositioning you for sex at the moment . . . Now is not the time for words like 'augment.'" Her hand skirted lower and I placed my palm over it to stop her, knowing if we went any further I'd lose eighty percent of my capacity for rational thought.

"I know. I mean . . ." I shifted so I could catch her eye. "What if when we got home, we kept . . . enjoying each other."

"You want to keep hooking up?"

It was amazing that in all my years of experience as a human, I'd never had to find the words to really ask for this. "Yes, but more. Like we could be . . . together."

Gia stilled. Not only the path of her hand, but her whole body went rigid, and apparently I'd asked for it in the wrong way. "Like a couple? You want to date me?"

"I . . ." I searched my mental archives for some other conversation to pull from but came up blank. "You talk in your sleep," I said in response.

"What?"

"You talk in your sleep and it's cute. I like it. I like that I know that about you."

Gia pulled back a few inches and was quiet before pulling her body into a seated position next to me, the sheet pulled over her chest. "I'm confused right now. You like my night rambling?"

I made a sound suspiciously like a growl. "No. I mean, yes. I mean . . . how do I ask you if you want to date me?"

The smile that crossed her lips was faint, and my stomach dipped. "That was a good way," she said quietly, as if speaking at a normal volume would disturb the sleepy city outside. "I'm just surprised. You think I'm too fun."

"And I'm no fun." I reached for her soft hand and she linked her fingers with mine. "Maybe together we could average out to a standard level of fun."

She worried the corner of her lip, which was something that normally drove me wild, but now made me brace for what she was going to say next.

"Or not," I added.

"We probably would average out to a standard level of fun," she said, her voice lilting up in what sounded like mock positivity. "But I don't want that. I can't want that right now."

"Oh," I said, wishing I had pants on. I could think better with pants on; even thin cotton pajama pants would provide some armor here. "Okay." I wanted to get off the bed and walk away, but we just had the one room, and in the small bed there wasn't anywhere for me to shift or move.

"It's . . ." Gia trailed off, and over her shoulder I noticed the first rays of sunlight warming the sky.

"No need for explanation," I said, holding up a hand and searching the floor next to the bed for my boxers. "It was just a thought." I found them and swung my legs off the side of the bed. "Of course you don't want an average level of fun. Who wants that?"

I stood and ran a hand down my stomach and made sure I'd gotten whatever emotion might be on my face in check before I turned to face Gia.

"Felix . . ." She was studying me when I turned, but she didn't correct me. She didn't need to, and I already regretted the absurd idea. "We work together. I can't date a colleague, and it just wouldn't work."

"Of course not. You're right. Forget I brought it up." I walked past her toward the en suite. "Give me just a few minutes and then the bathroom is yours." I needed to splash cold water on my face. Maybe I needed to dunk my head in some frigid water. As the door closed behind me, I knew she was right. She didn't want someone who wasn't fun to balance her out, just like she didn't want to date someone she worked with in a male-dominated environment. Still, I looked into the mirror and scrubbed a hand down my face, remembering with stark clarity how Gia's nails felt digging into my skin.

This flight home is going to be very awkward.

17

Gia

I NORMALLY LOVED Fridays—everyone was a little friendlier, a little more conversational, and everyone cruised uninhibited toward the weekend. Normally.

> GIA: At what point are things so awkward between two people that moving to Switzerland to escape is justifiable.
>
> BENNETT: It's 8am.
>
> GIA: You were up. I think I-slept-with-a-coworker-and-then-refused-to-date-him might be bordering close to justifiable.
>
> BENNETT: I hear the chocolate in Switzerland is good.
>
> GIA: Can you have your beautiful wife pick me up some truffles from that chocolate store in the airport?

BENNETT: Because you're sad?

GIA: Because I'm hungry.

I glanced across the conference room to where Felix sat next to the presenter, a doctoral student sharing his research with the faculty in the Friday salon after we returned early from the trip. It had been four days of awkward step asides and polite nods. I was slowly dying inside.

GIA: And I'm sad.

BENNETT: You could tell him how you feel.

GIA: If I knew how I felt, I could. It wouldn't work. It would have been cruel to get his hopes up.

BENNETT: I'm sure sleeping with him was a crystal-clear indication he should keep hopes low?

GIA: Rude.

BENNETT: I love you and will ask Ollie to pick up truffles today.

I didn't know the graduate student well—he was one of Felix's students who had come with him to Thurmond, and it was clear he was trying to mimic Felix as he spoke, even down to his posture and the way the slide deck looked so plain, so clean. Felix watched him with what I would have previously called cool detachment, but I thought I saw a little pride there, a touch of swagger that had nothing to do with him being arrogant. That was how I felt about my students when I saw them present, especially when they did well.

"Thank you," he said, shifting to a slide reading Questions. I smiled to myself at the period. It rang of Felix. I always ended mine with a question mark or no punctuation at all. I was all open possibilities and question marks. I spared a quick glance to Felix again, who was jotting something in his notebook. Felix was a period. A solid, no-room-for-doubt punctuation mark.

I'd missed the question posed by another graduate student in the room, but the presenter's eyes widened for a moment, the veneer of cool detachment falling away and plain terror painting his expression. It was a relief to see that Felix's graduate students weren't always one hundred percent all over everything. "That's a good question. I believe the model generated by Dr. Ennings offers the best direction. I haven't studied the results from Dr. Price's approach extensively, so I don't know if I can speak to that; however, Dr. Ennings is familiar with the studies, and perhaps he could speak on it."

That was a good BS answer. The academic way of saying *Dude, why did you ask me that? You're supposed to be on my team!* I might have said the same thing, and I braced myself as Felix eyed the screen before opening his mouth to eviscerate me. On the one hand, I wasn't a big fan of having my work publicly torn to shreds, and no one did it better than Felix, but on the other hand, that was normal, and I wanted normal so I didn't have to start looking for an apartment in Zurich.

Felix's gaze skirted over mine to look at the graduate student who asked the question. "Both approaches have merit and value. In this instance, it's a case of picking a direction to focus attention versus merging perspectives."

The question-and-answer portion of the presentation continued, but I stopped listening because I saw red.

GIA: What was that?

FELIX: Me answering a question my grad student should have been prepared to field.

GIA: They both have merit? What was that?

FELIX: Are you angry I said your work had merit?

GIA: Yes.

FELIX: That's absurd.

GIA: It's not. You never miss a chance to point out
how your approach is superior to mine. Are you
treating me with kid gloves because of what
happened on the trip? Because you think you
know me?

Everyone around the table clapped, and a low hum of conversation began as people packed up their things to head out for the weekend. My text was still unread, and now Felix was on his feet, talking in low tones to his graduate student, who alternated between matching Felix's stance and looking like he was going to wet himself. I tapped my foot, planning to have it out with Felix, to explain why this was the reason we wouldn't work, why it wasn't worth it for me to take a chance on him.

"Dr. Price, a moment?" Christopher's hand hovered over my shoulder and I nodded, giving Felix one more glance. He never called me Dr. Price. Our department was casual and most everyone was on a first-name basis, so it stood out.

Christopher's office down the hall overlooked the campus quad. Outside the leaves had started changing colors and hung in that moment between brilliant bright colors and brittle brown leaves abandoning gnarled limbs.

I fell into the chair next to Christopher's desk instead of the one across from it. I wasn't sure why he even had a chair there—the proximity of people to his space, to his level, always seemed to put him on edge. "What's up?"

His hand was halfway to the chair on the other side of his desk when he noticed I'd taken the seat already. "Yes, well. This is kind of . . . delicate."

"Is it about the trip? We know the rescheduling couldn't be helped. It won't be a problem to move some things around, especially since I'm only teaching one course this fall."

"Yes." He arranged a stack of papers on his desk. "It's about the trip, but not that. I think it would be best if Alexander did the last leg on his own."

Golson College had been the stop I was most looking forward to, the institution that was doing genuinely cutting-edge work and had the results to support it. I wasn't looking forward to traveling with Felix again, but it would be worth it to visit. "Why?"

"Well, he's the more senior colleague and established in the field, a bigger name. You know," he said, straightening the papers again.

"Perhaps, but I'm the one who has led every step of the trip, done the research, built the partnerships to take what we learn and bring it back to Thurmond." I leveled him with a steel in my gaze I didn't feel. "And you know that."

"Gia, no one is discounting your work, but . . ." He finally set the papers down. "This is none of my business, but a colleague from Douglas University mentioned the . . . interactions between you and Alexander." He held his palms out toward me. "None of my business, but I think it's in the best interest of the department to put forward our most professional presence."

I breathed his words in through my nose to keep from reacting, but my face heated regardless. "And the most professional presence is . . ."

"I think Alexander alone will be most effective."

I nodded, deciding how to play this, as torrents of anger, frustration, and indignation warred with the feeling of being caught. As soon as I told Felix I didn't want more, it felt wrong. While I knew

I needed some time for casual and fun after the breakup with Elena, and I knew dating a colleague could be disastrous, it still felt wrong to turn him down, because part of me did want to try with Felix—our average level of fun was more enjoyable and felt more right than anything else. "If your concern is that our flirtation was unprofessional, why am I the only one you're talking to?"

"C'mon, Gia. I'm not interested in what you two do together, but the dean and president are up my ass about us participating in this, and Alexander is less likely to embarrass us."

There are moments when time slows and you know you're making a choice and that choice is violence. I blinked, nodded, and leaned back in the chair, crossing my legs. My foot got kind of stuck on the edge of the desk, but I didn't think it marred the effect. "Your double standards are showing, Christopher. As far as I know, my ticket is booked and I'll be getting on that plane. Pass that on to the dean. As for embarrassing the department?" I flicked my eyes down his shirt. "You missed a button and your fly is unzipped."

Christopher wasn't at a loss for words, but I stood before he could get any out, hustling back to my office to fume and ferret out how much I might regret my response. I was almost there when Felix stepped out of his office and we ran into each other, his hand moving to my arm to steady me, probably before realizing it was me.

"Oh," he said, in his normal, stiff, Alexander Felix Ennings way.

I stepped around him. "Excuse me." My attempt to mirror his blasé tone wasn't successful; there was too much anger creeping in from his flippant comment in the meeting and Christopher's directive.

"You're angry with me." His voice was low, and I noticed how his fingers twitched after he pulled them away from me.

"You've gone back to being a condescending jerk," I said in a hushed tone. *Okay, just choosing violence left and right this afternoon, I guess.*

"I never stopped being a condescending jerk."

I wanted to laugh. It was funny and it was kind of true, but laughing would be giving him hope something would happen between us, and it couldn't work. Nothing had hammered that home faster than him passing on the opportunity to critique my research. "I'll see you at the airport," I said instead, walking around him to my open door.

18

Felix

"ARE YOU SURE you're not going?" Christopher's face was twisted, his forearm resting on my door, which stretched his polo shirt and gave him the look of an aging fraternity brother.

I glanced up from my computer monitor, giving him the exact level of care in my tone that I felt was warranted. "Yes. I'm far too busy."

I had a lot of work to do. I was under deadlines for a book chapter and two articles in addition to the graduate courses I was teaching, but I hadn't thought to back out of the last leg of the trip until the day before, until Gia had leveled me with the coldest stare I'd ever seen on her face. I didn't like how unsettled the look had made me.

By all accounts, she turned me down. I was under the impression that if anyone was the injured party, it was me. But she'd ignored my joke, she'd walked away from me, and I'd still wanted to pull her into my arms. "I don't have time to spend another three days traveling. It's not worth the effort."

"Well," Christopher said, scrubbing his hand down his face. "I gotta say, that makes my life a little easier."

I bit back the urge to tell him I didn't care about how easy his life was, but midwestern niceties and all, so I just nodded, which he took as an invitation to come in, close the door, and settle into the chair across from me. *Damn midwestern niceties.*

"I kinda stuck my foot in my mouth and told Gia I thought only you should go," he said, like we had these informal chats all the time.

"Why?" I glanced back at my screen as if it were hard to look away from these revisions, but his words piqued my curiosity.

"A colleague of mine mentioned you two were . . . well, that you looked romantically involved at Douglas." He held up his palms. "I don't want to know, but I figured that wasn't the impression we wanted to make, and if it was just you, it would be more professional. Gia is too . . ." He searched for the right term. "Well, she's just generally too much. Unpredictable."

I held his nervous stare without speaking. It was a skill I learned from my dad. He wasn't a big man, but his silent stare would bring anyone to their knees.

"I mean . . . c'mon. You're not the most effusive guy. I'm sure most of what they saw was her, but anyway, you don't want to go, so we'll deal with Gia alone, and I won't have to fight her on it." He smiled and glanced away, proof the stare was doing its job. "Win-win."

I forced myself to slowly pull my glasses off my face and set them gingerly next to the pen holder on my desk. In another life—hell, two months earlier—I would have been horrified to learn I was the fodder for gossip, that colleagues might see me as anything less than competent, imposing, and professional. That wasn't my concern in that moment, though. "Christopher, you've gotten the wrong impression of me."

"Seriously, you and Gia hooking up is an HR issue I don't want on my desk. I really don't need to know."

"No," I said, sitting taller. "You don't, but this casual sexism, this *bro-to-bro* misogyny you're employing right now, is certainly an HR issue I'd be happy to make sure lands on your desk." An entire childhood of pointed conversations with my dad came back to me in an instant, and I relaxed my hands, laying them flat on the table in front of me, though I wanted to make a fist. "You seem to think that Dr. Price is a second-string option here. She's the one who did the research, who already drafted a report about changes to implement here, the one who has contacts across the country related to teaching in STEM. She's not *too much* of anything, and this department is lucky to have her." And I was lucky to have had her.

I thought back to her indignation when I went easy on her in the graduate student's presentation. She was right. It was an opportunity I would have normally taken to point out the shortcomings of her purely experimental approach, and the only reason I didn't was because despite her shutting me down, I remembered how her neck smelled and the way her lips felt against mine.

Christopher blustered. "This is not sexism or misogyny."

I remained silent but my gaze didn't leave his, even as I replayed Gia's response, how it might have made her feel, how she might have thought I was like this guy. I'd advised mentees and former students tons of times to keep their work and personal lives separate, to remind themselves that they don't want to see someone in the hall every day who will distract them from the work. It was good advice and I should have followed it.

"You're blowing this way out of proportion. It's not like you need to report me or something. There's nothing here."

I didn't miss the furrow between his brows. "I wouldn't do that without first giving her the chance to do it."

"All I said was—"

"I was here. I heard what you said." I put my glasses back on and glanced back at my screen. "I recommend her name be listed first in any discussion you have about this project."

He rolled his eyes. "You want her getting more credit because you have a crush on her?"

I pushed back enough that he took his hands off the table, but mine were curled into fists now. "I am expressing my expectation that she be given more credit because she did more work. Are we done here?"

We held eye contact for a moment, but he muttered, "Sure," and walked out, closing my door harder than necessary. In the ensuing quiet, I realized Gia must not be in her office. There was no music, no laughter, no light hum as she sang to herself while she worked. I still didn't know what to say, other than saying I'd support her in challenging Christopher, but she was gone, probably to pack for her trip.

I started to type but paused. I'd gotten used to the hum through the wall, the faint echo of music. I'd gotten used to Gia being on the other side of the wall before I'd ever fallen for her on the trip.

Fallen for.

I leaned back in my chair and scrubbed a hand over the back of my neck at the realization that I'd been falling for Gia in some way or another since New Year's Eve. That she'd told me she wasn't ready for anything big and I'd ignored that, focused on the enormity of what I felt. That I wanted to be with her.

I glanced at my inbox, where the details for the canceled travel arrangements sat at the top of my unread email. Gia would be back the following Tuesday, which meant one day of a quiet office next week and the weekend to figure out what I wanted to do.

19

Gia

I TUCKED MY notes from Golson College into my bag and tried to spot the front of the long line at the coffee shop. It was already late morning, but I needed caffeine, this long, slow-moving line be damned.

Someone tapped me on the shoulder. "Do you know what time it is?" She was a little older than me, with shiny black hair that fell in waves down her back and over her bare shoulders.

"Oh, it's ten fifty," I said, glancing at my phone. I admired her smile, the kind that took over someone's entire face. "This line isn't moving very fast, though. If you're in a hurry, this might not be it."

"I've got some time," she said. "My phone and watch battery died at about the same time. It's maybe a sign I shouldn't be traveling today."

I returned her smile, noticing how her gaze flicked momentarily to my lips. "Maybe. Time to go back to bed?"

"Maybe, but how would I know?" She was my type—funny, outgoing, and friendly, curvy with flashes of her collarbone and belly showing. She laughed at her own joke in a way that made me smile. I should have already asked her name. She was checking me out.

"Good point."

"So, lucky I ran into you," she said, dipping her voice low, as if it were a secret.

It really should have been tempting to me. She was sexy and had kind eyes behind cool, funky red glasses, but I wasn't feeling the spark. Someone else was using all my mental oxygen. "Anytime." Her glasses were cooler than Felix's, but he was still living rent-free in my head. I glanced back toward the front of the line and my new friend seemed to take the hint, stepping back into line. *Who am I right now?* I never passed up a chance to flirt when I was single. I sometimes even fell into it when I was dating someone. It was fun. It was my happy place.

I stepped forward, antsy over the lack of movement in the line. I'd been antsy since we returned from our visit to Douglas, since I told Felix I didn't want more when I really did, and since I got on the plane without him. I turned again. "You're adorable," I said. "I love your glasses and I would normally be deciding if you were flirting with me."

"I was." She studied my face, a level of scrutiny I hadn't planned on that morning when getting ready. "Recent breakup?"

"Two of them. You could tell?"

She shrugged. "You have a little air of heartbreak about you."

I grinned at her moxie. I really was off my game. "I'm Gia."

She shook my hand. "Mazie. Tell me about your heartbreak, Gia. From the look of this line, I have time for a story and"—she leaned conspiratorially toward me—"there's no one else interesting to flirt with."

• • • •

"SO, WHAT ARE you going to do?" Mazie handed her now-empty iced-coffee cup to the flight attendant collecting trash. After talking in the long coffee line, we'd ended up being on the same flight and able to swap seats to sit together. It was so different from my recent travels with rule-following Felix, whose head might have exploded if I asked a stranger to swap seats.

"About Elena or Felix? I don't know if there's anything to do either way."

"There's always something to do!" She pushed her hair off her shoulder. "Start with Elena. You said you miss her, right? Miss being her friend?"

I nodded. "Yeah. I mean, I'm sad our relationship is over, but mostly I miss her being in my life."

"Duh. That one's easy. Text her. Figure out how to be her friend again." She put her hand on my forearm, her funky nail colors vivid against my skin. "You know you want to. Just bite the bullet and do it."

She was right. I did miss talking to Elena, back in the time before we were in love and were friends. I hadn't been brave enough to try very hard. "You give good advice."

"I get it from my mother, but don't tell her I admitted it. Now, for your man. It's not against the rules at work for you two to date or bump uglies or whatever you decide to do?"

I snort-laughed at the phrase. "There's nothing ugly going on there," I said in a hushed tone to avoid further scandalizing our seatmate, who was pretending to ignore us.

"Bump lovelies, then."

I laughed again, choking on the drink of Coke I'd finished. Mazie was like a mirror, like all my energy and humor was being reflected at me. Maybe my heartbreak was a good thing, because Mazie and I together might start fires. Not the kind born of hot passion but inadvertent, though actual, fires. "There's no rule," I answered. "It's frowned upon, but that doesn't matter. I can't do my job and be with him if he starts to take it easy on me."

"That's the part I don't get." She fastened her seat belt at the ding. "You want him to keep being a hard-ass?"

"It's like . . ." I leaned my head back against my seat. "In academia, when you turn in an article, you get feedback from other people in the field. Usually at least two people read it."

She cocked her head to the side and I had to remind myself I was referring to something pretty specific to universities and the fellow grown-up nerds who made professing their career.

"Their identities are confidential, but reviewer two symbolizes the person who is nitpicky, critical, and sometimes unreasonable."

"Ah, so your boy is reviewer two."

"Yes," I said. "Except he's not unreasonable, usually."

"Maybe you could just tell him to take off whatever kid gloves he thinks he needs?"

"People don't stop underestimating you just because you ask them to."

Mazie shrugged. "In my experience, the right people do."

I thought back on my life, on the people I'd loved, the people I wanted to love me. I thought about Elena and how I never told her it bothered me when she said I wasn't serious enough. I just assumed Felix wouldn't change his mind. He was so unyielding about everything else. It didn't even seem like an option. When he asked me for more, to try for something real, I just assumed he'd end up underestimating me, too. The cabin lights pulsed in time with my revelation, and it was like a lightbulb went on. "Mazie, I think you might be a genius."

She grinned. "You mean a hot genius."

I laughed. "Of course I do."

I checked my watch and did the mental time-change calculations. We'd land in an hour and a half and I was going straight to Felix's place to hash it out. I didn't know where he lived, but I'd figure something out as soon as I had cell service and a 5G connection. An hour and a half to decide what I wanted from Felix.

20

Felix

FOR THE TENTH time, I balled my fists and walked back toward the security exit. That time, I'd barely taken one step before returning to my spot. I didn't realize grand gestures took so much psyching up, but the first time I'd reminded myself this idea was ridiculous, I'd almost gotten out of baggage claim.

A woman next to me corralled three small children, all of whom seemed adamant in their desire to drop their WELCOME HOME, DADDY signs on the ground.

On my left a guy a little shorter than me spoke to himself and reached into his pocket every fifteen seconds, trying out different iterations of "I'm sorry and will you marry me?"

I wasn't alone in this grand-gesture-at-the-airport thing, and I almost stepped away again, but then I spotted her in the distance, pulling a roller bag behind her and tapping on her phone. She looked like she'd been traveling all day, but she looked like Gia, and my heart gave an unfamiliar lurch in my chest.

GIA: What's your address?

I stared at the message and swung my gaze back to Gia, who was intent on her phone. Intent on me, or intent on my text thread. I'd had this idea in my head that Gia's focus was always moving from thing to thing, be it her personality or her brain chemistry, but she looked focused, and now she was focused on me.

> FELIX: Are you sending me a postcard?
>
> GIA: I'm subscribing you to a pool aficionado magazine.
>
> GIA: I want to come by your place. We should talk.

She was getting closer, coming down the hall at a leisurely pace with a woman next to her, exchanging what looked like jokes. Gia's head tipped back in a grin.

> FELIX: I'm not home.
>
> GIA: I guess it is the middle of a weekday. No problem. When is a good time tonight?

I could hear her laugh now even over the wails of the toddler forced to greet their father instead of drawing with crayons on the tile. I couldn't see her—the family blocked my view, and on the other side, a flash of blond hair flew by me and into my neighbor's arms, his incessant practicing blessedly paused only to be replaced by loud, wet kisses. That they could be heard over the screaming children was saying something.

I began typing my reply. Well, it takes about forty-five minutes to get home from the airport, but before I could hit send, my head snapped left as the blonde hit the floor, her tote bag toppling, and as she was rubbing her backside, my neighbor shouted, "Oh my God! I dropped you! How is your butt? Will you marry me?" but it came out in one long stream of syllables. *OhmyGodIdroppedyouHowisyour buttWillyoumarryme?*

"Baby," she said from the floor, pausing mid—bend and stretch to collect her spilled items. "We've only been dating for six weeks."

I felt for the guy—he looked stricken, holding the ring box out like it was a deadly spider he needed someone to take off his hands. "Is your butt okay?"

"Yes," she said with a smile. "And yes!"

In an instant, he was on the floor with her and the loud kissing had commenced, only this time over my shoe.

I glanced back at my phone and hit send, then heard Gia's voice from behind the family who were momentarily blocking the walkway. "The airport?"

> FELIX: I'm past the big family with the screaming
> kids. Next to the couple making out on the floor.

She squeezed past the family who were now dragging along a six-year-old who decided going limp was the best form of protest. Gia smiled as she maneuvered around the family, glancing at me and then back to the kid. She called over her shoulder. "Hey! I think the Paw Patrol is still at baggage claim. I'm going to try to hurry so I can see them!"

Like that, the kid was mobile again, and all three children were dragging their tired-looking parents out of the way.

"Very slick," I said as she walked closer.

"Oh, I was serious. I need to hurry if I want to catch the show." She wore a plain yellow T-shirt that made her skin look even more luminous. "What are you doing here?"

"I wanted to see you and do something . . . something you would do."

One member of the couple on the floor groaned between kisses. "Baby, I'm glad we don't have to wait."

"Maybe you could wait long enough to get off my shoes?"

"Oh," the guy said, pulling back, red-faced. "Sorry, man. It's just that she said yes."

Gia's voice filled my senses. "She said yes, Felix. Don't be a stick-in-the-mud." Gia winked and gave me a wide-eyed smile as I took a step around the once-again lip-locked couple. "I would do something like that," she said, quietly stepping with me. "But I hope that's not what you have planned."

I cleared my throat. "No. You're very attractive, but not so attractive I could forget how dirty that floor probably is."

"Is this reviewer two?" The woman Gia had been walking with peeked over her shoulder.

"Reviewer two?" I glanced between them as Gia nodded at the woman. "You're telling people I'm reviewer two?"

She nodded and grinned. "I mean, you are." Behind her the woman made a "call me" motion with her hand and then slipped away.

"I . . . don't have a response for that." I reached into my pocket. "But it doesn't matter. I wanted to give you this," I said, holding out the envelope.

Her fingers brushed mine when she took it, but she didn't open it, looking to me instead. "What is it?"

"It's a list of everything about your work with which I disagree. Your dogged adherence to a purely experimental approach leaves chips on the table; your assumptions are playing fast and loose with what I and other scholars have established; your research methods fly in the face of established norms. You left out key nuances when summarizing my work in your last paper, and your conclusions, though interesting, could be so much bigger." I took a breath, taking in her unchanged expression. "And you play your music too loud in the office. I don't actually mind that one so much anymore. It was too quiet while you were gone."

"Man, you're supposed to say nice things," the new groom-to-be said from the floor.

"Yes. Thank you," I said, regretting doing this in the airport for so many reasons. A wobbly suitcase wheel made a *clack-clack-click* as it rolled by. "But I won't say nice things about your research when I should criticize it just because you're so beautiful and I can't get you out of my head. And I'll never underestimate your capacity to challenge me professionally just because you challenge me to think bigger." I glanced down at her hands. I wasn't sure why. She was still holding the envelope, the red paint on her thumbnail in stark contrast to the white paper of the envelope. "You're a tornado of chaos," I said, glancing back up to meet her eyes. "And I'd really like to take you out on a date where no one will interrupt us to report abandoned luggage."

She looked down at the envelope with her name scrawled across the front. "And you wrote all that down here?"

I nodded. "There's more written down, along with citations."

She laughed, the sound wrapping around me like a hug, and she stepped into my space, her free palm sliding up my chest. "Of course there is. I'd like to go on a date with you." She bit the corner of her lip and I waited for some other pin to burst this balloon. "I'm sorry about how I reacted that morning at the hotel. I was scared."

"You're not anymore?"

She raised her palm, her fingers skirting along my neck. "Who's afraid of reviewer two?"

My lips tipped up and my shoulders relaxed, making me realize how I'd been holding them stiffly. "Not you?"

"Not me." Her lips brushed mine and I let my hand fall to her waist, pulling her close and feeling just an ounce or two of kinship with the couple on the floor.

"Attention, passengers, please keep walkways clear so everyone may move safely through the airport."

"I think that's our cue to get out of here," Gia said, looking up at me as her fingers found mine and we stepped away from the security exit area.

"I've never known you to be a rule follower," I said, squeezing her hand.

"I guess I've picked up a thing or two from you," she said, bumping her hip against mine. "Now, tell me more about how you can't stop thinking about me."

The automatic door opened with a whoosh and cool air hit us as we stepped outside the terminal. "That's outlined on the list, too."

FEBRUARY
One Year Later

Epilogue

Gia

"WHAT IS WITH us and flight delays?" I looked up at Felix, who was pacing in the gate area, the crease between his brows showing his own . . . well, not frustration. Maybe anxiety. He hated being late.

"This one is my fault," he grumbled. "I booked too tight a connection."

There were some aspects of dating a control freak that I enjoyed, like when we decided to get away for Valentine's Day, he booked and managed our arrangements and I could just be along for the ride. "No big deal. The next one is only another ninety minutes." I snagged his hand as he walked by. "You want to read that latest article from Simmons together?" Recently, a seeming devotee of Felix's model had utilized my experimental approach as the foundation of his latest study.

His forehead crease disappeared and I got the tiny lip twitch I had hoped for. There was a time when I would have been disappointed without the full smile, but two years after meeting Felix, I knew it was special. "You want some coffee?"

I nodded and stroked his hand before he walked down the concourse. I glanced the other way. Pre-Flight Paws was closed today, which was a shame—I'd hoped to catch up with Ollie and Jess during our layover. Just past their shop was my favorite candy shop, and I snatched up my carry-on bag and hurried that way, tapping a message into the group chat with my unlikely hype squad.

> **GIA:** I'm gonna do it tonight!
>
> **MAZIE:** Get it girl!
>
> **ELENA:** So excited for you!

"WELCOME TO JULIANNA'S Candy Shoppe," the young woman behind the counter chirped. "What can I get you?"

I perused the case. Bennett made fun of me, but this was the best chocolate shop in the country as far as I was concerned. "I'm getting a mix of my and my boyfriend's favorites. Can I get a box of a dozen?"

She smiled. Her name tag read TEAGAN and she looked about the age of a lot of my students, maybe a little older. I started pointing out truffles—some dark chocolate for Felix, white chocolate for me. "Special occasion?" Teagan waited patiently as I decided between options.

"I'm going to propose to him tonight," I said, enjoying the feel of the words. We'd been together ever since our trip the year before, and he was my person. We'd talked about the future, about moving in together, marriage, maybe becoming foster parents. The person behind the counter didn't need my life story, but I was bursting to tell someone. "I'm a big-public-spectacle kind of girl, but his style is more wine and chocolates in private, so . . . might as well get the best chocolates!"

"Well, these are new and they're my favorites," she said, tucking two pink-flecked white chocolate truffles into a bag and then adding two similar ones but with green flecks. "And these are my best friend's favorites. We're not married but we've been besties forever, so maybe they'll bring you luck."

I ducked down to look at the tags. "Raspberry and pistachio. These look amazing!"

"These ones are on the house," she said, handing them over. "Good luck," she said with a smile as she swiped my credit card for the box and held up her crossed fingers.

I didn't see Felix at the gate when I returned, and I tucked the chocolates into my bag, pressing my lips together. The gate seemed fuller and I tried to see over some guy's head to check out the screen for a flight update, but the gate agent's voice crackled through the speakers. "Attention in the boarding area, Flight 893 with service to Myrtle Beach will depart in about an hour. Until then, we'd like to do something special, since it's Valentine's Day."

I grinned. I loved this airline's sometimes playful approach to flying. I was surprised Felix chose them, because their style was usually too "loosey-goosey" for him, and I did mock him mercilessly for using that phrase. A pop song I recognized immediately came on.

"You're welcome to dance with us." Two of the gate agents nearby began swaying their hips, and four little girls began twirling in the open space between seats. I tapped my foot and looked around as husbands, wives, and kids were slowly cajoled out of their seats by their flying companions and the boarding area became a little party. An older woman next to me leaned over and said, "I wish we had dance partners!"

I grinned and held out my hand for her as the impromptu dance party picked up steam and people from neighboring gates began to join in as the song played. The woman laughed and took my hand, letting me spin her, and we bopped to the beat until the song ended and another began, an old Bruno Mars song I couldn't immediately place.

"I think you have an admirer," the woman, whose name was

Greta, said, pointing behind me, and I turned, expecting to see Felix rolling his eyes at this silly display, but I screeched when I saw Bennett and Ollie.

I threw my arms around them. "What are you doing here?"

"Dancing with my wife," Bennett said, pulling Ollie back toward him.

I opened my mouth to ask more questions, but my dance partner tapped my shoulder and I turned again, recognizing that the song was "Marry You" by Bruno Mars and the shoulder tap hadn't come from Greta but from Felix, who looked at me with a raised eyebrow, and I laughed.

"What's going on?"

I shrugged. "I have no idea. Ben and Ollie are here, though!"

"Cool," he said, looking around, and then he took my hand, spinning me to the beat of the song. I caught a quick glance of Bennett and Ollie, and of Greta, who'd found a nearby businessman to twirl her around the unplanned dance floor. I ended the spin against Felix, my hand on his chest, mid-laugh. Our eyes met and I pulled his face down to kiss him.

"Thank you for dancing with me."

"I didn't want you to have to dance alone." The chorus of the song kicked up as we swayed together after the kiss. I loved kissing Felix. It wasn't like kissing anyone else, and I thought about the chocolates in my bag. "I want to ask you something tonight," I said. "When we get to the hotel."

"Okay," he said, body bouncing to the beat with mine. "The song's almost over."

"Just drinking coffee during the rest of the delay is going to be a real letdown," I joked.

"I didn't get the coffee," he said, spinning with me.

"Line too long?"

"No." He bit his lower lip and sank to one knee as the song and crowd swirled around us. It was like being in the middle of everyone and being in this private bubble, too. The title lyrics from the song played, and he didn't say anything for a moment.

"You hate this stuff," I said, holding a hand to my mouth.

"I hate this stuff," he confirmed, holding my hand in his as he reached into his pocket. "But you love it." Felix held out a ring in a beautiful combination of rubies and diamonds that caught the light. "And I love you."

"You planned this?"

"Ollie helped. Glad people danced or this would have been awkward."

I fell to my knees in front of him and wrapped my arms around him. "I was going to ask you tonight alone in our room," I said, tears filling my eyes.

"Is that a yes?"

I laughed through my tears and nodded as he slipped the ring on my finger. "I can't believe you did this."

"I brought a copy of Simmons's paper to read aloud if the dance party didn't take off," he said, pulling me to him.

"Read that to me later," I said before pressing my lips to his, back in the airport where everything started, and things for us would never be the same again.

The
Sweetest
Connection

For Brian and Matt. Every person should have phenomenally kind, supportive, and funny friends who can also rock sweater-vests or no-veto you into a nine-hour bus tour of Manhattan.

1

Video Chat

SEVEN YEARS AGO
A FRIDAY

FACILITATOR: Welcome, everyone! We're so excited to have all these amazing leaders join us from colleges across the state for this leadership conference. Because of the bad weather, we're doing this virtually. We know it's new for everyone, but we appreciate you joining us from your computers. First, we're going to send you into breakout rooms to meet the person you'll be paired with for the rest of the weekend. Instructions are in the chat, and we'll see you back here in five minutes.

You've been added to breakout room twenty-seven

Silas: Hey

Silas: I think you're muted.

Teagan: Sorry! It's so weird to talk via a video call. Not sure I'd ever get used to this.

Silas: Yeah, I guess new technology.

Teagan: Anyway, hi! I'm Teagan, she/her, and I'm a freshman at State.

Silas: Hey, I'm Silas. Um, he/him, and I'm a freshman, too. I go to Thurmond.

Teagan: Looks like you're my buddy for the weekend. We're supposed to . . . let's see, introduce ourselves and play two truths and a lie. Are you a good liar, Silas?

Silas: *(Laughs)* No. I don't think I've ever been able to keep anything from anyone.

Teagan: I can hide things for years. Stick with me.

Silas: Okay. You go first, then.

Teagan: Let's see . . . Are you watching my face closely to see if I give anything away?

Silas: Intently.

Teagan: Okay. I love to travel. I want to write mysteries. My favorite color is pink.

Silas: Hmm . . . I think the first is the lie.

Teagan: Wrong! I mean, I haven't gone anywhere really cool yet, but if there's a chance to get on a plane, I'm there. And I hate pink. There is nothing pink in my wardrobe, and as far as I'm concerned, there never will be. It's the worst color.

Silas: I guess I wasn't watching your face close enough.

Teagan: What about you?

Silas: Umm . . . I love candy, I speak French, and I'm afraid of spiders.

Teagan: I think . . .

Teagan: You don't speak French.

Silas: Not a word. How did you guess?

Teagan: I can just read you. We'll have to spend more time together so you learn to read me, too.

Silas: We should have a lot of time to figure it out during the conference.

Breakout will end in thirty seconds

Teagan: Oh, we're going to be best friends, at least for the next two days.

2

Silas

PRESENT DAY
SATURDAY

THE WOMAN'S PHONE crackled with the voice on the other end and she held it away from her face, pushing down the neck pillow clinging to her scrunched cheeks. In my opinion, using speaker-phone in a crowded setting was tantamount to public indecency, only this drew more annoyed glances than walking through the terminal pantsless might. Her tie-dyed T-shirt read TEQUILA MADE ME DO IT, and she had the unmistakable look of someone who had been pushed a few inches past her threshold for patience. The voice from the other end of her call erupted again. "What the hell is taking so long?"

"I'm stuck in the damn airport and if one more airline employee son of a b—"

"Good afternoon," I said with a smile, interrupting and pretending I hadn't heard every word of her conversation from three feet away. "How can I help you?"

"You could get me out of this damn airport, for starters." She thrust her crumpled boarding pass over the counter, disdain and frustration rolling off her in waves.

I was mostly immune to that after working in customer service for the airline for a few years. "I'm sorry your travel plans have been interrupted," I said, entering her information into the computer. Over her shoulder, Teagan shot me a wry grin from across the hall in the entrance of the candy store where she worked, and I ignored the impulse to shoot my best friend a sideways smile.

"You should be sorry," she said with a harrumph. Her posture and the set of her jaw conveyed that it was my fault the storm had knocked out flights through New York. "I don't know how the planes ever take off with this level of incompetence in the—"

"I'll get you rerouted to Boston," I interjected with a practiced but firm positivity. While I reassured her, I pulled the basket of individually wrapped candy from under the counter. "Would you like a chocolate truffle while you wait? They're from the shop across the way and they're quite good. The ingredients are listed there."

You would have thought I offered her a cigarette or Henry Cavill's phone number from the way her expression softened immediately. "Well, thank you," she said, popping the candy into her mouth. Teagan knew I only pulled out the basket for certain customers, and in my peripheral vision, she chuckled.

"We know the delay is an inconvenience and appreciate your patience. I can get you into Boston by nine tonight, with a connection through Chicago. Is there anything else I can do for you?" She shook her head, chewing on the candy, and I returned her nod as I handed her the new documents. "Have a nice day."

Still chewing, she nodded, gave me a wave, and walked off, as the person on the phone interrupted the silence with "Are you still there?"

"I don't know why you give them candy," James said. He hadn't been on the job long, and I didn't think he'd make it; maybe I just didn't want him to. He flirted with Teagan a lot, and he wasn't a bad guy, but it still bugged me. "Does it make them less angry or something?"

Teagan waved and walked back to the counter of the shop, tugging on the pink apron she despised, but Julianna, the shop's owner, insisted all staff wear it. The first thing I ever learned about Teagan was that she hated pink. She'd told me during that first video chat when we were freshmen in college seven years earlier. I hadn't even wanted to attend the conference, but my adviser convinced me, saying it would help me broaden my horizons. Joke was on her—I met Teagan, who quickly became one of the only stars in my sky. James was still staring at me expectantly, and I tucked the basket back under the counter. "Nah. It stops them from talking."

James laughed, pressing his hand to his stomach. "Seriously?"

I shrugged. "That caramel is really thick." I didn't give them to everybody, and I happened to have a hookup with a discount at the candy place. It was worth it to cut off angry people's rage midsentence, and though it usually stopped them from talking, it had the pleasant side effect of sometimes making an angry customer's day a little brighter. "Usually works."

James clapped me on the back, pulling my attention back from the shop. "You're a genius, man. I'll stop over there and pick up a couple before my next shift when we're expecting weather delays. You think your girl would hook me up?"

Teagan was leaning over the counter handing a customer something, and the woman's face lit up. It was their new raspberry and pistachio truffles. She insisted they were my favorites, so she'd bring them over to my apartment all the time, but she'd end up eating half of them. I didn't really mind—she'd been suggesting new candy options to Julianna for years and this was the first one the older woman had decided to try. They were good. Teagan was back in school studying writing, but I told her she'd missed her calling as a candymaker.

"You know, your *girl*," he said, nudging me with his elbow before stepping up to the counter as a family approached.

"Teagan." I tapped at the screen, updating the information. "She's just my friend, though. Not my girl." I'd made sure that was the case years before, and my hackles rose at the idea of James and her together.

"Yeah," he said, his gaze wandering back across the concourse. "She's single, right?"

We'd been mobbed for more than an hour, and now it was quiet at the service counter. I almost wished neck-pillow woman would come back to complain about her flight to Chicago. "She's single. She's leaving the country in a few days, though." *A week from today.*

"I remember her mentioning that." James leaned toward me, his voice pitched low lest our manager pop in out of nowhere and get on us about personal conversations behind the service counter. It wouldn't happen. Our manager, as far as I could tell, had been taking only brief breaks from his napping schedule for the last decade.

"Yeah, she's back in school to finish her degree and doing a semester abroad." France, with long trips to Ireland, England, Spain, and Prague planned. She'd gone over the itinerary and her hopes for side trips at length for months, and there was a map hung in her apartment over the bed.

"Erin must be excited to get more of your time," he said, returning to his own station. "I mean, that's one cool girlfriend to be down with you spending so much time with another woman."

Before I had to answer, Ada interrupted. "Afternoon, boys." She strode toward us and we both returned her greeting. Ada left the operations office and took a walk through the terminal every day she worked, saying she needed to get out of her office and stretch her legs. "Silas, isn't this your day off?"

"This guy can't manage to leave work, ma'am. He picked up shifts from a coworker with a sick kid," James said. I glanced over

Ada's shoulder at the candy shop. My coworker had needed someone to cover, but I'd also wanted to be where Teagan was as much as I could this week.

I shrugged. "What can I say, I can't get enough of this guy." I clapped James on the shoulder and earned a laugh from Ada. "What about you?"

Ada was probably in her mid-fifties, with a smoker's voice and wide smile.

"Looking for my walking buddy," she said, looking around. "I can usually find him lingering near that candy shop if he's on a break." She glanced behind her and I followed her gaze to Teagan. "Guess I'm on my own today. Later!" She waved and walked down the corridor. We didn't see a lot of the central office staff, but Ada was a favorite of mine.

"She's funny," James said, returning to his work, and I hoped he'd drop the Erin and Teagan thing.

Luckily, a large group all in matching T-shirts that read MILTON FAMILY REUNION approached the counter at once and I was saved from having to respond to James while we tried to get thirty people to Akron. Erin's reactions to Teagan and vice versa had left me in too many awkward corners already; I didn't need to seek them out when neither woman was around.

3

Teagan

I SMOOTHED DOWN the front of the god-awful pink apron and checked my watch. The amount of time until the end of my shift hadn't really changed from when I'd looked thirty seconds earlier. I'd never imagined a pink apron when I used to think about being in my mid-twenties, but I was finally getting my life back on the track I'd planned on. I was back in school, about to take the trip of my dreams, and hoping to ditch the apron permanently very soon.

"Don't let Julianna catch you checking your watch like that." Martin leaned on the handle of the push broom he was carrying, smiling like he was preparing to tell me a joke. I loved Martin, one of the members of the custodial staff. He'd been in the airport even longer than Julianna and was like a fixture. He had great stories about all the unbelievable things he'd seen over the years.

"Hey." I glanced around and then handed him one of his favorite dark chocolate truffles coated in coconut. He was the only person I gave freebies to besides Silas, but I'd learned his favorite from Julianna, who, despite being a demon with a sweet tooth, couldn't resist Martin's charms any more than anyone else. "When are you going to let me write a story about you?"

He laughed, nodding in thanks for the candy. "So much to write. How'd a budding author like you end up working here?"

I shrugged. "I needed a job and Julianna was hiring." I'd been lucky to find a job at all—it had been a tough time to search, and I'd loved the idea of being so close to international travel, even if it was just watching other people take off. The job got a hundred times better two years later when Silas took the customer service job with the airline. Getting to know people like Martin made the gig a little sweeter, though.

He adjusted his belt. "Aren't you flying off to France to write stories? Why would you need mine?"

I cocked my head to the side and leaned toward him. "Don't act like you haven't gotten up to some stuff in this airport."

His big booming laugh made me instinctively try to catch Silas's eye. He said he always knew where Martin was because of that laugh, but a crowd of people swarmed his and James's counter. "You know I have, but you're too young to hear any of those stories. Julie would have my behind if I corrupted her young employees." He motioned toward the gates near us, where people were dancing. "You see the hullabaloo down there? Maybe they're having another dance party like that one on Valentine's Day. Never a dull moment." He glanced toward the gates. "I'm gonna go check it out. You want me to toss that?" He motioned to the other side of the shop where a slip of paper was on the floor.

"Nah. I'll get it. We were rearranging some things, might have fallen out of a box."

"I'll report back if the hullabaloo is anything interesting." He shook his hips as he walked out and called over his shoulder. "Just might cut a rug myself."

I waved and wiped my hands again before walking to pick up the paper. I was hungry for something exciting, anything to break up the monotony of my days. I wasn't in any classes until my trip, so I went to work and sold candy, which wasn't a bad job, but I was so tired of standing still. The thing about working in an airport was you were constantly seeing new people, but it still often felt like seeing the same people day in and day out. People who were going somewhere else and seeing somewhere new. I couldn't wait to be one of them. When we weren't too busy, I loved to learn where people were going and imagine going there, too.

I had a to-do list a mile long to get ready for my trip, including cleaning out the fridge and scrubbing the bathroom of my apartment, and I ticked off the items in my head as I picked up the sheet of paper. It was a printout from an email, though the address wasn't visible, and I gave it a quick glance, ready to throw it in the trash and check my watch again.

Before I tossed it, the headers caught my eye. "Pros." Then "Cons."

PROS

- She's my best friend.

- Seeing her is the best thing about working here.

- I could listen to her stories for hours.

- I'm in love with her. I think I always have been.

CONS

- If I lost her, I don't know what I'd do.

- I'd have to see her in the terminal all the time if it didn't work out.

- She doesn't know I'm in love with her, and it might be too late to tell her.

Silas was leaning against the counter when I looked up, the light catching the metal on his name tag, and the dark blue of the lanyard around his neck stood out against his shirt. "You're not studying your itinerary again, are you? I know you have it memorized." He made fun of me for being so excited about my trip, but there was never real bite in it. He knew how much I wanted to travel, and now that I had a second chance, I was obsessed with being prepared to make the most of it. He was always reticent to tell me about his own travels, worried I'd be jealous he was able to go and I wasn't. "Or have you moved on to sketching out the next three trips?"

"Very funny," I said, setting the list on the counter. "What are you doing here?"

"Shift is over. Want to get dinner?" He scratched the side of his neck the way he did when he wanted something to do with his hands. Silas had nice hands, with neat nails and long tapered fingers.

"Won't Erin mind? We've had dinner together a few times this week already and her birthday is soon, right?" I liked Erin; I just didn't think she was particularly interesting enough for Silas. But I couldn't say that to him.

"It's today." He shrugged one well-developed shoulder and skirted my question. "But she's out of town and you're leaving in a week. Pizza? What's that?" He pointed to the list on the counter and I had a moment of panic wondering if I should hide it or play it off. Another wild hare tickled the back of my consciousness. *What if Silas wrote this?*

"I found it on the floor," I said, holding it away from him. "It's a pros and cons list."

"For what?" He made a grab for it anyway, his fingers sweeping it from my grip. *Damn him and his big hands.* "Hm," he said, reading through it as I searched his face for some flash of recognition even though I knew not to expect one. "I wonder what the person was deciding to do."

"Kind of sounds like telling someone how they feel or maybe starting a relationship?" I took the paper back, drawn in by the words. "I don't know. You think it's someone who works here?"

He shrugged again. "Dunno. Pizza tonight?"

"Si, why aren't you interested in this?" I swatted at his arm. "It's a mystery."

"It's . . . trash."

I rolled my eyes, smiling at a couple lingering near the entrance who then decided to walk on. "I blame Erin if you are this unmoved by a potential love story." My brain was waving hands wildly at my mouth, the universal sign to indicate "Stop talking. What is wrong with you?" I rarely listened to my brain in those moments.

"It's not a love story; it's someone's discarded decision-making tool." Silas swatted at my arm as I had his and tried to grab the paper out of my hands, but I snapped it back.

"It's the *possibility* of a love story. What if someone dropped this and they have to make this decision soon? What if their happily ever after is hanging in the balance?"

His brown eyes narrowed, those brows that had no business looking as manicured as they did furrowed. "The list isn't that long. I'd hope they could re-create it or work from memory."

"You're missing the point," I said, tucking the paper into my apron.

"The point being you're nosy and bored?"

I leaned on the counter, catching the clock out of the corner of my eye. My shift was almost over. "What if you had to make some critical decision about the woman you loved and you were talking yourself into the right decision, then lost this?"

"That doesn't sound like me." He handed me a stick of gum from his pocket. Julianna didn't let us chew it in the shop and I always craved something minty at the end of my shift.

"Humor me. Maybe this person is taking losing this list as a sign from the universe that they shouldn't act on their feelings."

"Teag, I really think you're reading too much into this."

I met his stare head-on, lifting one of my much less impressive eyebrows. "I'm invoking the no-veto rule."

Silas stilled, his lips parting. Damn those full lips. "The no-veto rule . . . for this?"

The summer after sophomore year, we'd gone on a road trip through the Midwest. At the time, it felt like a grand adventure, but mostly it was cheap motels and an inordinate amount of gas station snacks as we took in the world's largest, oldest, best, et cetera. It was the best and worst days of our friendship, and we'd created the no-veto rule. Each of us got to choose one thing we both had to do, and the other couldn't say no. We kept it going, each year the clock resetting and each of us getting one new no-veto card to play. Over the years, he'd made me do *Star Wars* cosplay, eat octopus, and spend Thanksgiving with him and Erin. I'd made him take a nine-hour bus tour of Manhattan, watch the entirety of *Gossip Girl*, and go skinny-dipping. I'd been grossed out by the octopus and he'd considered never talking to me again when we almost got caught skinny-dipping, but we always had fun whatever we were doing together.

Silas sighed and held out his hand. "Okay. This is low stakes for no-veto, but let me see it again."

"And pizza sounds great," I said, beaming and tapping his nose with my fingertip. "Extra pepperoni."

"Like you had to specify."

Four

Video Call

SIX YEARS AGO
A SATURDAY

Teagan: So, what happened?

Teagan: A shrug doesn't tell me anything.

Silas: She dumped me. She wasn't happy, and "kissing me had become like kissing her brother."

Teagan: Ouch. I know you really liked her. Want me to drive out there and egg her car?

Silas: I don't think the petty vandalism is worth the three-hour drive.

Teagan: Says you. I love petty vandalism. And breaking my friend's heart is not a petty offense.

Silas: Save the eggs for an omelet.

Teagan: I never learned how to make one. So, how are you doing?

Silas: We were good friends since high school. We never should have dated in the first place.

Teagan: Are you sure you don't want me to pick up some eggs?

Silas: *(Laughing)* I'm sure. I don't get the sense we'll be talking anymore. Just remind me to never date a friend again, okay?

Teagan: Okay. I mean, there will be a point when you find me irresistible, but I'll remind you.

Silas: The first night we met in person, I held your hair while you threw up cheap beer and whipped cream. I think we're safe.

Teagan: That was a fun party.

Silas: If by fun you mean loud and out of control.

Teagan: I did mean that when I said fun. So, I was thinking . . .

Silas: Uh-oh.

Teagan: It's not a bad thing.

Silas: What is it?

Teagan: There's this study abroad program that has connections with both our campuses. Do you want to go to France with me next spring?

Silas: I don't speak French.

Teagan: I remember, but the program instruction is all in English and we'd have almost a year to learn some French.

Silas: I don't know . . .

Teagan: Think about it—we'd get to spend five months

together, and we've lived three hours apart since becoming best friends.

Silas: Since you decreed we were best friends.

Teagan: And I was right about that, so I'm probably right about France.

Teagan: Just think about it!

5

Silas

PRESENT DAY
SUNDAY

I OPENED MY eyes slowly, my face warmed by the sunlight from
the open window. I had an alarm set, but I usually woke ahead of it,
like my body knew the sun was up and it was time to go. I still
braced for the loud chirping of Erin's alarm, which she'd snooze and
then silence again seven minutes later. This time it was only the
heavy breathing of my best friend asleep on the other side of my bed.
I'd told her once she snored and she'd insisted it was just normal
breathing. Teagan's normal breathing shook the walls, and it was
one of my favorite sounds.

I rolled to find her sprawled over my comforter, her worn T-shirt
riding up to reveal a sliver of her lower back. As soon as I realized I
was thinking about how warm and soft her tanned skin would feel
beneath my fingers, I climbed out of bed to walk away. I didn't need
to be thinking about the skin on Teag's back, and I scrubbed my
palms down my face as I walked to the bathroom. We'd both passed
out on the most uncomfortable couch on the planet the night before,
and I'd told her to crash with me in the bed instead of driving home
at three in the morning or waking up to a sore back. We'd started
watching a movie after pizza and both fallen asleep after dissecting

the pros and cons list she was so interested in. I still didn't understand, especially her making it a no-veto pick. She was leaving the country, leaving me for months, and I figured there'd be something bigger, more significant, for her to use the rule on.

When I returned from the bathroom, she was stirring, sliding back and forth on the pillow the way she did when she didn't want to wake up.

"C'mon, sleeping beauty," I said, swatting at her calf peeking out from under the blanket. "Rise and shine."

"Sorry," she said, rubbing her eyes and pushing her hair off her face. "I didn't mean to fall asleep. Why didn't you boot me out?"

I pulled boxers and a T-shirt from my dresser, my uniform already pressed and hanging in my closet. "Because it is physically impossible to wake you up. I tried once and you kicked me in the groin. You sleep like an ogre."

Teagan grinned, knowing it was true. "Still, you could have rolled me onto the floor. Your girlfriend will not appreciate me sleeping over."

I glanced back into the drawer, pretending to search for socks. "It's not a big deal." I didn't want to talk about Erin, not with Teagan, and not really at all. "What time do you have to be in today?"

She rolled off my bed and walked toward the bathroom door. "Not until this afternoon. I want to take another stab at that last French language lesson. I can't believe I remember so little from college." She pulled her phone from her pocket and tapped away. "And . . . *et nous avons un mystère à résoudre!*"

"I never spoke French very well, Teag." I shut the drawer, casting a glance at the list I'd pulled from her sleeping fingers and set on the nightstand.

She called over her shoulder before closing the door. "We have a mystery to solve!"

I rolled my eyes and set my things on the dresser, wandering over to the list and the handwritten notes she'd scribbled the night before of potential list writers, staff who might have been near the candy shop, and a game plan for figuring it out. She was going to talk to Julianna first, which I would have paid money to see. I didn't know the shop's owner well, but if anyone could be described as severe, it was her. She was like a cross between the personality of Ursula the Sea Witch and the face of Mary Berry from *The Great British Bake Off*, and I couldn't think of anyone less likely to inspire the kind of romantic angst reflected in that list. I reread the beginning of the last item. *She doesn't know I'm in love with her.*

Behind the closed door, Teagan was singing a Beyoncé song while washing her hands, her off-key voice coming through the closed door, and my chest tightened. She wasn't meant for me. I'd decided that a long time ago, and she was leaving the country so she didn't need to know what I had been thinking about. "My neighbors are going to complain about the noise," I said instead when she came out.

"Your neighbors love me." She pulled one of my hoodies from the closet and tossed it on the bed. "Well, maybe not love me. But the one really likes me."

Erin had introduced them at a party we threw the year before, saying she thought they'd be cute together despite my protestations. I'd finally agreed, swallowing the bile in my throat when they left the party together. "That one moved. The new neighbors are an older couple, so you'll have new people to charm."

She raised her eyes and laughed before pulling the shirt over her head, planning to wear it home without asking, the way only she would. "What if the letter is about Julianna? Can you imagine being in love with her?" She pushed the cuffs of the sleeves up.

"I can't, but I guess there's a lid for every pot."

She searched the floor for her shoes, which I'd set neatly next to her bag. "I used to tell you that and you didn't believe me. Julianna would need one hell of a lid." She spotted the shoes and fell onto the floor to tie them. "Anyway, it's too bad Erin had to be out of town for her birthday. Are you going to celebrate when she gets back?"

I gathered the stack of clothes, looking away. "Maybe." My chest tightened again, this time at the lie. Erin was out of town, but I only knew that because she'd told me it would be another few days before she could pick up the box of her things I'd found at my place. "I don't know. It's just a birthday. It doesn't really matter."

"Si, you need to be a better boyfriend. Maybe it matters to her."

I swallowed. It had mattered, and if we hadn't broken up a couple of months earlier, I would have paid attention to the day, gotten my girlfriend of several years flowers and presents. I would have thought about buying a ring and probably put it off again. Instead, we'd ended it, and she told me she didn't want to keep competing for my affections, knowing she'd never be the woman I loved more than Teagan.

"I brought this for Erin," she said, pulling a candy-shop box from her bag. "For her birthday. It's some of her favorites."

I opened it on instinct, and it was full of white chocolate options plus peanut brittle and gummy bears. "Ouch!" I pulled my hand back when she smacked it.

"Not for you," Teagan said. "Don't eat your girlfriend's birthday present, you sugar fiend." She stood from her cross-legged pose and tossed her bag over one shoulder. "I'll get out of here so you can get ready." She swiped the list off the nightstand. "And I'll let you know what Julianna says."

"*Au revoir,*" I said with a wave.

"Hey, that's my line!" She blew a kiss and trounced out of the room, probably en route to my kitchen to make coffee before leaving, but I felt her absence immediately. It was a relief. Since Erin had left, I'd been worried I'd let too many things spill. It was right to break up. She wasn't the one I was in love with. Trouble was, the woman

I was in love with was in my kitchen making coffee and a mess, and there was nothing I could do about my feelings because that ship had sailed the day I reaffirmed having my best friend was more important than entertaining a what-if. Thinking about more than friendship wasn't an option. No mystery there.

6

Teagan

JULIANNA LOOKED UP from the paperwork in front of her when I walked into the shop. Her silver-streaked hair was short and pushed off her face with a soft headband. The combination of soft pinks and purples in her outfit might have made her look grandmotherly, but it was a ruse. "You're early. That's a first."

I nodded. "Well, I'm here." I straightened the boxes of chocolates on a shelf nearby and strode behind the counter, plucking the pink apron from the hook inside the back room. "I wanted to ask you something, if you have a few minutes."

"You can't take any time off. I know you're leaving in a few days, but I can't just be giving people time off to prepare to gallivant around the world as a creative writer. You're already leaving me in the lurch." She hadn't looked back up at me yet somehow communicated complete disdain through her posture. I'd told her about the trip months earlier, as soon as I found out I could go, but I ignored her tone.

"I'll work all my shifts." I settled next to her behind the counter. I'd actually picked up more shifts this week to make a little more money for the trip. Working every day was a lot, but it was worth it to squeeze in a little more money. "Could I ask you a personal question, though?"

Julianna signed something with a flourish and then stacked the papers. "I can't guess why you'd want to, but fine."

I tried to imagine someone besotted with the woman in front of me, toiling over a pros and cons list about wooing her, and I came up empty. "Are you dating someone?"

Her eyes narrowed slightly, not in her normal derision but like she was trying to tease out my hidden meaning, before she laughed, a genuine belly laugh. "Why on earth would you ask that?"

I hadn't expected the humor, the delight in me asking that question. I could have pulled the list from my bag, but I paused. If I showed it to her, she'd tell me it was trash like Silas had. It was trash, but I didn't want to let it go. I was saved from having to answer when a customer entered and I helped them decide between three kinds of truffles. My answer was always to just get all three and try a few more because who didn't need more chocolate, but apparently others had more restraint than me. Candy was the one thing Silas had no restraint around. He never bought it himself, but when I'd bring some over to his place or with us to a movie, he was a man on a mission to eat it. When I first told him I'd gotten the job here, after I had to leave school, his eyes lit up like a kid's on Christmas morning. Total sweet tooth.

By the time I'd finished with the customer, who finally decided on one white chocolate cookie butter truffle and one dark chocolate espresso for their flight, Julianna was gathering her things to leave. "So, not seeing anyone, then?" I asked, peeking my head into the office.

"Girl, why are you asking? Is this for one of your stories or something?"

I bit my lower lip. "No, just heard about a budding relationship between staff in the terminal. I thought maybe it might be your love story."

She hoisted the world's largest purse onto her shoulder and grazed a hand over the desk. "Gossip. It's probably one of those annoying pet-grooming women, who treat this place like their personal dating show." She checked her watch. "Ask Martin. He always knows all the rumors. Gossips like an old hen, too. If there's something going on, he'd know."

"Okay, thanks." I smoothed down the apron and clocked in for my shift on the computer, entering my employee code. "I'll ask him." I glanced at the customer service counter across the way. Silas wasn't there but James was, and he caught my eye and waved. James was cute and a nice guy, but it was always hard to pay attention to him when Silas was nearby.

Alone in the shop once Julianna left, I texted an update.

> **TEAGAN:** Not Julianna.
>
> **SILAS:** Not surprised.
>
> **TEAGAN:** She said to talk to Martin.
>
> **TEAGAN:** Where are you? I can only see James.
>
> **SILAS:** Stalker much?

He walked into the shop, all long legs and easy strides, pushing his copper-colored hair back off his forehead. "I was on my break." He set a notebook down on the counter between us. "I started this." Since I had met Silas over a video call, I'd been surprised months later when we met in person and I saw his full height. I'd seen his photos on social media, but I still wasn't prepared for the size of him.

I took the notebook, reading through the list of people quickly. "You made a list of suspects?"

Silas scratched the back of his neck and shrugged. It was the thing he did when he wanted to play something off like it wasn't a big deal. He'd always done it, like when he'd told off a drunk guy who wouldn't leave me alone at a bar, or when he'd changed my tire when I went to visit him for a weekend in college, or after that night we'd never seemed to fully get past. "You seem to care about figuring this out, and we only have a few days. There aren't that many people, but maybe it's a start," he said, motioning to the list and then picking up a toothpick from our free sample tray.

"They're chocolate-and-caramel-dipped crispy rice treats," I said as he examined it. "They might be good for your difficult customers in the future."

Silas didn't respond as he chewed the sample, and I laughed at his yummy noises, pushing forward with the task at hand. "Jess at the pet-grooming place," I said, reading the first name. "I love her. She's divorced, so maybe this is a second chance! Ooh, I want this to be her epic love story."

Silas chuckled. "You would."

"Why is everyone so cynical? I asked Julianna if she was seeing someone and she reacted like I'd been practicing a stand-up set."

"I think it's just that you believe in love stories more than most people." He took back the notebook, turning it on the counter and reading his own notes. "That's not a bad thing. It's why you're such a good writer. You look for stories."

I toyed with the corner of the page, our fingers brushing briefly, the spark I'd been feeling for longer than I could remember lingering under my skin as it always did when we touched. "I know life isn't a fairy tale or a rom-com, but imagine there being one person you're meant to be with no matter the obstacles, no matter the cons on the list. It would be nice to live in that world."

He didn't look up. "Sometimes the cons on the list are what we should pay attention to."

"Yeah," I said, pushing thoughts of him and Erin from my head. "Anyway, Jess is a start. Who is Ada?"

"Works with operations. She takes a walk through here every day and has talked about her walking buddy. I don't know his name, but he's in security and she seems kind of into him. She said he comes in here sometimes."

I nodded, scanning his list. "This is great, Si."

He shrugged again. "Well, if we're going to make sure love wins out, we have to get going." He nodded toward James. "I gotta get back."

I was excited about my trip, more excited than I'd been in years, but he kept reminding me I was leaving, and the distance it would put between us made me a little sad. I had a fantasy that he went with me. The first time around, we'd always planned to do it together.

7

Phone Call

FIVE YEARS AGO
A SUNDAY

(BUZZING)

Teagan: You're the only twenty-year-old who still calls anyone.

Silas: I'm sure I'm not the only one.

Teagan: Even my grandma texts me at this point.

Silas: Well, I'm driving. Leave me alone. What are you doing?

Teagan: Packing. I can't get this damn suitcase to close!

Silas: Packing for what?

Teagan: Um, our study abroad trip to France. You know, the semester-long excursion we've been planning for months?

Silas: The excursion that we leave for in over a month?

Teagan: I needed a practice run to see if it will all fit.

Silas: Of course. Packing usually requires rehearsal. I'm guessing it doesn't all fit?

Teagan: I'm going to hang up on you.

Silas: No, you won't. What did you overpack? Notebooks? You don't need that many. They sell paper over there.

Teagan: What if I'm walking down the boulevard de la Croix-Rousse and I'm struck with inspiration but I don't have my favorite notebook with me because I had to make room for underwear?

Silas: So, does that mean you're currently deciding between packing notebooks and going commando across Europe?

Teagan: You're funny, Si. Do I ever tell you that?

Silas: Not enough. I'll make you a deal. You can pack a few notebooks in my suitcase if you promise to take underwear with you.

Teagan: This is why you're single. *C'mon, you stupid thing. Zip!*

Teagan: Don't laugh at me.

Silas: I can't help it.

Silas: And I'm single because I spend all my time wrangling my best friend to make sure she's not going to flash her creative writing professor.

Teagan: I would totally flash my creative writing professor. He's hot! And your standards are too high.

Teagan: *Yes! Got it! It zipped!*

(The sound of a car blinker in the background)

Silas: Having standards isn't the same as them being too high.

Teagan: I'm just saying, maybe you should worry about some other woman's underwear. Or what's inside them. You might meet the girl of your dreams and then you could call her on the phone like an old man instead of calling me.

Silas: Yeah, yeah, yeah.

Teagan: *Yeah. Yeah. Yeah.* What kind of a friend am I if I don't do my best to get you laid and find you love?

Silas: I'm not interested in finding love.

Teagan: Ah, but you are interested in getting laid. See, Si, this is why you have me around. There's a lid for every pot, but I'll shift my focus from you falling in love to you falling into bed.

Silas: Great, does that mean you're changing your no-veto so we don't have to go look at the Pont des Arts in Paris and can instead go to a club?

Teagan: Never! Literal tons of padlocks affixed to the bridge by couples in love? I would never miss that.

Silas: You're not going to find some French dude to fall in love with just so you can add a padlock, are you?

Teagan: Here's hoping. I think I could be pretty good at falling in love in French. *L'amour. C'est grand.*

8

Silas

**PRESENT DAY
MONDAY**

JAMES HELD UP a hand, indicating he was taking his break, and I nodded, moving my hips along with the hold music while I waited for the agent to get back to me. The song wasn't exactly a bop, but the longer you listened to it, the easier it was to imagine it wouldn't be bad with a better bass line. Teagan made fun of my dancing, especially when I started trying the dance trends on TikTok. She still joined me sometimes, usually both of us laughing too hard to finish the video. I saved them all, though, and would rewatch sometimes when I couldn't fall asleep.

Martin approached, sweeping the area on the other side of the counter.

"Morning," I said, holding the phone with my shoulder.

"And a beautiful one at that," Martin said, leaning on his broom. "It's kind of quiet today." He glanced around the mostly empty terminal, the relative quiet promising an onslaught of people at any moment.

I looked across the hall at the candy shop. I couldn't see Teagan, but I glanced back at Martin. "I have a weird question for you, if you have a minute."

"Always have a minute for a weird question." He leaned an elbow on the counter and he smiled under his bushy mustache. "Hit
me, but I bet I might know what's coming and my answer will be
yes."

I cocked my head to the side, curious, but asked anyway. "Do
you know of any budding relationships between staff? Probably
someone who would be around this part of the terminal?"

He straightened. "Well," he said with a laugh. "That was not the
question I was expectin' to ask."

"Yeah, I know. It's for Teagan, really." I motioned across the hall.

"Oh, well . . . that maybe makes more sense." He held his chin
in his hand and stroked the short beard. "Why does she want to
know about couples?"

"It's a long story involving a love letter. She roped me into it. I
just figured if anyone would know, you would." I'd never been particularly self-conscious, but I felt like a preteen, standing next to
Martin asking what felt like a very dumb question.

"Let me think . . . there's two kids who work in the coffee place
who I've seen making eyes at each other, and between you, me, and
the counter, I think Jess at the dog groomers might be interested in
the owner of that new luggage store on the D concourse, or he might
be interested in her. I've seen them together, but I don't know for
sure."

I jotted down the notes next to the short list I'd already made for
Teagan, circling Jess's name. "Thanks, Martin."

"I mean, then there's the other obvious one."

"Obvious one?" The hold music still played in my ear.

Martin grinned like he had some good information. "I'd say
pretty obvious."

"Want to share?"

"Boy, anyone with two eyes and a few minutes of spare time
could see you're in love with our sweet Miss Teagan over there." He

nodded toward the shop without looking and I checked over his shoulder on instinct, making sure she didn't see us.

"We're just friends."

"Yeah," he said, laughing and pushing the broom again. "I have friends, and I ain't never looked at them like you look at her." He tipped his head. "Well maybe a few of them, but only because I'd hoped we might be more than friends. I figured you were going to ask me if I thought you should make a move."

The hold music suddenly stopped, half a second before the anticipated beat drop, and I was left with a dead line. "Damn it," I muttered, setting the handset back in the cradle.

"For the record, I would have said yes, 'cause she looks to be in love with you, too." He shrugged. "Just one old man's opinion, of course."

"We're just friends," I repeated, glancing over his shoulder again and wondering what he saw on my face when I looked at Teagan and if she saw it, too. "Wouldn't risk a great friendship for a chance at something more."

"Why the hell not?" Martin held up a hand. "I know times are different, but where's your courage, man? I've loved three people. One I married, one turned me down, and I hope one will eventually cave to my charms." He rapped his knuckles on the counter twice. "The good stuff comes with risk."

Teagan reappeared from the back office in the candy store and flashed me a smile from behind the counter.

"Ah, see?" Martin raised his eyebrows. "Your whole face just lit up. I bet you caught a glimpse of her." He laughed to himself and began sweeping past me toward the next area. "Act like I can't tell what's plain on your face. C'mon, now." He waved as he left, chuckling to himself.

I scratched the back of my neck and scanned the monitor screen, my face feeling roughly two hundred degrees, and I was glad James had stepped away. Unbidden, the memory of Teagan's lips on mine slammed into me. I let myself look up and take in her expression as she helped a customer. If I was honest, the memory didn't slam into me so much as remind me it was there, like it did all the time. We'd gotten through the fallout of that kiss, but it almost destroyed our relationship. How I felt about her now was just something I had to ignore or get over because I would never risk that again.

"Hey, I'm back!" James stepped behind the counter next to me, interrupting the memory.

"Hey. Didn't miss much." I glanced down the hall after Martin. I had the notes in front of me and knew Teagan would be excited for me to share what I'd learned. I pushed the memory of the kiss out of my head and intentionally did not look into the candy store as I got back to work. If Martin knew, then she might suspect, too. It was why I hadn't told her I'd ended things with Erin. She was really the only person I spent time with, and if I really lost her, I'd be lost.

Jess and the baristas at the coffee shop. Maybe that's where we'd start. I tapped at my keyboard and attempted my call again. If solving the mystery made her happy and distracted me, maybe that was the best possible outcome I could hope for.

9

Teagan

I WALKED THROUGH the parking garage, going through checklists in my head. It was hard to believe my trip was coming up so soon. I'd been up since seven that morning, running errands and generally freaking out. I didn't remember feeling this frantic about leaving the last time, but I'd been younger and life had been a little easier. I stepped to the left to give a wide pickup truck the berth to pull around and tripped on a bit of uneven pavement. The truck near me caught my fall, and as I twirled to get my hand off it lest I set off a car alarm, I spotted Jess from the grooming place walking ahead of me.

For some reason, Julianna didn't get along with Jess or her business partner, but I thought both women were kind of sweet. I guessed Jess was in her late thirties or early forties, and she reminded me a little of my mom when I was a kid—all soft curves and long legs. I hoped the letter was about her.

I started walking again, staying back because even if I didn't have sunglasses and a trench coat, if I was going to lean into solving a mystery, I was going to lean all the way in. I hadn't gotten to talk to Silas for long the day before. He'd left in a hurry when his shift was over, but he'd texted me what Martin said, and it felt serendipitous to follow Jess in from the parking garage, though I wasn't sure what I expected. I pulled out my phone.

> **TEAGAN:** Are you on your break? Jess is walking in front of me.

> **SILAS:** Wasn't there any other hobby you could pick up this week besides sleuthing? I don't know if I like this side of you.

> **TEAGAN:** Yes, you do.

> **SILAS:** Well, did you ask her if the note is about her?

> **TEAGAN:** I can't do that! If it's her, maybe she doesn't know.

I rolled my eyes instead of including the emoji. Silas thought this whole thing was silly, but he'd play along. He'd help because I asked him to, even though I hadn't explained all the reasons I wanted to figure this out before I left.

Watching Jess walk ahead, though, made me think about my mom, and about my parents. They'd weathered hard financial times when I was in college and after I dropped out, but they'd made it through. I loved my parents, but my mom had told me about the plans she had when she was young, how she'd take the world by storm, but then life happened, and she never saw her quiet home life as much of a storm. I promised myself I'd never set my dreams and plans aside for any man. And I hadn't. Unfortunately, so far that meant I hadn't gotten a love story, either.

I stepped out of the way again, letting two cars get through before I kept going, being more careful of the uneven concrete this time, part of that old conversation playing in my head.

Ahead of me, a lanky man stepped out of a car and called to Jess, and when she whipped around, a smile all but exploded on her face. *Jackpot.*

They chatted as he walked toward her. They didn't kiss or embrace, but he approached her eagerly, angling his body in a way that looked like he wanted to kiss her cheek or wrap an arm around her.

TEAGAN: They're so cute together.

SILAS: Doesn't your shift start in ten minutes?

I glanced at my watch. *Damn it!* I sped up and ended up at the elevator with Jess as the man slipped into the stairwell.

"Good morning," I said. The doors slid open just as I arrived, and I took it as a good sign from the universe.

"Morning," she said, hitting the button for us.

This is where my lack of planning bit me in the butt because I was always friendly with Jess, but we'd never had any substantial conversations that would let me casually, in the length of an elevator ride, find out if the man from the parking garage was secretly in love with her.

I said the first thing that came to my mind, and it wasn't my best work. "That guy you were talking to looks so familiar. Is he an actor or something? I swear I've seen him on TV."

Silas would have hung his head and laughed at my bald-faced, poorly acted lie, but I was fairly certain Jess didn't know me well enough to think I was being anything other than strange.

She gave me a curious expression and let out a small laugh. "I don't think he's ever acted. He just opened a luggage store on the D concourse."

"Must just be one of those faces," I said, racking my brain. I'd hoped for a little more information, like he just opened a luggage shop *and we kiss on the weekends*, but she hadn't tacked anything on. "That's cool, though. You two are friends?"

The doors opened with a *whoosh*, and her phone rang as we stepped off. She glanced at the screen with a grimace. "I need to take this, but yeah, we go way back." She stepped away and I waved, hurrying toward the shop and determined to fill in Silas as soon as I got the chance.

In the years since I'd started working in the airport, I'd had a few fantasies. One was the superhot TSA agent giving me a very thorough pat down and the other was a faster way to get through security to get to work. As I took notice of said hot TSA agent two lanes over, I realized the odds of either happening were about the same. I tapped my foot and waited in the line for staff. I'd really wasted time trailing Jess, but death, taxes, and the TSA were on no one else's timeline, so I followed the young woman in front of me with the bouncing ponytail and her friend who had dark hair. They looked familiar, and I listened to their easy banter about work. It sounded like they worked at one of the coffee kiosks.

I was in my head because now I immediately jumped to whether they were a couple and if one of them might be considering confessing their romantic feelings. Maybe Silas was right. I did look for love stories.

"Late for work?" Martin called out when he saw me power walking to the candy shop. "Julie's not going to be too happy about that."

"You're the only one who calls her that."

Martin shrugged. "Call it a perk of age."

"Perk of beauty," I said with a wink, hurrying by.

"You know, you're right," he said. "Tell her not to be too hard on ya."

"Would that work?" I called over my shoulder.

Martin laughed. "Nah. Can't imagine it would."

10

Teagan's Dorm Room

FIVE YEARS AGO
A MONDAY

(PHONE BUZZES)

Teagan: Shh! Will you turn that down? It's my mom.

(Phone buzzes)

Teagan: Hey, Mom. What's up? You're on speaker.

Mom: Hi, honey. Just checking in. Are you leaving for home soon?

Teagan: Yeah. Silas is here, and he's going to give me a ride on his way to his parents' place. We'll leave in a couple hours.

Mom: Hi, Silas!

Teagan: You're on speaker, Mom. You don't have to yell.

Silas: Hi, Mrs. Jones.

Mom: Don't underestimate me, young lady. Just because you're going to be traveling the world doesn't mean you know more than me.

Mom: Oh, hold on. Your dad just walked in.

Teagan: My mother just put me on hold.

Teagan: Why are you watching plane crash videos?

Silas: There's so many of them.

Teagan: You're afraid to fly. Stop it.

Silas: I'm not afraid.

Silas: Stop looking at me like that. I'm not *unduly* afraid. Look at this! There are legitimate reasons to be hesitant about flying.

Teagan: Do you want me to hold your hand during takeoff and landing?

Silas: You wouldn't hold my hand.

Teagan: Sure I would.

Silas: Hey, I was watching that.

Teagan: You're done watching it. What if my mom comes back on the line and just hears the audio of chaos and destruction? She'd be in her car and halfway here before you clicked the next "World's Most Dangerous Airport" videos.

Silas: What are you doing?

Teagan: I'm holding your hand. Here, close your eyes and imagine you're in a plane and you're freaking out.

Silas: I'm not going to be freaking out.

Teagan: But you can squeeze my hand like this if you do.

Silas: This is ridiculous.

Teagan: Squeeze, man!

Silas: Your hand is too small. I would crush it if I actually squeezed.

Teagan: I think you're giving yourself a little too much credit, but fine. This way with our fingers linked. You can still squeeze and you won't crush my hand with your Hulk Smash grip.

Silas: Hm.

Teagan: What?

Silas: It's . . . nice.

Teagan: Yeah? You feel less anxious?

Silas: I didn't feel—

Silas: Yeah, I do. Is that some kind of trick? Moving your thumb over mine like that?

Teagan: Oh, I, uh, didn't realize I was doing that. Sorry.

Silas: Don't be. It felt . . . good.

Teagan: I told you I'd take care of you. You should trust me.

Silas: . . . I do, Teag. I always have.

Teagan: Yeah?

Silas: Yeah.

Teagan: You have soft hands. Why are your hands so soft?

Silas: I . . . have no idea. Why are your hands soft?

Teagan: I moisturize on the off chance I have to walk a friend through a simulation of air travel.

Silas: What if . . .

Teagan: What?

Silas: Never mind. It doesn't matter. Did your mom forget about you?

Teagan: She'll be back eventually. What were you going to say?

Silas: Just . . .

Teagan: You just tightened your fingers around mine. Is it the flying? It's really going to be okay. I'll be with you the whole time.

Silas: No . . .

Silas: Teagan, what if—

(Click)

Mom: Teag? You there?

Teagan: Sorry, yeah, Mom. I'm here. Was just talking to Silas. Are you okay? You sound upset.

Teagan: No. You're not on speaker anymore.

Teagan: Oh my God!

Teagan: I'll be home tonight and we can talk, okay? I love you.

Teagan: Bye.

Silas: Are you okay?

Teagan: It's bad, I think.

Teagan: You don't need to keep holding my hand.

Silas: I know, but you can squeeze my fingers if you want to.

11

Silas

**PRESENT DAY
TUESDAY**

"DO YOU MISS the sweater-vest when you finish a shift?" Teagan ran a finger over my shoulder, which was covered in the synthetic fibers, and I ignored the flare of sensation that simple touch left on my skin when her hand trailed down my arm. We were walking toward the food court because I insisted she have Americanized Chinese food before leaving the country, and she would never turn down the offer when I was treating.

"I look good in the vest," I said, gently swatting at her hand and then adjusting my tie.

"I will admit, there aren't a lot of people who can really pull off this look, but I think you're one of them. Nerd chic suits you well."

I shot her a look. "When you hang with a former communications major and current deeply uncool adult, this is the best you get, my friend." The airport was buzzing, but we'd caught the food court at a decent time and the lines weren't atrocious. I nodded toward the place we were going to grab food. "Aren't you going to miss this?" I said, motioning to the window.

"Overpriced, inauthentic Chinese food? I'm guessing I'll be able to find that in Europe, but otherwise, no, I don't think I'll miss it."

She gave a little smile and I noticed the three freckles like a constellation across the bridge of her nose.

"Even the egg rolls?"

"Okay. Yeah." She nudged my shoulder with hers. "I'll miss those."

I didn't expect the lump to form in my throat at her words. I swallowed thickly, but I heard a familiar voice behind me and turned. Ada chatted amiably with her walking buddy behind us, a few inches closer to him than I thought I might walk with just a friend.

"Well, hello there!" Ada's warm voice was chipper. "Looks like we weren't the only ones craving fried food for lunch," she said to her buddy. I looked him up and down, a guy a little shorter than me with gray hair at his temples. He wore the security uniform and Ada grinned at him like he'd invented the fried food she was craving.

"Hey," I said. "Teagan, do you know Ada?"

Teagan held out her hand. "Nice to meet you." She pivoted to the man. "I know this guy, though!" They did a multistep handshake and the man's face cracked into a smile.

"Where's the pink apron?" His voice was deep like James Earl Jones's, and I weirdly felt like we were in some kind of competition for the affections of my friend.

Teagan cringed. "Don't remind me. Four more days and I am apron-free."

Ada glanced between them. "How do you two know each other?"

"She works in Julianna's shop," he said. "I can't resist those peanut butter cups."

"He's one of my best customers," Teagan added, turning to Ada. "I'll make sure he buys you some next time."

I watched Ada's smile turn girlish, her cheeks pink, and even though Teagan was the one who was supposed to notice these kinds of things, I saw the crush on her face, the clear adoration.

"I'll try to lock it in up here," he said, smiling down at Ada and tapping his temple. They held eye contact for a few moments and then he glanced at his watch. "I don't think I'll have time for egg rolls. Later this week, Ad? I gotta get back to my shift."

"Oh!" She looked at her own watch. "I didn't realize we'd been walking for so long. You're right." She stepped back along with the man, whose name I still hadn't caught. "Nice to see you kids."

I watched them walk away until Teagan tugged on my arm. "Oh my God, what if it's them!" She leaned in close and hissed, her eyes sparkling. "That would be so cute!"

"Why cute? They're like fifty."

She punched my arm and we stepped forward to order. "Don't be a jerk. Couples of all ages are cute!"

"I don't think they're a couple," I said, though I remembered the look on Ada's face.

"Not yet," Teagan said, and the lump in my throat returned as she ordered her favorite. She glanced over her shoulder at me. "I hope he buys her something sweet she loves. I would totally do that for a boyfriend."

I was about to remind her she did it for me all the time, but I closed my mouth and let her keep talking as we waited for our food.

"I feel like you can tell a lot about a person by their favorite candy. About how they are in a relationship."

I laughed. "Because you're such an expert?"

She elbowed me in the side. "More than you. Think about it. I know if someone picks a fun flavor combination, like whiskey chocolate or bacon and potato chip, they're probably a little adventurous." She ticked off her fingers. "And if they pick safe choices, like solid milk chocolate or white chocolate truffles, they're super reliable and steady. Like Erin," she added, and I bit my tongue again at the mention of my ex. "Olivia, the dog groomer. Do you know her husband always picks up his best friend's favorite chocolates for her whenever he flies to Chicago? How sweet is that? He's one of the reliables, too."

She talked faster when she got excited about a new idea. "Then there's the I-like-everything people. They're the ones who will rock your world or break your heart. Maybe both. They're the ones who want it all."

The kid at the counter handed us our food and we walked the short distance to the seating area. "But I like everything. You make me sound kind of reckless."

Teagan mulled that over and bit the corner of her lip in the way that always made me want to watch her mouth. "You like *almost* everything."

"Well, only a sociopath would want black licorice." I set our tray down on a table, using a napkin to brush crumbs away. "What kind of person am I in a relationship if I like everything except black licorice?"

"I'll have to think about that. At the very least, not a sociopath. That's something. I'm sure that's at least part of why Erin loves you."

I skirted the comment and tossed away the napkin I'd used to clean the table. When I returned, Teagan was digging into her meal. "So," I said, as I joined her at the small table. "How are you feeling about leaving? Are you ready?"

Across from me, she unceremoniously shoved an egg roll into her mouth, deep-fried flakes falling across her pink apron and taking up residence over her breasts.

I glanced down at my own bowl, trying to ignore how I'd taken in the shape of her out of habit, examined how the flakes dotted her chest.

"I'm not," she said with her mouth full. "But let's talk about the list."

I raised an eyebrow before I knew I was doing it. "Is this whole thing a distraction so you don't have to think about actually leaving?"

She broke her chopsticks apart. "Of course it is. Thinking about someone's love story is way better than thinking about whether or not I canceled my cable and what is worth packing."

"Are you packing underwear?" I jumped back when her soy sauce packet squirted, and I narrowly missed getting hit. By the time I looked back to Teagan, her eyes were wide.

"Um, yes, I'm bringing underwear. Why would you ask that?" She lowered her voice. "What do you think I plan to get up to in France?"

I laughed, the memories from years ago coming back effortlessly. "Back in college, you told me you were going to give up packing underwear so you could fit in more notebooks."

Teagan snort-laughed and her hand flew to cover her mouth, almost knocking over her soda in the process. "I'd forgotten about that. How do you remember that stuff?"

My face warmed. It felt like I remembered everything when it came to her, and I always had. The fantasy of my best friend leaving her underwear at home had plagued my thoughts more than I'd wanted it to those months I was in France. "It was memorable."

"Well, lucky for you I have succumbed to the electronic age and one notebook will suffice." She eyed me thoughtfully. "Well, it won't make a difference for you, but lucky for the French citizens who will be saved a view of my butt."

"Attention in the boarding area. Flight 344 with service to Detroit is now boarding."

"I'm sure some French citizen will probably still get to see it." I froze the fork halfway to my mouth before shoving the rice in. I wasn't sure why I'd said it, and even though Teagan laughed, my stomach clenched at the thought of her finding someone while over there.

She shrugged. "I mean, you met Erin when you went, so maybe luck will be on my side."

"Anyway," I said, moving the conversation along after swallowing too much food at once. "We've got Ada and . . . what's his name?"

"Sam," she said. "He comes in all the time, so he could have dropped it."

"So, Ada and Sam, and then Jess and the luggage guy."

"And the two baristas—I can't shake the feeling they're pining for each other, like how they look at each other. It's so telling."

"Do you know them?"

"I'm just guessing after seeing them a few times. It's so obvious."

I glanced down at my food on instinct. *Do I look at her a certain way?* "Okay. Where do we start first?"

She bit her lower lip and looked around. "I get off at four. Want to get some coffee?"

"And spy on baristas?"

She placed two palms on the table and I noticed the dark purple nail polish, which was new since the last time I noticed her hands. "That's my love language, Si."

I laughed and handed her a few napkins from the stack I'd grabbed, knowing she was moments away from popping up to find some. "Being nosy is your love language?"

"Duh." She picked up a second egg roll and grinned. "Part of me doesn't want it to be any of them so we can keep looking for the owner. This is kind of fun."

"Except you're leaving in a few days."

She shot me a look over her bowl. "Buzzkill."

"That's *my* love language."

"Maybe you do secretly like black licorice."

12

Teagan

SILAS LEANED OVER the café table, lowering his voice. "This is creepy."

I sipped my mocha and glanced over his shoulder. "It's only a little creepy."

"We're pretending to drink coffee to spy on two twenty-year-old baristas. I think that fits the bill for creepy." Silas's eyes darted around as if everyone knew what we were up to or would care.

"For the record, I'm actually drinking mine." I took another sip, enjoying his twitchy discomfort with more glee than I would ever admit. "And look on the bright side: If it's these two, then we'll return the note and you won't have to play my game anymore."

He grumbled something unintelligible and sat back in his chair.

Mara, the barista with swept-back brown hair, stepped up to the counter and set down two disposable cups. "Half-caff Americano and a caramel latte with oat milk!" Our view of the counter was momentarily obscured by the suited duo who approached to grab their drinks.

"Have either of them been in the shop?" He looked over my

shoulder again, and as much as he grumbled, I was pretty sure Silas was excited about solving the mystery.

"Not that I remember, but there's lots of times I'm not there." I followed his gaze to where Mara was laughing with the other barista, whose name tag we couldn't see when we ordered. "Look at them. Ah! Silas, what if we found the owner of the list? There is some serious pining happening between those two."

He looked back at me skeptically. "How can you tell?"

"The way they're leaning in toward each other, how the one on the left is pushing their hair behind their ear. I think this is it."

"I kind of think you're seeing what you want to see. That's how James and I look when we work together."

Her eyes met mine and she blinked slowly, lowering her long lashes. "First, I see you guys all the time and you don't look like that. Second, are you pining for James? Because if so, I have questions. Namely, does your girlfriend know, and would you like me to turn James down the next time he asks me out?"

He leaned forward again and I had to clutch my cup to stop it from toppling at his sudden movement. This was the second time in one day that I was in danger of losing my beverage because of Silas.

"James asked you out?"

"That's what you took from that?"

He picked at his thumbnail and I absently let my gaze wander the even trim of his short beard. "But he asked you out?"

James was sweet and kind of cute, but I'd turned him down since I was going to be leaving soon. "Last week, but I asked for a rain check until I'm back in the country."

Silas's jaw worked and he bounced his clenched hand on the table.

"He was polite. It's not like he catcalled me in a stairwell. Why do you look so ragey?"

"I'm not ragey," he said, unclenching his fists, his long fingers awkwardly stretching on the table between us. "I just didn't know he asked you out is all."

"Well, at the time, I didn't know you were pining for him, but I'll proceed accordingly."

"If I was pining for James, you'd be the first to know." He took the first drink of his black coffee and winced. "Cold," he muttered.

We'd been sitting there for fifteen minutes and he hadn't touched it, so I wasn't shocked it wasn't piping hot anymore, but in that moment, the last customer in line moved aside and the line was blessedly empty. "We're coming back to the James thing," I said, finishing my drink and standing. "C'mon."

"C'mon, what?"

"Let's go ask them!"

He shook his head, his vehement disagreement with my plan written on his face. "No way. What are we going to say? 'We've been watching how you flirt. Is one of you in love with the other?'"

"I'll be smoother than that," I said, tipping my head to the counter. "No veto, remember?"

He grumbled but stood. After all the years I'd known him, I still wasn't used to Silas's height or the way his long limbs unfurled like a giant's when he stood. I wasn't short, but he had a good eight inches on me, and I loved the rare occasions when I had reason to get a hug from him and his long body wrapped around me. I always wanted it to last longer.

The first time I connected the dots of wanting more of his hugs to wanting more of him, period, we'd been on a video chat. I'd been upset about some guy who'd ghosted me, and he said he was sorry he couldn't give me a hug. I remembered thinking how much I wanted one from him and knowing he really would hug me if he wasn't several hours away. It was such a small moment in the course of our friendship, but that's when that first spark of attraction started. I'd been with other guys, some seriously, and he'd been with Erin forever, so I'd learned to ignore it, but it was always there, that feeling that Silas's arms around me would always make things better. His solid body near me always had.

Now he was in a grumpy mood since I made him spy with me. So I got a stiff, awkward Silas next to me as we approached the counter.

"How can I help you?" Mara greeted us. The gold name tag said SHE/HER under her name. "Refill?"

"No," I said, glancing over my shoulder. Silas wasn't going to help me at all, and I guessed I deserved that. "This will sound odd, but I'm just wondering if either of you lost a note in the candy shop down the hall."

Mara looked confused and shook her head. "Katie, did you lose a note in the candy shop?"

Katie approached the counter, and I didn't care what Silas said—there were vibes between these two. "Nope. Never been in there. What kind of note?"

I was a little relieved the note wasn't theirs, only because it meant we got to keep trying to figure it out and it distracted me from the realization that I was going to be leaving Silas for five months. "Dang," I said, looking at Silas for a moment before turning back to them. "We found a pros and cons list. Looks like someone was deciding whether to tell someone else who also works in the airport how they felt, and we wondered if it might be you two."

Mara glanced over her shoulder at Katie and then back to us. "Uh, nope. Sorry. Why did you think it was us?"

Silas poked me out of view of the baristas, since he'd already made fun of me for not having a great answer other than creeping on them.

"We're just asking everyone at this point," I lied.

Mara glanced at her friend and then back to us with a shrug. "I hope you find the owner. It's really hard when you can't tell someone how you feel about them."

"You're right," I said, avoiding a glance at Silas. "Thanks anyway!"

I reluctantly turned on my heel, tugging on Silas's arm.

His voice was pitched low so they couldn't hear us. "Sorry it's another strike."

"Me, too. I—" I stopped and slowed my pace, listening in on the two baristas behind us.

I was pretty sure it was Mara who spoke first. "That was kind of weird."

"Yeah." Katie's voice was a little higher. "But, um, funny thing is . . ."

I was moving at a glacial pace now, waiting for Mara's response. "Really?"

The disembodied voice reminding people to keep an eye on their luggage and sounds of coffee brewing in the background were the soundtrack to the baristas' heart-to-heart, and I reached behind me to swat Silas's poking finger away as he tried to prod me forward, our fingertips brushing.

"We're such good friends, so I wasn't sure, but, yeah . . . I've been into you for a long time."

I swallowed my "aw," pressed my fingers over my smile, and poked Silas back, subtly motioning to the counter.

"I've . . . been into you, too." The two grinned at each other and their fingers almost touched. "I never knew how to say it."

Silas cleared his throat and I could have killed him for ruining the moment, not that either of them seemed to hear us. Really, he was just ruining my ability to spy on the private moment. "We should probably leave them to it, Teag."

We walked away toward his counter and the shop, Silas still

holding his cold coffee. "Well," I said. "I think an 'I told you so' is in order."

"You could not have predicted that would happen. You got lucky. That could have been super awkward."

I brushed off his comment, though he was right. "Young love, though! And just blurting it out like that? Admitting it? I'm impressed. I've never been that brave."

I bit the inside of my cheek because I'd maybe said too much. There'd been a time—there'd been lots of times—when I thought about telling Silas I wanted more than friendship, but then he was attached or I was attached and it wasn't worth the risk. Our timing was always off.

In my periphery, Silas straightened his tie, his hand moving down toward his taught stomach. He'd gotten into working out during the last few years. Before then, I'd always liked that he was a little soft in the middle, but from the few times I'd seen him without a shirt on or when he'd posted on social media, I knew Silas was now kind of ripped. I averted my thirsty gaze and looked back at his face. "Anyway, you know I avoid awkward through sheer force of will."

He looked at me, eyes soft but assessing. "Yeah," he said, looking ahead again. "I know."

13

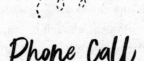

Phone Call

FIVE YEARS AGO
A TUESDAY

Teagan: You could have texted.

(Sound of windshield wipers swishing)

Silas: I'm driving. How is it going?

Teagan: *(Sighs)*

Silas: Bad?

Teagan: Really bad. My dad got laid off, and he'd made some big investments that went south. He didn't tell my mom about any of it. They're so mad at each other. They're not talking.

Silas: How are you?

Teagan: I'm okay.

Silas: How are you really?

Teagan: I don't think I can go on the trip. I don't think I can even stay in school.

Silas: Oh no. Is there any way with financial aid?

Silas: Don't cry, Teag.

Teagan: I'm not crying.

Silas: I can hear you crying. Your snot noises are ricocheting off the inside of my car.

Teagan: (*Laughing through her tears*)

Teagan: I was being quiet. It's weird you know me this well.

Silas: Not that quiet. And who else could know you like I do?

Teagan: No one.

Silas: Well, if you're not going to France, I'm not going, either. I'm sure I can cancel.

Teagan: No!

Silas: I don't want to go without you. I wouldn't know anyone else on the trip anyway.

Teagan: You're going.

Silas: The whole thing was your idea. I'm staying.

Teagan: Don't make me fight you. I won't play fair, and I'll win.

Silas: What will you do if you're not in school?

Teagan: Get a job, I guess. I think it's going to be all hands on deck for a while. I have no idea what you do with half an English degree.

Teagan: It's . . . people go through a lot worse. Not getting to go to Europe isn't exactly the end of the world. I know that.

Silas: It's okay if it feels like it is, though.

Teagan: They're not sure we'll be able to keep the house. It's like everything is disappearing.

Silas: You still have me. Even if I'm thousands of miles away.

Teagan: I know. Besties for life.

Silas: No veto.

Teagan: Where are you driving, anyway? It sounds like it's really coming down out there. I didn't realize this storm spread so far across the state.

Silas: It didn't. I'm here.

Teagan: Where?

Silas: Your driveway. Come let me in.

Silas: I thought you could maybe use a hug or a hand to hold, or we can go egg your dad's car if you want.

Silas: Well, I told you not to cry.

Teagan: It's just that you know I love petty vandalism. I'll be out in a second.

14

Silas

PRESENT DAY
WEDNESDAY

MY SHIFT WAS ending in a few minutes and James had arrived early to relieve me. "Hey, man," he said, logging in to the system.

Despite Teagan's insistence that it was not a big deal, her revelation the day before had stuck with me. "Hey," I said, finishing what I'd been working on. My tie felt too tight and I wanted to hit the gym when I left, needing to burn off some energy. I briefed him on the few issues he might end up dealing with during his shift and caught his gaze wandering across the hall, where Teagan was getting ready to close the shop. "Uh, hey. So, you asked Teagan out?"

James didn't look up from the computer. "Yeah. Why?" He froze. "Oh shit. That's okay, isn't it? I know you two are . . ."

"We're not together or anything. Just didn't know you'd asked her out."

James shrugged. "She shot me down, if that makes you feel better." His gaze lingered again on where she had bent over near the counter, and I clenched my fist to stop from smacking his arm. "What's up with you two anyway? I know you're with Erin. You've never . . ."

"Just friends." I made sure my phone, wallet, and keys were in my pockets. "She's leaving the country in a few days."

James didn't respond, and when I looked up, his face held a bit of amusement. "You sure you're just friends?"

"Yes," I said, wondering what had changed that made everyone start doubting this all of a sudden. Well, rightfully doubting it, but still.

Before she had to drop out of school to help her family, Teagan had visited me one weekend during our sophomore year. I was freshly dumped by my first girlfriend, who had been my best friend through high school, and I was basically a storm cloud in a hoodie. In retrospect, that relationship was doomed to fail—we were young and inexperienced—but we weren't friends after the breakup, which was the hardest thing to deal with. When Teagan arrived, she took one look at me and made me change out of the hoodie, shower, and go to a party. It was my campus and not hers, so I didn't know how she even found the party, but hours later we were a little drunk on the porch of some random house. "Here's the thing," she said all of a sudden, breaking the combination of the silence of the evening and the party behind us. "You're going to find someone new because you're amazing." She slurred her words a little and I studied her face. I'd always known Teagan was pretty, but I'd never thought about it much since I had a girlfriend. She was actually beautiful.

"I might not find someone new," I said, my own words slurring as I leaned against the nearby wall. "What if that was my one chance at love and it's over?"

She leaned against me, so I felt the sharp angle of her elbow until she shifted and fit with me like a puzzle piece. "You're nineteen. Highly unlikely." Teagan smelled like oranges and beer, and my arm fell around her. "But if it's true, then sadly you'll be alone forever," she said sweetly. It took a second for me to register her playful tone. "Which is a shame because I think you would have liked sex."

"You're mean." Her sarcasm was really the furthest thing from my mind. I was nineteen, and her saying the word "sex" coupled with her snuggled against me was all it took to send my mind down a dangerous path. Her hand rested on my stomach and her head was against my shoulder and I couldn't remember what my ex felt like against me in that moment. It was all Teagan. That random house party, her hair tickling my chin, was when I first knew I wanted Teagan and that I'd never have her. We'd fallen back into drunken silence until she spoke again.

"But now you have me, so you might be a virgin forever, but at least you'll never lose your best friend again."

I pushed the memory out of my mind and answered James. "Yeah. Just friends. Since college, so it's kind of like you asking out my sister."

James's smirk fell. "I got it, man. Like I said, she turned me down, so no harm, no foul."

"You ready?" Teagan strode toward the counter with a smile as he finished. "Hey, James."

"Hey," he said without looking up, and I shrugged when I caught Teagan's confused expression. She'd murder me twice if she knew I was going all alpha male on someone interested in her.

"See ya, James," I said with a wave, and we headed toward the exit. I was giving her a ride home since she'd lent her mom her car to use while she was in France, and she let me guide her away from the counter without saying anything else to James.

"Is he mad I turned him down?" She sounded concerned, and my guilt returned.

"I don't think so. Just had an angry customer," I lied, hoping she hadn't been watching the counter too closely.

"Oh, because—" She paused and stopped abruptly. Her voice was a hiss and she nudged me against the nearby wall. "Look!"

I followed the direction of her nod and saw Jess from the dog-grooming place glance left and right and then step into the luggage store at the entrance to D concourse. "Teag . . ." When I looked back, I could see on her face that she was already plotting. "No."

"Yes," she said. "We'll just walk by and maybe . . . pop in. I'm about to be traveling, after all," she said.

"Yes, every college student is bargain hunting in a high-end airport luggage shop."

"They don't know I don't have any money." She took my hand; her soft palm fit perfectly against mine, and she linked our fingers. It was so she could drag me toward the shop, but I got lost in the feel of her hand on mine for a moment. "C'mon!"

I eventually slowed my pace and pulled her back. "It will take us a few minutes to even get down there, and she might not even be there anymore."

"Then we should get moving."

I leveled her with a stare. "Why does it matter?"

"You didn't see them together. There was chemistry! Don't you want to know?"

I cocked one eyebrow and resisted the urge to go with her when she tugged on my hand again, our fingers still linked.

"I'll buy dinner if you do this with me," she said, tugging my hand one more time. "And I'll let you pick the place."

"I'll pick sushi."

She made a face but nodded and tugged on my hand again, her grip stronger than I expected, and I reluctantly followed her.

"Will you pick up the pace?" she said over her shoulder.

"I agreed to help you spy. I did not promise to be excited about it."

The interior of the store smelled like leather, and one of the clerks was near the front helping someone decide between two bags.

"Where did she go?" Teagan leaned into me as we neared the back of the store, pausing to look at a rack of luggage tags. Like all shops in the airport, the place wasn't big, and we slowly made our way along the wall of luggage options, looking around like Jess might appear while the clerk was mercifully busy with someone who looked like they might buy something.

"Are you sure she came in here?" I asked.

"I didn't see her leave."

"Maybe she slipped out while you were agreeing to eat sushi with me," I said with a laugh.

Teagan didn't have time to answer because we both heard the muffled groan from the other side of the closed door to what must have been a back office or storage space. Our eyes met, hers wide with recognition, as mine must have been.

"Was that . . ." We both heard the sound again, followed by a soft moan, and I tugged on her hand to pull her toward the exit.

"That was definitely . . ." We'd gotten almost all the way out of the store, but the person deciding between bags was blocking the path; then we heard the door open behind us. I wanted to crawl into one of the suitcases.

"Hi, folks. Can we help you?" The man approaching us smiled and adjusted his tie, though he didn't reach out to shake our hands. *Noted.* Behind him, Jess from the pet-grooming place emerged, running a hand down the front of her shirt, her cheeks a little pink.

"Oh, hi, Teagan," Jess said. I thought she sounded a little breathless, but I might have imagined it. "What are you doing here?"

"Oh," Teagan said, fixing her face. I knew she wanted to be squee'ing, and it was all I'd hear in the car on the way back to her place. "You know, I'm taking a trip soon and wanted to check out what was in here." The lie rolled off her tongue so easily, I was jealous . . . and a little frightened, but then I remembered the lie I'd been telling her for months.

"Did you know my ex-husband ran this shop? Jack, Teagan works at that candy place that's so good, a few gates from us."

Ex-husband. Teagan's lip twitched at the realization, but she smiled and greeted the man.

"Will you excuse me? I need to get back to the salon." She kissed Jack's cheek and they shared what looked like a pretty heated gaze. "If I don't see you, have a good trip, Teagan!"

We walked out, too, Teagan saying she'd think about the bags we'd supposedly looked at. She practically vibrated next to me as we walked out. When we were almost to my car, she turned. "Are we not going to talk about what they were doing behind that door?"

My body had reacted to it the same as I imagined hers did . . . or fantasized hers did. "Do we really need to debrief it?"

"Um . . . people were having sex five feet from us. Yes, we need to debrief. How often does that happen?"

I shrugged and hit the button to unlock my car. "Admittedly, not since I had a roommate in college who didn't respect boundaries."

"How is Caleb anyway?"

"I have no idea, but I overheard enough of his partners to be pretty confident he's making someone somewhere very happy."

"I really should have gotten to know him better," she mused. She said it to get a rise out of me, but it still worked.

"I'm sure it would have changed the course of your life," I said dryly. "The best and loudest three minutes you'd ever had."

"Just because you weren't hooking up in college doesn't mean you have to sound so snarky about people who were."

"What makes you think I wasn't hooking up in college?"

"Because you weren't. You would have told me. What girl were you spending time with besides me?"

"I didn't tell you everything," I said quietly. I hadn't told her when I lost my virginity or the few times I'd had sex after because it wasn't good, and if I was honest with myself, I'd been thinking of her the entire time.

"Silas, I am shocked. How did I not know?" She met my gaze

over the top of my car before climbing in. "I told you about all my hookups."

I cracked the knuckles on my left hand as I climbed into the driver's side. I hadn't exactly minded when she told me, but I never liked it. I'd chalked that up to us being so close and me feeling protective, but after a while, it was jealousy. It was the same feeling I had when I learned James had asked her out. "It's not a big deal." I shrugged and started toward the exit.

"Anyway, what do you think they were doing?" She drummed her fingers on the cup holder. "They weren't in there long enough to do much, were they?"

"I have no idea, Teag." Also, I didn't like how my body reacted in pretty obvious ways to her talking about sex.

"Maybe just fingering or something . . . She definitely looked like she was flushed." Teagan gripped the handle when I swerved at her words, then played it off like I thought a car was backing out. "I can get off pretty fast from fingering if it's done right," she mused, looking out the window, and I hoped she wasn't looking down, because I was now cruising through a parking garage with an erection, thinking about how fast I could get my best friend in the world to an orgasm with my fingers.

15

Teagan

I PUSHED OPEN the door of my apartment and shivered, searching for the sweatshirt I'd stolen from Silas that I kept near the door.

"It's freezing in here," he said, walking in behind me and rubbing his arms. "What's up with your heat?"

"I'm trying to save as much on utilities as I can before I leave," I said, pulling on the sweatshirt, the familiar weight and softness surrounding me. "And it's not usually this cold." I glanced around my one-bedroom apartment. The benefit of living near campus was that it wasn't hard to find someone to sublease it while I was abroad. A math major who would be returning from her own study abroad trip needed something furnished for the remainder of the year. I loved that cramped little home, though—it had been my first place all on my own—no roommates, no parents, just Silas visiting and the occasional Tinder date coming home with me.

"You know, I might want that back someday." Silas plopped down on my love seat and motioned to the sweatshirt.

"I think the statute of limitations has passed." I tossed him a fleece blanket from the arm of the couch. "It wouldn't fit you anymore anyway." I hadn't planned to let my gaze drop from his face to his now well-developed chest and arms. It wasn't usually what I was attracted to, but on Silas it worked, not that I hadn't liked how he looked before.

"I'm taking something of yours, then." He looked around and I grinned at his assessment. "This blanket," he finally said. "It's mine now until you return the sweatshirt."

"Okay," I said, taking the short walk to the kitchen and pulling two beers from the fridge. Silas, despite all his laid-back qualities, was a beer snob, and I had a couple of bottles of his favorite microbrew still in my fridge.

"Why did you give in to that so quickly?" He had the blanket over him. It really was cold in the apartment.

"I stole that from you, too." I settled on the arm of the love seat, taking a drink after I handed him his beer. "You let me use it during a camping trip, and it ended up going home with me." I'd kind of forgotten about that until he mentioned it.

"Teag . . . I'm concerned you're in this friendship solely to steal from me." His neck stretched when he took a drink from his own bottle, and I watched his throat work like a creeper. He had a nice throat.

"Oh, I am. No doubt." I set my bottle aside on the end table and rubbed my upper arms to generate heat. "That and to get help with solving mysteries. Was that not clear before?"

"I feel so used." He eyed my movements and then lifted the fleece fabric. "C'mon, get under the blanket with me. You're shivering. Can I Venmo you some money so you will turn your actual heat on?"

I slid down the arm of the couch and under the blanket with him, the heat from his body already warming the space under the thick fabric where our bodies were pressed together. That had happened thousands of times in our friendship, and it shouldn't have meant anything, but I had an inkling of a feeling and I pushed it back. "Nah, no need for Venmo. I'll just take it from your wallet." I nudged my shoulder against his, and his arm fell around me, like it had a hundred times before.

"So," he said, pulling his phone from under the blanket. He thumbed to a photo of the list we'd made. "Looks like our leads are coming up as dead ends." I leaned against his arm and looked at the list. Silas's biceps were solid against my cheek.

"Well, not total dead ends. Julianna laughed at me, but the baristas seem happy together, and Jess seemed . . . really happy." My face heated thinking about our conversation in the car about Jess and her ex-husband. We talked about everything, but I'd tried to back off on sexy things since he'd gotten serious with Erin.

"True," he said, zooming in on the list, "but we're no closer to finding the owner of this."

"Maybe—" I paused when a notification flashed over the screen, and we both stared at it.

ERIN: Thanks! I'll be by later tonight.

He dismissed it quickly, but I pulled out from under his arm, suddenly aware this was too close, no matter how familiar it felt.

"I can't believe you're letting me off the hook for sushi. Do you want something else to eat?" I walked back into the kitchen, eager for some excuse to step away from my very attached friend.

"No, thanks." He was still looking at his phone. "Maybe Ada and Sam? You said he comes into the shop sometimes, right?"

I opened the fridge—there wasn't much in it besides eggs, whipped cream, cheese, some questionable cold cuts, and beer. "Yeah, we could look into that. Will you go on another fact-finding mission with me?"

He looked up, pinning me with his brown eyes and raised eyebrow. "Do I have a choice?"

"No." I settled back on the arm of the couch and Silas eyed me curiously.

"Do you want back under here?"

"Nah. That's okay." I stuffed my hands into the hoodie's front pocket. "When is Erin coming over? Do you need to get out of here?"

He glanced back at his phone. "Uh, I have a little time."

I nodded and reached for my beer. "So, she's back in town? I bet it will be nice to see her again!" I was going for positive, but I'd veered a little far into maniacally peppy.

He nodded and glanced down at his phone. "Yeah, I guess so." He wasn't a guy who spent a lot of time staring at his phone, but he spoke again without looking up. "Couldn't we avoid spying on people and just ask Ada or Sam directly?"

I ignored his question because he was giving off a weird vibe. "Why are you being weird?"

"Says the woman who refuses to turn on her heat." He held up the blanket for me again. "Will you get under here? You're clearly cold."

"I don't think we should snuggle on the couch. Your girlfriend would hate it, even though nothing is happening."

He looked away again. "She won't care."

"She hates me. She would definitely care."

"She doesn't hate you. And it doesn't matter if she does. You're my friend." He reached for my ankle, tugging my leg toward him and under the blanket.

The space under it was warm through my socks and I let him pull my other foot under the blanket, resting his palms over my toes while I kept my perch on the arm. "It matters because you love her and I'm your friend, because I respect boundaries—a few of them anyway."

Silas was looking down at where my feet had disappeared under the blanket, and I appreciated not seeing his reaction. He always looked so conflicted when it came to me and Erin, and I worried I hadn't made enough effort to get along with his girlfriend.

"Anyway," I said, wiggling my toes under the blanket. "I'm glad you have her."

"Teag," he said, looking up, his brown eyes flashing.

"I know. I know. Just let me say this, okay? No veto."

"You already played your no-veto card for the year."

"Yeah," I said, rubbing my arms through the sweatshirt material. "But don't you think I should get two?"

He rolled his eyes but held his arm out in the "carry on" motion. "Why are you glad I have her?"

"She makes you happy, and I like you to be happy. It's good you have someone besides me." I pushed my hands between my thighs to warm them, and I wondered if it might be time to cave on my cost-saving measure of keeping the heat off. "And you being with her made it impossible to ever . . . slip up, like we did before you left all those years ago."

He gave me a very Silas look, so I knew he had something to say but also wasn't going to say it out loud.

"Which is a good thing," I reassured him. "When it was bad between us, and then awkward . . . that was hell. I don't ever want that to happen again."

He finally spoke, holding up the blanket and tugging on my leg. "Will you get under this damn thing? You're freezing. Stop being so stubborn."

Silas was warm and the blanket was warm, and even though on a few levels I knew I shouldn't, I slid under the fabric and his arm fell back around my shoulders.

"Happy now?" I asked, ignoring the warm sensation moving through my body that had nothing to do with the blanket.

He didn't answer immediately, but his arm over my shoulder

tensed. "For the record, that would never happen again, us being awkward and weird together. Even if we were both single."

"But it could. What if you got drunk enough to think I was attractive, or you wore those suspenders I think are so weirdly sexy?"

"They were my grandfather's, and I only put them on as a joke." His body jostled with his low chuckle, and I smiled. "And I wouldn't have to be drunk to know you're beautiful."

I ignored his words and the flutter I felt in my chest at hearing them. "But since you have Erin, it doesn't matter. We won't slip up and ruin everything."

When I glanced over, he was staring at a spot on the blanket, jaw set.

I nudged his side with my elbow. "You should probably get going. I'm sure you want to shower before she gets to your place, and I want this blanket all to myself. I've decided I'm not giving that back either."

I thought he'd laugh, but he gave me another Silas look before finally nodding.

16

Phone Call

FIVE YEARS AGO
A WEDNESDAY

Silas: Hey, it's Silas. Leave a message.

Teagan: Hey, stranger. Remember me?

Automated response: If you would like to keep your message, hang up. If you would like to delete and rerecord, press 1.

(Beep)

Automated response: Rerecord your message.

Teagan: Hey, it's me. I can't believe it's been two months already. I want to hear everything, and can we forget about the whole me-making-out-with-you-at-the-airport thing?

Automated response: If you would like to keep your message, hang up. If you would like to delete and rerecord, press 1.

(Beep)

Automated response: Rerecord your message.

Teagan: It's Teagan. Are you even checking this voice mail? I hope so. I miss you. I really miss you. I'm sorry I kissed you. It was a huge mistake. I was just swept up in the moment, but it was so wrong.

Automated response: If you would like to keep your message, hang up. If you would like to delete and rerecord, press 1.

(Beep)

Automated response: Rerecord your message.

Teagan: It's me and I miss your face. I'm sorry for what I did. I kissed you and you kissed me back and I think we both just got swept up, but then I ran away without saying anything. I tripped and fell down the stairs in front of a hundred strangers while running, if that makes you feel better. It probably doesn't because you're usually a better person than that, but on the off chance it helps, my butt was bruised for a week and the contents of my purse flew everywhere, so I had to retrieve tampons from where they landed in front of a bunch of hot military guys. And I know you called me a bunch of times and I didn't call back. I'm the worst kind of friend. I don't have an excuse, but I promised you'd never lose me as your best friend, and you haven't. If you still want me. I hope you do because, as previously stated, I miss your face. And I know you're not living in your hoodie because I stole it from you, but I hope me being a jerk didn't ruin your trip. Call me back so I can grovel properly?

(PHONE BUZZING)

Teagan: Hi!

Silas: Hey.

Teagan: You got my voice mail, then.

Silas: Yeah.

Teagan: How is France? Is it amazing?

Silas: It's good.

Teagan: . . .

Silas: What?

Teagan: This is so awkward—and I hate it.

Silas: I hate it, too.

Teagan: The military guys were really cute, and one of them had to tell me someone's discarded gum was stuck to my shirt from my fall.

Silas: *(Laughs)*

Teagan: So, that has to make up for me being a jerk a little, right?

Silas: You kissed me, like really kissed me, Teag. And then took off, like . . . what happened?

Teagan: You were leaving and I realized how much I'd miss you, and I was so sad I couldn't go. And it's not like I hadn't thought about it before.

Silas: You'd thought about kissing me?

Teagan: I mean . . . it doesn't mean anything, it's just . . . thoughts. It doesn't have to mean anything.

Silas: It sucked, Teag. You ghosted me and it was like getting dumped by my ex all over again.

Teagan: I know. I freaked out.

Teagan: Some of the gum got in my hair, too.

Silas: That helps.

Teagan: Are things going to be awkward until we're eighty now?

Silas: With as fast as you drive, there's no way you're making it to eighty.

Teagan: With as slow as you drive, you'd think you were already eighty.

Silas: *(Chuckles)* Okay. I was being awkward.

Teagan: I deserve it. But I promise I'll never let anything get in the way of us being friends again. I'll never let it happen. Are you okay, though? Is someone there to make you get drunk and forget about girls who mess with your head and kiss you sloppily when they're sad?

Silas: It hasn't been great, but it's getting better.

Silas: And it wasn't a sloppy kiss. For the record.

Teagan: It wasn't. It was actually a—

Woman's voice: Silas, *êtes-vous prêt à partir?*

Teagan: Are you ready to go where? Who is that?

Silas: Yeah. Give me a minute.

Woman's voice: *En français!*

Silas: That's Erin—she's the other communications student here with the group. We're going out to dinner.

Teagan: *Très bien.*

Silas: *(Chuckles)* Can we talk this weekend?

Teagan: *Oui.*

Silas: I miss you.

Teagan: *En français!*

Silas: *Tu me manques, mon amie.*

17

Silas

PRESENT DAY
THURSDAY

THE CONVERSATION FROM the night before was still on my mind as I brushed my teeth. I'd left Teagan's place so close to telling her how I really felt and in dire need of my car's seat warmer. Her apartment really was freezing. I thought about inviting her to stay at my place until she left, but since I was leaving her to meet with my ex-girlfriend, that felt like a bad idea, too. As I went through my morning ministrations, I replayed the rest of the evening.

As much as we could be, Erin and I were still friendly. After dating for six years, many of those including the foregone conclusion that we'd be together forever, it was hard to not be friends, and we'd shared a long hug when she stopped by. Hugging Erin was different from hugging Teagan, and that I'd always made that comparison on some level was a reminder that I should have ended things with her sooner.

"Hey," I said when we pulled apart. She didn't look anything like Teagan, which was what had first drawn me to her when we met on our study abroad trip. Erin had dark blond hair, was on the short side, and had a beautifully round body. She had a great laugh, and I'd loved her on some level. On that study abroad trip, she'd been a friend and then more when I didn't have anyone, and then I realized I liked being with her because it was safe. I wasn't ever risking anything. Now we stood a few feet apart, but I didn't long to be closer. "I packed up the things of yours I found," I said finally, nodding toward the kitchen, where a box of her stuff was organized.

"Thanks," she said. "I appreciate you keeping it all together." She looked around the apartment. We'd never moved in together, but she'd practically lived here, and I at her place. The untangling part had been harder than I imagined, especially because the person I'd normally confide in didn't know I'd ended the relationship with Erin.

"You want something to drink?" I invited her into the small living room. The box of chocolates Teagan had left for Erin's birthday sat on my table.

"Sure. Beer if you have it." Erin settled on the far end of the couch, which had been her spot, and traced a finger over the box.

The bottle was cold in my hand when I handed it over, and it made me think of Teagan's cold apartment. "Help yourself." I probably should have told her the box was hers, but I realized with a cold clarity that Teagan got her something and I didn't, and the words lodged in my throat. I'd make sure she took them with her.

"You and your candy," she said, accepting the bottle. "How is Teagan?"

I knew I wouldn't hear bitterness or vindictiveness in her voice, even though they'd never gotten along. She knew how important Teag was to me, but that didn't stop the guilt from gnawing at me.

"She's good. She's taking that study abroad trip finally. She leaves in a few days."

"Ah, *c'est bon pour elle*," she said before sipping from her bottle. I did the quick translation in my head. "Good for her" could have sounded sarcastic from someone else, but I knew Erin meant it. She slid into French sometimes—it had always made me smile.

Unlike me, Erin had really wanted to be in Lyon, kept up with her French, and did a lot of business internationally. Once things were kind of resolved with Teagan, I'd had some fun, but Erin and Teagan looked at travel like the ultimate experience. For me, those five months were a trip I took once. Neither woman ever understood my ambivalence.

Erin set her beer on the table. "You're sad she's leaving?"

The question was so direct, I took a sip from my beer instead of answering. "I'm glad she's finally getting to go."

"You didn't answer my question, but that's okay." She gave me a small smile and looked at her lap. "So, I wanted to tell you I started seeing someone."

"That's great," I said unconvincingly. "Who?"

"We work together. You don't know him. It's nice to be in something new. It's different." She leaned forward on her knees, tracing the writing on the top of the box. "Did you tell her yet?"

I shook my head and she nodded like she knew that answer was coming. "I don't think I'm going to."

"Silas. I say this with love," she said. "Because I think part of me will always love you, but you're being a dumbass."

"Don't sugarcoat anything."

"I won't," she said with a cheeky grin. "You said too much of your heart was with her, that that's why you couldn't stay in a relationship with me. That hurt, but you were right. I deserve to be with someone who can give me their whole heart."

"You do. I'm sorry, Er—"

She held up a hand. "I'm okay, and we did that part already. What I'm saying is, why are you denying yourself the chance to be happy?"

"That's not what I'm doing."

She eyed the candy box and her smile saddened. "Do you realize our entire relationship, anytime I brought you candy, you only let yourself have a little at a time? I thought at first you were just being healthy or not having too much sugar at once, but it wasn't that. You never want too much of a good thing at once."

I didn't have an answer, so I glanced at the box, too. "I like to savor it. Make it last."

"You know people don't work like that, though, right? You love her. Holding that in doesn't make anything better."

"It's more complicated than that."

She arched a brow and took a last swig of her beer, setting the bottle on a coaster. "Is it?" She let the silence of her question mark hang in the air before rising to her feet.

I'd never told Erin everything that had happened and how gutted I'd been for most of the time in France after things with Teagan got so weird. When we started dating, I could mostly ignore that gutted feeling, and by then, Teag and I were getting back to okay.

"Fine, fine," Erin said. "Don't answer, but I know I'm right. I should get going, but I hope you tell her. For what it's worth, I think she probably feels the same way, but you guys are closer than any two people I know. Even if she doesn't feel the same, you'll figure it out."

I handed her the box of the things I'd found. A hairbrush, a half-empty bottle of her expensive conditioner, a few books, and knickknacks. It wasn't heavy. I held out the box of chocolates to her. "These are actually for you."

"Thanks, but you keep them," she said, balancing the box of her things on her hip. "Eat some candy, Silas. There's no prize for leaving it in the box."

I sat on my couch in the quiet of my apartment for a while after she left, mulling over what she said and not coming to any conclusion, but I ate a few of the truffles from the box on the table. She was right—I'd been letting myself have only a little at a time. Unable to resist, I let my mind wander to what it would be like to have more of my best friend all at once.

18

Teagan

"HI, JAMES," I said, sidling up to the customer service counter after my last shift at the shop.

James startled and glanced away with a mumbled hello. *What is up with him?* He'd been flirting with me for months and was a friendly guy, and now it was like I'd tripped him in the parking garage or something. "Silas," he called over his shoulder to my friend, who had his back to the counter working on something. We'd been busy all day and hadn't had a chance to really see each other, but he looked tired up close, with faint dark circles under his eyes.

"Hey," he said, tapping at something on the keyboard. "You're a free woman. Ready to go?"

I nodded, still eyeing the heaviness in his eyes. "You don't have to help me pack. You look like you need some rest."

He waved me off and snatched his messenger bag from the counter before saying goodbye to James and the petite woman with a high ponytail who'd shown up to replace him. "I'm okay. Who else is going to force you to finish packing?"

We weaved through the crowds toward the exit. Ahead of us, two people held hands, their twin tan complexions and floral shirts giving the impression that they were coming home from vacation together, and I shoved my hand in my pocket because I wanted to be holding someone's hand, and that someone was Silas, whose hand was spoken for.

Silas must have seen my examination and lowered his voice. "We're not following random travelers to see if they lost a love note."

I laughed. "Even I'm not that much of a romantic."

"I wouldn't put it past you," he said, his elbow nudging my arm as we moved through the crowds until we could veer toward employee parking.

IT WASN'T AS cold when we walked into my apartment, but the relative warmth was balanced by the visible chaos of my life turned upside down. "Teag," Silas said, dragging out my name. "What the hell?"

I took in the mess. "Well, I was packing for the trip and then deciding what I needed to box up and take to my mom's before the subletter arrived, then I decided to organize some things, and, well . . ." I motioned around.

Silas dropped his bag next to the door and pushed up his sleeves on his forearms, revealing the fine auburn hairs on his arms. "Where do we start?"

"With wine," I said. "I need to finish a bottle before I go."

"I mean . . . I won't fight you. Is there food to go with the wine?" Silas walked into my kitchen and opened the fridge. I admired how his back muscles looked under his shirt after he'd peeled away the sweater-vest. "You have . . . eggs, cold cuts, sliced cheese, and whipped cream."

"Omelet sundaes?" we said at the same time, and I laughed, looking for my corkscrew. "I love us," I added.

He pulled the egg carton and the cheese from my fridge but left the whipped cream to me.

I watched him work and poured glasses for us. "Who is going to cook for me in France?"

He snort-laughed. "No one. You're going to have to fend for yourself. I'd pay to see it."

I grabbed the whipped cream can and hopped onto the counter to the left of the stove, watching him work. "Want to be impetuous and chuck it all to come with me?"

"So I can make you eggs and Kraft Singles in a new time zone? I'm good." He whisked the eggs with a fork, searching my counter for seasoning, and I handed him the salt and pepper shakers. "I wasn't in love with France the first time."

"I'll never understand that." I admired the soft red stubble covering his familiar jaw and how his movements were so quick and precise in my kitchen.

"By the way, I ran into Ada today."

I gulped. "I ran into Sam."

"Kismet," Silas said with a smile. "Ada said they weren't together but she was hopeful. She's been single since she and her husband divorced. I know I got on you about saying people were cute, but she was really . . . I don't know. Sweet about it."

I opened the Kraft Singles for him, peeling back the plastic and spraying a little whipped cream on my finger before licking it off. "Ugh."

Silas's eyes dropped to my lips for a split second. He usually teased me for eating whipped cream from the can, but he didn't comment. "Ugh? I thought you'd be thrilled. You love this stuff."

"I do," I said, licking another fingerful. "But I talked to Sam, too."

"What did he say?"

"Well, I showed him the list and he immediately started naming people he thought it could be. Why do the middle-aged and older men in that place know everyone's business anyway?"

Silas shrugged one broad shoulder, pouring the eggs into the heated pan. "Airport illuminati?"

"Maybe so." I tapped my fingertips on the surface of the laminate counter before filling my finger again. "But Sam didn't write it." I held my finger out to offer Silas some of the cream—he always declined, but his gaze fell to my finger like he was considering it before turning back to the pan.

"No . . . no, thanks." He flipped the omelet, adding the cheese as best he could with what I gave him to work with. "So, I guess we're out of leads."

When I finished sucking the sweet cream off my finger, he was looking at me again. "What? Is there some on my face?"

Silas shook his head and returned to the eggs. "Sorry we didn't solve the mystery. I know you wanted to before you left." He slid the food onto a plate but didn't make a move to get forks. Instead, he watched me spray more whipped cream. "It was fun to investigate with you, though."

"We always have fun." My stomach did a weird flip-flop at the way he looked at me. I'd wanted someone's love story to work out, for the letter to mean something, but now time was up and maybe I'd been putting too much symbolism into all of it. I held out my finger again, waiting for his rebuff, but just before I pulled my hand back, Silas turned off the burner and his fingers wound softly around my wrist.

"Yeah, I'll try some."

"You will?"

His lips wrapped around my index finger, his tongue sliding along the pad of my finger and sending chills through me. More than the feel of his mouth or the intimacy of the gesture, his eyes were on mine the entire time, and my body warmed. "It's good," he murmured, his fingers still holding my wrist, the hold loose but unmoving.

My brain was rearranging itself, sitting there in the tiny half-packed kitchen with the ghost of Silas's mouth on my finger. Maybe he was calling my bluff or he just wanted some whipped cream, but it felt like more. My voice was small when I spoke. "Did you know when I first found the list, I wondered if you wrote it?"

"You did?"

I nodded. "Isn't that horrible?"

"No." He didn't elaborate.

"You've been dating Erin for years," I said, pulling back my hand, my senses coming back to me as I realized how wrong it was to feel the things I was feeling. "How could I hope for even a moment you'd be thinking those things about me?"

His brows pinched together and his hands stilled.

I lifted the whipped cream can. "I know. I'm a bad person. You are lucky I'll be in a different time zone for the next several months." I didn't want to put a wet blanket on what little time we had left, so I sprayed the whipped cream directly into my mouth, alleviating me from having to say anything or acknowledge how long I'd wanted Silas to touch me like that.

Silas's lips tipped in a grin once my mouth was full. "I broke up with Erin."

I stared, incredulous. "Last night? What?" The words came out as a garble because my mouth was still full.

"A few months ago," he said, interpreting my nonsense, his voice still low. He wanted to look away, I knew he did, because he always did when I was angry, but he kept his eyes trained on mine. "I didn't tell you because . . ."

I swallowed the rest of the whipped cream. "What happened?"

Silas sucked in a deep breath but didn't answer my question. "You have some here." He swept his thumb under my lips, his gaze following the movement. "I ended it."

"But why?"

Silas stepped closer and I placed my palm on his chest, feeling his heartbeat. "Because I didn't write that list . . ." His thumb still ghosted near my lip, sweeping back and forth in a slow arc. "But it wasn't fair to her that I *could* have written that list."

"What are you saying?"

He shook his head slightly. "I don't know." Silas cupped my jaw, one soft palm against my face, warm and solid. Our mouths were so close together, foreheads almost touching. "I don't know what I'm saying because you're my best friend but I want to kiss you."

"My mouth is going to taste like whipped cream."

His chuckle was low and his chest vibrated under my hand. "That's better than tasting like the cheese."

"Can you imagine an American cheese kiss?" My voice was a whisper, but now we were both laughing, pressed together in my cramped kitchen.

"A French-cheese kiss." Silas's finger stroked the shell of my ear.

I shivered at his touch. "A camembert smooch."

His finger trailed slowly, achingly slowly, down the side of my neck.

"I've never talked about cheese this much when someone was about to kiss me." Our lips were close and our breaths mingled, our noses almost touching. "That might have ruined the moment."

"No." His lips brushed the corner of my lip. "It didn't." The teasing sweep was maddening, and I tipped his head, seeking his lips fully against mine. "I've wanted this since the first time." He dipped his head and teased his lips over my jawline. "I never stopped thinking about it."

"Silas," I murmured.

"You're my best friend," he said, holding my face so our eyes met while he repeated my words from all those years ago—but I'd meant them then to stop us. Now they felt like a lit match near kindling, and his lips lowered to mine.

19

Silas

AS MANY TIMES as I'd fantasized about kissing Teagan again, I thought I would have been prepared for the feel of her lips and tongue, for the way she sucked in a breath when I settled my hand at her back and pulled her against me. I wasn't prepared for any of it, and my head was clear of any thought except to keep touching her. It felt like we kissed for hours, me standing in her kitchen and her on the counter, the food, wine, and packing and all the reasons we shouldn't be kissing forgotten.

Her skin was smooth under the hem of her T-shirt, and when I lowered my kisses to her neck, she dragged her fingertips across the back of my neck, her short nails barely grazing the skin. I could have moved into the crook of her shoulder because of how intoxicating it was to kiss her neck and find the secret places that elicited an intimate sound. "Si," she groaned, tipping back her head when I found one.

I kissed her there again, hunched over to get the best angle. It wasn't exactly comfortable, but I couldn't have cared less. Her legs were spread wide at my hips and she ground against me, stretching her neck the other way.

The sound of a bang startled me.

"Shit! Ouch!"

I snapped back to see her rubbing the side of her head. "What's wrong?" I slid fingers gingerly over her hair.

"I smacked my head into the cupboard," she said, her fingers under mine as I stroked where she'd hit. "You never told me you were so good at this."

I linked our fingers and slid her hand to behind my neck. "You never asked."

"I wondered," she said, tracing a fingertip up my neck. "What else are you good at?"

Throughout the course of our friendship, Teagan had touched me thousands of times, but the gentle brush of her fingertips on my neck made my mind spin, and I crashed my lips to hers again, pressing between her thighs, my hand on the back of her head to keep her from banging it into the cupboard again. "Is your curiosity satisfied?"

She grinned and pulled my lips to hers again. "Not even close. What else?"

"I've been told I'm good at . . ." I stroked the back of her thigh, pulling her leg up my hip. "Packing."

"Don't even joke." Teagan wrapped her other leg around me. "Bedroom."

My cock jumped at the word and I pulled her to me. "That's bossy."

She bit her lower lip. "I actually like it if you're a little bossy. Do you like that?"

I lifted her, settling my hands under her thighs and her ass as she clung to me. "Yeah, I think I do." It's hard carrying someone down a hall when that hall is filled with boxes, and I tripped twice, Teagan clinging to me harder and both of us laughing as I made my way to the bedroom, thankfully without dropping her. "Your apartment is dangerous," I huffed, lowering her to the floor.

"We made it," she said, pulling her T-shirt over her head, revealing a yellow lacy bra over the breasts I'd dreamed of for years. "You're staring."

"I . . ." I slid my hands up her ribs, stopping just before my thumbs stroked the underside of the bra. "Yeah. I am."

She tucked a finger under my chin and lifted my gaze until our eyes met. She unhooked her bra and tossed it aside before sliding her hands back to my chest. "Show me what else you're good at, Silas."

My world could have ended in that moment. If lightning had struck her unpacked bedroom, I'd have died at my happiest, with Teagan's bare chest against me, her plump lips slightly parted. I kissed her again, savoring the feel of her lower lip before spinning her around so her back was to me. Her short gasp at the spin and at my breath on her bare shoulder was a shot of adrenaline. She said she liked me in charge—that was new for me.

"I know everything about you," I said against her neck as my splayed palms slid over her stomach and up her ribs. "But I don't know how you like to be touched." Her breasts were heavy in my palms as I cupped them, letting a thumb play over her nipples. It was sheer luck that I hadn't come in my pants at the feel of her body. It felt like the culmination of half a decade of foreplay, and she wiggled against me as if issuing a challenge.

"Like that, but harder. I can't see you."

"I know. You can feel me, though. Close your eyes." I rolled her nipple between my finger and thumb, adding more pressure with each twist, seeing what she reacted to. "I'm here."

"You're always here," she murmured, sliding one of my palms over her heart.

My own heart was unexpectedly full at the realization that the same was true for me, and I tried to think of the best way to say it, except my brain was otherwise engaged with the feel of Teagan's body. She saved me the emotional moment when she pushed my hand lower. "But maybe tonight you can be here, too."

I laughed against her shoulder and let her guide my palm down her body, over her stomach, and under her pants. "I thought you wanted me to be the bossy one."

She shrugged. "I'm unpredictable."

"I know," I said against her neck. "I like that about you." I slid my hand lower and hers fell away. The heat at the apex of Teagan's thighs was what I'd dreamed of, and I slid past the waistband of her underwear, inching closer. I dragged my fingertip over her mound, only brushing over the side of her already swollen clit and then up the other side, my finger sliding along her wet folds easily. "Teag," I groaned against her neck. "I can't believe we're doing this."

"I've wanted it for so long." She looked over her shoulder, and I caught her lips as I continued to explore her with my finger while still cupping her breast.

"Hold still," I said into her ear, and I moved in front of her, kissing her again because I needed to kiss her. I felt like I'd always need it. I fell to my knees in front of her and tugged down her pants, looking up to catch her dreamy expression. "These are in the way," I said, enjoying her hand on my shoulder as she stepped out of them. "On the bed, baby."

She climbed onto the bed after pushing a packed suitcase to the side. She stretched out in front of me but scrunched her nose. "Baby?"

I settled between her legs, my shoulders nudging her thighs apart. "I was trying it out."

"Silas?"

I traced kisses down from her belly button before lifting my head and meeting her hooded gaze. "Yeah?"

"You're my best friend."

I nipped at her thigh, then kissed the spot. "But you don't like 'baby'?"

She laughed, a perfect throaty laugh that shook her body under me, and her fingers traced through my hair. "I really don't."

Her laugh was still in my ears when I dragged my tongue along her folds, holding her hips in place. Teagan was sweet on my tongue, her body wrapped around mine as I explored her with my lips and tongue and fingers, giving her everything I had and not able to make her wait. She reacted to every touch, every lick and kiss, guiding me with her fingers and her body. I would have stayed there forever and drowned between her legs.

She climaxed hard and fast, thighs pressing against me as the ripples of her core squeezed the finger I'd slipped into her eager body. I wanted to do it again, but she'd gone limp, her expression dreamy as she looked at the ceiling, and I kissed up her body, pulling her into a kiss.

"Si," she groaned, clutching me, her hands sliding over my back. "Why are you still dressed?"

"I didn't know how far you wanted to go, and I was too busy to get undressed."

Her fingers were already working at the buttons on my shirt, her leg on my hip. "You taste like me," she said, pushing the sleeves off my shoulders.

"Better than whipped cream," I said, and she laughed, her cheeks tinting pink.

Teagan's hands moved over my chest, tracing the line of hair down my stomach to my belt.

"We don't have to," I said, resting my hand over hers. "This is a lot. A good lot, but we can just . . ." I searched my brain for a way to say "stick with oral" that sounded nicer.

"Do you not want to?" Neither of us was particularly new to sex, but I felt like I was, a little, with Teagan, like with us it was all a little new. I couldn't explain why that made me smile.

I arched against her hand, the contact forcing me to close my eyes against the desire to explode. "No, I want to." I didn't move away from her touch but dipped my head to meet her eyes. "Just to be clear, I want more than this, though."

"I don't know if we have time for anal," she teased. "I still have to pack."

I kissed her smile, inhaled her laugh. "Unzip my pants, smartass," I said, rolling to my back. As I moved, something shiny caught my eye, a padlock tossed on the top of her half-packed suitcase.

I reached for it. "You kept this?"

Teagan was working my pants and boxers down my thighs, and my straining cock glistened at the tip. "Of course," she said, stroking me, her warm, sure hand moving over my sensitive skin.

She moved up my body, dropping kisses over my stomach and up my chest, and I set the familiar lock back down, stroking the back of her neck as she met my lips, her thighs against mine. "It reminds me of you."

"There's no bridge to hang it on now," I said, reaching into her bedside drawer and praying to God she hadn't packed there yet. *Success!* I pulled a condom from the drawer and began sliding it down my length. "Ride me, Teag." I guided her thigh over mine.

She grinned, and I had a good idea she liked being on top. "I don't need a bridge to hang it on." She hovered over me before sliding down.

"My God." I saw stars, actual stars in my vision, as she lowered herself onto me and her heat surrounded me.

"I know," she said, beginning to rock, her hands on my chest.

I let her lead, despite every fiber of my muscles wanting to pump up into her, and my palm settled at her hip as I worked my thumb against her, willing her to break again before I did. I wanted to say something sweet and romantic and confess my love in three languages, but all I could do was hold on to her gaze as our breaths quickened and we both fell over the edge one after the other.

Teagan fell onto my chest, her fingers linked with mine over my heart, and I pulled her to my side, reaching for the padlock behind her.

"It might be a little early to incorporate locks into the bedroom," she teased, touching her fingers to the lock and studying it with me. "It always reminded me of you and that once you thought of me in a place so filled with love stories," she said softly.

"I love you," I said, matching her tone, but the words felt like they exploded from me, like they couldn't be held in. "I always have."

"I love you, too," she said, sliding her fingertips against mine.

"We still have to pack your apartment, huh?" I hugged her to my side.

"Oh yeah," she said. "This was totally a bribe to stay and help with Bubble Wrap."

I squeezed her against me and kissed the top of her head. "It was a good bribe. I'm not going anywhere."

20

FIVE YEARS AGO
A THURSDAY

Teagan: You're online!

Silas: Sorry I haven't been on much.

Teagan: That's okay. How's it been?

Silas: Okay.

Silas: Took this photo for you.

Teagan: The Pont des Arts! OMG! You went!

Silas: I got Erin to go with me.

Teagan: Ooh. You two have spent a lot of time together.

Silas: Uh, yeah. Sad news about the bridge, though—they're shutting it down.

Teagan: No! Why?

Silas: The weight of the locks is messing with the structural integrity of the bridge or something. They're going to cut them down and replace the rails with glass.

Teagan: I can't believe I'll never get to see it. Do you have more pictures?

Silas: I knew you'd ask. Here are three more photos.

[photo]

[photo]

[photo]

Teagan: Aww. You even took a selfie. You hate selfies.

Silas: I thought you'd want one.

Teagan: Did you take one with Erin?

Silas: No.

Teagan: Why not?

Silas: I don't know. It was your thing, and it felt too weird.

Silas: I'm sorry you don't get to see the real thing.

Teagan: All those love stories.

Silas: All those padlocks.

Silas: People still have all their love stories.

Teagan: It's symbolic.

Silas: Sometimes a symbol is just a symbol.

Teagan: You're the most unromantic person I've ever met. Tell Erin she should be looking for some swoony Frenchman and leave you behind.

Teagan: Where did you go? I was just teasing you.

Silas: We are kind of seeing each other a little.

Teagan: Oh wow. I was just kidding, but that's great.

Teagan: I told you you'd find someone in France. My mission is complete.

Silas: I don't think you can take credit.

Teagan: Sure I can. You needed me to make it so awkward that you had to find someone else to spend time with.

Teagan: Did I make it weird? I made it weird, huh?

Silas: Yes.

Silas: Anyway, I picked something up for you.

[photo]

Teagan: You got me a padlock?

Silas: There was a vendor there selling them. I figured even though the locks would be gone when you got here, you could still symbolically toss the key into the Seine.

Teagan: I take it back. You have your moments, even if you don't believe in symbols.

21

Teagan

WHEN THE ALARM buzzed, I flailed my arm to silence my phone, but I didn't find it on the nightstand and I forced my eyes open. "Where is my phone?" I tried to push the haze of sleep from my brain and looked around the floor.

"You can't snooze this morning," Silas said from the other side of the bed, holding up my phone and then sliding his thumb across the screen to silence the alarm.

He rolled to his side, a forearm tucked under his cheek, and grinned at me. His gaze unabashedly swept over my body, pausing on the bare skin of my shoulders and legs. "Good morning."

I lay back down and pulled the covers around us, scooting closer to him. "Why can't I snooze?"

Silas stroked his finger down my arm, making the tiny hairs stand up, until he pulled me closer. He shifted, tucking me against his chest, his fingertips still sliding over my back and down my neck. "Because you have a lot to do today and you leave the country in ten hours."

"I stayed up late," I whined, enjoying the feel of his chest and stomach under the blankets in our cocoon.

"We could have gone to sleep earlier," he said, lips grazing my forehead.

We'd managed to pull ourselves from bed, shower, make more eggs, and pack most of my things. By the time we finished, it was past midnight and we'd fallen into my bed again. "I didn't want to," I said, crossing my forearms over his chest and remembering his murmured voice, telling me about the view of Mont Fourvière from Footbridge St. Georges and how he'd go there and think of me. Then he'd kissed me and we'd been up even later.

Silas gave a little laugh, and I rested my head on his chest again, listening to the steady *thrum-thrum* of his heartbeat until he spoke. "Ten hours isn't a lot of time." He drew circles on my shoulder blades.

"No," I said, tracing my own circles on his chest. "I was thinking about it and maybe I can cut back on some of the things I planned for the trip so there's more time for us to . . ." I chewed on the words. "To be together even while we're apart. And I was planning to take some side trips that would extend my trip, but I could cut back on those. Nothing is set. I don't want to be with you and not make time for you."

"You've been waiting for this for so long." Silas was quiet, only the way his breathing changed giving away that something was wrong. "I don't want you to do that. I don't want you to change your plans for me."

"You're my plans," I said, enjoying the warmth of him against me and snuggling closer.

He didn't reply, and when I finally looked up, he had a wry smile on his lips. "That's a good line."

"Thanks. I wrote it myself." I rested my chin on my forearm so I could meet his gaze.

His expression turned serious. "I'm not your plan, though. And you weren't mine. I swore I'd never let another friendship be ruined by dating, and when we kissed in college and then I left . . ."

I stretched my arm so I could trace the line of the hair along his jaw with my fingertips.

"The way you took off and then wouldn't respond. Then when we reconnected, I didn't think it meant anything to you. It seemed like you just lost your head and kissed me because you were sad. It drove me nuts. I couldn't focus. My head was all over the place because I kissed you back because I *wanted* to. It made me feel . . . used or like a prop. I know you didn't ever mean to make me feel that way, but I did. I really thought it didn't mean anything to you."

"It meant something to me," I said, remembering how at home I'd felt in his arms, how seen and cherished I felt when his lips were against mine. "But I knew you were so broken when your ex broke up with you and you lost your friend."

"I was."

"So I ran because I was scared and I didn't know what I was feeling. When we reconnected, I never wanted you to worry you'd lose me as a friend. Plus then you had Erin, and I dropped it." I scooted higher on the bed so we were face-to-face and I could cup his jaw. "Are you worried about that now? Losing me?"

"No." His hand fell to my waist, and I thought about how much I loved learning this new side of him, the side that needed to touch and be touched. "I meant what I said last night. I love you. I mean, that's scary to admit, but it's nice, too. It's honest. I think loving you is the one thing I've been certain about for a long time, and not telling you just to keep things the same just isn't sustainable. I love you, Teag."

"I love you, too. But you want to leave this until I get back?" The warm cocoon we'd formed began to feel a little cooler, and I didn't understand what he was getting at. Hitting the brakes felt wrong down to my toes.

"I mean . . ." Silas shifted his big body until I rolled to my back, my flimsy tank top riding up, and he propped himself on his elbow.

"We waited this long." He traced a line down my sternum to my belly button, and I tensed as his fingers brushed the waistband of my sleep shorts, but he brushed his fingers back up my bare stomach, making goose bumps rise on my skin.

"What would waiting even look like? What would we wait for?" I lay still, feeling the rumpled sheet below me and Silas's fingertip moving achingly slowly up and down, teasing at my waistband each time. "Because we already *didn't wait* a few times."

His voice was low and throaty and full of Silas humor. "I remember."

I rested my palm over his, stilling it low on my belly, and met his gaze. "Tell me what you're thinking. I know you've been thinking about this. I can tell from the crease between your eyebrows."

"It's like . . . you found that pros and cons list and you worried the person who lost it would take it as a sign, right?"

"Sure."

"Well, back then, last time . . . I felt like that. Like, we were so far apart, it was a sign that the kiss was a mistake we couldn't come back from." The warmth from his palm radiated through my body. "And I thought I'd lost you."

My breath hitched when his palm edged lower. "Okay. And now?"

"Now we're talking about it." When he dropped his other hand from under his head to stroke my hairline, the combination of touches put me on edge in the most delicious way. His fingertips slid under the waistband of my shorts and I went limp with anticipation, imagining where his touch would land next. "I want to do this right, though. Are we setting ourselves up for failure starting a relationship the day you leave the country?"

"It's hard to think when you're doing that," I said, wiggling under his hand, attempting to nudge him further.

"Sorry," he said, grinning and stilling his hand. "I think we should talk; it's just hard to stop touching you."

I studied his expression, his cheeks a little pink, eyes that were hooded focusing on my face. "We'll talk and then touch," I said, soaking in the warmth of his hand.

"Go to France and do all the things you planned on doing, and I'll be here when you get back. I'm not running and neither are you."

"You don't want to talk while I'm there? It's going to be months."

"Maybe we could talk once a week or something. I don't want to be the reason you don't take time to do everything you want to do while you're in France and during all your side trips. You've waited so long for this, and I don't want to be a distraction that keeps you from soaking it all in." He dropped a kiss to my shoulder, and I smiled that his decision for us not to touch was abandoned so quickly.

"Si . . ." I knew he was right. There was so much I wanted to do, and I'd want to virtually tell him about what I'd seen all the time. "What if we hate only talking once a week?"

He kissed my shoulder again, brushing the skin. "I was lying awake last night and listening to your snoring shake the walls."

I poked him in the side where I knew he was ticklish, earning a laugh.

"And I thought about how we've been inseparable since we met. You've been a constant in my life since I was eighteen, and I in yours. If we hate it, then we'll make a new plan, but maybe being apart before we're together wouldn't be a bad thing."

"You want to date other people?"

His eyes widened in surprise. "No! I mean, do you?"

"No . . . unless he's hot and rich and French."

"Obviously. Same." Silas smiled, and I felt his palm slide incrementally lower. "But we could talk once a week and you can do all your adventures and I'll do my thing here, and save the emergence of a hot, rich Frenchman in either of our lives . . ." His hand dipped lower, fingers grazing my needy places.

"You're touching me again."

"I know." He slid his fingertip in slow circles that made me groan, and then he spoke close to my ear, the feel of his breath like more fingers on me. "When you get back, we can figure out what happens next. I know you'll want to keep traveling when you finish school, and who knows what will happen if I move up with the airline. Maybe this will be good preparation."

"Okay," I said, letting my legs fall apart, writhing already under his teasing touches.

"Okay?" His eyes met mine as his fingers worked me into a frenzy.

"Yes, but please, just—"

Silas grinned and slid under the blankets in a flash, wriggling like an oversized garter snake and making me laugh as his mouth found me under the blankets.

"That." I stared at the familiar ceiling as pleasure rolled through my body, and I tried to imagine what it would be like to talk to my best friend only once a week.

22

Silas

"FLIGHT 93 WITH service to LaGuardia at Gate D12 is now boarding all passengers, all rows."

"Guess it's time to go." I handed Teagan her bag from the floor. Her eyes were wet, and I wrapped my arms around her again. "Are you crying because you'll miss me or because you'll miss Julianna?"

Teagan laughed against my chest and I held her tighter, blinking back my own emotion. "You're a better kisser, I imagine," she said, pulling back so our eyes could meet.

"God, I both hope so and hope I never have to compete with her for your affections." I brushed her cheek with my thumb, wiping a tear from her skin. "I love you. I just wanted to say it again." I cupped the back of her neck and lowered my lips to hers.

When we pulled apart, she hugged me again. "She's just a little better than you, but she's had more experience."

I laughed and dropped another kiss on her lips. "Let me know when you get there?"

She nodded and pulled her phone from her pocket, the mobile boarding pass visible on the screen. "Here we go," she said with an exhale and a longing look toward the boarding door.

"You got this," I said, dropping one more kiss on her lips.

"You, too," she said before stepping back from me, ready to board. "I love you, Si."

"I love you, Teag."

"HANG IN THERE, man." James patted me on the back before leaving our customer service desk. He'd covered for me so I could see Teagan off for her flight. When she'd shown up to the airport in my old hoodie, I'd wanted to laugh and tear up and pull her into a hug, and I'd done all three. I'd questioned my plan all day, still unsure if suggesting we step back from each other was the right thing. That morning in bed with her body in my arms, it felt like a smart decision, but now with her plane on the way to France, all I could wrap my head around were worries that things might fall apart.

"So, how goes the investigation?" Martin walked toward me. "Uncovered all the hidden dalliances going on around here?"

"You know, I don't think we scratched the surface." I leaned forward on the counter, catching some of the early morning sunlight that flooded the gate area nearby this time of morning. "You gave good tips, though. The baristas sure looked like they were on their way to dating when we walked away, and it turns out the luggage guy is Jess's ex-husband."

"Well, hey. Look at that. You two were playing Cupid!" Martin smacked the surface of the counter with a good-natured *thwack*. "Who'd the letter belong to?"

I shrugged. "We never found out."

"You're giving up?"

I glanced across the hall at the stranger standing there in a pink apron. "Teagan's flight left about an hour ago."

"Ah," Martin said. "And she took the fun of this with her on the plane, along with your heart?" Before I could respond, Martin laughed. "I told you, boy, it's as clear as day." He held up a palm. "And I know you said you're just friends, but I'm just telling you I think you're lying."

"She did take my heart, but I think she'll bring it back."

Martin slapped his thigh. "I knew it! Told Julie the other day, and now she owes me five bucks."

I tried to imagine how the unlikely friendship between Martin and Julianna looked and I couldn't make the pieces fit together, but it didn't matter. "We were all out of ideas about who it could belong to anyway."

"Hm . . . maybe I can help. Can I see this letter? You have it? You didn't actually tell me much about it the first time."

I pulled my phone from my pocket and scrolled through to a photo of the list. It had been printed from someone's email, but the original information about the date and who sent it was missing. "It's really not a love letter, more of a pros and cons list."

I handed it over to Martin, who zoomed in and dragged his finger along the screen while he read. I glanced around the space again. I thought about the love stories we'd seen play out since beginning the investigation—young love, old love, unrequited love. Teagan teased me all the time about how little credence I gave symbols and metaphors. It wasn't that I didn't understand them. I just didn't think they were signs from the universe, but when she told me there was a job open at the airport that I'd be great at, she'd tried to sell me on the beauty of so many stories coalescing in one place. At the time I'd been more interested in the health insurance, but now I saw it.

Across the hall, the stranger in the pink apron prepared to close the shop, checking things behind the lowered gate. It would take time to get used to Teagan not being there, not being within arm's reach all the time. She'd always been there. Even when I was in France, she was still always there, on my mind and on the other end of a call.

Martin was still reading, scrolling up and then back down, a faint smile on his face. "Well," he said finally, setting my phone down. "You should have showed me this in the first place."

"Yeah?" I slipped my phone back into my pocket. "You saw some clues?"

"Better than that," he said with a grin. "I know who wrote it."

23

Video Chat

**AFTER ONE WEEK IN FRANCE
A SATURDAY**

Teagan: I have a thousand things to tell you. A week is an eternity.

Silas: I know. Do you feel French yet?

Teagan: I missed you. Are you sure about this distance and space thing?

Silas: No, but I still think it's a good idea.

Teagan: I guess you're right.

Teagan: So, these weekly chats . . . they can involve sexy times?

Silas: I could be interested in that.

Teagan: And let's discuss this. When did you get good at sex?

Silas: I've always been good at sex.

Teagan: Lies. I taught you about the G-spot and clitoris junior year.

Silas: With a grapefruit. How could I forget.

Silas: Visiting you was always so memorable.

Teagan: Your future girlfriends all thanked me.

Silas: I think my next girlfriend appreciates you.

Teagan: Thanks, self. You're a VIP.

Silas: By the way, I dropped everything from your apartment at your mom's place.

Teagan: You repacked it, didn't you?

Silas: I don't know if you throwing everything in garbage bags because we spent too long in bed counts as packing in the first place.

Teagan: It wasn't just that we spent so much time in bed. We were in the shower, too.

Silas: What am I going to do with you?

Teagan: Why are you laughing at me? It's true!

Silas: Yes, I repacked all your stuff. And cleaned the shower, so everything is ready for your subletter.

Teagan: You're really great.

Silas: I know.

Silas: Great at sex, as you said.

Teagan: I said "good."

Silas: I'll buy some grapefruits to practice on while you're gone.

Silas: Speaking of you being gone . . . you ready for the first day of class?

Teagan: No! I'm nervous. Can I just spew my anxiety at you?

Silas: Of course.

Teagan: Okay, so . . .

24

Video Chat

AFTER FOUR WEEKS IN FRANCE
A SATURDAY

Silas: Hey, you.

Silas: You're muted, sweet cheeks.

Teagan: Ugh, why do I always do that? Also, sweet cheeks?

Silas: I'm trying to find the right pet name for you.

Teagan: Well . . . keep trying. Sweet cheeks ain't it.

Silas: Noted. You look exhausted. Everything okay?

Teagan: I truly love that you went from "sweet cheeks" to "you look like crap." *(Laughing)*

Silas: You look gorgeous and sexy and only a little rough. Late night?

Teagan: Yeah. We decided at the last minute to take a train to Paris and partied and explored all weekend, so I was up late last night finishing my part of a paper I put off. I need to get it to my group members today.

Silas: Isn't Paris like five hours from Lyon?

Teagan: Only two on the train, so I could have worked on the paper then but . . .

Silas: You made friends with strangers instead?

Teagan: Not strangers, just friends I hadn't met yet.

Silas: You didn't meet that rich, sexy Frenchman, did you?

Teagan: A couple of them, but they don't eat grapefruit, so you're safe.

Silas: Whew! I was worried. Glad you're meeting new people and doing all the things you want to, though.

Teagan: You, sugar butt, don't look exhausted at all. You're glowing, if I'm honest.

Silas: Sugar butt? Is that payback for sweet cheeks?

Teagan: Sucrose glutes?

Silas: Much better! As for the glowing, you might make fun of me.

Silas: I went to a day spa with Ada. We got facials.

Teagan: Like . . . Ada from the airport?

Silas: Her sister backed out at the last minute and she was teasing me about being lonely with you gone, and I ended up agreeing to go with her. It was kind of fun. Did you know Ada was in the navy and is a drummer in a band? James and I went to see her perform, and she's good.

Teagan: I still can't believe we didn't find out who wrote the list. I was sure we'd figure it out. For a minute, it felt

like it was mirroring our story, and I wanted a happy
ending.

Silas: I'm, um, still working on it.

Teagan: Give me updates!

Silas: I'll tell you when I get something good. I promise. It's
not Ada or Sam, though. She's way too good for him, and if
I was into women twice my age and didn't have you . . .

Teagan: She's cooler than me and I'm in France. Shoot
your shot.

Silas: I only have eyes for you.

Silas: And even exhausted you're the most beautiful woman
I've ever seen.

Teagan: You're going to make me cry. And I love that
you're getting out and doing things. I was worried you'd
stay home without me there to drag you out.

Silas: I did, for a while, but yeah. This has been good.

Teagan: James isn't mad you stole me after he asked me
out?

Silas: Yeah, James . . . has way more game than I ever
knew. Going out with the guy is like being at a casting call
for a modeling agency. I can safely say he's moved on from
you.

Teagan: I so want to see you in a club playing wingman!

Silas: I'll take some video next time. We've been hanging
out a lot.

Teagan: Silas! You made friends!

Silas: Shut up . . . I'm not a total hermit.

Teagan: You are, but in a good way. Like a sexy hermit.

Silas: It's amazing you mock me like this and I still want to kiss you.

Teagan: Yeah?

Silas: Yeah. Tell me more about Paris.

25

Video Chat

AFTER THREE MONTHS IN FRANCE
A SATURDAY

Teagan: Hi!

Silas: Hey, honeybun.

Teagan: Keep googling nicknames, syrup rump.

Silas: I like syrup ru—

Teagan: Silas? I think you're frozen. Can you hear me?

Teagan: You still there?

———

Silas: Teag, sorry. I don't know what happened, but everything froze and then I couldn't get back on. I got your voice mail, so you're probably in bed now. I'm so bummed to have missed you tonight. Can we talk tomorrow instead? I love you. Sleep well.

A MONDAY

Teagan: Hey, it's me. I was hoping I could catch you before you went to work. Things are nuts here, but it's so amazing.

I wish you were here and I could show you everything. I took a day trip to Vienna and I felt so inspired. I just couldn't get the words down fast enough. It's like when I was in Barcelona last month. I just felt inspired. I'll tell you about it soon. I hope we can catch each other. I love you.

A TUESDAY

Silas: I went to Vienna when I was there. Do you remember me telling you about it? I can't wait to read all this writing. I had to work a double shift so I'm sorry I missed you again.

A WEDNESDAY

Teagan: This is hard. I guess we'll just connect next week at our normal call time. I got an A on that last paper. My professor talked to me about graduate school. He thinks I'd have a shot at a good MFA program in creative writing. Can you believe it?

———

Silas: I'm so proud of you. I can believe it. And yeah, it's harder than I thought. I didn't realize how much time we spent together until you were gone. I think I count on you to make me . . . interesting, and I've had to figure that out with people on my own. I don't know. Anyway, I love you. I know you're in class now, so . . . we'll talk soon.

A THURSDAY

Teagan: You were always interesting. Hey, I took this picture for you the last time we took the train into Paris. After I snapped the selfie with it next to my face, three people reminded me I couldn't attach the padlock to the bridge. I told them I didn't need to. I'll talk to you tomorrow at our normal time.

———

Silas: This is the cheesiest message I've ever left, but you aren't the only one with a padlock, and I know you'll appreciate that after taking this selfie with it over my heart, I accidentally hit myself in the nose with it. Have a good night.

26

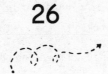

AFTER ALMOST FIVE MONTHS IN FRANCE
A SATURDAY

Teagan: Where's your video? I can only hear you.

Silas: Just a bad connection. What's wrong?

Teagan: How do you know something is wrong?

Silas: I hear it in your voice.

Teagan: I loved this trip but I want to be back near you. I'm tired of waiting and growing and becoming our own people. We did that, but now I want to be *with* my person.

Silas: I know. Me, too. Soon, though. Only another month.

Teagan: I wore out my vibrator. I didn't budget for replacing it.

Silas: Do you need to buy some grapefruits so you can reacquaint yourself with driving a manual transmission?

Teagan: *(Laughing)* No, I bought a new one. I'll just go without food for a couple weeks. Priorities.

Silas: Your vibrator costs what you'd theoretically spend on food for a couple weeks?

Teagan: Clearly you're not spending enough time searching for high-end toys.

Silas: I guess not. You are still actually eating food, right?

Teagan: Of course. I'm waiting for dinner to get delivered. Hey, you want to know something weird?

Silas: Of course. Is it related to high-end toys?

Teagan: No. I actually miss Julianna's chocolates. Can you believe it?

Silas: They're good! Should I send you some?

Teagan: Yes! A whole box of my favorites, please.

Silas: I'll get on that. Um, do you want to know what I found out about the list?

Teagan: Yes! You found a new clue?

Silas: Okay, so . . . don't be mad at me.

Teagan: That makes me assume I'm going to be furious.

Silas: I've known who wrote the list for a while.

Teagan: How long is a while?

Silas: . . .

Teagan: You're very lucky there's an ocean between us. How long?

Silas: Um . . . I found out the night you left.

Teagan: You've known for five months!?

Silas: I swear I had a reason for not telling you.

Teagan: Spill it. You're on probation.

Silas: Well, Martin wrote it.

Teagan: Martin? No way! About who?

Silas: It was like two years ago, and he wrote it about . . .

Teagan: Say it already!

Silas: Julianna.

Teagan: No way. Not possible!

Silas: He said they were getting close and he wrote the pros and cons list and he sent it to her, like via email.

Teagan: You're messing with me. Not possible.

Silas: That's what he said! She must have printed it and, I don't know, it ended up behind a box or fell or something, but I guess that's how you found it.

Teagan: She said she wasn't seeing anyone.

Silas: Well, that's why I didn't tell you. He was into her and made the list, but they tried for a month or so and it fizzled. Didn't work out.

Teagan: Oh.

Silas: And you were so convinced the list was a sign of it being like us. I didn't want you to take it as a bad sign.

Teagan: Martin and . . . Julianna? Wow.

Silas: That's what he said. They decided they were better as friends, and that's how it is now.

Silas: You still there?

Teagan: Yeah, sorry. I think my food delivery just showed up.

Silas: No problem. So, what do you think about the end to the mystery? Kind of a letdown?

Teagan: Just a little, but I guess it's okay. I like the idea of the list being a symbol for us, but I don't think it is. I mean, that's why we waited, right? To take some time apart to make sure being together is what we want, and I do want that. Hey. Hold on, my food is here.

(Door opens)

Teagan: *Bonsoir. Merc—*

Silas: Did you know my employee discount can be used for international flights?

Teagan: I can't believe you're here!

Silas: I made a pros and cons list about coming.

Teagan: This is unreal. You're on my doorstep. Come in!

Silas: Do you want to hear the list?

Teagan: No, I want to kiss you!

Silas: I want that, too, but can I read it to you first?

Teagan: Can you read it fast? Because what I want is to tackle you to the ground.

Silas: Con: You'll probably steal all my stuff. Pro: I won't have to worry about checked luggage.

Silas: Con: I'll owe James big for covering my shifts at the last minute. Pro: I can brush up on my French.

Silas: Pros: I want to kiss you awake in the morning and make you omelets, and I want to call you the woman who is the most important person in my life instead of just thinking it. I want us, and I don't want to wait anymore.

Teagan: You didn't say the last con.

Silas: There isn't one. I—

(Knock on the door)

Teagan: Oh, that's my food. Uh, hold on.

Teagan: *Merci.*

Teagan: Sorry, that kind of spoiled the moment. Our timing is always bad, isn't it?

Silas: Nah. I think we've always been right where we needed each other at the right times.

Teagan: Can I tackle you to the ground now?

Silas: Definitely. Oh, and I brought you these.

Teagan: Julianna's chocolates.

Silas: Who knows you, sugar?

Teagan: I'm going to kiss you now in hopes you eventually come up with a better nickname.

Silas: Might take a lot of kissing.

Teagan: Might take a lifetime of it.

Silas: No veto.

Epilogue

Martin

"ATTENTION IN THE boarding area. Flight 706 with service to Phoenix is now boarding."

I settled against the counter and accepted the second truffle Julianna handed me. "Thank you." I eyed the new flavor. "What is it?"

"Just try it." She was annoyed when I asked before taking a bite, like she always was. Probably the reason I always asked. "It's not like I'm gonna hand you something you don't eat or try to poison you."

"True," I said with a chuckle. "You'd've poisoned me a long time ago if you were planning to." I bit into the milk chocolate, the shell cracking and a combination of strawberries and peanut butter filling my mouth. "Mm. Julie, this is good."

She brushed her hands down her apron. "Of course it is." I saw the grin at the corner of her lips, that secret smile she tried to hide when I loved one of her new creations. "It's one of the ideas Teagan tried to sell me on before she abandoned us to travel the world."

I glanced out the front of the store, giving a wave to the two girls from the coffee kiosk walking by hand in hand. I didn't know them well, but young love always showed up on my radar. "You ever wonder why there's so much love in this airport?"

Julianna rolled her eyes at my observation and began cleaning the counter. "Because a lot of people are horny toads?"

I touched my fingers to the back of her hand to still her scrubbing of an already spotless counter. A few days earlier I'd chatted with Silas on his way to catch his flight and finally go get his girl. I never understood why they put off being together while she was away, but I was happy they'd gotten over the 'finding themselves' thing. "Jess from the grooming place and her husband are back together, and remember how her business partner met her husband right here near the C gates?"

"Oh, don't mention the dog women to me." She brushed off my hand and kept cleaning, holding on to her old grudge against the women who'd moved into the storefront her old friend had occupied for years. I was pretty sure the grudge didn't have teeth anymore. Julie just liked to look tough and unyielding.

"Then that couple got engaged at the gate with that crazy dance party? Love is all around us." I gazed down the hall before looking back to her and accepting one more of the peanut butter and jelly chocolates.

"Are you drunk?"

I winked. "Not yet. You wanna grab a drink on the way home?"

Julianna met my gaze with an annoyed look that cracked quickly, and I earned another of her small smiles and a shrug. "Sure. I could use a glass of wine."

I helped her lock things up and we walked toward the parking garage, the route toward the exit as familiar to me as the back of my own hand.

When we reached the exit, the summer air swirled around us, blowing one lock of gray-and-black hair around Julie's face. I always liked watching her hands when she brushed her hair off her face. She had a soft side; it just only came through in those kinds of moments. "I've been meaning to ask you something, old man."

I nodded. "As a gentleman, I won't remind you that we're the same age."

"Why did you tell those kids it didn't work out between us?" She reached into her pocket and fiddled with her key fob when we neared the garage.

I'd told her all about the conversation I'd had with Silas when he finally showed me that list. I hadn't thought about it in more than a year, and it was wild to see my words on the page. I shrugged. "A little white lie. I knew it wasn't gonna change how over the moon he was for that girl. I was right, by the way. He ran off to France to see her, and I'm calling it now—they're engaged by next year. And anyway, you told me you'd skin my hide if any gossip about you and me ever started."

"I guess I did." She looked around and then stepped close to me, touching my cheek with her delicate fingers. "I can't believe you were able to keep your mouth shut this long."

I pulled her to me next to her car. "A man does a lot of things for the woman he loves that he won't do for anyone else."

"Holding in juicy gossip is a feat for you." She gave me a quick kiss before we climbed into her car.

"It is. You know I'm a born storyteller." I fastened my seat belt and inhaled the scent of her car, which was always a little floral mixed with the aroma of chocolate. "You gonna let me make an honest woman out of you one of these days?"

She signaled as we worked our way out of the garage. "You got a ring in your pocket or something?"

I laughed. "No, ma'am. You also said you'd skin my hide if I ever proposed inside the airport."

"Yep. This," she said motioning toward the terminal, "is not my idea of a romantic place."

I followed her gaze and then linked my fingers with hers, pulling them to my lips. "On that we disagree, beautiful. On that we disagree."

Acknowledgments

Attention in the terminal, luggage full of gratitude and appreciation for bringing this collection of stories together has arrived at baggage claim. Please check your departure city, as many bags may look alike, but all were packed with heartfelt appreciation.

✈️ DSM

Thank you to my home, comfort, sanity, and fellow mess-makers. Husband, Tiny Human, Best Dog, and Worst Dog, you keep me feeling loved, inspired, and caffeinated. I love you.

✈️ OMA

I am lucky to have a family of people who both exemplify beautiful love stories and fully embrace air travel. Maybe it was kismet that I would write airport-based love stories? Thank you to Mom and Dad, who put me on my first international flight as an infant; to Jay (sorry I told you turbulence meant the plane was going to crash when you were six!); and to Amanda, John, Jovie, Barb, Tim, Allison, Kaitlin, Crystal, Bruce, Jean, Mike, Melissa, Xander, and the best aunts, uncles, and cousins from Sea-Tac to RSW.

✈ 🚄 LGA→JFK→EWR

Some of the people most responsible for this book being in your hands live or work in New York. None of my books would happen without them. Thank you to Kerry Donovan, my editor and someone whose love of stories shines through in her work. Thank you to Dache' Rogers, Bridget O'Toole, Hannah Engler, Mary Baker, Liz Gluck, Alison Cnockaert, Farjana Yasmin, Rita Frangie, and the rest of the Berkley and PRH teams—I would give up an available outlet after a long flight for any of you.

I will forever share my Biscoff cookies with my agent, Sharon Pelletier, who also came up with the title of this book. Thank you for being amazing all the time, without fail and in every way! Thank you also to Lauren Abramo, Andrew Dugan, and Gracie Freeman Lifschutz at Dystel, Goderich & Bourret, and Kristina Moore at UTA.

✈ 🚄 LGA→ATL→LAX→DFW

These books came out in audio versions first, and I owe a special thank-you to Karen Dziekonski, Maureen Monterubio, and Jessica Kaye, plus everyone on the PRH Audio Team. I am eternally in awe of narrators' abilities to bring our words as authors to life. Thank you to January LaVoy, Shane East, Jakobi Diem, Zenzi Williams, Angel Pean, and Teddy Hamilton for taking a trip to the airport with me and delivering the captivating performance you did with Ollie, Bennett, Felix, Gia, Teagan, and Silas.

✈ MCO→DSM→WRWA→AUS→PHX→RDU

My dear friends who make my stories better and my heart happier are across the country and all over the world. Thank you for helping me fine-tune these stories, reading early versions, and joining me in biweekly meltdowns that usually devolved into sharing funny Tik-Tok videos. I couldn't do any of this without Bethany, Allison Ashley, Katie Golding, Jen DeLuca, and Libby Hubscher. Thank you also to Brian, Kristine, Matt, the 2020 Debuts of Color group, Rosie Danan, Jane Igharo, Priscilla Oliveras, and so many other gorgeous souls.

✈ SEA-TAC→ORD→DCA→ARN

Thank you to Cass Newbould, Taj McCoy, Charish Reid, and Alicia Sparrow, my Better Than Brunch crew! Our Sunday writing groups and DM thread are lifesavers, and you are all beautiful writers and even more beautiful people.

✈ BWI→BOS→MKE→PDX

I would not have made it through 2021 and writing these stories without Romance Fight Club. Thank you to Beth, Allie, Tova, and J, and our main men, T & Victor. I love you all to pieces (except T, whom I would relegate to the back of the plane).

✈ PHL→PIA→CYOW

In these books I decided to speak French, speak chemistry, and speak with a British accent. Thank you to my tutors. Margo Ryan explained chemistry basics to me like I failed freshman chemistry (because I did), and she was gracious, lovely, and insightful in her suggestions for *The Missed Connection*. Suzi Vanderham helped me edit *The Love Connection* to get Bennett's voice right, and she is also a consummate cheerleader. Thank you for being a lover of books, a true friend, and a fellow pancake fiend. Thank you to Lydia M. Hawke for my French lesson in preparation for *The Sweetest Connection*. You saved me from Google translate. *Merci beaucoup!*

AMW

I love my job as a writer, but I also work full-time on a college campus with some of the best people in higher education. Thank you for always having my back, current and former MSA family, Emily, Tera, the Cardinal Women, Matt, Haley, Rachel Mans McKenny, Jen, Ann, Jenn, and all my romance-loving colleagues who share book recs before (*cough* during) meetings. Thank you to Dog Eared Books in Ames and Beaverdale Books and Storyhouse Bookpub in Des Moines—local bookstores are phenomenal and critical for so many reasons, and I never feel more at home as an author than when I'm in your shops.

Finally, thank you to my Juicy Readers and everyone who has welcomed my stories into their lives. Let's share a pretzel on a moving walkway together someday!

Keep reading for an excerpt from

Do You Take This Man

1

RJ

I DIDN'T BLAME Maddie Anderson for scowling at her soon-to-be ex-husband.

He appeared calm and collected in a somber Italian suit, remaining quiet and deferent, and seeming reasonable. He almost looked bored by the proceedings and the minutiae of his marriage ending. I made note of the gray at his temples and supposed it was easy to look dignified as a fifty-seven-year-old sitting next to one's twenty-three-year-old wife, and probably easy to look bored when you'd done this a time or two before.

Behind the makeup, Maddie's eyes were puffy, and the cuticle on her thumb looked shredded, like she'd been nervously scratching it. Since walking in on her husband with not one but two women during their son's first birthday party, she'd been through a lot. The hurt and embarrassment were clear in the woman's mannerisms, but Mr. Anderson didn't seem to care.

I'd never been in Ms. Anderson's shoes—today, a pair of crystal-encrusted pink stilettos. I'd learned young that people were rarely worth trusting, and baring your teeth was easier than baring your soul only to be shown you weren't worth someone's time. It didn't make me bitter, but it made me careful. It also made me enjoy these little moments when I could help someone else bare their teeth.

Granted, my client huffed anytime opposing counsel spoke. I glanced at the clock on the far side of the wall and estimated how long this would take. Despite the eye-rolling, gum popping, and faint smell of a perfume probably marketed to teenagers, Maddie Anderson was going to leave this office a very rich woman.

Twenty-five minutes later and before rushing back to my desk, I smiled at Maddie, whose philandering ex-husband was not as covert in his affairs as he'd hoped, and who'd chosen the wrong woman to underestimate.

"Everything should be finalized by the end of the month." I shook Maddie's hand to interrupt the hug coming my way and shared her smile. One point for the wronged woman and one more win for me. I rushed down the hall, trying not to look like I was in a hurry even though it was five fifteen and there was no way I was going to be on time.

"RJ." The smoky voice of one of the senior partners left me cursing in my head as I turned to greet her. Gretchen Vanderkin-Shaw would have scared the crap out of me if I didn't admire her so much. Really, she still scared the crap out of me, but as a named partner before forty with a success rate through the roof, she was a force to be reckoned with, and she liked me. Gretchen was the lawyer I wanted to be, and I was gathering my courage to ask her to be my mentor.

She nodded toward the conference room. "The Anderson case?"

"We were able to come to a resolution that worked in our favor." That was code for crushing them like tiny little bugs and then doing a victory dance that might involve some light professional twerking.

She nodded, a faint smile on her lips because I'd learned the victory dance from her. "Excellent. Eric mentioned you wanting to talk to me. I have a free hour now."

I stole a quick glance at my watch, because nine times out of ten, if Gretchen asked to meet, we did. Hell, if she asked me to hop, I'd have gone full Cha Cha Slide.

"Do you have somewhere to be?"

I could have lied and said a conference call or a client meeting, but what was the point? Everything I was doing was happening because the firm wanted to keep a client happy. Well, mostly. "I have to be downtown at six."

Her mouth formed into a thin line, and I knew she'd decoded my reason for needing to be downtown. She nodded. "Well, you'd better go. You know how I feel about this, though, RJ. You're better than some publicity stunt."

I fumbled with a response, biting my lower lip. That wasn't characteristic of me—I held my shoulders back and chin up on the regular, and I never backed down from anything. I made powerful people want to cower, and I was good at it. She was right, and I was better than a publicity stunt, but I had to admit, I enjoyed this particular stunt. "Thank you for checking in. I'll talk to your assistant and make an appointment."

I hurried into the back of a waiting Uber, with plans to change clothes modestly in the back seat. Was I telling myself I would be modest, knowing that I was about to give anyone looking a bit of a show? Absolutely.

> PENNY: Where are you?
>
> RJ: On my way. There's traffic.
>
> PENNY: You're killing me.

I sent her the knife emoji. *Top of my class in law school and this is my life now. Event planners harassing me as I strip down in the back of an Uber.* My phone buzzed again from the seat as I brushed powder onto my cheeks and checked my edges in a compact.

PENNY: But I love you.

RJ: I know.

RJ: You have the mic set up how I like?

PENNY: Yes, but if you're late, you're getting a
handheld with a tangled cord.

I pulled out the binder where I'd prepared my script. All the
pages were in plastic covers with labeled tabs just in case, a copy of
all pertinent information in the back folder and a Post-it Note reminding me of everyone's names and pronouns tucked in the front.
I climbed from the car and repeated the opening phrase to myself as
I hurried toward the stairs of the venue. I spoke part of the line to
myself. ". . . the promise of hope between two people who love each
other sincerely, who—"

Suddenly I was hurtling toward the sidewalk, not sure whether
I should try to save myself, my bag, or the notes. I clutched the binder
to my chest as I hit the concrete, scraping my leg, my palm stinging
with the impact. The clothes I'd hurriedly shoved into my bag after
changing fluttered around me, and I took in the large form who'd
been blocking the sidewalk.

In a movie, this would be the start of a how-we-met story. The
tall guy, his features obscured by the sun at his back, would lean
down and help me up. Our eyes would meet. He'd apologize, I'd
note something like the depth of his voice or the tickle of the hair on
his forearms, and we'd be off. That might have happened for other
people, but though our eyes met, I was not in the market for cute,
and now I was about to arrive late and bruised to perform this couple's wedding rehearsal.

2

Lear

I STEPPED OUT of my car and stood looking up at the wedding venue as if I were standing on some great precipice. My phone buzzed again, and against my better judgment, I looked at the screen.

SARAH: I just need to know you're okay.

She hadn't texted for a while. Someone must have told her I'd gone home. I'd never planned to return to Asheville, North Carolina, and yet there I was, living in my cousin's basement after doing my best impression of someone trying to self-destruct for the better part of a year.

I tapped the delete icon with more force than it needed. I imagined the sympathetic face she'd probably made while typing out the text, with her lower lip out, eyes soft. When I didn't respond, she'd sigh in exasperation. She told me once that nothing drove her crazier than when someone didn't respond to texts, and I made it a point from then on to never leave her hanging. One of the many things I did to make sure I was everything she wanted, something I'd done with everyone since I was a teenager.

Done with her sympathy. Done with her. Done with being a nice guy. My phone buzzed again, but this time it was my cousin.

> **PENNY:** Did you go back to LA or something?
> Can you still cover this?
>
> **LEAR:** Got held up. There in a sec.
>
> **PENNY:** You're killing me.

I shoved my phone into my pocket, clearing my head so I could take on my first task as Penny's assistant wedding planner. The title required a second deep breath, because my old job, planning events for a professional football team—my dream job—was across the country, and it wasn't mine anymore. With Sarah's text fresh on my mind as a reminder that falling in love was the first step off a cliff, I headed into my first day as a wedding professional. I'd helped my cousin with setup earlier in the day, but now my only task was to woo a prospective client and her mother. I sucked in a breath. *Here goes my new life.*

A fast-moving body stopped my progress when it rammed into me, the voice of its owner high pitched as they cried "Motherf—" but hit the ground before completing the expletive.

The woman was sprawled on the pavement, the contents of what looked to be her entire life strewn around her. Her shocked expression quickly shifted, lips pursed and brow furrowed.

"Dammit," I muttered.

She was dressed professionally, but the grass near her thigh was littered with a few tampons, a balled-up shirt, a stick of deodorant, a small bottle of maple syrup, and nine rolls of butter rum Life Savers. I lost focus on her haughty expression and tried to figure out why a person would have these things just with her. If she wasn't still muttering curse words under her breath, I would have really taken a moment to appreciate the randomness of the maple syrup and the audacity of that many Life Savers.

She looked up at me like I owed her something, eyes narrowed and expression incredulous, and I lost interest in the contents of her bag. I didn't have time for this, but I tried to sand the edge from my voice. "You should watch where you're going," I said in what I hoped was a playful tone, holding out a hand only to be met with a deeper scowl.

"Speak for yourself," she said in a huff, pushing away my hand and scrambling for balance. Her face was pinched, annoyed, and she turned in a flash to collect her things. "And manners. Have you heard of them?"

"You ran into me."

"Because you were standing in the middle of the sidewalk, not moving."

I still held out my hand to help her. Ten years in LA hadn't completely robbed me of my Southern home training, but this random angry little woman was pissing me off. I reminded myself that I left the nice-guy thing back in California, along with everything else. I shook my outstretched hand at her, letting any veil of politeness slip. "Will you take my damn hand so we can both get going?"

She scowled again, and the entitlement running off her petite frame in this brief exchange hit me in waves, even from a few feet away. "This is not what I needed today." As she pushed herself to her feet, she ignored my outstretched hand, and I stepped back.

Her hands flew frantically over her clothes and swiped at her hip. She muttered to herself as she tried to pick everything up, swatting my hand away when I tried to help. "Assholes just standing in the middle of the sidewalk," she muttered to herself. "The last damn thing I needed today . . ."

I'd never heard that combination of whisper-quiet cursing. My instinct was to offer help again, to apologize again, and to smile until she walked away, but if the last several months had taught me anything, it was that my instincts weren't all that great.

"Good luck with that." Without another word, I turned to walk away, but not before deciding I could truly go against everything my gut told me to do, to hammer that last nail in the coffin of the old me. I called over my shoulder, "You know, you should smile more."

I regretted it immediately. My sister would have my ass on a plate if she knew I'd uttered those words. I thought briefly about turning back to apologize, but I was already pressing my luck after getting lost. My phone buzzed in my pocket again, no doubt my cousin.

I pushed the woman from the sidewalk out of my mind and reminded myself that being a nice guy was not on my priority list anymore. I'd probably never see her again anyway.

THE VENUE HAD been a bank once upon a time, and the old architecture framed the entryway. Following a complete renovation years ago, it was an event space now and today would host a wedding rehearsal. I wondered if the vault was still in place and if anyone held parties there.

LEAR: I'm here and waiting for them. Fear not.

PENNY: You're my favorite cousin, but if you fuck this up, I'll end you.

LEAR: Noted. Love you, too.

The door opened, letting in a swath of sunlight. A pang of anxiety hit me that it might be the woman from outside, and I ducked my head, intent on examining the pattern on the marble floor. Instead of the angry growl someone had briefly introduced me to outside, a voice that sounded more like chirping filled the space.

A stylish younger woman chatted with an older woman, both adjusting their blond hair. Catching my eye, the younger woman beamed. "Are you Penny's cousin? She said you'd be tall and well dressed and, oh my, you are. How lovely. She didn't say you'd be so good-looking, but of course you are." She talked without pause, her words flowing from her nervous laughter. I flashed an easy smile at Melinda and Victoria Matthews, daughter and wife of Richard Matthews. The family apparently owned one-third of North Carolina.

"Nice to meet you," I said smoothly, taking the younger woman's hand. "Lear Campbell." I wanted to make a good first impression, but I also wanted her to stop rambling. From what Penny had said, the bride wanted to copy and paste the next day's wedding, but we wanted her to feel like she was just getting inspiration. Her wedding was over a year away and it seemed silly to be concerned with how the rehearsal venue's lobby and gardens might work, but Penny's words played in my head. *Make them feel special. Don't disparage any idea they love, no matter how bad the idea is. Make it seem like you can move mountains.* She'd also added *Don't make that face,* but I was fairly certain that was her being my older cousin and not my boss.

"This is so beautiful!" Melinda twirled around in a circle, looking at the space. She also seemed to end every sentence with an exclamation point, her voice high and excited. She reminded me of a teenager or a terrier.

"It's a beautiful venue. You chose well." My compliment on her excellent taste was met with a beaming smile from both mother and daughter. Penny didn't give me quite enough credit. It wasn't like I didn't have to schmooze and make people feel important working in professional sports. "We can visit the gardens. That space isn't in use now."

"We are just so excited. I can't believe—" Her voice halted and her eyes grew wide.

Over my shoulder, I saw the woman from the sidewalk hurry out of the restroom across the vestibule. I snapped my head down before she caught my face. She'd put herself back together, clothes straightened and her hair, which had come loose when she fell, pulled back into a bun that showed off her neck. She had a nice neck. She was short but in sky-high heels and a black dress that subtly highlighted her rounded curves. She looked better when she wasn't scowling at me from the ground. It was a wonder I hadn't seen any of that outside. *Well, maybe not a wonder. She was pretty adamantly insisting I was an asshole at the time.*

"Mom," the girl hissed. "That's her! The woman who performed Alejandro's wedding! I love her." Mrs. Matthews followed her daughter's gaze.

"Who is Alejandro?" Her voice was sweet and slow. Her accent reminded me of my aunt, and I smiled, also interested to learn why the bride knew who the woman from outside was.

"Alejandro Calderón proposed to George O'Toole in the park and it was totes cute, just, like, all the feels. Their families were there, and he said all these nice things. Mom, I was seriously bawling." The woman bounced on her heels, her energy like a gale force wind.

"Melly, you know I don't know who those people are," her mother interjected.

I'd been in a hole for almost a year and even I knew who they were. The two men had played opposite each other in a superhero epic a couple years earlier, and when the country's new favorite hero and most reviled fictional villain started dating, it was big news.

Melinda fiddled with her phone and held it out to her mom. "You remember. They were in the Interstellar Man movies. I had the biggest crush on Alejandro when I was a kid and had all these posters." She took a breath, and I slid into the conversation, because this was taking us way off course.

"Weren't those movies great?" I asked smoothly, sidestepping Melinda's trip down Middle School Crush Lane. "So, they got married?"

"Anyway, this woman was in the park where it happened and could perform weddings, so they did it that day. She was amazing, like, such a beautiful ceremony that she wrote on the fly. Absolutely everyone has seen the video. Mom, we have to get her. Can you imagine if the same woman who married the coolest couple in Hollywood married me and Sam?"

I peeked over my shoulder again as the woman strode toward where the wedding would be held, hands smoothing down the front of her outfit.

"Well, you know your father and I would prefer you use our pastor, but it's your day, and if you want this woman, it's fine with us." She turned to me. "Can you check on that?" I did not know the answer to her question and would rather have talked up an anti-deodorant activist with a new multilevel marketing obsession than show my face to that woman, but Penny had told me to make them think we could move mountains, so I nodded.

"She's completely popular, but everyone on the wedding websites says she doesn't take new clients. How cool is it that she's attending this wedding?" the younger woman exclaimed, her smile spreading. "If you could get her, I would be the happiest bride in all North Carolina."

As the woman I'd left scowling on the sidewalk reached the door, a slip of paper fell out of her binder, and I jogged over to her. *Turn on the charm. Apologize. Move mountains.*

"Excuse me?" I bent to pick up the yellow Post-it Note from the ground. "You dropped this."

At my voice, she turned, her smile genuine. "Oh, thank—" She stopped when she saw my face, her soft eyes snapping into cold daggers and her smile turning into a tight line of full, pressed lips.

I held out the note and smiled anyway.

"Thank you," she said coolly, taking the slip of paper but being careful not to touch my hand, as if I'd peed on it or something.

"Listen, I'm sorry about what I said outside. I was way out of line and—"

She interrupted me with practiced skill. "Can I help you with something? I'm in a hurry."

"Yes, I just wanted to apologize. I'm Lear Campbell," I said, holding out my hand.

She looked at it like I'd just offered her an old gym sock. "Lear? Like King Lear?"

"It's a nickname," I said, pulling my hand back for a moment. "My client over there is interested in working with you on a wedding." I motioned to the embodiment of fangirling, her blond ponytail bobbing while she bounced on her heels. "Do you have a card, or can I call you about your availability?"

"Did you hear me say I'm in a hurry?"

"Sure—"

She interrupted me again. "Are you familiar with the phrase?" She arched one eyebrow in a way that made me feel two inches tall despite having a good eight on her.

This might be the least pleasant person I've ever met, beautiful body and stunning smile be damned. "I am," I gritted out. "If I could just get your card."

The door to the anteroom pushed open, and Penny slipped out. "RJ. Thank God. I was about to send out a search party. You're never actually late." She glanced between us. "And you met Lear," she said to her with a sideways glance at me. "He's just starting out with me. Lear, RJ Brooks is the officiant."

Oh shit.

I noted the binder RJ held, the one she'd clutched to her chest outside. The officiant for this wedding. That made sense and was so much worse for me. "It's nice to formally meet you," I said, holding out a hand again.

She raised that eyebrow again and then turned away from me, a fast-moving polar vortex taking over the space where she'd stood. "I ran into something unpleasant on the way in. Sorry. I'm ready." She flashed a smile to my cousin and didn't give me a second glance.

Penny flicked her eyes to me in a way I knew meant *What the hell did you do?*

My first day was off to a great start.

Photo by D&orfs Photography

DENISE WILLIAMS wrote her first book in the second grade. *I Hate You* and its sequel, *I Still Hate You*, featured a tough, funny heroine; a quirky hero; witty banter; and a dragon. Minus the dragons, these are still the books she likes to write. After penning those early works, she finished second grade and eventually earned a PhD in education, going on to work in higher education. After growing up as a military brat around the world and across the country, Denise now lives in Iowa with her husband, son, and two ornery shih tzus who think they own the house.

CONNECT ONLINE

DeniseWilliamsWrites.com

🐦 NicWillWrites

📷 NicWillWrites

f AuthorDeniseWilliams

♪ NicWillWrites

Ready to find
your next great read?

Let us help.

Visit prh.com/nextread